love
under
cover

Also by Jessica Brody

The Fidelity Files

love
under
cover

Jessica Brody

ST. MARTIN'S GRIFFIN ⚏ NEW YORK

This is a work of fiction. All of the characters, organizations, and events portrayed in this novel are either products of the author's imagination or are used fictitiously.

LOVE UNDER COVER. Copyright © 2009 by Jessica Brody. All rights reserved. Printed in the United States of America. For information, address St. Martin's Press, 175 Fifth Avenue, New York, N.Y. 10010.

www.stmartins.com

Library of Congress Cataloging-in-Publication Data

Brody, Jessica.
     Love under cover / Jessica Brody. — 1st ed.
         p. cm.
     ISBN 978-0-312-38364-0
   1. Women private investigators—Fiction.   2. Adultery—Fiction.
3. Chick lit.   I. Title.
     PS3602.R6357L68 2009
     813'.6—dc22

                                                              2009017045

First Edition: November 2009

10 9 8 7 6 5 4 3 2 1

To Charlie,

*One of the few men in the world
who has the patience
to live with a writer.*

I love you.

1

bare witness

The girl in the slinky black dress and matching stiletto heels was perched on the edge of a high-backed bar stool at the far end of the bar. She was trying hard to blend in with the rest of the Thursday night crowd. Unfortunately, God had given her certain features that made blending inherently difficult.

Of course, the dress didn't help either.

She fidgeted anxiously with the metal strap of her black designer clutch with one hand while the other fingered the ends of her lusciously long blond hair, twirling them around the tips of her fingers as if she were skillfully performing some type of lesser-known crocheting technique. It was the nervous habit of a girl who had blossomed late in life, never being able to fully develop the confidence of those who had always been beautiful.

Whether or not she was really *that* girl was irrelevant. She played the part flawlessly.

With a despondent sigh, she reached into her bag and pulled out a small silver cell phone. Her fingers wrapped tightly around the helpless device, suffocating it mercilessly as she mustered enough courage to glance at the screen. The thought that a tiny envelope-shaped icon was her last and only hope for salvation struck her as ridiculous and sad, but at this point, she was clearly beyond naïve expectations.

The screen was blank.

Just as it had been five minutes ago and five minutes before that. The tiny icon that had promised to save her from the conclusion she feared most was defiantly absent.

After one final hopeful glance around the hotel bar, the girl in the black dress tossed the cell phone on top of the bar and reluctantly resigned herself to the idea that whoever was supposed to occupy the bar stool next to her was not going to show. She sighed and took a sip of her Pinot Noir, which until this moment of defeat had remained untouched.

It was becoming clearer with each passing moment that tonight she would be drinking alone. But certainly not by choice.

The man who had been watching this entire spectacle from across the hotel bar suddenly felt a surging rush of confidence. The girl in the black dress had intrigued him immensely. Not only because she was so strikingly beautiful . . . and blond (he had always had a secret thing for blondes), but because she seemed so lost. So fragile and endearingly powerless. It had been such a long time since he'd encountered someone of such beauty displaying such vulnerability out in the open.

It was, in all honesty . . . *refreshing.*

He eyed the empty bar stool next to her. Marveling at how an inanimate object could suddenly appear so welcoming. So inviting.

It was practically begging him to take it.

Everyone in the room was waiting for me to speak.

It was the only reason I had been brought here in the first place. A messenger of words. A linguistic savior.

It was a title I had become familiar with in recent months.

The air was hot and sticky. An unusually muggy day for New York in late October, and the air-conditioning had seemingly given up trying to keep up hours ago. But truth be told, I wasn't sure if the tiny beads of sweat on my forehead were due to the humidity in the room or the burden of my purpose here.

It would have been easier if I were completely impartial. Prepared to accept the inevitable outcome regardless of which side it landed on. But I couldn't do that. As much as I wanted to, I couldn't *not* care.

The uniformed guard standing to my left finally spoke. "Do you swear to tell the truth, the whole truth, and nothing but the truth, so help you God?"

"I do," I stated, keeping my gaze locked on a white marble statue situated in the back of the room. It was the only neutral thing here. Half of the people staring at me wanted nothing more than to see me fail. Watch me break apart and stumble for words. The other half were looking to me for salvation.

Neither was a comforting expectation.

But then again, it wasn't *their* expectations I was worried about.

"You may be seated," the bailiff informed me.

I sat down, trying to ignore the hard, splintery surface of the wooden chair beneath me.

There was a brief silence in the room, and I refused to make eye contact with anyone. Especially not him. The man in the light gray suit sitting diagonally to my left. The one with invisible laser beams shooting out of his eyeballs.

For the most part, I was used to it. It wasn't the first time I'd found myself the direct target of a glare like that. Especially from someone occupying his seat.

The tall, redheaded woman in a knee-length pencil skirt and silk blouse stood up from the opposing table and made her way toward me. In her hand she held a yellow legal pad, which she referred to briefly before addressing me. "Can you please state for the record what it is you do?"

I nodded with practiced confidence and spoke in smooth, even tones, keeping my sentences brief, limited to no more than ten words. After doing this four or five times, brevity starts to become second nature. "I run an agency."

"And what does this agency specialize in?"

I cleared my throat. "We offer a service called a 'fidelity inspection.'"

I heard a groan from the other side of the courtroom, and out of the corner of my eye, I saw the man in the gray suit roll his eyes. His lawyer quickly shot him a subtle yet warning glance.

"A fidelity inspection," the female lawyer repeated. "Can you explain to the court what that is?"

I took a deep breath and spoke the same words that I repeated nearly every day. To anyone who entered my office in search of answers. "It's an undercover test to determine whether or not the subject in question is capable of infidelity."

"So," the woman said, holding on to her legal pad with one hand and using the other to animate her words with large circular motions. "Basically you send out a decoy, or *bait,* in the form of a beautiful woman to see if a man will cheat on his wife?"

"Basically," I replied.

She nodded, as if she were digesting this information for the first time, even though I had already explained it to her numerous times over the past week. "I see," she continued. "And can you tell me, was my client, Mrs. Langley"—she paused and pointed to the thin, harsh-looking woman sitting behind her—"one of your agency's clients?"

I stole a quick glance in the direction of her finger. Mrs. Langley sat stony faced, her tightly pulled skin and high-arched eyebrows refusing to give up any emotion. She had the kind of unforgiving face that you expect to see on a headmistress at a strict boarding school, and I wondered if the plastic surgery had been intended that way. Maybe her job as the CEO of a Fortune 500 corporation demanded nothing less than severity. Maybe she had found that a cruel, harsher beauty went further in this male-dominated world than the softer variety.

Her dark, serious eyes focused back on me with only a fleeting hint of expectation. She wasn't the kind of woman who willingly relied on others. Or if she did, she wasn't the kind of woman who wanted people to know that. A spitting image of the person who had entered my office with poise and confidence only a few short months ago.

"Yes," I replied, opening a glossy crimson folder on my lap and checking the notes inside. "Joy Langley hired the agency to test her husband, Todd Langley, on June twenty-fourth of this year."

"Why?" the lawyer asked simply.

I looked down again. "According to my notes from our initial meeting, Mrs. Langley was concerned about her husband's ability to cope with the success of her rising career and feared that his feelings of inadequacy would lead him to stray."

Mr. Langley snorted his disapproval and mumbled something that sounded like "Conceited bitch," but I wasn't close enough to confirm.

Mrs. Langley's lawyer continued as if she had either failed to hear the underhanded comment or simply chosen to ignore it. "So you sent out one of your *associates* to either prove or disprove her suspicions?"

I continued to sit tall in my seat, trying to keep movement to a minimum. I knew that the opposing counsel would be studying my body language for any signs of uncertainty. Any reason whatsoever to poke holes in my testimony or question my credibility. And I refused to allow an innocent slouch to sway the outcome of this case.

"Yes," I replied.

The girl in the black cocktail dress downed the last of her red wine with one smooth gulp. The man who had just casually slid into the empty seat beside her watched out of the corner of his eye as she brought her glass down against the top of the bar with a purposeful clank.

"Thirsty?" he asked as a rush of adrenaline coursed through his veins.

He had never been as smooth as he would have liked in these kinds of situations. The James Bond–esque superhero who had championed similar scenarios in his head was nowhere to be seen now. And the real-life version of himself was decidedly less impressive.

She turned her head toward the stranger and flashed a disheartened grin. "Yeah, I guess."

"Can I get you another?"

Her head fell into a grateful nod. "Yes, please. It's an Estancia Pinot."

At the mention of these words, the man's face brightened. "Estancia? That's my favorite vineyard."

The girl nodded her enthusiastic agreement, or as enthusiastic as her self-pity party would allow her to get. "It's all I drink."

"Two glasses of the Estancia," he announced to the bartender, pleased that this conversation seemed to be off to a smooth start. Then he turned back to the girl in the black dress, silently taking in the way her long golden hair seemed to fall in perfect waves around her shoulders. Almost as if it had been styled *especially* to his taste.

She immediately noticed him looking, and her mouth twisted into a blushing smile.

It melted him.

The wine arrived and they clinked glasses, toasting to something generic like health or good fortune or new acquaintances.

Silence quickly fell between them after the initial sip, a heavy silence filled with anticipation and the fear of rejection. But that's the way it had to be. She could probably think of two dozen conversation starters that would easily put his fears to rest, but she wasn't there to start conversations. She was there to follow them. Sometimes the hardest part is the *not* speaking. The quiet before the storm. The *waiting*. But she knew the process was designed that way for a reason.

And she also knew that it would probably only take another seven seconds before—

"Are you waiting for someone?" he asked. His head bobbed back and forth, surveying the bar with only semi-genuine curiosity.

The girl sighed and fingered the stem of her wineglass as her eyes narrowed and her face sank into a practiced display of defeat. "I *was* waiting for someone, yes. My boyfriend. But I guess he's not going to show up . . . ever again."

"I'm sorry," the man offered with a weak attempt at sincerity. "I didn't mean to—"

"No, no, you're fine," she rushed to interrupt. "It's probably better this way. He wasn't right for me anyway." She tossed in a sigh. "Or at least that's what I'll try to tell myself."

"Were you together long?"

The girl in the black dress seemed to find unusual humor in this question, and she laughed quietly to herself. "Not really. Almost a month. Which is fairly typical of all my relationships. I mean, I guess it's probably not even long enough to call him my 'boyfriend.' At least that's what my friends tried to tell me. Lesson learned, right?" She pulled her wineglass toward her lips and sucked down another long gulp.

Never had there been a better opportunity for an introduction. And never had he been so eager to make one. "I'm Todd," he said, reaching his hand out toward her. "Todd Langley."

She shook it with a kind smile. "Keira Summers. It's a pleasure to meet you."

"So the entire evening is a setup?" The lawyer in the pencil skirt and silk blouse was all over the room now. Pacing back and forth in front of me as she spoke, as if she were running some sort of courtroom lap-a-thon to raise money for cancer research. "Nothing is real. The story she tells, the way she tells it, not even her name."

I nodded, feeling somewhat accosted by the question but hiding it well. This was how it worked. How all of them worked. She interrogates my methods in an attempt to discredit my testimony, then when she fails to do so, the opposing counsel isn't left with much else to do.

But even though I was familiar with the strategy, it still made me cringe slightly on the inside.

"Yes," I asserted, dabbing at the moisture on my forehead with the tip of my finger. "The associate gives the subject a fake name and a pre-scripted story or background about herself based on what he is likely to respond to. It's designed to facilitate conversation."

"So you have multiple associates working for you at your agency?" she asked, stopping in front of me.

It was more of a statement than a question, as had been most of her inquiries, but I answered it anyway. "Yes," I replied again. "Both women and men."

"*And* men?" she repeated, slightly amused by my response.

I nodded. The truth was there was only *one* man who worked for me. As of right now, anyway. If demand increased, I would certainly hire more. But I preferred not to divulge any specifics about the inner workings of my business. After all, it was supposed to be an undercover establishment. Which was why the lawyer pacing in front of me had agreed not to divulge the name of the agency.

"Really?" she confirmed. "So husbands come to you requesting fidelity inspections as well?"

The opposing counsel flashed an aggravated look and raised his hand in the air. "Objection. What's the relevance of this?"

Mrs. Langley's lawyer addressed the gray-haired female judge who sat directly to my right. "I'm only trying to establish the witness as a nonbiased party whose company offers support to both genders equally."

The judge nodded in reply. "Overruled. You may continue."

"Thank you, Your Honor." She turned back to me, not bothering to repeat the question, just waiting for me to respond.

"Yes," I stated. "I've had several husbands hire us to test their wives."

"And you've also testified at some of the resulting divorce proceedings as well, am I right?"

I didn't approve of her use of the words *resulting divorce proceedings*. As if my agency alone were responsible for the divorce rate in this country. It's true most of these couples would still be together had their husbands or wives not failed the fidelity inspection, but I liked to think of it more as "awakening" people to the truth rather than "inspiring" divorce.

Of course, I didn't voice my opinion on her word choice. I simply responded, "Yes."

"And what is your role in these inspections?"

"I meet with the client, gather all the details, then I assign the case to the associate I feel is best equipped to handle it."

Mrs. Langley's lawyer set her legal pad on the table so that she could now use both hands to animate the intricacy of her next statement/

question. "So in other words, you *match* each subject, in this case Mr. Langley, with his *ideal* . . . fantasy."

I shrugged. "I guess you could put it that way."

"Yes or no," she prompted me in return.

I paused, looking fleetingly around the courtroom, my eyes falling upon the empty jury box. I immediately wondered what twelve of my so-called peers would have thought about what I was about to say. Would they have judged me for it? Or would they have respected me because I was genuinely trying to help people? The same way I was trying to help Mrs. Langley today, in this humid, air-conditioning-forsaken courtroom in Westchester County.

"Yes."

"Uh-huh." Mrs. Langley's lawyer picked up her ballpoint pen and began using it as a prop to enumerate the points in her next sentences. "So, Mrs. Langley comes into your office, tells you that she's worried about her husband's *behavior* on business trips, you choose the associate that you feel best fits his ideal woman, then she meets him in a hotel bar in Seattle, tells him her name is something that it's not, strikes up a conversation with him based on made-up facts that he is likely to respond to, and waits to see if he'll cheat on his wife with her."

"It's actually an *intention* to cheat that we test for, not—"

The woman flashed me a look that urged me to just say yes so that we could move on.

"Sorry, yes."

She contorted her face into a disgusted expression and let out a small snort. "But isn't that entrapment?"

"Objection, Your Honor," Mr. Langley's lawyer cut in again. "Leading the witness. She's trying to discredit my argument."

"I'm just asking the question that I think *everyone* in this court-room is dying to know the answer to," Mrs. Langley's lawyer argued calmly.

I looked anxiously to the judge sitting next to me. She appeared completely immersed in this interrogation. "Overruled," she decided after a moment of deliberation. Then she turned to me. "You may answer the question."

I exhaled quietly, relieved that this particular question would not be left hanging in judicial limbo. "It's not entrapment," I stated in an unwavering tone. This was an issue I took very seriously. There's a fine line between inspecting someone and entrapping, and I took all precautions to make sure my business remained on the right side of it. "My employees are given explicit instructions to follow, not lead," I continued. "As was the case with Mr. Langley, the associate was not allowed to initiate anything. Any and all suggestions of further intimacy were left solely to his discretion." By the end of my sentence, I realized that my voice had started to sound somewhat defensive.

I paused and took a deep breath, reminding myself not to get too worked up. I had a tendency to do that when someone brought up the E-word. Let's just say it was a sore spot. "In other words," I began, calmer and more in control, "Mr. Langley made a conscious *choice* to cheat on his wife. He did not fall victim to a trap."

Two hours had passed since Todd Langley first sat on the bar stool next to the beautiful and delicate Keira Summers. They had covered every topic from religion to politics to pop icons. He now sat close enough to touch the bare skin of her arm or shoulder with just the slightest reach. And he *had* touched it. Numerous times. Nearly every sixty seconds for the past hour, in fact. Every joke, every shared opinion, every seemingly genuine connection, had, in his mind, been grounds for another fleeting contact with her soft, flawless skin. He simply couldn't get enough of it.

And the fact that Keira hadn't seemed to mind in the least only fueled his resolve to touch her again.

Todd motioned toward the bartender and ordered another two glasses of Pinot Noir, but Keira quickly interrupted him with a slightly intoxicated giggle and said, "Actually, I think I've had enough." She checked her watch. "Plus, it's getting kinda late."

In reality, she could have easily drunk twice as much as she had and still managed to successfully convince a police officer that she'd been drinking soda water all night. A high tolerance to alcohol was a standard prerequisite for this job. The girl who got tipsy and giggly and uninhibited after two glasses of wine was only an illusion. A physical embodiment of everything his wife was not.

"Why? What time is it?" Todd asked.

"Eleven forty-five," she replied, gathering her things and pushing herself off the bar stool. "I should really head home. And didn't you say you had an early flight back to New York tomorrow?"

But he didn't answer. He had a hard time forming a coherent sentence at this point. Even if it just consisted of the word *yes*. Because his brain was focusing on only one question: *Could he really let a woman like this walk out of here?*

The answer appeared evident immediately. Even though the fading photographs of his wife and children seemed to burn a hole right through the leather of his wallet and the cloth of his pant leg, threatening to scorch his skin. If anything, those burning photographs only made him act faster. Before they could leave any permanent scar tissue.

"Maybe you could come upstairs?" he blurted out, abandoning any and all attempts at sounding suave or urbane.

Keira giggled bashfully at the invitation. It was the perfect reaction. Awkwardness could not be met with complete confidence. Particularly with a man like Todd Langley, who was all too used to encountering nothing but overbearing confidence at home. No. Awkwardness had to be met with mutual awkwardness.

The most endearing kind.

"Sorry," he began, stumbling to find his next words. "I didn't mean that the way it sounded, it's just that—"

"Okay," Keira replied, looking at the floor.

"Okay?"

She nodded timidly, tucking a strand of her hair behind her ear. "I could probably use the distraction tonight."

Todd let out a sigh of relief as a huge smile beamed across his face. "Okay."

He put his hand gently on the small of her back and guided her out of the hotel bar, through the lobby, and into a waiting elevator that had nowhere to go but up.

⸏⸏⸏

A sly smile had just appeared across the face of Mrs. Langley's lawyer. "Are you saying that Mr. Langley *failed* his fidelity inspection?"

I looked back down at my notes. It was a superfluous move at this point. I had been preparing for this afternoon for the past two weeks. But something compelled me to do it. Perhaps the notes made me feel more credible. Better prepared. Or perhaps it was because this single, one-word answer was really all I was here to give.

"Yes."

"I have no further questions, Your Honor," she stated confidently before taking her seat next to Mrs. Langley and pulling her legal pad in front of her. She held her pen in her left hand, poised and ready. As if that one writing instrument was all it was going to take to defeat the enemy sitting on the other side of the room.

I glanced off to the left and saw Mr. Langley's lawyer begin to rise from his seat. He reached down and fastened the single button on his suit jacket before making a long, slow approach to my little wooden box.

My intuition warned me that he would be nothing but ruthless. I could read it on his face, in the way he sauntered toward me. Intimidation was the way he lived his life. The way he raised his kids, spoke to his secretaries, sent back food at a restaurant. Above all else, it was the way he cross-examined his witnesses. I knew it shouldn't have bothered me. I'd dealt with intimidating men plenty of times. And lived to tell about it. But I couldn't help feeling anxious . . . nervous, even. It was that damn partiality rearing its ugly head again. If only I didn't care. If only I didn't feel as though I needed this victory just as much as Mrs. Langley did.

If only . . .

"What did you say your name was?" he asked once he had arrived in front of me.

"Ashlyn," I stated simply.

He flashed a condescending smile. "I mean, what is your *real* name?"

Before I even had time to react, Mrs. Langley's lawyer shot out of her seat like a rocket. "Objection, Your Honor. The witness has agreed to testify anonymously, as confidentiality is an integral part of her business, not to mention the safety of her associates." She tapped at a stack of paperwork on the table. "I have five precedent cases here that document the court allowing the witness to give an anonymous testimony under similar conditions. She should not be pressured to divulge any personal details about herself, as they are irrelevant to this case."

Mr. Langley's lawyer threw up his hands in frustration. "I'm just trying to establish witness credibility! If she won't give us her *real* name, how can we even trust that she's giving us *real* facts?"

"Objection sustained," the judge decided. "The witness's real name has no bearing on her testimony. Next question."

Mrs. Langley's lawyer settled back into her seat, seemingly satisfied. She gave me an encouraging nod of her head.

"Fine, *Ashlyn,*" the man in front of me began, doing little to hide his mocking tone. "Were you present during my client's 'fidelity whatever you call it'?"

"Fidelity *inspection,*" I clarified, struggling to mask my annoyance. "And no, I don't attend most of the inspections."

"And why is that?"

"Because I trust my employees wholeheartedly, and therefore I find no reason to fly halfway across the country for each one. Plus, there are far too many for me to be present at all of them. I would have to be cloned . . . many times over."

Mr. Langley's lawyer nodded, pursing his lips in deep thought. "Hmm. Lots of distrustful people out there, huh?"

I replied with a noncommittal shrug.

"So how do you even know what goes on during these assignments?"

I folded my hands in my lap. "My associates are required to provide me with detailed accounts in the form of notes and post-assignment reports. In addition, we have weekly staff meetings where all associates

verbally recap the results of their assignments. I have no doubt that
I can effectively recount, in comprehensive detail, the events of Mr.
Langley's case."

"So let me get this straight," he began, drumming his finger con-
templatively against his bottom lip. "Basically you're implying that
we should base the division of Mr. and Mrs. Langley's life assets on
your word, which is in turn based on someone *else's* word?"

"Objection!" Mrs. Langley's lawyer shot up again. "Do I even
need to object to that?"

The judge nodded. "Rephrase your question, Counselor."

Mr. Langley's lawyer turned to the judge with fabricated aggrava-
tion in his eyes. "I'm sorry, Your Honor, it's just that we're here to
decide whether or not my client, a loving and devoted husband and
father, is entitled to half of his wife's earnings. A sum not short of
three point five *million* dollars. And all we have to go by is this
woman's *notes*? I'm honestly not even sure why we're still here."

"I appreciate your opinion, Counselor," the judge replied calmly,
"but I will decide whether or not her testimony is useful. I think
you should just continue to question your witness."

The man bowed his head slightly in submission. "Of course, Your
Honor. But based on my strong *opinion* that this witness bears no
credibility, I have no further questions."

The judge nodded and then turned to me. "You may step down."

That wasn't so bad, I thought, surprised, as I tucked my notes into
my briefcase and snapped the top flap closed. I had expected a much
more valiant display from this guy. And from the confusion on Todd
Langley's face, I'm guessing so did he.

I felt good about my testimony. Confident. *Hopeful.* It was an
emotion I wasn't used to attaching to aspects of my job. I had always
made a point of avoiding "hope" when it came to the lives and relationships of others. Because there are just too many factors outside of
your control. But recently, somehow "hope" had managed to sneak
past the radar. And by the time I realized it was there, it was too difficult not to cling to.

Bottom line: I wanted this win.

The backs of my legs rejoiced as I stood up from the uncomfortable wooden chair, and I heard a small pop come from the middle of my lower back. But as I took my first step down the stairs toward freedom, I heard Mr. Langley's lawyer say, "Actually, I do have one more question."

The judge nodded, and I stifled a groan and sat back down.

Mr. Langley's lawyer leaned against the table and feigned deep contemplation. The palms of his hands pressed together, and the tips of his fingers rested on his chin. "You mentioned earlier in your testimony something about an 'intention' to cheat. What exactly does that mean?"

⚬⚬⚬⚬

The pressure of Todd's lips on hers was intense.

He paused momentarily and took a moment to admire the woman who now lay on his hotel bed before leaning in to kiss her again. She tasted like heaven mixed with Estancia Pinot Noir.

She moaned slightly, and this gave him the courage to press further. His hand began to reposition itself under her dress.

But it never quite got there.

"Wait—" Keira pushed lightly against his arm. "Are you sure you want to do this?"

Todd let out a deep, lustful sigh. "More than you could ever imagine."

She placed a single finger on his lips and whispered, "Then I'll be right back."

She sat up and scooted to the edge of the bed. Her movement was so fluid, so *practiced,* it almost alarmed him. But not quite. His blinding anticipation was strong enough to block out any alarming thoughts. The light from the bathroom flickered on and splashed a murky shadow across the room. He heard the sound of water running from the faucet, and he rolled onto his back and stared up at the ceiling, a silly, boyish grin spreading across his face as he waited impatiently for Keira Summers to return.

Or more important, for the promise of what was to come when she did.

Little did he know . . . she was already gone.

The light in the bathroom remained illuminated and the water continued to run for at least five minutes before he decided to check on her. But by then, the girl in the black dress and all traces of what she represented had vanished. Even her lingering smell had begun to fade. And after shutting off the faucet and standing perplexedly in the middle of the bathroom, staring at the cold white tiles on the floor, he even started to wonder if she'd ever been there to begin with. Maybe she'd been a figment of his imagination. A drunk and desperate apparition.

And even though he wouldn't fully understand the true implications of her sudden absence until a few days later, when he came home to find that his key wouldn't turn in the lock, a faint buzzing sound was already sounding in his ears. A warning bell signaling that something was not as it should be. That beautiful blondes in slinky black dresses didn't just simply appear and disappear without reason.

<hr />

"So in the end, you have no *physical* proof whatsoever that my client, Mr. Langley, would have actually gone through with sexual intercourse?"

I could feel the defensiveness seeping back into my voice. "The fidelity inspection is designed to make absolutely sure that the intention of infidelity is—"

"Yes or no is fine," Mr. Langley's lawyer interrupted, a smug grin plastered on his face.

I sighed, my shoulders slouching slightly. "No. I don't."

"So theoretically, had your associate not left before the deed was done, Mr. Langley could have easily stopped it himself."

"In theory, yes, but—"

"Thank you," he interrupted again, clearly not overly concerned with common courtesies at this point. "So I guess the only question I have left is why the witness thinks an *intention* to cheat is the same thing as cheating. An unfaithful *tendency* is not an act of adultery. It's simply one person's judgment of character. And probably not even an accurate one."

I took a deep breath and spoke with as much conviction as I could muster. "My associates don't engage in any sexual activity. Otherwise it would be prostitution. I run a legitimate business. And that's why my employees test the subjects for an *intention* to cheat only. But I am fully confident that had my associate not left Todd Langley's hotel room that night, he would have had sex with her."

"Well, thank you for that," Mr. Langley's lawyer offered condescendingly after a short pause. "But if the witness has no *physical* proof of infidelity to share with us, then I have no further questions, Your Honor."

The judge nodded. "You may step down," she informed me for the second time, and then turned her focus to the rest of the courtroom. "We'll reconvene tomorrow morning, and I'll have a decision by then." She gathered her paperwork and pushed her chair back from her desk.

"Actually," I interrupted, raising my hand tentatively. "Can I just say one more thing?"

Mrs. Langley's lawyer shot me a "What do you think you're doing?" look, but I ignored it and spoke directly to the judge. Because she was the only audience I cared about at this point. The one who had control over all those outside factors that used to keep me at an emotional arm's length from situations like this.

"Go ahead," she allowed.

I didn't know if what I was about to say would help at all. But I was fairly sure that it probably wouldn't hurt. So I decided it was worth a shot. "I've learned in the course of my life that cheating is a subjective term. Sex often has nothing to do with it. Mr. Langley may not have *physically* cheated on his wife—at least not with my associate—but the betrayal was there long before she ever walked into his hotel room."

A long silence followed. And it was only now that I dared look into the eyes of Todd Langley. The man who had seduced one of my associates, invited her up to his hotel room, touched her skin, kissed her mouth, and showed every intention of doing exactly what he had promised to never do. His thoughts spoke to me as clear as day. He felt justified in the choices he had made with Keira Summers.

Entitled. The faint smirk on his face told me that he was not sorry for what happened—only sorry that he had gotten caught.

Then I looked at Mrs. Langley. Her hardened features hadn't revealed anything throughout this entire testimony. And they certainly weren't revealing anything now. Here was a woman who had fought her way to the top despite all the odds stacked against her. Despite all the tension her superior salary had caused at home. And now her soon-to-be ex-husband was trying to claim half of everything she had worked for. Even though it had been *his* actions that had put them in this courtroom in the first place. I didn't need to see pain scrawled across her face to know it was there. The woman who never breaks on the outside always feels it twice as hard on the inside.

The judge finally responded to my declaration with a vague nod of her head. The kind that indicated only that she had heard me, not necessarily that she had listened. I searched her face for any sign of persuasion, but I might as well have been staring at an abstract painting hanging on the living room wall of some well-off art collector. A red canvas with a single black dot slightly off center. It was anyone's guess what that dot represented.

Apparently, I would have to wait until tomorrow to find out if my emotional wager was on the right side of the table. Just like everyone else in this room. All I could do now was step off this witness stand, walk out that door, and hope that I had done enough.

So I did.

2

the relationship virus

The next morning, I was back in Los Angeles at my three-bedroom condo in Brentwood, trying to get my friend Sophie off the phone without hurting her feelings. A fairly typical task in my morning routine. Sophie's wedding was less than a month away, and staying true to her neurotic self, she had officially become a bridezilla. I'd even considered submitting a hidden camera recording of one of her meltdowns to one of those cable reality shows, but I was pretty sure that went against every unspoken agreement in my maid-of-honor contract.

"So then the caterer goes, in this really snotty British accent, 'Perhaps we can just serve Van de Kamp's fish sticks if you're so unhappy with the seafood selection.' And then I was like, 'Well . . .'"

I attempted to zone out Sophie's voice as I tucked the phone between my ear and my shoulder and struggled to zip up the back of my skirt.

"Jen, can you believe that?" her voice screeched through the speaker, and I instantly regretted pressing the phone that close to my ear. I dropped it into my hand and held it up to my other ear as I tried to massage my bruised eardrum.

Then I proceeded to launch into the speech I had been giving for the past six months. "Soph," I began with intensity and a sprinkling of compassion, "I think you should just relax and let everyone do what you've hired them to do. If you keep trying to do everyone *else's* job, you won't have the time or the energy left to do your own. Which at this point is just one thing: transforming yourself into the beautiful blushing bride that all your friends and family are coming to see. Including myself."

It was a good thing I already had the speech memorized, because after having just walked out of a room in which two people (and their lawyers) were arguing over how they were going to *end* their marriage, the last thing I felt like doing was coming up with motivational orations about joining two *more* people together for "all of eternity."

Not that I was worried about my best friend ending up like that. I knew for a fact that Sophie's fiancé, Eric, was nothing like Todd Langley. Let's just say I had "proof."

"I guess you're right," Sophie conceded after my little speech. It was probably the fifth time in the past two weeks she had done so. It baffled me how every time I recited the same exact words, she acted like she was hearing them for the first time. As if it were a breath of fresh air when in reality it reeked of a stale, mildewed basement, having been recycled over and over since the start of this wedding planning process. Not that I was complaining. Sophie's selective amnesia was thankfully keeping me from having to come up with any new and inspiring speeches off the top of my head.

"I mean," she continued, "so what if the fish is tilapia instead of ahi tuna. Maybe she's right about it pairing better with the wine."

I stole a quick glance at the clock on my nightstand. It was already 9:45 A.M.

Shit! I'm late!

I tucked the phone under my ear again and balanced on one foot as I made a hasty (and rather acrobatic) attempt to shove my left foot into my favorite pair of slingbacks. "She's absolutely right," I replied, pulling the strap around my heel. "And I happen to *love* tilapia." The emphasis I placed on the word *love* might have been a tad over the top. As soon as the sentence left my mouth, I marveled at how much it sounded like a fifteen-year-old gushing over the latest bad-boy heart-throb, not a twenty-nine-year-old woman talking about a fish.

"You do?" Sophie asked, her tone clearly questioning my enthusiasm.

"Absolutely. In fact, I just read in some food magazine that ahi tuna is so last season. Totally overdone. It's all about the tilapia now."

"Oh," she replied with a satisfied realization, and I knew that it was time to execute my escape, before she had a chance to light another fire for me to put out.

"Yep, well, I should probably get going. Late for work. Talk soon!"

"Oh, okay. But are we still on for tomorrow night to finish the place cards for the tables? I told Zoë we could meet at your place and order pizza or something. Although I'll probably just have salad, 'cause, you know, I don't want to have to let my dress out . . . yet *again*. That cheesecake I had last week at Eric's birthday was a *huge* mistake! I practically felt like—"

"Yes, we're still on," I interrupted quickly, checking my reflection in the mirror and attempting to smooth down my long, chestnut brown hair. "How about eight?"

"Yeah, that sounds good. Oh, and I invited John as well. Well, I less invited him and more *surrendered* to his begging. He says he knows calligraphy, but I highly doubt that. You know how he can be. Is that okay?"

"Yes, that's fine. Look, I'm *really* late. I'll see you tomorrow and we'll chat more."

"Right. Sorry. Well, have a good day at work! Catch lots of cheaters!"

I laughed and pressed "End" on my cell phone. I still hadn't completely gotten used to my friends knowing what I really did for a living. Until about one year ago, they all thought that I worked for an investment bank. It wasn't until an unfortunate Web site popped up with my picture on it, warning men of my real motivations, that the lies slowly started to unravel.

I used to do this job all on my own. I met with the clients, I took on the assignments, and I executed them. Meaning I *personally* tested the fidelity of these women's husbands and fiancés. And no one in my life had any idea. My friends, my family, even random people I met on airplanes thought I sat in a cubicle for fourteen hours a day staring at thousands of rows of numbers on a screen. Which wasn't that much of a stretch since it was exactly what I *did* do prior to becoming a fidelity inspector.

But after the whole Web site fiasco, which I found out was sponsored by a very disgruntled ex-husband of a former client, I eventually had to come clean. I told them everything. My *friends,* not my family. Can you imagine telling your mother that you *almost* sleep with married men for a living? I don't think so.

Now that I run the agency and have five full-time associates hired to conduct the fidelity inspections for me, life has become a little easier. Although I still haven't told my family about it. They now think I run a domestic services agency that specializes in placing housekeepers, nannies, and private tutors with affluent Southern California families. Well, at least the "domestic services" part is somewhat true.

After hanging up with Sophie, I immediately opened up the e-mail application on my iPhone and began frantically typing a message to my assistant to tell her that I was running late and could she please inform everyone. While I typed with one hand, my other hand was helping my right foot slide into my second shoe. Unfortunately, I wasn't as skillful at the shoe administering as I was at the typing, and by the time I secured the strap of the slingback around my heel, I had completely lost my balance.

I reached out for something to break my fall, and my hand landed on skin. The soft skin of a well-formed upper arm.

It was Jamie. My boyfriend.

And he was standing just inside the doorway, his arm extended around my back as he effortlessly broke my fall. "Whoa there, Turbo. Multitasking again?" he asked with his usual irresistible smirk. Sometimes I wondered if he really loved me for me or just because I was entertaining to watch sometimes.

Jamie and I had been together for over a year, and now we practically lived together. He still had his own place in Century City near his office, but he spent most of his time at my condo. I think he liked coming here to get away from the whole corporate landscape of Century City. He could literally *see* his firm's building from the window of his loft, and ever since he'd been promoted to partner a

few months ago, he'd become more and more desperate for an escape at the end of the day. And trust me, never in a million years did
I ever think I'd end up here. In a near cohabitation situation with a
member of the opposite sex.

Before I met Jamie, love had never been on the agenda for me. I
kind of always thought that I would just casually skip over that part
of my life and continue on as though nothing had happened. You
know how some people don't go to college or some people find dogs
more fulfilling than children? Well, I was going to be the person
who didn't fall in love.

Honestly, I didn't see the point. And you can't exactly blame me
for that. As a fidelity inspector, the only relationships I ever encountered were ones that were falling apart. And my parents weren't
much good in the role model department, either. So it's pretty safe
to say that Jamie came as a bit of a surprise. He wasn't exactly part of
the game plan. I had always thought that I was immune to love and
all that mushy relationship stuff. Blessed with the impenetrable antibodies that protected someone from falling head over heels, from
trusting another human being wholeheartedly, from ever feeling
vulnerable.

But I guess those antibodies don't really exist. Or scientists just
haven't managed to perfect them yet.

So I caught the flu. I contracted the virus. The one that makes you
start sentences with the word *we* and end them with the words *isn't
that right, honey?* The one that makes you sick with anxiety when the
phone doesn't ring exactly when it's supposed to. It's a disease that
makes you dizzy, feverish, nauseated, clammy, and from time to time
even delusional.

Yet once I had caught it, I never wanted to be cured. I only
wanted to be with Jamie.

And that's one of the main reasons I no longer take on assignments myself anymore. In fact, I had made a promise to Jamie that I
never would. Clearly, you can't be in a trustworthy, committed relationship *and* be a fidelity inspector. It's kind of one of those either/or
situations. So when I came up with the idea for the agency, I convinced Jamie that I would be able to manage the entire process from

behind a desk. Or more specifically, from my office on the top floor of a midrise building overlooking the ocean in Santa Monica.

It was the perfect desk job for a retired field agent.

After I steadied myself and managed to get my other shoe on my foot, Jamie reached out and handed me a steel, lidded travel mug with a teabag string dangling over the side. "English Breakfast with milk and sugar, as usual."

I flashed him a grateful smile as I took the tea. "Thanks, babe." I slid open the small slit on the top of the mug and took a sip. "What are you still doing here?" I asked, eyeing his ensemble of boxer shorts, undershirt, and wet hair.

"I have a conference call with the London office in ten minutes. I thought I'd just take it here."

I raised my eyebrows playfully. "So you're gonna sit around my house and run up my international phone bill, huh? Typical."

He reached his arm back around me and pulled me close to him. I could smell the fresh scent of his aftershave as my nose brushed up against his smooth, freshly razored chin. "They're calling *me*," he clarified before kissing me and giving my left butt cheek a squeeze. "Hmm, I like this skirt."

I rolled my eyes and pushed him away. "I have to go."

His shoulders slouched as he watched me walk past him into the hallway. "But I still have ten minutes," he pouted behind me.

I laughed and grabbed my Louis Vuitton briefcase from the dining room chair. "But I don't," I reminded him. "And we both know it would take longer." I dropped my cell phone into the front pocket of the bag. "*Much* longer," I added with a flirtatious grin.

Jamie was tall and beautiful, with this distinguished, mature look about him that drove me crazy. What is it about worldly-looking men? They're so enticing. To me, Jamie was like George Clooney in *Ocean's Eleven*. Slightly older, with that coy smirk of his and those soft yet powerful eyes. His dark hair had just started to reveal the slightest shades of gray around the temples, and honestly, it was one of the sexiest things I'd ever seen.

But gray temples or not, I was still ridiculously late.

I clasped the pocket of my briefcase and headed for the front door.

But I only got halfway there before my phone started ringing. I groaned, thinking that maybe it was Sophie again, and I immediately regretted the day that I gave up my two separate cell phones in exchange for one single iPhone. I used to carry one cell phone for personal use and one for business. And at least back then, I always knew what kind of call it would be based on which cell phone was ringing. But ever since I opened the agency, there just didn't seem to be a reason for me to have two. Most clients only had the number to the office, and my assistant handled all those calls. Which worked really well in keeping my home life and my work life as separate as possible.

I set the briefcase on the edge of the couch and fished the phone back out of the bag. The number on the caller ID wasn't one that I recognized. "Where's area code 914?"

Jamie appeared from the hallway behind me and shrugged. "No clue."

Curiosity got the better of me, and I answered. "Hello?"

"Hello, Ashlyn?" replied the slightly familiar female voice on the other end.

Well, at least I could tell the call was work related from the name she used. If she had called me "Jennifer," I would have known it was personal in nature. I never used my real name for matters of business.

"Yes, this is she."

Jamie approached and kissed me silently on the cheek. "Don't forget about our plans tonight," he whispered before heading into the kitchen.

I held up one finger and nodded.

"This is Paula Porter, Mrs. Langley's attorney."

I could feel my body stiffen immediately. Of course—914 area code was Westchester County. Where I had been less than twenty-four hours ago.

This was it. The phone call I had been dreading since I left that courtroom yesterday. Part of me didn't even want to know what the outcome had been. Part of me just wanted to move on with my life and forget all about it. Maybe this was one of those things better left to fade away in the back of your memory. A burning question that, after a few weeks' time, eventually sizzles out until it's just a faintly glowing ember that's hardly worth talking about.

But the other part of me knew I would never be able to let it go. As much as I hated to admit it, I had made some kind of emotional investment in this outcome. Ever since I quit the fieldwork and began my "desk job," these courtroom testimonies were the only way I could be directly involved in my clients' lives. Sure, I greeted them at the agency, took their case, prepared their assignment, and reported back to them when it was all said and done. But there was something inherently lacking in that. Being the bookends of the process but never the book. On the surface, I knew I was still helping people, but I always felt one step removed from it. I was never *personally* involved anymore. And I'll admit, sometimes I missed it. The personal involvement. Not the almost sleeping with married men, obviously.

Becoming an expert witness seemed like a good solution. It was a way that I could make an impact on people's lives while at the same time keep my promise to Jamie that I would never actually be the one to conduct the fidelity inspections. Unfortunately, the last five testimonies I had given hadn't made much of an impact at all. Every single one of them had ended in a ruling that favored the cheater and not the cheated-on. I was hoping Mrs. Langley's case would put an end to my losing streak and reestablish some kind of faith that I actually *was* making a difference.

I realized it was a lot of weight to place on one phone call.

"Yes, hello, Ms. Porter," I replied softly, sliding into one of the dining room chairs.

"I just wanted to thank you again for flying all that way to testify on Joy's behalf yesterday. I realize it's a long flight, and we both really appreciate it."

"It's no problem."

"And I also thought you might want to know what the judge's decision was."

I tried hard to detect any traces of emotion in her voice. Did she sound happy? Sad? Disappointed? Elated? But I was left with no clues whatsoever. I guess that's what made her a good lawyer.

"Oh," I replied casually, as if the thought of this phone conversation hadn't even crossed my mind. "Sure, you can tell me if you like . . . since you already have me on the phone."

"Right," she began. "Well, as you said in the courtroom, cheating is a very subjective concept. It's difficult to determine what really constitutes it."

I could feel my hand start to wind in slow circles in front of my body, urging her to skip the fluff and just tell me what the decision was. "Uh-huh."

I looked over at Jamie, who had moved into the kitchen and was now searching my cabinets for something to eat for breakfast.

"So in order to get around issues of subjectivity, the legal system usually relies heavily on language."

What the hell is she talking about? Just tell me if the judge awarded him the money.

"The fact is, the language in the New York State statute pertaining to adultery is very rigid," Ms. Porter continued, her voice still not giving away anything. Which was frustrating to no end. "It specifically defines infidelity as *sexual* intercourse with someone other than the subject's spouse."

"And?" I prompted, desperation seeping into my voice. I was convinced that there had to be more to this phone call. She couldn't just call up and drone on about all this legal mumbo jumbo and not have a "but" coming. Now would be the ideal time for her to say something like "*But* despite all of that, the judge still feels that . . ."

But she didn't say that. In fact, she didn't say much of anything. All she did was echo my question right back at me. "And what?"

I felt my heart sink. I had already mentally prepared myself for this outcome. I had played it over and over in my head the entire flight back to L.A. just so I wouldn't be caught off guard. But here I was, stunned nonetheless. And feeling completely desolate.

I could hear Jamie rummaging through the pantry now, shaking a series of almost empty cereal boxes to determine if the remaining contents would successfully fill a bowl.

"So that's it?" I asked, my voice rising higher than I would have liked. I quickly composed myself again. "The judge couldn't do anything? She couldn't make an exception?"

"Afraid not. Her hands were pretty tied. New York *is* a fault state, but the language is just too rigid."

"But that's such bullshit!" I shouted, and then recoiled, immediately regretting the outburst because Jamie's head poked around the cabinet door and he eyed me with apprehension. I turned my back to him and clasped my hand tighter around the phone. I wasn't sure what to say after that. So I just seethed quietly.

"Look," she said, finally interrupting the heavy silence. "We all know that he cheated, regardless of the way it was defined in the state's legal code. And Mrs. Langley is still eternally grateful for the priceless information that your agency was able to provide about her marriage. Otherwise she would probably still be married to him."

"Right," I replied diplomatically. I knew I had to get this woman off the phone and go on with my day as quickly as possible. Distraction was the only option for me at this point. And there would be lots of it once I arrived at the office. "Well, thank you for calling, Ms. Porter."

"Who was that?" Jamie called from the kitchen as soon as I hung up.

"Oh, no one." I waved my hand in the air and slipped my iPhone back into my briefcase. "Just Mrs. Langley's lawyer."

"Ah," he responded, as if everything he'd overheard in the last three minutes suddenly made perfect sense to him. He closed the door to the pantry and turned to face me. "Not good news, huh?"

I shrugged casually. "You know, a lot of technical lawyer stuff. It's all really over my head, actually."

Jamie shot me a skeptical look. "Well, what did she say about the divorce proceedings? Did the judge make a decision about the division of assets?"

I shrugged again as I snapped my bag closed. "I guess he's getting off on a technicality."

Jamie's face fell, and he came over to me and wrapped his arms around my waist. "I'm sorry, baby. That *is* upsetting."

I scrunched my nose in confusion, as if I couldn't imagine why he would ever think that *this* of all things would be capable of upsetting me. "I'm not upset. It's not *my* problem." I forced out a faint chuckle.

"Yeah, but I know you were counting on this one. After the last five—"

"I wasn't *counting* on it," I insisted, trying to douse each word with credibility as it left my mouth. "Sure, it would have been nice for Mrs. Langley not to have to share everything she's made with her cheating ex-husband, but it doesn't really matter."

Jamie studied my face. It was obvious he didn't believe me. I felt uncomfortable under his scrutiny. "Look, I'm *really*, really late. We can talk more about this tonight, okay?" I grabbed the briefcase and my steel mug of tea and gave him a quick kiss on the lips.

But Jamie wrapped his arms around my waist and held me close to him, our faces only inches apart. "Remember, you didn't go into this business to protect clients' assets or punch holes in prenuptial agreements; you went into it to offer people the truth. And that's exactly what you did for Mrs. Langley."

I squirmed away from his grasp and hid my escape behind a sip of tea. "I know."

"She's better off now, regardless of what happened in that courtroom."

"I *know*," I repeated, this time with just a bit more indignation in my voice.

Jamie leaned forward to kiss me on the forehead. "Okay, just making sure. I don't like seeing you upset."

"I told you, I'm *not* upset." Another ambiguously true statement.

"Good. Then I'll see you tonight."

"Where are we going again?"

He grinned, quickly forgetting all about the Langleys and their court case, for which I felt overwhelmingly relieved. "It's a surprise."

I smiled as I made my way to the front door and opened it wide. "Oh, right. I forgot you're being melodramatic about it," I teased with a playful roll of my eyes.

Jamie shook his head and walked back to the kitchen. "Just meet me here at seven-thirty. And don't be late."

"I won't!" I called over my shoulder, and shut the door behind me.

3

the fantastic five

Being a fidelity inspector was the only real career I had ever known.

Sure, there had been jobs before it. In high school, I sold men's boxer shorts and undershirts at the Hanes outlet store in the mall. In college, I became an official Subway sandwich artist, trained in the fine art of processed meats and cheeses. And when I finally graduated at the age of twenty-two, I landed the prestigious and highly coveted analyst job at Stanley Marshall Investment Bank, where my life became a dizzying array of spreadsheets, PowerPoint slides, and working weekends.

But I never considered any of those temporary professions an actual "career." Because in my mind, a career is something you believe in. Something you work hard to excel at. Something that defines you.

And I think it's safe to say I never felt *defined* by men's undershirts, foot-long roast beef subs, or spreadsheets. These were just obstacles in my way of completing each and every day so that I could go home and do something useful with my time.

But then I stumbled upon a job that was like nothing I'd ever heard of before. In fact, I don't even think most people would call it a *job*. It's definitely not advertised on Monster.com. And you'll never find it listed in a brochure from your high school guidance counselor or on some form asking you to check the box that most appropriately describes your current occupation. In fact, *I* didn't even know it existed until I actually became one. To this day, I have no idea if there were others out there like me. Or if maybe I had been the only one. A Lone Ranger in a new frontier, paving the way for anyone who decided to stumble along after me.

I used to think of myself as kind of a mini-superhero.

I know it sounds pretty ridiculous. But I did have all the defining characteristics of a female superhero. I had the kick-ass costume (or wardrobe, rather) that effectively accentuated my legs, boobs, or butt depending on the assignment. I had the secret identity that nobody else knew about—my friends and family knew me only by my real name: Jennifer Hunter. But I couldn't very well use that name for my job. It was too risky. I dealt with too many unstable, untrustworthy people. So I came up with a code name: Ashlyn. And that was the name I gave out to all the unsuspecting men I met on a weekly basis.

And I even had a superpower. I guess technically I still have it. It's the kind of thing that doesn't just go away. I may not be able to leap buildings in a single bound, but what I can do is probably much more appealing to the eighteen-to-thirty-five female demographic.

I can decipher any man you put in front of me . . . in less than thirty seconds. I can read them like an open book. I don't know how or when I acquired this particular skill, it just always seemed to be there.

Clearly, it's something that used to come in handy when I worked in the field as an inspector.

Now it comes in handy when I'm preparing an assignment for one of my associates. I get a sort of "sense" about what a man's going to respond to just by talking to his wife. Of course, it's not exactly the same as standing right in front of him and being able to predict what he's going to do next, but I suppose it's still a good use for my so-called ability.

It doesn't work quite as well when I'm preparing the female fidelity inspections, but I do the best I can.

The drive from Brentwood to the office can take me anywhere from eight to fifteen minutes depending on traffic and how many red lights I hit along the way. Today I made it in seven.

Although I've been known to talk myself out of a few speeding tickets in the past, if a cop had caught me doing seventy down Wilshire Boulevard, I'm fairly sure I would have found myself trying to talk my way out of a jail cell.

But I was already fifteen minutes late to my morning staff meeting, and I don't like being late for anything unless there's a good reason. And I didn't think Sophie's tilapia meltdown or my boyfriend's sudden craving for a morning quickie constituted a good enough one.

I rode the elevator to the top floor and walked briskly down the long corridor toward the waiting double glass doors at the end. The same ones that I've walked through every morning for the past year. Suite 1207.

Hadley, my newly hired twenty-two-year-old assistant, was sitting in her usual seat at the front reception desk under a large chrome-plated sign that read, THE HAWTHORNE AGENCY.

Hadley was the kind of girl you wouldn't normally look twice at. Her dirty blond hair could have used some highlights, and her large brown eyes could have used a touch more makeup. My guess is she'd probably spent the majority of her life relying on her brains rather than her looks. She was fresh out of college and had been recommended by one of my associates, who assured me she was both hardworking and trustworthy. Obviously, the latter is one of the more important qualifications of this job, given the secretive nature of our business.

She had been here only a few weeks and was still learning the ropes, but she was eager, well organized, and a quick learner, so I couldn't complain. I'd hired her after my former assistant, Marta, told me she was leaving. Her resignation came as something of a surprise since Marta had been with me from the beginning. But when I tried to talk her out of it, she simply flashed me one of her knowing, motherly smiles and said, "I've helped you get exactly where you needed to go. Now it's time for me to help someone else do the same."

And I really couldn't argue with that.

Upon seeing me walk through the door, Hadley jumped out of her seat as if she were rising to greet a foreign dignitary. "Good morning, Ashlyn," she said with bubbling enthusiasm. "That costume you asked for was delivered this morning. I hung it up in the prop closet. And I left all your messages on your desk." Her eyes fell to a paper cup on her desk, filled with steaming hot liquid. "Oh!" she exclaimed, grabbing the cup and holding it out for me. "And I made you some coffee."

I smiled gratefully at her. "Thanks, Hadley. But I actually only drink tea in the morning. I save my coffee for the afternoon. When I need an energy boost."

Her large doe eyes blinked a few times as she digested this new information, and I was afraid that she might actually start to cry. But instead she placed the cup back on her desk and began scribbling something in a spiral notebook. "Tea morning. Coffee afternoon," she mumbled as she wrote. Then she looked up at me and smiled. "I'm sorry. I promise I'll get it right next time."

I had to laugh at her eagerness. "It's no problem. Don't worry about it. Is everyone already inside?" I asked, cocking my head toward the door to my right.

She nodded, and I headed into the conference room.

As soon as I entered, conversations faded away and five pairs of eyes focused their attention on me. I took my seat at the head of the table and pulled a stack of glossy crimson folders from my briefcase.

For the past few months, the success of the agency has grown exponentially. Hardly a week goes by that I don't have at least one assignment for each associate on my staff. And based on the fact that we advertise by word of mouth only, that's a whole lot of referrals being passed around out there. I guess news of a service like this travels fast.

"Good morning, everyone," I said, pulling my chair up to the table. "My apologies for being so late. Let's get started so we can all get out of here on time."

To my immediate left sat Lauren Ireland, a tall, slender brunette whom I had gotten to know quite well over the past year. Mostly because she was my first associate and actually part of my inspiration for opening the agency in the first place. After being the beneficiary of my services over a year ago, she was convinced that she wanted to devote her life to helping other women find the answers they were looking for. That's when she came to me and told me she wanted to become a fidelity inspector. And it didn't take long for me to figure out that there were probably others just like her out there. So I set out to recruit them.

Lauren is also the agency's technical guru. She knows everything there is to know about networking, databases, gadgets, you name it. And those kinds of skills definitely come in handy when she's in the field. The fact that she's beyond stunning *and* knows how to hack a Linux server makes her irresistible to a lot of men. She's the ideal fantasy for the Bill Gateses of the world.

Lauren's inherent technological skill set was actually the basis I used for forming the Hawthorne Agency. Because a little less than a year ago, when I was doing this job entirely on my own, I spent a lot of my free time researching and taking crash courses in everything from Web site development to car engines and poker in order to transform myself into hundreds of different male fantasies. I was constantly struggling to become a near expert in anything and everything in only a week's time. To avoid this kind of struggle when I formed the agency, I made sure that every one of my five talented associates came ready and armed with a unique skill set. That way, no matter what the clients think their husband or wife will respond to, chances are it already exists in this room.

Take Katie Morgan, for example, seated on my opposite side with her knees propped up against the edge of the table. She's a petite girl in her mid-twenties with shoulder-length blond hair that she often wears pulled back in a ponytail with jaggedly cut bangs sweeping across her forehead. I always know when she enters a room because she is constantly followed by the smell of strawberry bubble gum and the sound of punk music blaring from her iPod.

Katie is our resident guy's girl. She's feisty and sassy, and she loves to drink beer. She's got this cute "girl next door" look about her, but once she opens her mouth, it's quite another story. With her razor-sharp wit and cunning knack for verbal repartee, she can win almost any argument you put in front of her. She's one of those people who can convince you that you're wrong and then somehow also magically convince you at the same time that you should be grateful to her for pointing it out. It's nothing short of a Jedi mind trick. I hired her because she can outmaneuver men at all of their own games: poker, darts, pool, beer pong, fantasy football, even car racing.

Before joining the Hawthorne Agency, Katie did what every other good-looking blonde under thirty does in this town: She acted. But the few and far between one-liner parts that she did manage to land didn't exactly pay the bills. And when she learned that the money in this job is comparable to the salary of an established soap star, she didn't hesitate for a second. Plus, it gave her the opportunity to put her acquired acting skills to use on a regular basis. And because my "intention to cheat" rules clearly state that all physical intimacy with a subject is limited to what the FCC will allow on network television, I imagine this job is fairly similar to a typical recurring role on a popular daytime soap opera.

Seated next to Katie was the breathtakingly beautiful Shawna Miller. Although I think every one of my associates is irresistible in his or her own way, Shawna possesses the kind of classic, undisputable beauty that never fails to turn heads on the sidewalk. The moment I saw her, I knew she was perfect for this job. She has the kind of look that men lust after. Todd Langley is living proof of that. With long, wavy blond hair, a captivating smile, and the most perfectly straight white teeth I've ever seen, she inevitably cultivates a certain sense of "wow" that follows her everywhere she goes.

Shawna is also incredibly versatile, which affords me a lot of flexibility when placing her on an assignment. She can play the heartbroken and vulnerable Keira Summers one night and a raging party girl the next. But with her heart-stopping good looks, curves in all the right places, and a tolerance to alcohol that's through the roof, she's usually my go-to associate for bachelor parties. I've often overheard other members of the staff refer to her affectionately as "the final fling girl." And based on the actions of the soon-to-be husbands she encounters on her assignments, it's a fairly accurate nickname.

Sitting across the table from Shawna was Cameron Kelly. Cameron is the only male associate at the agency. He looks remarkably like Josh Duhamel, so much so that he is often mistaken for him by

fifteen-year-old girls and subsequently finds himself signing a lot of
"With Love, Josh Duhamel" autographs whenever he steps foot inside a mall. Obviously, I brought him on because men aren't the
only ones who cheat. Yes, the statistics are staggeringly higher, but
the bottom line is women cheat, too. And the high failure rate of his
inspections is indisputable proof of that.

Despite his protests, Cameron often finds himself wearing a
uniform of some kind. I've requisitioned uniforms from almost
everywhere—the navy, the marines, American Airlines, UPS, even
Sparkletts on one occasion when a client insisted that his wife had a
thing for the tall, handsome men who carry those five-gallon bottles
of water over their shoulders. Apparently, clichés are created for a
reason. And I can now tell you firsthand that married women . . .
like men in uniform.

Finally, at the far other end of the table, in her usual place, sat
Teresa Song, the sultry Asian siren. At least that's the way some of
the other associates like to refer to her. And I have to admit, the title
fits her to a tee.

Teresa is an enigma. She's cold, mysterious, and detached. But
that's exactly why I hired her. Because a lot of men like that kind of
thing. She's strikingly beautiful, with soft, feminine features, yet there
doesn't appear to be one warm, sympathetic bone in her body. But
men are just sort of awestruck in her presence. She definitely has the
ability to reel them in with only a look. Which I suppose is a good
skill to have in a "follow, not lead" business such as ours.

Teresa doesn't say a lot around the office, and as far as I can tell,
she's never made much of an attempt to get to know any of the other
associates. But she shows up for staff meetings on time, writes her postassignment reports with impressive detail, and is always extremely
professional, so I can't really complain. Plus, her aloof, indifferent at-
titude is exactly why I hired her.

That and her uncanny knack for real estate.

"Teresa," I said, launching into the meeting, "Larry Klein, the
real estate agent you tested last week. How did it go?" I pulled a yellow legal pad from my briefcase and flipped through a few scribble-
covered pages until I located a blank one.

"He failed," Teresa replied with her usual zero attachment.

"Care to elaborate?" I teased.

She shrugged apathetically. "I requested an appointment to see the property alone, and once we reached the bedroom, he just went for it. It's all in the report. I'll e-mail it to you by five."

"Great," I said, making a note on the blank page of my legal pad. "I only have one for you this week." I pulled a glossy crimson folder from the top of the pile, double-checked that the front page was inscribed with Teresa's name, and slid it across the table. Teresa caught it adeptly under the tip of her index finger without so much as a flinch.

"A businessman from Chicago," I explained as she leafed through the file. "He's staying at the Four Seasons in Beverly Hills. He likes to hire a private masseuse from a local Asian massage parlor when he's in town. His wife is afraid it's more than just a massage. I've made arrangements for you to go instead. Find out what he does— or tries to do—behind closed doors. Hadley located a geisha costume for you. It's hanging in the prop closet."

Teresa nodded ever so slightly and closed the folder. "Done."

I turned to my left. "Cameron, how'd it go yesterday with Jocelyn Sandover, the housewife in Santa Monica?"

"Pretty basic, really. We met up at her child's school, talked for a while, and then she invited me for coffee and eventually back to her place. It seemed to take her some time to get comfortable, but once she did, it was over pretty quickly."

I made another note on my pad. "Okay, and how'd you make your exit?"

Cameron took a sip from a Starbucks cup in front of him. "I told her I thought I'd left the lights on in my car."

Katie rolled her eyes and popped her gum. "How creative," she mumbled.

Cameron's hand shot up in protest. "Hey . . . it was the best I could come up with spur of the moment."

"Whatever works," I replied diplomatically.

In my days as a sole proprietor, I usually made a habit of telling the subject to his face that the entire night had been a setup, that I had been hired by his wife or girlfriend to test his ability to remain faithful, and that he had failed. Then I left behind a card with a toll-free phone number on it that the subject could call for more information. But because that approach sometimes got me into trouble, not to mention jeopardized my safety on a few rare occasions, I decided to abandon that practice and the cards when I started the agency. Now my associates were instructed to "make an exit" and never come back, leaving behind no explanation and no proof that they were even there to begin with. It was for their own protection. Plus, it allowed time for them to report back to me with the results. If the subject knew what had just happened, there's a chance he (or she) might try to interfere before I'm able to deliver the news to the client.

The assignment files that I distribute at staff meetings all contain more or less the same contents. On the first page is always the client and subject biography outlining the background and relevant information of the man or woman who hired us and the person we've been asked to inspect. Following that is the assignment report, charting out all the details of the associates' forthcoming inspection. Where to go, what to wear, who to be, what to talk about, and any other facts or particulars that I feel are relevant to the case at hand.

I pulled the next folder from the stack and handed it to Cameron. "Another housewife. The client is worried that she gets 'bored' during the day while he's gone and wonders how far she'll go to remedy that."

Cameron groaned as he took the file. "Please don't tell me I have to wear that damn UPS uniform again."

I flashed him an affectionate smile. "No uniform this week. But you will have to take your shirt off. You're going in as the new pool boy."

Everyone in the room snickered. Katie nearly choked on her bubble gum.

"Seriously?" Cameron said, leaning forward to get a closer look at the file.

I nodded. "You'd be surprised what bored housewives will do when a shirtless man comes to clean their pool."

After explaining a few details to Cameron, I continued moving around the table. Katie and Lauren reported two more failed inspections to add to my ever expanding database of infidelity, and I handed them both new case files for the week. A newly engaged software developer for Lauren and a guy who spends too much time at the track (according to his wife) for Katie.

At five before the hour, I finally landed on Shawna. I glanced down at my legal pad and flipped back a few pages until I reached my notes about her latest assignment. She'd been sent to Des Moines last Thursday to attend an election fund-raising event for a popular Republican senator. The subject, Richard Patterson, happened to be one of the campaign's largest contributors. His wife, Michelle, a life-long Democrat, was worried that their opposing politics were starting to become a problem in their twelve-year marriage. To determine the validity of her concerns, I sent Shawna to the fund-raiser, posing as a beautiful young diehard Republican who shared all of the subject's political views.

"Shawna," I stated in an even tone, glancing through my notes, "you were in Des Moines last week with Richard Patterson."

She nodded. "Yes."

"And what happened there?"

"He passed, actually."

My head popped up in surprise, and I stared at her for a stunned moment before speaking. "He did?"

"Yeah," she confirmed. "He didn't seem to want anything to do with me."

"Really?" I was having a hard time hiding my skepticism. I knew I should have been pleased with this result. It wasn't every day that I got to deliver *good* news to a client. But I'd had a strong feeling about the way this assignment would turn out from the beginning. And my initial instincts were hardly ever wrong.

But Shawna simply nodded again. "We were seated at the same table, we chatted for a while, and then that was pretty much it. Eventually he told me he had to get up for an early meeting and left."

I conducted another quick scan of my notes. "Did you talk about Prop 31?"

"Yes."

"And what about the death penalty and immigration?"

Shawna glanced uneasily around the room. "Yes," she said again. "All of those issues came up in our conversation."

"And did you research all the initiatives on the upcoming Iowa ballot? Because if you weren't fully knowledgeable on all the issues, he might have thought that you were after something else."

An uncomfortable silence fell over the room. Everyone was gaping at me, wondering where this second degree was coming from. Shawna fidgeted in the hot seat, shifting her weight around and running her fingers through the ends of her hair. "I . . . um . . . I think so. I spent the entire week preparing for it. He just . . . didn't seem interested in . . . you know, doing anything else but talking about politics."

I nodded, although I wasn't fully convinced. What if Shawna had missed something?

My logical side was telling me to let it go. That I was attracting too much attention and making everyone nervous. But there was another side of me that just couldn't seem to go along with that. Michelle Patterson would be using *this* information to decide the way she lived the rest of her life. If it wasn't one hundred percent correct, she could be making a huge mistake.

And then another thought struck me. And this one nearly knocked the wind out of me: Would it have turned out any differently if *I* had been the one at that fund-raiser?

I dismissed the notion immediately. Because it was beyond ludicrous. I hired Shawna because I knew she was well qualified and capable, and I had every bit of faith that she'd pulled off this assignment, as well as every other assignment, flawlessly.

But then where was this sudden paranoia coming from?

Was it possible it was just a side effect from the phone call I got this morning?

Well, I refused to let a former client's divorce proceedings interrupt my ability to do my job. Michelle Patterson would be ecstatic to know that her husband was every bit as faithful to her now as he had been the day she'd married him. And I would be just as ecstatic to tell her about it. End of story.

"Okay, then," I said, trying to sound upbeat as I picked up the last case file on the table. "Here's a local bachelor party for you. The groomsmen are taking the subject to a gentleman's club in West L.A. The client agreed to let her fiancé go as long as he promised not to get any lap dances. The only way to find out if he keeps his word is for you to pose as one of the girls at the club. Hadley signed you up for some private pole-dancing classes at a studio here in Santa Monica. Two or three sessions before the weekend should be sufficient."

Shawna tentatively reached out and took the file, her expression still uncertain. I could feel her eyes scanning my face for clues to unraveling my strange behavior. So I masked it with a bright smile and then turned my attention to the rest of the group. "Well, that's everything for today. I'll see you all next Tuesday. Don't forget to turn in your postassignment reports by five tonight. And be sure to call or e-mail if you have any questions."

I excused everyone and gathered my things before disappearing down the hallway into my office to get ready for my next appointment. According to my calendar, it was with a woman named Melissa Stanton, presumably coming in to discuss her concerns about Mr. Stanton.

I stopped just short of my office door and looked back toward the conference room, watching as everyone else filed out of the office and disappeared into their own private lives. I have no idea where they go when they walk out those double glass doors, and frankly, I don't care. Or better yet, I choose *not* to care. As long as they do their jobs and uphold the reputation and confidentiality of this agency, as far as I'm concerned, their personal life is their own business.

And I attempt to maintain the same level of privacy for myself. None of my employees even knows my real name. And they certainly don't know anything about my home life. They don't know about Sophie's wedding or my laborious maid-of-honor duties. They don't know that I have yet to tell my mother what it is I really do for a living and doubt I ever will. Or that up until a year ago, I had been completely estranged from my father.

And they definitely don't know anything about Jamie.

I just don't see the point in mixing your professional life with your personal life. That's why I leave my associates alone and choose not to worry about what they do outside of this office. The screening process each of them went through before being offered employment was extensive enough—background checks, drug tests, a mandatory two-week tail by a private investigator. They were trustworthy people. That much I knew.

And I didn't see any reason to learn more.

I was in my office for only a few minutes when the intercom on my desk buzzed and Hadley announced the arrival of my next appointment.

By the looks of her, Melissa Stanton was in her mid- to late thirties. If I had to guess, thirty-seven. But definitely no more than forty. Her hair was dark and long and swept away from her face into a half ponytail, secured with a black clip. She was medium height, slender, with smooth skin that showed hardly any lines.

I held out my hand to greet her. "Hello, I'm Ashlyn, president of the Hawthorne Agency. It's nice to meet you."

"Nice to meet you, too . . . sort of." She chuckled weakly.

"Please take a seat." I gestured to the white chenille sofa in the corner of the room. I sat opposite her on a matching armchair, holding my notepad in my lap as I waited for her to get settled.

She surveyed her surroundings somewhat uneasily. I've tried to make this room feel as welcoming as possible. But I also know that making someone feel comfortable in a situation like this was a near-impossible task.

When she didn't speak right away, I took the liberty of initiating the conversation. "Why don't you start by telling me why you're here?" I suggested.

Mrs. Stanton took a deep breath and forced a silly smile onto her face. "The truth is," she began, "I came here because I need to hire a nanny."

My smile immediately faded into a cloud of confusion that I fought to hide. "Uh-huh," I replied guardedly.

We were, after all, registered with the city of Los Angeles as a "domestic services" agency, a company that helps match families with qualified nannies, housekeepers, and tutors, but that was just a cover that I came up with for tax purposes and . . . parental purposes. Namely *my* parental purposes. We didn't *really* do that. The domestic services agency was a dummy corporation to mask the real services we offered.

I decided to tread lightly. If this woman really thought she was here to hire herself a nanny, then I would have to politely steer her in a different direction without giving away any unnecessary information. "And may I ask how you heard about us?"

Mrs. Stanton fidgeted in her seat. "I was referred by a friend. I told her about my . . ." She paused awkwardly. "Well, my current nanny situation, and she recommended I get in contact with you. She said you could help."

Yes, this woman was definitely in the wrong place. But what friend referred her? We'd never placed anyone with a nanny . . . or a housekeeper, for that matter. Why would she have been referred to us? It must have been some kind of mix-up.

"Well," I said with decisiveness, plopping my notepad onto the coffee table between us, "I'm afraid we're fresh out of nannies today, and it doesn't look like we'll be getting any more in the near future. But I'd be happy to call you if that changes. In the meantime, may I suggest you try another agency so your children aren't kept waiting?"

She looked at me as if I were crazy. As if she had absolutely no idea what I was talking about. But believe me, the feeling was mutual.

She shook her head. "No, no. It's not for my children. It's for my husband."

I cocked my head to the side and shot her a strange look. "You need a nanny for your husband?"

She nodded slowly and reluctantly, and I could see tears forming at the corners of her eyes. "Yes." She took a deep breath and cleared her throat. "I have reason to believe that he's slept with the past *three* nannies that I've hired. But I need to know for sure."

Slowly the cloud began to lift, and I suddenly understood what this woman was asking.

I leaned forward and picked up my legal pad again. "So you want us to send one of our associates," I confirmed with a tight nod of my head. "To pose as the new nanny."

She seemed relieved that I had caught on and she wouldn't have to actually explain what she had in mind. "Yes," she replied with a heavy sigh. "I figure the only way I can prove my suspicion is if the next nanny I invite to live in my home is there as a decoy."

4

déjà golf

When I arrived home later that night, Jamie was waiting for me in the living room. He was sitting on the sofa, his feet propped up on the coffee table, the TV playing softly in the background. The minute the door closed, he jumped off the couch and ran over to me, pulling me into an unusually long hug. "Hey! You're on time."

I laughed as I tossed my briefcase onto one of the dining room chairs. "Did you expect me to be late?"

He shrugged. "Kind of."

"Well, I'm happy I could disappoint you." I glanced over his shoulder at the flat-screen TV on the wall. A middle-aged bearded man was demonstrating how to hang a two-hundred-pound mirror with a paper-clip-size piece of metal.

"Are you watching infomercials?" I asked in disbelief.

He quickly grabbed the remote and zapped it off. "I wasn't really watching it. I was just kind of zoning out."

"So, how'd your conference call go this morning?" I asked from the hallway as I made my way into my bedroom. I pushed my feet out of my slingbacks and placed them in a cubbyhole in the back of my closet.

Jamie entered a few moments later and lay down on the bed, propping himself up against a stack of throw pillows. "Good. I'm pretty sure I convinced them to sign with us. It's a quarter-of-a-million-dollar gig, so the senior partners are gonna be pretty psyched."

"That's fantastic!" I called from the closet, trying to sound bubbly. But honestly, it didn't really work on me.

Which was why Jamie laughed in response. "So, how was work for you?"

I shrugged. "Work was work." I pulled my shirt over my head and tossed it into the clothes hamper. "I got the strangest request for an assignment today, though."

"Oh yeah?"

I stepped out of the closet and leaned against the doorway. "Some woman wants one of the associates to pose as a nanny in her house."

Jamie let out a laugh. "You mean like a live-in nanny?"

"Yeah. She thinks her husband has been sleeping with the nannies."

"Nann*ies* plural?"

"Hollywood Hills family. Husband is some big-time studio exec. Apparently, they've been through three in the last six months."

"Well, I guess it makes sense, then," Jamie mused. "Are you taking the assignment?"

"Yeah," I called as I walked back into my closet and sifted through hangers of clothes. I picked up a cassis-colored Diane von Fürstenberg dress and held it up against my body. "I just have to figure out who would be the best person to handle a job like that."

There was suddenly a long, awkward pause on the other side of my closet door, and then Jamie said, "What about you?"

I dropped the dress hanger down against my waist and glanced strangely toward the door. "What did you say?" I asked, popping my head out.

But he wouldn't look back at me. He kind of just stared straight ahead, and when I followed his gaze, there was nothing there except an old framed oil painting of Paris in the 1920s that he'd seen a million times. "I'm just saying," he replied, his tone bordering on chilly. "It's a highly unusual job. Nothing like the agency has ever seen before. And maybe it should be handled by a professional."

I stepped back into the bedroom and shot Jamie an offended look. "But my associates *are* professionals."

He tucked his hands behind his head. "But none of them have been doing this as long as you."

I wasn't exactly sure where he was going with this, but I didn't like the direction regardless. I sat on the bed, gripping the padded hanger in my hands. "But I *don't* do it anymore. You know that. I haven't done it for a year."

Jamie continued to avoid my stare. I finally got fed up and reached out to grab his chin and turn it toward me. "Hey," I said adamantly. "What's the matter?"

He shrugged evasively again. "Nothing. I'm just saying that if there were ever a time for you to come out of 'retirement,' I would think an assignment like this would be tempting."

I stammered, feeling helpless and insulted at the same time. Jamie had never acted this way before. He'd always said he was fine with my desk job. And his actions never suggested otherwise. But for some reason, *this* particular assignment was getting to him, and I wasn't sure why.

"Are you saying you *want* me to move into some stranger's house, pretend to be their nanny for three weeks to see if some horny, middle-aged man who can't keep his hands to himself tries to get it on with me? Is that what you want?"

"Is that what *you* want?" he shot back immediately, and I cowered slightly. His reaction surprised me. Not just the swiftness of it, but the traces of hostility that were lingering in its tracks.

"No!" I shouted as I shot up from the bed. "What are you talking about? Why would you even think that? I have *no* desire to get back into that side of this business."

Jamie looked up at me intensely. This time his gaze was penetrating, and I suddenly wished he'd go back to staring at the wall. "Even after what happened this morning?" he challenged.

I felt my fingers twitching against the hanger in my hands as I swallowed hard. "What about this morning?" I knew exactly what he was getting at, but I wasn't going to give him the satisfaction of confirming it. If he really wanted to go down this road, he would have to be the one to lead the way.

"That's six courtroom losses in a row," he pointed out, as if he were simply stating the score of a hockey game he cared nothing about.

"So?"

"So," he echoed, "I just thought maybe you'd be feeling a little . . . I don't know, helpless. Unfulfilled. Empty."

"Empty," I repeated, as if I were hearing the word for the first time, wondering what kind of meaning Jamie was attempting to infuse it with.

"Yeah," he insisted. "I mean, you spend two years fulfilling this crazy quest of yours. You know, to expose cheaters, find the truth, enlighten people. And then suddenly you have to take a backseat and watch other people do it. Sure, at first it's fine. You feel like you're still an active part of the process. But then a year goes by, you start looking for other ways to get *involved,* and they don't pan out. So where does that leave you? And how are you going to remedy it?"

I was speechless. His words struck an unnerving chord inside me. Not necessarily because they were right on target, but because they weren't entirely *off* target. Regardless, I wasn't about to move into some stranger's house and take care of her kids as I waited for her husband to try to sleep with me. And Jamie had to understand that. Or if he didn't, I had to *make* him.

I took a deep breath and reached out to grab his hand. "Jamie," I said softly, "that part of my life is *over.* Yes, I may have felt a little down because of the expert witness thing. But that doesn't mean I'm itching to go back to almost sleeping with married men. I made a promise to you, and I'm going to keep it." I paused and decided to rephrase. "I *want* to keep it. That's why I hired five very capable associates to replace me."

His eyes flickered up at me and held my gaze. "But what if the client doesn't want one of your associates? What if the client wants *you?*"

I stared at him, somewhat stunned. "I would say no."

His eyebrows rose. "Really?"

"Really," I assured him in a calculated whisper.

Jamie's face was very stern. I had never seen him look so serious before. And then, as if someone had flicked a switch inside him, it suddenly just softened. The intensity in his eyes faded away, his tightly pressed lips parted, and all the muscles in his face relaxed. Then he nodded as a soft smile broke through. "Okay," he whispered back. "I'm sorry. I guess sometimes I just need to make sure that it's what you really want. That I'm not holding you back."

I wanted to laugh. "Holding me back?" I sputtered. "Are you kidding? If it weren't for you, I'd probably be in some seedy hotel bar in Milwaukee or something right now. Trust me, baby, you have only pushed me *forward*."

This response seemed to please him immensely, and his small smile grew into a dopey grin. "I'm happy to hear you say that."

I leaned forward and kissed him deeply, trying to extract any remaining shred of doubt from his body with the power of my lips.

"Now," I said, a clear change of focus in my voice, "where are we going tonight?"

But he just smiled and shook his head smugly. "Still not telling."

I threw my free hand up in the air. "Well, how am I supposed to decide what to wear?" I held up the Diane von Fürstenberg dress in front of me. "How about this?"

He promptly vetoed it. "*Way* too formal."

I turned the hanger around and gazed longingly at my new dress. "It's not *that* formal. It's supposed to be a casual dress."

"Just wear something comfortable."

"Fine," I muttered as I disappeared back into the closet.

"And Jen?" Jamie's voice followed behind me a few seconds later.

I popped my head back out. "Yeah?"

"What do you think about giving up the expert witness gig for a while?" The question was serious, but his voice danced so playfully along the words, it almost sounded like a joke.

Either way, I knew what my answer had to be. "I think it's a very good idea."

Thirty minutes later, Jamie had already vetoed four different outfits, claiming that each was "not comfortable enough," until I felt like asking if I should just wear a pair of sweatpants and an oatmeal peel-off face mask. He had finally approved a pair of low-rise khaki pants and a black fitted V-necked sweater, and we headed to the garage, where Jamie's car was parked in the space next to mine. I had tied my hair into a tight ponytail so that he could put the top down. Jamie had bought his convertible Jaguar before we met, and I constantly teased him about owning a car so prestigious that it had its own special pronunciation guide: *Jag-yoo-ar.* But then I guess I wasn't one to talk. I drove a Lexus. But at least it was a hybrid. And at least the commercials didn't call it a *Lex-you-us.*

"Okay," I said as soon as we were out of the garage and the top was down. "Now are you going to tell me where we're going?"

Jamie laughed and shook his head as he flipped on his left turn signal and turned onto Wilshire Boulevard. "What's the matter? Your magic men-reading superpower not able to penetrate the wall of steel I've put up in my brain?"

"Ha," I replied sarcastically, wishing I had never divulged that particular secret to him. One year later and he still gives me shit about it.

But as it turned out, the two men who seemed to be completely immune to my keen men-reading abilities were Jamie . . . and my father. Ironically, the only two men in the world I would give anything to read.

Like right now, for instance.

"Very funny," I quipped. "It just so happens my abilities don't work in the car. Something about the asphalt on the road. I don't really want to bore you with the science of it all. It's quite complicated."

Jamie flashed me that award-winning smirk of his. "I see."

But as he skillfully navigated the streets of West L.A., I was trying desperately to narrow down our destination. With every turn he took, my mind was systematically eliminating possible locations. For instance, as soon as he passed Barrington Avenue, I knew that we weren't going to our favorite sushi restaurant. And the minute he turned right onto Sepulveda, I knew that it couldn't possibly be our favorite jazz club in West Hollywood. And when he finally turned left onto Pico, I was thoroughly confused. My only thought was that he was taking some mysterious alternate route to throw me off my keen sense of direction.

It wasn't until we reached the intersection of Pico and Overland that it dawned on me where he was heading. And once I figured it out, my mouth crept into a knowing smile and I looked over at him in amazement.

"No . . ." I shook my head in disbelief. "You are not seriously taking me there *again*."

He grinned. "Ah, so you've finally figured it out," he remarked as he pressed down on the accelerator and sped out of the intersection.

"Yes," I said, watching the familiar landmarks pass by. "But I'm just not sure *why* we're going there."

Jamie slowed the car and turned left into a parking lot. It was a parking lot I hadn't stepped foot in for over a year. And not because of bad memories associated with it. This parking lot actually held some of the best memories of my life.

It was where Jamie had first kissed me.

And directly adjacent to it was the golf course where we'd had our very first date. The fact that he had taken me to a golf course for a first date had actually surprised me. It was different and fun and even the slightest bit bold. I believe the original rationale behind the location selection was the idea that he'd be able to impress me with his golf skills. But that's not exactly how the story ended up going.

It wasn't like any date I had ever been on. Although that's not saying a great deal since I hadn't really dated much in my adult life. Particularly not after starting my fidelity inspection business. But I couldn't imagine a date being any better.

I remember the conversation being so fluid and natural. As if we'd been having conversations together all of our lives. Granted, I had made a living out of making sure that conversations flowed smoothly, but with Jamie, there was no effort necessary. I didn't even have to try. It just flowed.

I remember the dinner he bought me: hot dogs and Cokes at the golf course snack stand. Ironically, it was one of the best meals I'd had in a long time. And then he kissed me—right here in this parking lot—and every nerve ending in my body simply exploded. Of course, I hadn't seen it at the time, but it was pretty obvious looking back now that the night was going to change my life.

And it certainly did.

"We're *here*," Jamie explained as he steered the car into a parking spot and pulled up on the emergency brake, "because we haven't been here since the night of our first date."

"Yes," I agreed. "And if I remember correctly, that was a very painful night for you. I think I whupped your ass by about thirteen strokes. I would think this was the last place you'd want to return to."

Jamie bowed his head in shame. "Not one of my finer moments, I admit. But that's not what I remember most about this place."

He smiled tenderly at me, and I could feel my face blush. It still amazed me that he was able to do that. Make me blush with only a look. Even after a whole *year* of blushing. You would think that my body would have run out of whatever chemical it required to turn my cheeks red a long time ago, but it hadn't. I just kept on blushing.

"But this time," he began as he got out of the car and popped the trunk using the keyless remote, "I came prepared."

I peered inside and saw that he had brought both of our golf clubs *and* shoes. I let out a boisterous laugh. I hadn't used those shoes since he'd bought them for me the last time we were here. After it was discovered that golfing in espadrilles with wedge heels wasn't all it's cracked up to be. "Good thinking," I said to him. "How long did you have to rummage through my closet to find those?"

He shrugged. "Only about an hour."

Everything was exactly as I remembered it. I felt as though I had stepped back in time. Rewound an entire year and was now reliving the night all over again. We still managed to share a laugh at Jamie's subpar golf skills, the conversation still flowed naturally without skipping a beat, and I could still feel small traces of that same exhilaration I had felt when I was here with him for the first time. The kind of exhilaration that comes with something new and unknown.

Except now I was able to be myself. There were no more secrets between us. No fake jobs, no fake names, no fake alibis.

It was just me and him. And that's what made tonight an even better version than the one I remembered.

After the fourth hole of the nine-hole course, Jamie parked the golf cart in front of the snack stand, and I just had to shake my head and laugh at him. I was really enjoying this whole rerun episode from our life. "Let me guess," I said. "Hot dogs and Coke?"

He smiled and held out his hand to help me out of the cart. "Men-reading skills back?"

"Lucky guess."

Jamie walked up to the snack stand to order the food, and I took a seat on the same wooden bench we had occupied on the night of our first date. It was the strangest sense of déjà vu I'd ever had. As I waited for him to bring over the food, I tried hard to remember what it was like to be here with him a year ago, when all I could think about was making sure he never found out the truth.

I was grateful when I realized that I couldn't really remember what that felt like. I couldn't put myself back into the mind of the girl I used to be. The one who trusted no one and wanted nothing to do with love. Because in her experience, it always ended with pain. I knew now how far I had come from being that girl.

And that made me smile.

Jamie came over with the hot dogs and Cokes and sat next to me. "Ketchup only," he recited as he handed me the paper tray.

"Well, that's one thing that's different," I remarked.

He tilted his head to the side. "What do you mean?"

I pulled off my leather golf glove and took a bite out of my hot dog. "I mean," I began, chewing and swallowing, "last time we were here, you didn't know what I put on my hot dog, and now you do. But other than that, it's exactly the same night. Nothing is different."

Jamie shook his head. "What are you talking about? Everything is different!"

"Yeah, I mean, obviously *we're* different," I conceded as I popped the top of my Coke. "We see each other every day. We practically live together. But I mean *this* . . ." I motioned to our surroundings. "This night is *exactly* the same. Don't get me wrong, it's wonderful. I *love* how everything's the same. It even *feels* the same. Which is crazy!"

I took another bite of my hot dog and looked over at him. It was then that I realized he hadn't even touched his yet. He was just sitting there, staring at me with this far-off pensive look on his face as his "dinner" lay uneaten on the bench next to him.

"What?" I asked, instinctively reaching up and wiping away any stray crumbs or ketchup blobs from the corners of my mouth.

He shook his head slowly, his eyes never leaving mine. It felt like forever before he spoke again. And I wondered what was preoccupying his thoughts. I hoped it wasn't the same thing we had talked about in my bedroom earlier.

"I know something that might make tonight different," he finally said.

I took another bite of my hot dog. "What's that?" I mumbled through a mouthful of bread and kosher beef. "If they had switched to Pepsi?"

And then I saw Jamie push himself toward the edge of the bench and over the side until he was kneeling on the cold, hard cement of the cart path. I watched in slow motion as he reached into his pocket and pulled out a small navy blue velvet box. When he flipped open the lid and revealed a flash of sparkling diamonds, everything around me suddenly went fuzzy, and I felt my hand reach out to steady myself on the splintered wood.

"This," he said.

5

unlucky number seven

The piece of hot dog in my mouth wasn't chewed nearly enough, but I forced myself to swallow it anyway, wincing as it pushed its way down my throat.

Of course, I've thought about getting married before. Plenty of times. Maybe not as much as some girls my age do, but enough. You can't spend an entire year with someone and not have the thought at least *cross* your mind. Even if it's just a fleeting notion—there one second and gone the next—just passing through on its way to a more welcoming, make-yourself-at-home kind of place.

And that's how it always was for me. The thought would enter, I would acknowledge it, and just as quickly as it had come, I would excuse it as an idea that was still light-years away from turning into a reality. A futuristic concept, even. Like flying cars or a pill that stops the aging process. Never something that I would fully entertain at this moment in my life.

But now there it was, standing—no, *kneeling*—right in front of me, forcing me to entertain it.

I had no doubt that I wanted to spend the rest of my life with Jamie. I couldn't imagine spending it with anyone else. But did people really get married after knowing each other only one year?

My mind fluttered to Sophie. She and Eric had gotten engaged after only eight months. But that was Sophie. Sophie lived for that kind of stuff. I think she's seen *Father of the Bride* like fifty-two times. In fact, I wouldn't be surprised if she was watching it this instant. And taking diligent notes.

"I know you've seen a lot of marriages fall apart," Jamie began. "Including your own parents'. I know that what you do doesn't exactly lend itself to optimism when it comes to relationships. And I know that it's hard for you to believe in happily-ever-after endings. But I also know that I love you like I've never loved anyone before. And if you'll let me, I want to be the one to show you what a loving, trusting, *faithful* relationship is supposed to be like."

I could feel tears start to well in my eyes. I don't know where they were coming from. They were just coming. And I made no effort to stop them. Because I figured it was a normal reaction to a situation like this. And I've struggled so hard over the past year to be just that . . . *normal*.

"So what do you say?" Jamie asked, holding out the velvet box in front of me, the beautiful princess-cut diamond reflecting perfectly off the glare of the golf course dome lights. "Will you marry me, Jennifer H.?"

I laughed aloud at the nickname. He used to call me that when we first started dating. Because when we met on that fateful flight back from Las Vegas, I refused to tell him my last name. I gave him only the first letter.

Contemplation is never something you're supposed to do at a time like this. It's one of the most important decisions of your life, yet it's probably the only one that you're actually *expected* to make without thinking. Basing the rest of your life solely on your gut reaction. Because when a man is down on one knee, holding out a piece of jewelry that probably cost more than your first car, confessing his undying love for you, the last thing you want to do is make him wait while you mull it over.

So I closed my eyes and trusted my instinct. I refused to think. My heart was beating faster than I ever thought it could go without the threat of breaking down. But I knew that it was a sign. Something to keep me moving forward. To keep me from living in the past. So I said the first word that came out of my mouth, and as I did, I made a silent vow to myself never to second-guess it.

"Yes!" I shouted, throwing my arms around his neck and pulling him back up to his feet.

Jamie was beaming. I had never seen a smile on him quite like that before. It filled me with something soft and warm and comforting. As though someone had injected a huge mug of warm hot chocolate directly into my bloodstream.

As I watched him slide the large diamond around my finger, I found it hard to believe that I was actually shaking. In fact, I had a hard time keeping my hand steady enough for him to get the ring on. It's funny, I never imagined this being something that would make me nervous, after everything that I've done and seen. After every ring I'd seen *removed*. But then again, I'd never really imagined *this* to begin with.

Jamie laughed at my unsteady hands as he finally got the platinum band all the way up my finger. "You seem almost more nervous than me."

"You didn't seem nervous at all!" But then I stopped and remembered his little outburst earlier in the evening when I was trying to figure out what to wear. "Wait a minute," I said with a sudden realization. "Is this why you were prosecuting me about the nanny assignment?"

Jamie surrendered with a sheepish shrug. "I guess I just needed to make sure that you would still choose me over your former job."

"Well," I said, staring down at my left hand, "I hope you have your answer."

Jamie stood up and held both of my hands in his, staring deeply into my eyes. "I do."

He leaned in and kissed me then. I half expected to see fireworks light up the sky out of the corner of my eye. It seemed like such an appropriate accessory for this moment. But I suppose firework kisses only happen at the end of cheesy romantic movies.

I didn't exactly miss them, though. The fireworks, that is. Because it already felt like the Fourth of July was happening inside my stomach.

The minute Jamie and I got home from the golf course, we were ripping each other's clothes off like teenagers after the prom. We stumbled through the living room, desperately devouring each other's mouths as I pulled off his shirt and he unzipped my pants. My mind was still buzzing from the proposal. I had just agreed to marry someone. Me! Jennifer Hunter. The longtime inspector of fidelity had agreed to walk down the aisle, say, "I do," pledge forever in front of everyone I know. And then what? Babies? Preschool selection, high school graduation, a golf course–adjacent condo in a gated community in Florida?

I felt the dizziness start to take over. I told myself to slow down. One step at a time. No one was asking me to move to Florida. It was just a proposal. Nothing between us had changed.

We fell onto the bed, and Jamie's hands went for the back of my bra. He was kissing me everywhere, and I tried to wash away all of my doubts and anxiety and just live in the moment. Enjoy the feeling of his body on top of mine. I reminded myself that this was what it was all about. Just me and him. Nothing else mattered.

As soon as he was inside of me, the rest of the world just kind of faded away. Like magic. And all I could feel was him. Every part of him. The way he moved, the way he smelled, the way his hair felt between my fingertips. If this was what I was agreeing to for all of eternity, then dress me up in white and hand me a bouquet.

"I think we should go somewhere to celebrate," Jamie said as we lay in bed afterward, his arm draped under my neck, his hand gently rubbing the top of my shoulder.

I snuggled up next to him, the post-postengagement sex bliss washing over my entire body. "Where do you want to go?"

"I don't know. Cabo, Catalina, Hawaii."

"Mmm," I cooed in his ear. "I like the sound of that. Just you and me alone on an island somewhere."

"How about I book something for next weekend?"

I sighed euphorically. "Sounds perfect."

"So who are you going to tell first?"

"About our vacation?"

Jamie laughed. "No, silly. About the engagement."

"Oh, right." I nestled closer to the side of his body. "I don't know," I replied dreamily. "I guess my mom and my half-sister and my niece and then my friends."

He reached up and began stroking my hair. My eyes slowly started to close, and I could feel the warmth of his body overtaking mine. And just as my eyelashes hit my lower lids, he asked, "What about your dad?"

My eyes flew open again. I hadn't thought about him. Of course I would have to tell him. But suddenly, the thought of it made me want to change my name and move to another country.

I swallowed hard. "What about my dad?"

"Well," Jamie said with a certain air of precaution, as if he were handling this moment with the same care that you'd handle a test tube with biohazard cultures growing inside, "I was just thinking that this may be a good opportunity for me to meet your dad. And for *you* to meet your dad's new wife."

And then the nausea came. It felt as though my stomach had just taken three dizzying upside-down loops on an F-14 fighter plane while I was still here on the ground lying in bed, trying to enjoy what was once a very beautiful moment.

I had just rekindled my relationship with my father a year ago. And that relationship generally consisted of lunches, dinners, and an occasional Sunday matinee movie. We hadn't really reached the point of true father/daughter intimacy. He knew *of* Jamie, and I knew *of* his new wife, but we hardly talked about them, let alone had a face-to-face meeting. I couldn't imagine myself calling up my dad to gush about anything having to do with my love life. Particularly since the very reason we didn't speak in the first place was directly related to *his* love life. The thought of running to him to brag about my faithful, trusting, honest relationship seemed almost humorous to me.

My dad had gotten remarried about nine months ago to his *third* wife. And despite his persistent efforts to get me to come to the wedding, I had politely declined the invitations. The thought of watching my dad stand up on an altar and swear to be faithful to a new woman after the dreadful way he'd betrayed my mother just felt wrong to me. You're supposed to go to weddings to wish people well, support their commitment to each other, give them a big high five for finally settling down. That image didn't exactly compute when you inserted my father into the equation.

But regardless, my dad and I had actually managed to build something of a rapport these past twelve months. We avoided certain topics and relied heavily on others. It was as if there were an unspoken rule between us. Don't talk about relationships. Don't talk about cheating. And definitely don't talk about the past. Then, of course, there was the added unspoken rule that only I knew about: Don't talk about what you really do for a living. We stuck mostly to generic subjects like weather, news, sports teams, and politics. And that was the reason I had yet to meet his new wife and he had yet to meet Jamie. It's not that he hadn't suggested it . . . numerous times. As had Jamie. I just didn't feel we had graduated to that level yet.

Jamie had always been so supportive of my desire to take it slow when it came to my relationship with my father. But I had a hunch that my days of avoidance were going to come to an end very quickly.

"Yes," I said after another bitter swallow. "I guess you're right. This would be the perfect opportunity for everyone to meet."

The next morning before work, I called my mom, my half-sister, Julia, and my niece, Hannah, and told them the exciting news of the engagement. They all reacted pretty much the way I had expected. With my mom, there was a lot of shrieks and crying and even a few Godly praises, as if I had just told her that I had conceived immaculately.

My emotionally stunted half-sister, Julia, congratulated me politely, careful not to show too much excitement (presumably so she wouldn't hurt herself), and her daughter, my fourteen-year-old niece, Hannah, followed her breathless rounds of "Oh my God!" with three distinct and nonnegotiable requests: (1) "You have to let me help you pick out the dress." (2) "You have to let me be a bridesmaid." And (3) "You absolutely *have* to hire a professional makeup person."

When I hung up the phone, I knew that the next appropriate person to call would be my dad. Even if he hadn't been a part of my life for a good portion of my adult years, he was part of it now, and therefore I had to tell him.

And Jamie was right: This *was* a good excuse for everyone to meet. It would have to happen eventually, and the thought of waiting until the wedding day sounded even worse.

So I picked up the phone again, took a deep breath, and started punching in the number I had committed to memory, one slow, painful digit at a time. I don't think I could have done it any slower if I had been using a rotary phone.

3-1-0 . . . 5-5-5 . . . 2 . . . 1 . . . 2 . . .

The last digit was a 7. I knew it was a 7. There wasn't a single doubt in my mind that it was a 7. Yet I just couldn't press it. My finger touched the corresponding key on the keypad, but I just couldn't apply any pressure.

My breathing had gotten shallow, but I hardly noticed. I was too focused on that damn number 7 button. How had it suddenly become so menacing? It was just a stupid number on a stupid phone. There were nine others just like it, yet somehow this one number had taken on an entirely new meaning.

With one swift movement, I clicked off the phone and placed it back on the cradle.

This is stupid, I told myself. *You're a twenty-nine-year-old woman. You're fully capable of picking up the fucking phone and dialing a fucking phone number.*

I reached out and grabbed the phone again, holding it out in front of me and focusing intensely on the keypad, the way an aspiring mountain climber would stare longingly at Mount Everest.

"Who are you calling?" Jamie's voice filtered into the kitchen, causing me to jump. I quickly returned the phone to the cradle and spun around to face him.

"No one," I said brightly. "I just got done telling Hannah about the engagement."

This made him smile, and he came over to me and wrapped his arms around my waist. He was wearing nothing but a towel, and his fresh, wet skin smelled incredible. I inhaled deeply.

"And? How did it go?" he asked.

"She warned me about the pitfalls of home makeup application."

Jamie chuckled. "Sounds like Hannah. So you gonna call your friends next?"

I kissed him on the cheek and started for the hallway. "Nope," I replied casually. "They're coming over tonight to work on Sophie's place cards for the wedding. I figured I'd tell them all then."

"Good idea."

"I'm just gonna hop in the shower!" I called eagerly as I was halfway down the hallway. Once I had reached my bathroom, I couldn't get into that shower fast enough. I turned on the faucet, threw my shirt over my head, whipped off my sweatpants and underwear, and bounced into the stall.

I wasn't really that excited to take a shower. I was just trying to get as far away from that phone as possible.

After Jamie had left for work, I stood fully dressed and ready to go in front of my bedroom mirror. Everything about me—from head to toe—screamed professional businesswoman, from the dark gray pants suit over the black cotton camisole to the simple knot in my hair, twisted and pinned at the base of my head. The clean lines of my makeup, the unadorned strand of pearls hanging across my neck, even the Louis Vuitton briefcase I held in my right hand.

As with any other day, there were so many elements that made up my outfit selection. So many pieces that came together to form the meticulously designed representation of myself that I chose to display to my employees and my clients.

Yet today, all I could see was the big, fat, sparkling diamond on my finger.

It stood out like a beacon, drawing the attention of anyone in its vicinity. I may as well have had a spotlight pointed at my left hand.

I tried to imagine myself walking into the office with the brilliance and shine of this newly acquired accessory lighting the way ahead of me. There was no doubt it would be noticed. No, not only noticed. *Revered,* admired, gushed over, celebrated, and most of all . . . questioned.

Because before today, I was a mystery. My life outside of the office didn't even exist. Every time I walked through those double glass doors, I left all aspects of Jennifer Hunter behind. And until six P.M. I was known only as "Ashlyn." A woman who, as far as everyone else was concerned, had no dates, no prospects, no friends, and no family to speak of.

I stared into the mirror at the ring on my finger, my eyes nearly burning from its radiant reflection.

This ring makes me a different person.

The thought entered my mind so fast, I had no time to process the root of its origins. But where it came from didn't matter much. As soon as it was out there, I knew it was true. This ring *did* make me a different person. Not because I was, in fact, different just by wearing it, but because people's *perceptions* of me would change the moment they laid eyes on it.

I thought about the appointment I had later this morning with Camille Klein, the wife of the real estate agent Teresa had tested last week. She was coming in at eleven. How would she react when she saw this ring on my finger? Would she glance at it out of the corner of her eye but try to ignore it as she listened to me deliver the results of her husband's assignment? Would she judge me for wearing it while I gave her the most heartbreaking news of her life?

I would if I were her.

Because everyone knows a diamond ring on someone's left hand isn't just a diamond ring. It's a hopeful promise. Or in my case, a bold statement. Asserting to the world that I refuse to end up like the majority of my clients.

Even though I wasn't the one conducting the actual assignments anymore, I was pretty sure that being married or even engaged while running a fidelity inspection business was some kind of conflict of interest. I guess this is one of those rare industries where people trust you *more* when you're single.

And in one swift, fluid movement, I slid the ring off my finger, dropped it into an interior compartment of my briefcase, and closed the flap, keeping the *new* me safely concealed behind a wall of expensive Italian leather.

6

princess cut in an uncertain setting

"All right, let's get this over with," Zoë announced later that evening as she strode through my front door. "Bring on the glue sticks and the glitter."

Sophie entered right behind her, carrying three large shopping bags full of supplies. She groaned loudly, clearly not appreciating Zoë's sarcasm. "For the last time, Zoë, there is *no* glitter. It's my wedding, not my sweet sixteen."

"Whatever." Zoë waltzed into the living room and plopped down on the sofa. "Where's the pizza?"

"I ordered it about twenty minutes ago. It should be here soon," I replied, glancing curiously into the hallway behind Sophie. "Where's John?"

Zoë rolled her eyes. "He's out with his new *boyfriend*. He said he'd stop by later."

I stifled a frustrated sigh. I had been waiting to tell my friends about my engagement all day. Through two difficult and disheartening postassignment meetings. Camille Klein cried on my shoulder for ten minutes when she found out her husband had seduced Teresa in one of his for-sale homes, and Neal Carter had punched the wall when I told him that his wife had invited Cameron back to their home for coffee when his kids were in school. Then I had to call in a repairman to fix the dent.

I was looking forward to doling out some *good* news for a change, and I wasn't sure the information would stay trapped inside of me much longer. I was honestly planning just on blurting it out the minute everyone had crossed the threshold, but apparently, it wasn't going to work that way. And John would kill me if I didn't wait for him.

My shoulders slumped as I closed the door behind Sophie and watched as she covered my coffee table with newspaper and then proceeded to empty the contents of her shopping bags.

"Okay," she said, spreading out the supplies in perfectly divided sections across the table. "I've devised a system that should help this assembly process run smoothly."

Zoë shot me a look and then turned her attention to our bride-to-be. "Sophie," she began in her infamous "don't piss me off" tone, "they're place cards, not circuit boards."

But Sophie simply ignored the remark and began to explain to us the complicated inner workings of her carefully devised plan.

Thirty minutes into the evening, I was a nervous wreck. John still hadn't shown up, and I couldn't bring myself to eat any of the pizza that had been delivered because I was positive I'd just throw it right back up. Plus, I had already ruined four place cards (much to the dismay of Sophie) owing to the shakiness of my hands. Just for the record, hot glue guns and nerves? Not a good mix.

Sophie had divided the three of us into ministations. First she wrote the name onto the card in silver paint pen, then I hot-glued the stems and the flowers down, and finally Zoë was in charge of gluing down the thin strips of silver foil along the outer edge.

"What's your problem, Jen?" Sophie scolded me for the tenth time, possessively taking the hot glue gun from my hand and showing me the *correct* way to glue a flower to a stem. "Correct" meaning without getting glue all over the rest of the card.

"Sorry," I mumbled, setting a handful of dried daisies on the newspaper tablecloth and wiping my sweaty hands on my jeans. "I guess I'm not very crafty."

"I'll say," Sophie agreed.

The truth was, I didn't have the brain capacity at the moment to think about flower-and-stem placement. The only placement I *could* think about was my engagement ring conveniently tucked away in the top drawer of my dresser. I hadn't worn it all day and was somewhat antsy to put it back on. As if I were afraid it might lose its sparkle sitting idly in my drawer.

"Are you gonna eat that?" Zoë asked, pointing to the untouched piece of cold pizza on my paper plate.

I shook my head and nudged it toward her. "No. Go ahead."

She happily reached across the table and grabbed the slice, stuffing it into her mouth. "Oh my God," she began, her lips shiny with pizza grease, as though she had just applied a fresh coat of Chanel gloss. "I have to tell you what happened to me this afternoon in the parking garage at the promenade. . . ."

I only half listened to Zoë's dramatic road rage (or should I say *parking* rage) story because my eyes were darting back and forth between the place card in front of me and the door, waiting for a knock to come from the other side of it. I couldn't believe how late John was. My heart was thumping so loudly in my chest, I was certain Zoë and Sophie would be able to hear it and ask me what my deal was.

". . . but clearly I had been waiting for the spot, *with* my blinker on. So I totally rolled down my window and started yelling at the woman. . . ." Zoë was gesturing wildly with the hot glue gun in her hand, causing me to duck and lean repeatedly to avoid second-degree burns.

"And she was like, 'I don't fucking care if you were waiting for the fucking spot. I'm in a fucking hurry!' "

I knew Zoë well enough to know that the word *fuck* was not used quite as liberally in the original enactment of this story. Zoë likes to decorate her narratives with the F-word almost as much as Sophie likes to decorate little index cards with artificial flowers. But I kept my mouth shut and my eyes focused on not messing up "Jackson Henry's" place card. I didn't know who the hell he was, but I was positive he wouldn't appreciate a deformed flower next to his name.

"So then I'm just about to scream something back to her when she totally trips over a curb in the parking garage and like face plants on the pavement. And I'm like *fighting* not to laugh because that is just *so* karma in action right there, and I know if I laugh, I'll just be storing up bad karma for myself, so—"

"Zoë," Sophie interrupted sternly, nodding toward the place card in front of her. "You need to pay attention to what you're doing. You're holding up the assembly line."

Zoë looked down in front of her to see a pile of undecorated place cards stacked up next to her. "Sorry," she grumbled, and leaned back over her half-foiled card. "You know, you *could* help glue some of these silver sparkly things on yourself. Since you seem to be so efficient over there."

Sophie frowned. "But that would mess up the system."

I could see in Zoë's eyes that she wanted to escalate this argument, but I shot her a look and shook my head. All of us had been doing a lot of conceding in the past few months out of respect for Sophie's "big day." And we all suffered through it only because we knew that once that day was over, we could go back to mocking her obsessive personality as usual.

"Whatever," Zoë mumbled.

"It *was* a funny story," I offered her as a consolation. She looked up at me and gave me a grateful half smile.

By 9:45 P.M., John still hadn't shown. I could almost *hear* the engagement ring calling out to me from the top drawer. Begging for me to acknowledge it and set it free from its velvet-covered prison. Sophie, having become incredibly fed up with the hot-gluing efforts of her two minions, had officially taken over the entire assembly line, and Zoë and I were sitting on the couch, watching the end of a *Weeds* episode. But I could hardly concentrate on the dialogue of the show because I was far too distracted. I didn't know how much longer I could wait.

When the doorbell finally rang at ten o'clock, I bounded off the couch and yelled, "He's here! John's here!"

Zoë and Sophie both peered up at me with the strangest looks on their faces. "Okaaaay," Zoë stated hesitantly before turning her attention back to the television.

I ignored her and continued for the door, opening it with a wide swing and a relieved breath. As soon as John was visible, I practically leaped into his arms and hugged him. "You made it!" I cried passionately.

John just stood there, his arms hanging lifelessly at his side. He finally reached up and awkwardly patted the middle of my back with one hand. "Um, yeah. Nice to see you, too, Jen." He disengaged himself from my grasp and made his way into the living room. "What's with her?" he asked, pointing back to me as he plopped down on the couch.

Zoë shrugged. "Apparently she hates making wedding place cards even more than I do."

Sophie smacked her on the leg with the back side of her hand.

"So, Jen," John said, grabbing a piece of pizza crust off Zoë's paper plate and nibbling on it. "What's the latest?"

Well," I began hesitantly, still standing by the door, "I have some exciting news, actually. Yesterday—"

"Wait!" John's eyes immediately lit up with anticipation. "Don't tell me. Let me guess. One of your associates took a bribe from a subject to keep quiet? No! I know! The client showed up in the middle of the assignment and called the whole thing off!"

I sighed dramatically. I should have known that John had been asking about *Ashlyn's* life, not mine. Ever since last year when he found out (completely by accident) what I really did for a living, he's been the hugest pain in my ass. I guess you could say he's my biggest "fan." If I were a band, John would be my groupie. He always wants to know every tiny detail about every little thing that happens at the Hawthorne Agency. I think, to him, my work is like a reality show, and he's always on the edge of his seat waiting to find out who was last voted off the island. Or in this case, which cheating spouse got voted out of the marriage.

"Actually—" I started to say, but I was instantly cut off again, this time by Sophie.

"No," she interjected, obstinately shaking her head. "No talk of cheating this close to my wedding. It'll soak into the place cards and curse the marriage."

"Oh, please," Zoë begged. "Let us talk about *something* besides weddings. That's all we've talked about for the past six months!"

I looked down at my feet, shifting my weight nervously.

"Well, that's because I'm getting *married*," Sophie was explaining to Zoë, as if it were the first time she was being presented with this information.

"Well, *obviously*," Zoë replied, motioning to the various crafts supplies spread out on my coffee table. "But do we really have to *talk* about it twenty-four-seven? I mean, all I hear about nowadays is wedding, ceremony, reception, place cards, dresses, bridesmaids, flowers, caterers. Fuck, it's exhausting!"

"Well, excuse me for caring about the most important day of my life," Sophie shot back. "Excuse me for—"

"I'm getting married!" I finally blurted out, unable to stand there any longer waiting for my friends to take notice of the fact that I had something to say.

Everyone fell silent and stared at me.

The first one to make any sort of noise was John. But it wasn't exactly the kind of noise I expected. I thought he would react the same way he had reacted to Sophie's engagement announcement last year—with a loud, girly scream. One that only a gay boy living in West Hollywood was capable of generating. But he didn't.

Instead, he *laughed*.

Actually, it was more of a cackle.

"Yeah, right," Zoë added with a slight chuckle of her own. "Imagine that. Little Miss Fidelity Inspector walking down the aisle."

"Jen," Sophie stated seriously, "that's not funny. I don't find that amusing at *all*! Yes, I know I've been kind of hard to deal with lately. But I'm sorry. It's my wedding. And I'm allowed to be a bitch before my wedding. Do you know how stressful it is to plan a wedding?"

I stood in the middle of the living room, absolutely speechless. I couldn't believe what was happening. I had been waiting to tell them all day, and when I finally do, they think it's a joke!

Apparently, my engagement was a concept that simply refused to stick. Hot glue gun or no.

Sophie continued ranting. "I've had *three* different DJs back out on me in the last six months, and I'm really starting to think I should be taking it personally, and *then*—"

"No!" I screamed in frustration, interrupting Sophie's diatribe. "I mean, I'm *really* getting married. That's what I've been trying to tell you since John walked through the door. Jamie proposed to me last night. We're engaged!"

There was no laughing this time, just more staring. And the three of them looked at one another, trying to gauge whether anyone else in the room was actually buying this.

Sophie crossed her arms over her chest. Clearly, she was in no mood for April Fools pranks in October. "Really?" she challenged me. "So if you're engaged, where's your ring?"

I looked down at my empty left hand. And then, without another word, I raced down the hallway at warp speed, threw open my top dresser drawer, and yanked out the navy blue velvet box. I tore the ring out of its holder and shoved it onto my finger.

"You mean this ring?" I asked indignantly as soon as I came back into the living room. I stuck out my hand and brandished it in their faces.

I had never seen three jaws drop in such perfect synchronicity in all my life.

There was a really long silence. Sophie actually reached out to touch the rock on my finger, as if she were making sure it was real and not just one of those cool hologram illusion tricks.

After all the grief they'd given me over the past few years about my "intimacy issues," you'd think I would get a more welcoming reception.

Finally, one of them spoke. It was Sophie. But she wasn't exactly eloquent. "Jen! W-w-why didn't you . . . I mean, how . . . when did this happen? I'm sorry. I'm kind of in a little bit of shock."

The rest of them just nodded their agreement.

"Yeah, I can see that," I said with a laugh as I plopped back down on my white sectional couch, hugging a green throw pillow to my chest. "I'm still kind of in shock myself. It happened last night. He took me to the golf course where we had our first date, and he asked me right outside of the snack stand."

"That's pretty fucking cute," Zoë finally said.

I nodded. "Yeah, it was. And he's taking me to Cabo next weekend so we can celebrate."

"But you have your final dress fitting that Saturday!" Sophie protested, and then immediately thought twice about it and shrank back in her seat. "I mean, I'm sure we can move it," she offered.

I laughed endearingly at her. "Don't worry. I'll call the tailor myself and reschedule."

"Just don't eat too many carne asada tacos down there," she warned me. "That dress cannot be let out. It can only be taken in."

I reached out and laid my hand tenderly on her shoulder. "I won't."

She took hold of it and pulled it up to her face. "It's a beautiful ring," she finally conceded.

Then I waited for the screams, the jumping up and down, the perfectly timed simultaneous gasps. But there was none of it. They all just stared at me, their faces still blanketed with shock.

"I just can't believe this," John said dazedly. "With you two gone away to live in Coupleville, I guess it's just me and Zo left." He threw his arm around Zoë's neck, and she quickly pulled away with a horrified look on her face.

"Great, you two are getting hitched and I'm gonna be stuck with the young, the gay, and the restless over here."

"I resent that," John said, crossing his arms over his chest. "I am *not* restless. I'll have you know, I am getting plenty from my new boyfriend, Danny. And he is oh so—"

"Okay, we get the point," Zoë interrupted. "You're getting laid. Congratulations."

John squinted suspiciously at Zoë. "More importantly, it sounds like someone is not getting *any*."

"I get plenty," Zoë shot back defensively.

And just like that, the subject was changed. But I didn't protest. A part of me actually felt relieved.

"From who?" John challenged.

"No one in particular," she replied.

Sophie's face brightened. "That's *great* news!" she exclaimed with a bit too much enthusiasm. We all shot her a questioning look.

"Jeez, Soph, you act like I've been on a three-year dry spell or something."

Sophie giggled. "No, I mean that's not why I'm excited. I mean, I *am* excited that you're . . . you know, having sex. It's just that this means you'll have a date for my wedding. You finally have a plus one!"

Zoë thought about that for a second. Sophie's statement seemed to perplex her, as if she had been caught in an awkward dilemma. "But I already RSVP'd for just one."

Sophie waved this away with her hand. "I know, but I marked you down for two anyway. I knew you'd eventually find a date. So what's his name? We can make him a place card right now!" She reached across the coffee table and pulled a blank card from the stack. She popped the cap off her silver paint pen, like an Old West bandit on the trigger, and sat poised and ready to write.

All eyes were on Zoë, and for the first time in her life, she actually looked *uncomfortable.* I had known this girl for years, and never had I seen such a distraught look on her face. She was always so sharp, so quick with a comeback, so seemingly immune to typical girly drama. She always knew what to say, and she was always comfortable saying it. And now she looked as if she had just walked into a surprise party thrown three and a half months *before* her birthday.

"What's the matter, Zo?" I asked. "Do we know him or something? Is it someone's ex-boyfriend?"

John's eyes lit up. "I knew it. It's that guy I dated last year. That Byron guy. I totally knew he was straight!"

Zoë shook her head. "No . . . it's not that," she stuttered. "It's just . . ."

Sophie gestured exasperatedly with her paint pen. "So just tell me the name already."

"I'm not taking him to the wedding," she finally declared.

"Why not?" Sophie sounded insulted.

"I . . . um . . . I just don't think we're ready for that." Zoë reached forward and grabbed her half-eaten slice of cold pizza and took an oversize bite.

I studied her, intrigued. This was definitely not the Zoë I knew. Something was up. She was never one to follow any sort of society-accepted dating rules. That was much more Sophie's department. When Zoë wanted to sleep with a guy, she slept with him. When she wanted to say "I love you," she said it. And when she wanted to take him to a wedding, she took him. There were no games in Zoë's world. It just wasn't her style.

"You do realize that *she's* the one walking down the aisle," John commented, pointing conspicuously at the top of Sophie's head. "All you have to do with the guy is dance to a few slow songs and share a piece of cake. It's not a lifelong commitment or anything."

Zoë shrugged, swallowing her mouthful of pizza. "No, I know. I just don't want to bring him, okay? Can we drop it now?"

Sophie frowned in confusion as she slipped the top back on the pen and threw it into her shopping bag. "Okay, whatever you say. But if you change your mind, you can always—"

"I won't," Zoë stated firmly, and we all took that as a sign to change the subject yet again.

The night eventually wound down, and one by one, my friends offered me a hug and another round of stunned congratulations and then drifted out the front door. Sophie with her one hundred and sixty perfectly (or close enough) glued place cards, Zoë with the last piece of pizza and apparently some kind of chip on her shoulder, and John with his stories about the size of his new boyfriend's package. Until it was just me . . . left alone with my big shiny ring.

Jamie was staying at his own place tonight, and it felt almost sur-real sitting alone in my living room, staring down at my finger, and imagining what my life would be like from here on out, all because of a little piece of jewelry.

I sat on the couch, admiring it for a moment. I had never actually looked that closely at it before. I mean, *really* looked at it. I had no idea how many carats it was, because frankly, I knew nothing about that kind of stuff. But I did know it was beautiful. No, beautiful didn't quite do it justice. *Spectacular* was closer. Perfectly square and seated on a thin, gleaming band of platinum. Just looking at it made me want to run out and get a manicure.

With a sigh, I pulled myself off the couch and began to clean up the living room. I ran the empty pizza box out into the hallway and threw it down the trash chute. Then I crumpled up all the newspaper that was lining the coffee table and tossed it into the recycle bin. Finally, I brushed my teeth, washed my face, shut off all the lights in the house, and climbed into bed. For some reason, I half expected these everyday, mundane little chores to feel different, maybe even novel. Because now I was doing them as an *engaged* person. As a soon-to-be *married* person. But they felt exactly the same. Brushing my teeth was still just brushing my teeth. Even with the massive diamond that flashed brilliantly in the mirror with every stroke.

Despite everything that had happened in the past day, it all kind of felt like a dream somehow. As if I were living someone else's life. Someone who was, apparently, engaged to a beautiful man, with a beautiful ring on her finger. I figured I just needed more time to let the whole thing sink in. It was a big adjustment. I'd spent the last few years of my life convinced that marriage wasn't for me. That's not something you can just flip a switch and change. You have to ease into it.

That's why I didn't really blame my friends for not believing me. If someone had told me a year ago that right now I would be engaged, I probably would have laughed, too.

I guess a lot can change in a year.

7

two-timing

I tapped the stack of crimson folders against the conference room table to kick off Tuesday's staff meeting. "Good morning, everyone. We have a busy week ahead of us, so let's get started."

I had been engaged for exactly seven days now, and it still didn't feel any more real. I had spent the past week playing hide the engagement ring. I'd wear it around the house and out to dinner when I was with Jamie, and then in the mornings, as soon as I got within a block of the office, I'd slide it off my finger and hide it in the interior compartment of my purse or briefcase. I'd keep it off all day when I was at work and then slide it back on again as soon as I returned home.

Yes, it was something of a hassle pretending to be one person during the day and someone else entirely at night. But what could I do? I wasn't about to let the five people in this room know that I was engaged to be married.

"Lauren?" I turned toward my technical guru. "How'd it go last weekend with the recently engaged software developer in Minneapolis?"

Lauren pulled her attention away from a small PDA device that sat in front of her, half-dismantled, and replied, "Fine. The assignment went smoothly. I approached him at the cocktail party after the sales conference ended and commended him on his speech. He seemed apprehensive of my attention at first, but he continued to lead the conversation, and the more beers he consumed, the less apprehensive he became. He asked me to join him for dinner, and afterward he asked if I wanted to see a beta version of his new Web project. I said yes and followed him up to his suite. He wasn't extremely bold or assertive. I think he was waiting to make sure I would reciprocate an advance before he made any. He took me through the basic foundation of the software on his laptop, and the more I reacted to the programming, the more aroused he seemed to become. And then he eventually asked to kiss me."

I noted this down on my legal pad. "Interesting that he asked. What time did you finally leave the room?"

With lightning speed, she reassembled the device in front of her and tapped on the screen a few times. "One A.M. I met him in the conference center at six-thirty, so it was a fairly long night."

"All right, then," I said, continuing to scribble on the page. "I'm sure his fiancée will find this information useful, since she was about to put down a hefty deposit on the venue rental for the wedding."

I picked up the folder on the top of the stack and flipped it open. "How much do you know about an online role-playing game called . . ." I squinted at my notes. "Intergalactic Battle Quest?"

Lauren shrugged casually. "It's all right. Graphics need some updating and the interface has several bugs, but it's very popular among the young twenty-somethings."

"And apparently a few thirty-somethings as well." I handed her the file. "Jarod Cunning. He's an avid player. His avatar is 'Quelth Commander.' According to his girlfriend of five years, he's a bit obsessed."

Lauren nodded understandingly. "It's easy to do. Especially if you're bored with your life."

"Find him online," I instructed her, "and build up a rapport. Make sure you set up a player profile with your photo and a location in Seattle, so that he thinks you're local. Wait for him to request a meeting."

"No problem," Lauren confirmed, flipping through the contents of the folder. "I'll even set up a few dummy sites with my alias and photo and index them through Google. Just in case he searches for me online."

I flashed her an approving smile. "That's why I hired you."

She grinned back and then set off on disassembling her device again.

"God, you're a dork," Katie said jokingly, picking at her fingernail. "I can't even figure out how to pimp my MySpace profile."

"Well," I said, turning to Katie and moving on with the meeting, "fortunately, for your next assignment there is no computer knowledge necessary. Although I must ask, do you have any experience with children?"

Katie shot me a befuddled look. "No. Um . . . why?"

"I need you to go on a long-term undercover assignment . . . as a nanny."

After a few instants, the entire room (minus Teresa, whose nose was buried in the latest issue of *Vogue*) cracked up laughing. I fought hard to keep my composure. I suppose it was a bit funny, the thought of Katie running around after two small children. But she was the best associate for the job. After all, she was the one with the acting experience. If anyone could handle a long-term cover like this one, it was Katie. The most difficult part was the fact that I didn't have any idea how long this assignment would take. If Mr. Stanton really was sleeping with his nannies, who knew how long he usually waited to make a move. Did he get to know them first, build a relationship, and throw in some harmless flirtation for a few weeks? Or did he just go for it the first week on the job? And if he didn't show any signs of inappropriate behavior, then it was only a matter of how long Mrs. Stanton wanted to wait (and pay) before she felt confident that he was, in fact, trustworthy.

"You want me to do what?" Katie repeated, dumbstruck.

I smiled patiently. "I know you're probably not much of a kid person, but with your acting skills, you're the best person for this job. You could be there for a while, and I need someone who's capable of pulling off a lengthy cover."

My flattery seemed to persuade her somewhat, but she still looked hesitant. "Don't you have a nice little poker game or another trip to the track you could send me on?"

I walked the file over to Katie and placed it on the table in front of her. Then I gave her a reassuring pat on the shoulder. "Don't worry. The client knows that child care is not your primary responsibility. She assured me that you will never actually be alone with the children."

Katie reluctantly flipped open the folder and studied the picture clipped to the inside cover. It was a family portrait supplied by the client: Mr. and Mrs. Dean Stanton and their twin sons. "How old are they?" she asked, scrunching up her nose as if she had just taken a whiff of bad cheese.

I referred to my notes. "Nine." And then for good measure, I threw in, "A really fun age." Not that I knew anything about boys at the age of nine. Or any boys under the age of eighteen, for that matter.

Katie took a deep breath, and I tried once again to ease her mind. "Don't focus on the kids. Focus on the husband. That's who you're there for. You'll be posing as a twenty-two-year-old college student who's taking time off of school to figure out which direction she wants to go. Dean Stanton, the husband, is a high-profile movie studio exec. He runs New Edge Cinema. Pretty big deal. Just pretend you've been hired to play the role of the nanny on a popular sitcom or something. You don't *really* have to take care of the kids. You just have to *act* like you can."

She considered this and finally surrendered a weak shrug. "Fine. Whatever. Bring on the little demon children."

"That's the spirit," I offered back with an amicable grin. "I'll need updates twice a week. To be safe, you and I will only make contact via e-mail. But keep your phone on just in case."

"No problem," she muttered.

After Teresa and Cameron had reported that both their subjects had, in fact, expected happy endings—in Teresa's case from his Asian masseuse and in Cameron's case from her new pool boy—and I handed them each new assignments for the week, I finally landed on

Shawna Miller, the beautiful blond bombshell seated to my right. "Shawna, how did it go at the strip club in West L.A. this weekend?"

Shawna shook her head. "He didn't keep his word."

"So he went for the lap dance?" I confirmed.

"Yes. When I came around to the table, his friends offered to buy one for him, and he didn't hesitate for a second. And he didn't exactly want to stop there, either."

I noted this down. "I see. So what was your exit?"

"I told him it was against club policy for me to sleep with the customers, and then he just kind of smirked and said, 'So when do you get off work?' It was pretty slimy, actually."

"Well," I replied, exhaling, "I guess the client will get some use out of *that* information." Then I picked up the final two files on the stack. "I'm afraid I had to double-book you on Saturday night," I explained as I passed her the folders. "With Katie out for at least a week, we're gonna be a little short-staffed around here. Fortunately they're both in Vegas, so you shouldn't have any problem with timing. The first one is a bachelor party at the MGM Grand. Ken Littrell is getting married in a few weeks, and . . . well, you know the drill. They're going to a Halloween party at Tabú. Hadley is working on getting you a costume."

"No fair. I want to dress up," Katie pouted with her arms crossed.

"You are," Cameron pointed out, clearly mocking her. "You're going as Mary Poppins. I'm sure you'll be able to find an umbrella in the prop closet."

Katie scowled back at him. "Very funny, pool boy."

I cleared my throat. "And the second assignment is Benjamin Connors, who often comes into town by himself to play blackjack. He's staying at the Palazzo."

Shawna listened, taking diligent notes as I spoke.

"I would have postponed this one, but it's a bit of an unusual situation. The client came to see me yesterday. She and her husband are trying to adopt a baby. They've been on the waiting list for almost two years now, and they're finally meeting an interested birth mother next week. But apparently the client's sister claims that she saw the husband try to make a pass at someone at a neighborhood party after he'd drunk too much. Now the client is freaking out and doesn't know if she can trust him. And she doesn't want to bring a baby into the equation until she's sure."

"Wow," Lauren mused. "That's pretty intense."

I nodded my agreement. "It is. And a very worthy cause. Shawna, I'm going to book you a suite at the Palazzo. You can get ready there and then head over to the MGM to meet Ken Littrell, who should be in the club by nine, nine-thirty. Afterwards, you can head back to the Palazzo to play blackjack with Benjamin Connors. His wife says he often plays until four or five in the morning when he comes to Vegas. So you should have plenty of time. Find him at the tables and let him teach you how to play. Call me if you have any questions."

Twenty minutes later, I was sitting at my desk when I heard a knock on my office door. "Come in!" I called with my head bent over a mountain of paperwork.

I heard the door creak open, but when no sound followed, I looked up to see Hadley standing timidly in the doorway with an unsettled look on her face.

"Yes?"

"Um," she began hesitantly, her eyes blinking at an unusually rapid pace. "Lexi Garrett, your first appointment, is here."

I eyed her warily. "Is she all right?"

Hadley's face softened. "Oh, yes. No. I mean, she's fine."

I nodded. "Okay, then go ahead and send her in."

But she didn't move. This is the part when she usually moves. Nods her head, smiles graciously, and then ducks out to finish whatever it was she was doing before she was interrupted. But instead, she just kind of stood there in the doorway, staring at me with a blank expression on her face.

"What's the matter?" I asked.

Hadley stammered slightly, shifting her weight awkwardly from one foot to the other. "The client," she began, her big brown eyes barely meeting mine. "She's young."

I laughed at her endearing naïveté. "Oh, that's all right, Hadley. Sometimes we get younger women in here. In fact, Lauren took a case just a few months ago where the client was a college student. I think she was only about twenty."

"No." She shook her head adamantly, and I could have sworn I heard a chill seep into her voice. "I mean, she's a *child*."

8

child's play

I have seen a lot of things in this job. But nothing had prepared me for what I was about to encounter.

The girl who stepped into my office couldn't have been older than twelve. Maybe thirteen. But her eyes reflected the life experience of a forty-year-old. She was small and slender; the oversize black-and-red backpack that was strapped to her shoulders looked as if it weighed twice as much as she did. She had scratches on both sides of her face, the kind you get from climbing trees, scaling forbidden walls, or playing touch football with the boys during recess. Under any other circumstances, I would have found the entire situation endearing in a way. A young girl, out on her own in the big city of Los Angeles with nothing but her backpack and her tough-girl scars. But at that moment, all I could think was, *What on earth is she doing here?*

I was too speechless to invite her to sit down, but it quickly became apparent that she didn't require an invitation. She sauntered through the doorway with poise and confidence and immediately took a seat on the white chenille couch in the corner of the room. Then she shimmied out of the straps of the oversize backpack and placed it by her feet. She looked up at me, her face showing no signs of distress or anxiety. Those were the expressions I was used to seeing on that couch. But then again, this obviously wasn't just another eleven o'clock meeting. This promised to be something far more complicated.

At first I was convinced that she was in the wrong place. Dialed the wrong phone number, written down the wrong address.

So I decided to play dumb. It was the only way I could get her to tell me what she was doing here without having to divulge any real information about the agency. I smiled politely, grabbed my notepad, and took a seat on the matching white armchair that faced the couch. "Hi," I said brightly, coming out of my speechless trance. "How are you?"

Her face revealed nothing. She didn't return my smile. Nor did she respond to my attempt to make small talk. She simply stared straight into my eyes without a trace of fear or apprehension and in an unforgiving tone said, "I know what you're thinking, but trust me, I have good reason to be here."

I swallowed hard and struggled to maintain my plastered-on smile. "And what might that be?" The only comfort I was able to give myself was my certainty that the question would be returned with something completely unrelated to the subject of infidelity. Or any other word spoken on a regular basis within these walls.

But apparently I was wrong.

"I need you to prove that my dad is a cheater."

I coughed loudly, choking on my own disbelief. "Excuse me," I managed to get out after I'd finished hacking up an imaginary chicken bone caught in my throat. "What did you say?"

"Let's just cut the bullshit," she said in all seriousness. "I know exactly what it is you do here."

I glanced nervously down at my notes. "*You* are Lexi Garrett?"

The small-framed girl who occupied my couch nodded confidently. "Yep, that's me."

I still couldn't believe what I was sitting across from. That couch was usually reserved for suspicious fiancés, distrustful wives and husbands, maybe the occasional long-term girlfriend with serious doubts in the back of her mind. But never anyone like this.

"And, how old are you?" I asked, trying to figure out how this girl even managed to get an appointment. Hadley was instructed never to ask for specific details over the phone, but she *had* to have at least heard how young she sounded.

"I'm almost thirteen," she said proudly, as if this were some kind of major accomplishment. And I'm sure for an almost thirteen-year-old, it was. But for me, it was like a stake in my heart.

"Uh-huh," I said, staring at her as if I were seeing a child for the very first time. Well, for all intents and purposes it *was* the first time. The first time in this office, no doubt. Not even my niece, Hannah, who had just turned fourteen, had ever been allowed to step foot in here, let alone know about what it is we actually do. "And why aren't you in school?"

Lexi shrugged. "I forged a doctor's note."

I coughed again, grasping at my throat like a choking victim. "Wow, it must be really dry in here. I think I need some water. Do you want some water?"

The girl shook her head as I jumped up and practically dived for the intercom on my desk. "Hadley, would you mind bringing us a few bottles of water?"

"No problem," her voice came obligingly back through the speaker.

I sat back down in the armchair, shifting restlessly in an effort to get comfortable. But I knew it was probably a futile attempt. There was nothing *comforting* about any of this.

"So, um . . ." I struggled to find the right words. Did they even exist? Somehow I doubted it. "How did you hear about . . . the . . . um . . ."

"About the Hawthorne Agency?" she completed my thought, and I felt a small shiver run up my spine.

"Yes."

"From my best friend, Elisa," she said matter-of-factly. "Her mom hired you guys about six months ago. Elisa overheard her mom telling her aunt that you completely changed her life. I need you to do that for my mom."

"So your mom knows that you're here?" I asked, half hoping and half dreading that it was the truth. Because as much as I wanted to think that this girl didn't come here to interfere with her parents' marriage on her own accord, I wasn't exactly thrilled at the idea of a mother sending her *child* to hire a fidelity inspector, either.

"Hell, no," Lexi replied. "She would never do anything like this. And that's the problem. They've been together since they were eighteen. She doesn't know anything else but him. And she trusts him so blindly. She's clueless! She goes through life with her eyes closed. She doesn't see any of the signs."

"And what signs would that be?" I asked, a chiding condescendence seeping into my voice.

Lexi rolled her eyes at me, clearly losing her patience. "The signs of a cheater!"

I nodded slowly, trying to absorb the words that were coming out of this young girl's mouth. "But *you've* seen them?" I asked doubtfully. "These . . . signs."

"Yes! They're *so* obvious. He works a lot. Or so he says. One night he came home at like eleven-thirty and he totally smelled like a bar. I think he's out prowling for chicks with his friend Rob, who just got divorced. *And,*" she continued dramatically, waving her finger in front of her face to make her point. "He's always texting on his stupid little BlackBerry. Like *all* the time. And I've heard him talking on the phone at two in the morning when my mom is asleep. He's talking to a girl. I just know it."

Hadley entered quietly, balancing two bottles of SmartWater and two glasses of ice on a tray. I bypassed the glass and went straight for the bottle, unscrewing the top and swallowing half of it in one long gulp. "Thanks," I said breathlessly as she slipped back out the door.

"Well, Lexi," I began, uncouthly wiping my mouth with the back of my hand. "Adult relationships are complicated, and sometimes things may not *seem* appropriate to childr— I mean, to *younger* people. But—"

"Trust me," she insisted. "Something's just not right. I can *feel* it."

"I'm not doubting your instincts," I continued warily, feeling extremely awkward having this conversation with someone else's daughter. "But isn't there a chance that your father really is just working late and that maybe he's using his BlackBerry for work purposes?"

"No," she replied blankly. "If he had the opportunity to cheat on her, he would. If he hasn't already. They've been together for too long, and he's bored with her. Some things you just know."

The resolve in the young girl's voice startled me slightly, and I felt myself taking a deep breath in an attempt to recover my slipping patience. "Well, have you talked to your mom about your concerns?"

She rolled her eyes again. "Hundreds of times. She won't listen. She thinks he's a saint. She doesn't even believe me when I try to tell her about the late night phone calls. She says I watch too much *Gossip Girl*."

"Well, perhaps she's right," I said, placing my notepad and pen on the coffee table in front of me and folding my hands in my lap. "TV shows do make it seem like cheating is more prevalent than it really is."

What the hell was I talking about? If anything, TV doesn't do the real statistic justice. But of course, I couldn't admit that to *her*.

"Don't be like that," the girl pleaded with me, narrowing her eyes. "I get enough of that at home. I came here because you help people, and I need help. Well, my mom does, anyway. I can't stand watching her live in this dreamworld. Someone has to show her who he really is. Someone has to wake her up."

"Some people don't want to be woken up," I stated simply, feeling the hypocrisy of my words bear down on top of my head. The truth was, I got into this business for one reason and one reason only: to wake people up. Because I had convinced myself that the truth is always better than the lie. No matter what people try to tell themselves.

The girl's eyes bored into me for a good five seconds before she reached down to the floor and unzipped the front pocket of her backpack. She pulled out a white letter-size envelope and smacked it down on the coffee table between us. "Here's your fee. In cash."

I stared quizzically at the envelope, trying to figure out if I even *wanted* to know how an almost thirteen-year-old girl could get her hands on that kind of money.

"Look," she continued, interrupting my thoughts. "If I'm wrong, then there's no harm done. You don't even have to tell my mother that I was here. But if I'm right and he does, you know, take the bait . . ." Her voice trailed off, and she paused dramatically before completing the sentence. "Then you just saved my mom from a lifetime of delusion." She leaned against the back of the couch and folded her arms contentedly across her chest, watching me as I continued to study the mysterious white envelope.

There was a long, heavy silence in the room as my brain battled out the decision that was literally lying on the table in front of me.

Finally, I picked up the envelope, feeling the burden of the heavy cash in my hands, and handed it back to her. "I'm sorry," I said gently. "But I just can't take this case. If you bring your mom in here, we can talk to her about her options and possibly convince her to hire us herself. But I just don't think it would be ethical for me to take money from you."

Lexi flashed me a dirty look that only a twelve-year-old girl with scratches on her face could possibly pull off. "Fine," she said as she rose and marched toward my office door, envelope of cash in hand. "But this isn't over. You *will* eventually change your mind. And next time, I'll come back with hard evidence."

I nodded politely but didn't respond.

"And by the way," she added, the anger in her voice suddenly replaced with the wisdom and peaceful poise of a spiritual shaman. "Anyone that you care about *deserves* to be woken up."

9

failing the WATs

1. Describe the setting of your ideal wedding ceremony (i.e., beach, garden, desert spa, mountain lodge, house of worship, yacht, private home, backyard, golf course, etc.).

2. Describe your ideal wedding cake (shape, color, flavor, frosting, filling, tiers, designer or classic, decorations). *Please attach any photographs or magazine cutouts if applicable.*

The next day, I was sitting in the pastel-colored waiting room of Willa Cruz, wedding planner extraordinaire. Jamie had gotten a rave referral from someone at his office who had recently gotten married and employed Willa. Apparently, you just "can't plan a successful wedding without her." And so there we were. Although personally, I thought it was a bit too early to be talking to wedding planners—I was still getting used to the engagement part—but according to Jamie's colleague, it's *never* too early to start talking to a wedding planner, which made me wonder if I should have booked this appointment back when I was sixteen.

I tapped the backside of my engagement ring against the plastic clipboard in my lap. The questionnaire attached to it read, "Questions for the Bride." Ten minutes had passed since I'd reluctantly accepted the daunting document, and the only question I had managed to answer was, "How long have you and your fiancé been engaged?" And the only reason *that* answer was fresh on my mind was that when I had read the question that preceded it, my first thought was: *I've only been engaged for a little over a week. How am I supposed to know what kind of cake I want?*

I was still reeling from yesterday's meeting with Lexi Garrett, the twelve-year-old Dalai Lama of relationships. She had caught me off guard, in more ways than one. She had made such an unnervingly valid argument for me to test her father.

And the most unsettling part of all was that something was telling me she was right. That at twelve years old, this little girl had been able to see something in her parents' marriage that her mother had missed. Sometimes it takes an unbiased eye to notice the nuances of a relationship, but that was the most confusing part. Lexi wasn't an unbiased eye. She was their *daughter*. If anyone had anything to lose from the outcome of an assignment like this, it was her.

But the sheer synchronicity of it all was what was really haunting me. She was twelve years old. *Twelve*. The exact age I had been when I first found out about my dad's affairs. And I did nothing about it. Then magically, seventeen years later, into my office walks Lexi Garrett. And she wasn't about to let her dad get away with anything.

Was the universe sending me some kind of sign? A bizarre chance at redemption? Or was it just a really annoying coincidence?

I sighed and tried to push the idea from my mind. I had to focus on the task at hand. Which right now was this impossible wedding planning questionnaire. And thinking about twelve-year-olds who suspect their fathers of cheating on their mothers seemed highly inappropriate at this moment.

> 4. Describe your ideal wedding theme (i.e., Hawaiian luau, enchanted forest, fairy-tale fantasy, butterfly garden, winter wonderland).

If I had known there was going to be a test, I would have studied first. I glanced to my right and stole a quick peek at Jamie's clipboard. Under the heading "Questions for the Groom," I caught sight of:

1. What is your favorite color?

2. What is your favorite kind of music?

3. How many people are in your immediate family?

Okay, now *those* were questions I could answer. I glanced at my clipboard and searched for anything that resembled an inquiry about my favorite color. But I couldn't find one. I was being asked whether I wanted an enchanted forest or a fairy-tale fantasy, and Jamie got to decide if he likes pop/rock better than punk?

What kind of lopsided wedding questionnaire was this?

And what had I been doing all of my life when clearly I was supposed to be thinking about this kind of stuff? And apparently organizing a collection of magazine clippings of wedding cakes in my spare time.

Great, I thought. We've only been engaged a week and I already suck at it.

I reluctantly glanced down at question number four.

4. Describe your ideal wedding dress.

Underneath, I wrote the word *White* and moved on, content that I'd finally gotten to one I could actually answer.

I glanced down the rest of the page. It went all the way to question ten. Then I flipped to the next page and the page after that and the page after that. I felt as if I were rifling through a legal brief. How far did this thing go?

I finally got my answer on page five when I read the final question:

47. Do you have any specific vineyards that you would like to special order your wine from?

This was officially the most brutal test I'd ever taken. It was worse than the SATs. Way worse. It was the WATs: the *Wedding* Aptitude Tests. And I could only imagine the little piece of paper I would get in the mail six to eight weeks later informing me that I was *not,* in fact, apt to have a wedding. Although I was starting to believe that I didn't exactly need to take a test to figure that out.

Jamie snapped his pen down against his plastic clipboard with a startling clank. "Done," he announced with pride. As if we had been racing.

Of course he was done. He had five preschool-level questions and I had forty-seven Ph.D. thesis–style essays.

"Good!" I forced out brightly. Then I flipped through the four remaining blank pages of my own novel/questionnaire and set down my pen in defeat. "Me too, I guess."

Jamie leaned over and attempted a glance at my top page. "How'd you do?"

I tilted it upward toward my chest, blocking the forty-five gaping blank spaces from his view. "Pretty well, I think."

"What'd you put for 'favorite type of food'?"

"Uh," I said, tapping my fingernails against the back of the clipboard. "I don't think I had that question."

I was afraid that Jamie would insist on looking at my answers, but fortunately, a door to our left swung open just then and Willa herself emerged, looking like Wedding Planner Barbie with her perfectly coiffed layers of wavy blond hair and dressed in a lavender-colored suit with matching lavender pumps.

"Jennifer! Jamie!" she proclaimed passionately, opening her arms to us as if she half expected to engage in some kind of group hug. But instead she rapidly curled back her manicured fingertips and beckoned us into her office. "Come in, come in! We have exciting things to discuss!" With this, she crinkled her nose slightly and flashed me a coy little wink as if we shared some intimate secret that Jamie was not privy to.

Jamie took my hand and we entered another pastel-colored room and sat on a pair of matching baby yellow armchairs. As I warily took in my surroundings, I felt as though I had just walked into an Easter basket.

"So," Willa said, sitting pretty in a twirling desk chair. "Let's talk about the big day. Do you have a date in mind? Or a time of year, perhaps?"

Jamie looked at me, and I continued to stare straight ahead. Maybe it was too soon for wedding planners. I failed my questionnaire, and we hadn't even talked about a date yet.

"Well," Jamie began, "I was thinking maybe next summer would be good. Would that give us enough to time to plan everything?"

I stared at him in surprise. *Next summer?* We hadn't talked about that at all. Or did I just sleep through that conversation?

Clearly, he could feel my confusion and turned to me to ask, "What do you think, babe?"

But who was I to argue? I couldn't even decide if I wanted a butterfly garden or a winter wonderland. What good was I? "Um, yeah!" I said, trying to sound upbeat. "Summer sounds great."

Willa scribbled something in a lavender notebook, and I couldn't help but wonder if she had a corresponding book for every pastel-colored suit in her closet or if we were just fortunate enough to catch her on a particularly coordinated day. "I just *love* summer weddings," she gushed. "And where were you thinking of having this blessed event?"

Jamie looked at me again, and I just shrugged. "I don't think we've really talked about it yet," he offered sympathetically, and I felt relieved that I hadn't also apparently slept through our conversation about wedding locations.

"Oh, that's totally *fine*!" Willa elongated the word *fine* as if it were actually made up of three elaborate syllables as opposed to just the boring one. "We'll come up with the absolute best location for you two. Now, did you fill out your questionnaires?"

Jamie produced his and handed it to her with a glowing grin while I continued to cling to my clipboard, keeping it tight against my chest. "Uh, I'm not really done with mine yet. I have so many ideas, I just couldn't figure out how to organize them into this short little questionnaire." As soon as the words came out of my mouth, I knew I was doomed. I had no idea where they even came from. They just sort of snuck past my bullshit radar and sprang forth into the room, running around the office like rambunctious children who had been fed too much sugar. And now it was impossible to reel them back in.

"Great!" Willa exclaimed. "The more ideas the better. You just take your time and fax it over to me whenever you're done."

Thirty minutes later, after the lady in lavender had thoroughly explained to us the value of what she referred to as her "stress-free, all-encompassing Wedding Extravaganza Package," Jamie and I left Willa Cruz's office with a handful of brochures, a portfolio stuffed with sample wedding invitations that were guaranteed "to die for," and a second appointment scheduled for two weeks from today.

"So, I spoke with my Realtor yesterday," Jamie said as he sat in the driver's seat and fastened his seat belt.

"About what?" I asked, flipping through my iPhone and skimming all the new e-mails I had accumulated over the past hour. Hadley had scheduled three new client meetings for this week alone. Was it just me or were fidelity inspections becoming increasingly more popular?

"About putting my loft up for sale."

Suddenly, my new e-mails were no longer of any interest. "Why would you do that?"

"Well," Jamie began, placing his hand tenderly on my knee. "I mean, we're engaged now, and I practically live at your place anyway, so . . ."

"You want to move in with me?" I asked with sudden realization.

"Don't you want me to?" Jamie asked. But for some reason, it didn't sound like a question. It sounded more like an accusation.

"Uh," I stammered. "Yeah, I guess so." Although I really hadn't given the subject too much thought. But now that he mentioned it, I suppose it made sense. I mean, we *were* engaged. And engaged people were supposed to live under the same roof, weren't they? But then again, the only engaged people I knew besides Sophie were usually not engaged for much longer after I met them.

"I mean, we could sell *your* place, but I figured since mine was so much smaller, it would be easier to—"

"No, no," I quickly interrupted. "You're right. Living in my condo makes more sense."

"And then," he continued with an abrupt spike in enthusiasm, "I was thinking in a year or two, maybe we could spring for a house."

I could feel my head start to spin. How did we go from planning a wedding to buying a house in less than five minutes? Next he was going to tell me that I was pregnant.

When I didn't reply to the house comment, Jamie spoke again. "So I told my Realtor he could give some interested buyers a sneak peak while we were in Cabo this weekend."

I nodded somewhat absently. "Well, good. That sounds good."

"And after we get back, I'll start moving some of my stuff in."

"Great!" I managed. But it felt so forced and insincere, and I immediately wondered why.

Of course I wanted to move in with Jamie . . . eventually. I guess I just didn't think eventually would come this soon. But my mind *had* been pretty occupied lately with work matters. Planning Katie's long-term undercover at the Stantons', scheduling Shawna's upcoming double-booked night in Vegas this weekend, and now the desperate plea for help from a preadolescent girl. It was definitely a full-time job that required the majority of my time and energy. And that would most likely account for why I hadn't given any of this other stuff much thought in the past week. I supposed it was a good thing that Jamie had seemed to take the reins on everything else. The wedding planner, the wedding date, selling his loft to move in with me. I was glad that he was so on top of everything. Especially because based on my test scores, I was clearly much better at breaking up marriages than I was at planning them.

10

cabo, interrupted

By the time Jamie and I arrived in Cabo San Lucas for our posten-gagement getaway on Friday night, I was more than ready for a vacation. The last two days had been filled with nonstop client meetings, and two nights in Mexico was exactly what I needed. Time away from everything and everyone. No cheating spouses. No wedding planners. Just me and Jamie and a suite at the Marquis Los Cabos. Everything had gotten so complicated in the last week and a half. It was nice to just relax and remember what was really important. And that was Jamie. Whether we had a wedding cake with cream or fruit filling didn't matter in Cabo San Lucas. All that mattered was the fact that we were together.

By Saturday afternoon, my skin was already a good shade-and-a-half darker, and Jamie and I had claimed a cabana on the beach that had become our temporary home away from home away from home. We had our breakfast and lunch delivered there along with *several* piña coladas and bottles of Corona.

The sun was warm. The ocean was a brilliant shade of blue. And the waiters were extremely attentive. It was pure paradise.

Until my phone started ringing.

I groaned audibly as I pulled it out of my bag and answered, "Hello?"

"Look, I know you're on your prehoneymoon, postengagement

whatever thing, but I *have* to talk to you and it can't wait." Zoë was speaking considerably faster than usual. And for Zoë, that was saying a lot.

"What?"

"Sophie has completely lost it. I think she's about to have a stroke. Everything is falling apart over here, and I don't know what to do."

I took a deep breath and flipped onto my stomach. "What seems to be the problem?" I asked diplomatically.

Zoë's piercing voice continued to melt my eardrums. "She's freaking out because Eric's sister, who's one of the bridesmaids, showed up at the dress fitting today with her hair dyed this obnoxious color, and Sophie claims it doesn't match the dress. But Eric's sister is refusing to dye it back."

I furrowed my eyebrows in disbelief. "She actually *asked* Eric's sister to dye her hair back?"

"Yup. And now they're in this huge terrible fight, and Eric's sister is threatening not to come to the wedding at all."

I pushed myself up onto my elbows. "Well, did you try to talk to her about it? And tell her very *nicely* that she was overreacting?"

"Yes!" Zoë cried, exasperated. "But she refuses to listen. She wanted to call you, but I insisted that she not ruin your weekend. I told her it would be much better if *I* called you instead. You know, calmer and less stressful."

I wasn't so sure about that.

"Uh-huh." I rolled over onto my back again and shielded my eyes from the sun. "Okay, what color is the hair?"

Zoë scoffed into the phone, "What does that matter?"

I was starting to get impatient. "Just tell me."

She sighed loudly. "Fine. It's like a red. But you know, not that strawberry blond red but *red* red. Almost magenta."

I thought for a moment. "Okay, here's what you're going to do. Call Sophie back, tell her you spoke to me and told me what the problem was. Then tell her that *I* said that I saw a model wearing her same bridesmaid's dress in a bridal magazine and she had the exact same color hair."

"Ahh," Zoë said, slowly coming around to comprehension. "I get it. A little mind trick."

"Exactly."

She sighed in relief. "Okay, thanks, Jen. You're the best. Go back to paradise."

I hung up the phone and tossed it back into my beach bag before resting my head back down on my towel and closing my eyes.

"What was that all about?" Jamie asked from his nearby chair.

"Not even worth repeating."

I was just drifting off into a nice little catnap when my phone rang again. I sat up reluctantly and pulled it out of my bag. "I should have guessed," I said, looking at the caller ID. "Hi, Soph."

"What magazine was this? I have every single bridal magazine on the newsstand, and I have never seen a girl with magenta hair wearing *my* bridesmaid dress."

I kept my eyes closed in an attempt to conserve composure. "I'm not really sure," I replied casually. "It was at the airport. I think someone left it in the terminal."

Sophie did not sound convinced. "People do not just *leave* bridal magazines lying around airport terminals."

"Sure they do," I said flatly. At this point, I could care less how persuasive I was sounding.

"You're lying."

"No, I'm not."

"Yes, you are!"

I shot up in my seat, the frustration finally reaching a boiling point despite my previous efforts to keep it at a low, unobservable simmer. "Okay, Sophie. I'm on vacation. I don't really want to play these childish games with you. I'm not concerned with the hair color, and neither should you be. You should be concentrating on—"

"I know! I know! Myself! You've been telling me that for the past six months."

And here I thought she wasn't absorbing any of it.

"It's easy for you to say the hair color doesn't bother you because *you* haven't seen it!"

I inhaled deeply and reminded myself that there would be only *two* more weeks of this crap and then it would all be over. Well, until Sophie got pregnant, anyway. But for the sake of my own sanity, I was pretty damn close to walking over to one of the local churches in town and saying a prayer for Eric's infertility.

I decided to try a different approach. "Well, just think how much better *you'll* look walking down the aisle after everyone sees Eric's sister and her hideous bright red hair. You'll look like a goddess compared to that!"

I could almost hear the gears turning in Sophie's head. "Huh," she finally said, intrigued. "I guess I never thought of it that way. That does make me feel a *little* better," she admitted.

I fell back against the chaise longue with a relieved sigh. "Good, then I'm hanging up now."

And I did.

Afternoon faded into evening, the sun set spectacularly over the water, and after four more rounds of back-and-forth phone calls between Zoë and Sophie and one very unpleasant conference call among the three of us, Jamie and I packed up our stuff and headed inside for dinner.

He suggested that I leave my cell phone in the hotel room while we were eating, and after what had just happened on the beach, I couldn't think of a better idea.

The restaurant in the hotel was small and intimate, only twenty tables total, with soft lighting, taupe linens, and three-pronged candlesticks that reminded me of something from an old Hollywood mansion. We both ordered the fresh fish of the day, and it was exquisite. I had to hand it to Jamie. From hot dogs and Coke on the golf course to this five-star restaurant in Cabo San Lucas, the man definitely knew how to dine.

After cocktails, appetizers, wine, entrées, dessert, more wine, and endless conversation, what I had expected to be at most a ninety-minute dinner had turned into a three-and-a-half-hour dining experience.

By the time Jamie and I left the restaurant, it was already 10:45 at night and we were both wasted. Although it feels inherently wrong to use the word *wasted* when describing our state after such an elegant and lavish evening. So let's just say we were "luxuriously intoxicated."

There once was a time, not so long ago, that I would have had to fake this kind of inebriation. Back when going from sober to tipsy in a matter of hours was just another part of my unusual job description. But since I gave up my glamorous days of strappy black dresses and a different married man every night of the week, my tolerance to alcohol had fallen back down to normal levels.

We stumbled back to the hotel room in a clumsy, unchoreographed dance of kissing, laughing, and playfully grabbing each other's asses. As soon as we were behind closed doors, Jamie backed me up to the bed and fell on top of me. He began to kiss the sides of my face, moving down to my chin and eventually landing directly on the small crevice between my neck and shoulders.

I giggled with pleasure, sliding Jamie's dinner jacket off his shoulders and unbuttoning his shirt.

His hand reached down and landed on my knee before wandering up the inside of my thigh and under the hemline of my dress. I shivered with delight. The wine was making every inch of my skin feel alive and tingling with desire.

With his other hand, he slid the straps of my dress off my shoulders and gently kissed my collarbone. I turned my head to the side and wrapped my arms around the back of his neck, pulling him closer to me.

My eyes opened for a second, and it was during that moment that I noticed my iPhone sitting on the nightstand. The screen was illuminated to alert me of an awaiting voice mail. I sighed and closed my eyes again, trying to erase the outside world from my conscious mind and just be in this incredible moment.

But I was quickly sucked out of it again by the sound of ringing. A shrill, high-pitched, unfamiliar noise that sounded like an old-fashioned rotary phone.

Jamie groaned and looked up at the nightstand. "It's your cell phone again."

"That's not my cell phone," I mumbled dazedly. "My ringer doesn't sound like that."

Jamie looked up again. "Yes, it is. I can see it lighting up."

And then I remembered. The wine haze slowly cleared from my head. "Oh yeah," I mumbled with frustration. "It's the ringer I programmed for blocked numbers."

"Well, do you want to get it?"

I wrapped my hands around the back of his head and pulled him toward me. "No," I cooed. "It's probably a wrong number. Besides, no one who would need to get hold of me at this hour has a blocked number."

Jamie was happy to oblige and leaned in to kiss me again. I moaned, and his lips pressed deeper into mine. I started to unbutton his shirt.

The phone rang again. And for some reason, this time it seemed even more insistent. Maybe that's because this time I was even more annoyed than the last.

"Okay," I resolved, sitting up and pushing Jamie off to the side. "I'm shutting the damn thing off."

I grabbed the phone and jabbed at the red "Ignore" button on the bottom of the screen. The piercing sound finally stopped, and my ears had never been more grateful. "I'm gonna have to change that ringer," I vowed as my finger reached for the power button. But just as I was about to hold it down, the screen switched over, revealing my list of missed calls. Ten in the past fifteen minutes. All from a blocked number.

"That's strange," I muttered as I stared down at the phone.

"What?" Jamie asked, rolling onto his back and letting out a displeased sigh.

"Ten missed calls." I tapped over to the voice mail screen. Five voice mails, all without a caller ID. "This better not be Sophie blocking her number," I grumbled as I selected the first voice mail. But just as I was about to tap "Play Message," the phone rang again. The sound startled me, and I nearly dropped the phone as I fumbled to press the "Talk" button with drunk (and somewhat anxious) fingers.

"Hello?"

A hysterical voice came on the line, and I struggled to keep up

with the influx of words that were pouring into my ear faster than I
could make sense of them, let alone place them in any comprehensible order. "And I don't know how they . . . I'm sure it was one of . . .
I swear it's not . . . can't believe . . . really scary . . . dirty . . . cold . . .
smells . . ."

After a few seconds, I was finally able to recognize the woman's
voice. And it wasn't Sophie calling to discuss various shades of red
hair color.

"Shawna," I asserted softly, "you need to slow down. I can't understand you."

Panic started to tighten my chest, and I could feel my breath
quicken as I remembered that she was juggling not one, but *two* assignments tonight in Vegas. I glanced at the clock on the nightstand.
It was eleven P.M., ten P.M. in Vegas, which meant that right now she
would be in the middle of her first assignment—a Halloween party
at MGM Grand with subject number one, Ken Littrell—and would
be getting ready to relocate to the Palazzo to commence her assignment with subject number two, Benjamin Connors, in a few hours.

My mind flooded with all kinds of possible worst-case scenarios
for what could go wrong on a double-booked night, and I scolded
myself for leaving the phone in the room. I had been so anxious to
escape Sophie's pre-wedding dramas for one night that I had completely forgotten about all the people who might really need me.

". . . with the bachelor . . . suddenly I'm . . . won't listen . . . took
my phone . . . so sorry . . ." Shawna continued to babble incoherently into my ear, and I reached out and switched on the lamp by the
bed. As if *light* could possibly help me *hear* better.

"What's the matter?" Jamie asked, sitting up and holding his head
to steady the room, which was undoubtedly spinning from all the
alcohol. It was spinning for me as well, but I was too pissed off at
myself to notice.

I shook my head back at him and pulled the phone away from my
mouth. "I don't know. I can't understand her. She was double-booked
tonight. Something must have gone wrong.

"Shawna," I repeated again, my voice slightly less calm this time,
"take a deep breath."

She stopped talking abruptly, and I heard the irrefutable muffled hissing sound of air being blown into the phone. It was honestly the first thing I understood.

"Good, now tell me what's going on."

When she spoke again, her voice still trembled, but at least her pace was finally clear and comprehensible. "I'm so sorry to bother you, Ashlyn. I didn't know who else to call."

Despite the warm, tropical ocean breeze blowing through the open window of our suite, the terror in her voice chilled me to the bone.

"It's no bother," I stated numbly, my body frozen in fear. "What happened?"

As I listened to her speak, I could swear I heard the soft splashing sound of her tears falling against the receiver. Her usual sweet, light-hearted voice sounded tiny and scared, like a small child's. Even though my heart wanted to leap into my throat, I urged myself to remain calm and composed. I knew that any unnecessary emotion from me would only send her into another round of hysterics.

I listened patiently as she recounted the events of her night between choked-up sobs. And then, before I could even fully digest what she was saying, I was on my feet, scouring the room for my shoes and the hooded sweatshirt I had worn on the plane the night before. I grabbed my purse and began throwing random contents into it, ignoring Jamie's inquisitive looks.

Right now, there was only one thing on my mind: getting the hell out of this hotel room.

"Don't worry," I said to Shawna before hanging up. "I'm on my way."

11

11:59 to vegas

There were no direct flights from Cabo San Lucas to Las Vegas, and the last flight that got me even remotely close left hours ago. But I called Hadley from the cab on the way to the airport, and she managed to find a charter jet that could get me there in less than three hours. So I charged the $10,694 one-way fare to my corporate American Express card and directed the cab to the private terminal.

I was wearing a faded yellow hooded sweatshirt from the Gap over my black-and-white-striped M Missoni rope halter minidress and red Jimmy Choo sandals. It wasn't exactly the ensemble I'd always pictured myself wearing on my first flight on a private jet, but appearances were the last thing on my mind right now.

The cab dropped me off in the middle of the tarmac and I was met by a young Hispanic man with a clipboard, who confirmed my identity and welcomed me onboard the beautiful Learjet that was idling nearby.

I stepped onto the plane and seated myself in one of the plush leather chairs, buckling my seat belt with shaking hands. My wine buzz had already worn off but my nerves were still raging.

As soon as the plane took off, my thoughts fluttered back to Jamie. After I'd hung up the phone, he'd followed me around the room like a scared puppy. "What's the matter? Where are you going? What happened?"

But my brain wasn't functioning properly, and I couldn't process his questions and figure out how I was going to get to Las Vegas tonight at the same time.

Finally, his frustration got the better of him and he yelled, "Will you slow down for one second and tell me what the fuck is going on?"

I took a deep breath and faced him. "Shawna's in jail."

His eyes squinted in confusion. "What do you mean, 'in jail'?"

I threw my hands in the air and continued searching for my missing second shoe. "I mean in jail. She got arrested for prostitution."

"What?!" Jamie spat out.

"Not for *real* prostitution. Somehow one of the guys from the bachelor party figured out who she was and what she was really doing there and told the club's security that she was soliciting sex. She's completely freaked out right now, and I have to go bail her out."

Jamie immediately sprang into action as well, throwing his dinner jacket back on and reaching for his shoes. "I'm coming with you."

But I placed my hand on his chest and gently pushed him back down onto the bed. "No, you're not. That's really sweet of you to offer, but this is a *work*-related problem. And you know I never mix work with my personal life."

Jamie's eyes pleaded with me. "So you're gonna fly to Las Vegas at this time of night all by yourself."

I ducked down and finally located the other shoe under the bed and began to slide it onto my foot. "Relax. I've been to Vegas plenty of times on my own. I met *you* on a flight back from there, remember?"

His shoulders slouched. "No, I know, it's just that—"

I hurriedly kissed him on top of the head as I slung my bag over my shoulder. "I don't have time to talk about this. I'll see you back in L.A. tomorrow. I'm really sorry to cut our weekend short. I'll make it up to you, I promise."

And with that, I was out the door.

I felt guilty about leaving him there alone. But I knew I had no other choice.

The pilot informed me that the flying time to Vegas was a short two hours and fifteen minutes, but I had to check my watch repeatedly for confirmation because to me, it felt like an eternity.

When we landed, I jumped into the first available taxi and arrived at the Clark County Detention Center in downtown Las Vegas at two in the morning local time. I hadn't slept a wink on the plane, but I was still wide awake, completely hyped up on that same dose of adrenaline I got from Shawna's phone call four hours ago. Evidently, it was stronger than a double shot of espresso. And lasted twice as long.

"Shawna Miller," I breathed heavily to the guard at the front desk. "I'm here to bail out Shawna Miller. She was brought in a few hours ago for"—I shuddered—"for suspected prostitution."

The heavyset uniformed man who sat at the guard station looked up from his ten-inch TV screen long enough to peer at me from behind his smudged horn-rimmed glasses and say in an impassive voice, "No bail posts after midnight."

Sheer panic rocketed through my body as my knees wobbled and I grabbed on to the edge of the counter for support. "No!" I pleaded. "I need to get her out of here tonight. There must be something you can do!" I urged him.

But he continued to stare at the TV screen, which I now noticed was playing a rerun of *The Golden Girls.*

"You mean she has to spend the *night* in here?" I realized in horror.

His eyes remained glued to the screen as his hand shot out and pointed to a blue plastic sign that sat on the counter. The faded white letters etched into the surface read, NO BAIL AFTER MIDNIGHT.

"You can't be serious! She did nothing wrong. It was all a huge mistake."

But he didn't respond. He simply shot me a look that I interpreted as, "Save your breath."

"Well, what time does the bail window open tomorrow?"

"Nine A.M."

I sighed heavily and leaned into the counter. I had just left my fiancé in a hotel in Mexico, paid ten thousand dollars for a private jet, and traveled across international borders in the middle of the night, and it was all for nothing? She still had to spend the night in jail? I could feel the frustration bubbling up inside me, but I fought to keep it under control. Something told me this guy wasn't the kind of person you wanted to get into a fight with. Or I'd probably be spending the night in that cell with her.

"Well, can I at least talk to her?" I fought back helplessly. "To tell her that I'm here?"

"Sign in," he replied mechanically, nodding toward the clipboard in front of me.

I eyed the paper clipped to the board and scribbled my name on the next available line. I set the pen down with an obstinate thump. If unnecessarily loud movements were the most I could do to protest this inane system, then I was going to make the most of it.

The guard glanced at my signature and then turned his attention back to the TV. I stomped my foot impatiently against the hard, cold floor. "Well?"

He didn't move. I craned my neck over the counter to catch another glimpse of the show he had clearly deemed to be more important than my request. Blanche was saying something about seducing one of the new neighbors. The live studio audience laughed, as did the overweight security guard. Although it sounded more like an amused grunt.

I rolled my eyes. I couldn't believe my poor, innocent employee was locked up in a cell, wondering if I was ever going to show up, while this guy was watching four old women talk about their sex lives.

Finally, a short jingle played over the picture—indicating the end of the act—and a commercial break commenced. Only then did Mr. Personality pick his fat ass up off his seat and lead me toward a locked door behind his desk. He swiped a plastic card with a magnetic strip through the lock, and the door opened. Then he held it open for me and muttered, "Last cell on the left. You have five minutes."

He stood just inside the doorway and watched me carefully as I started down the long hallway. As if he were making sure I didn't slip someone a crowbar or something. As I walked, I was careful not to touch anything or make eye contact with the diverse assortment of individuals that occupied the overnight holding cells of the Clark County Detention Center on a Saturday night. When I finally reached the last cell on the left, I saw Shawna sitting alone on a bench, her head buried in her hands. She was scantily dressed in a purple bikini top with seashells covering her breasts and a shimmering green sequined skirt that hugged her hips and flared at the bottom. Her stomach and shoulders were completely bare.

It took me a minute to remember that tonight's assignment took place at a Halloween party. A Halloween party gone very, very bad. And now Shawna was nothing more than a desolate mermaid, sitting alone in a cold, dirty jail cell far, far away from her home by the sea.

Upon sensing my presence, she lifted her head and her face brightened immediately. She jumped up and rushed toward me, stopping just short of the rusted metal bars. "Oh, Ashlyn! Thank God you're here. This place is so disgusting."

I glanced around and nodded. "Yes, it is." Then I reached through the bars to touch her shoulder. It was then that I noticed I was still wearing my engagement ring. I jumped slightly at the sight of it and quickly recoiled my hand, hiding it rather conspicuously behind my back as I managed to wiggle the ring off with my thumb and drop it inside my bag.

Shawna, thankfully, didn't seem to notice. "Is it over now? Can I go?"

My heart broke as I looked into her big blue eyes and shook my head sadly. "I'm sorry, Shawna. I did everything I could to get here as quickly as possible, but the bail window closes at midnight and the guard won't make any exceptions."

Her whole body seemed to crumple, and she staggered back to the wooden bench and fell onto it. "You mean I have to *sleep* in here?"

I sighed painfully. "I'm afraid so. But I promise I'll be back first thing in the morning to bail you out."

Her head returned to her hands, and she sat like that for a few moments in complete silence. There was nothing I could think to say that would possibly comfort her right now, so I just said, "Do you want to tell me what happened?"

She picked up her head again and shrugged. "One of his friends somehow caught on to what I was doing there, and he got . . . upset."

I eyed her surroundings and nodded. "How did he find out? Did something slip out?"

She shook her head and fought back another influx of tears. "No. I didn't say anything, I swear. I have no idea how my cover was blown. One minute I was dancing with the bachelor, and the next minute one of his friends was yelling at me. Saying he knew exactly who I was and what I was doing there. Then he told me I would be sorry. I thought he was going to clobber me or something. I thought I would have to break out my kung fu in this ridiculous costume."

I smiled weakly at her attempt at humor.

"But before I even had time to react, some security guard was leading me out of the club by my elbow, mumbling something about soliciting sex to those guys and how he better not see me in his club again. It all happened so fast. It was a total blur. It wasn't until the cops were putting me in the squad car that they told me I was being arrested for prostitution." She sighed and ran her fingers through her teased blond hair. "I couldn't even fathom the words coming out of his mouth. I couldn't even argue. I was too speechless. I don't even know how this could happen. How can you arrest a person based solely on somebody else's word?"

I shook my head. These were exactly the kinds of questions I had asked myself the entire flight here. And I, too, was at a loss. I was hoping Shawna would be able to provide more insight. But apparently she was just as confused as I was.

"Obviously there's been some kind of misunderstanding," I assured her. "But don't worry, we'll get it all sorted out in the morning."

She squeezed her eyes shut, and I could tell she was searching for her last ounce of inner strength. Something she could use to get her through the rest of the night. When she opened them again, the small, childlike voice had returned. "I'm sorry," she murmured.

I forced out a laugh. "You have no reason to be sorry. This was *not* your fault."

"No," she replied. "I mean about Benjamin Connors."

I knew the name sounded familiar, but my mind was coming up blank. "Who?"

She shot me a strange look. "My second assignment tonight."

I blinked a few times, and all the memories came flooding back. Since the moment I'd picked up the phone four hours ago, everything else in the world seemed to have become a big, messy, indiscernible blur in the back of my mind. I had completely forgotten that right now, Shawna was supposed to be six miles away getting a blackjack lesson from Benjamin Connors. And because of this little incident, he was now playing blackjack alone.

"It's fine," I said, trying to mask my concern with a fake air of confidence. "Don't worry about that."

But the truth was, I couldn't help but be worried about it. In the three years that I'd been in the fidelity inspection business, no assignment had ever been abandoned. Everyone who was scheduled to be tested *was* tested. Every fidelity inspection that was bought and paid for was conducted. But I supposed there was a first time for everything.

"I'm sure we can reschedule," I said brightly, hoping my voice would ease her concern.

But Shawna just stared back at me from across the rusty bars. "No, we can't," she replied adamantly. "He and his wife are meeting the birth mother of their adopted baby next week, remember? The file said she wanted to make sure he really was faithful before she brought a child into the marriage. Does any of this ring a bell?"

I nodded absently. It did ring a bell. In fact, it rang far too many bells. Suddenly there was a cacophonous chorus of them in my head, chiming at an earsplitting volume. I pressed my palm into my forehead to try to make them stop, but they just kept on ringing.

The messy, indiscernible blur in my mind suddenly dissolved, and I could see the scene in front of me as clear as day. My meeting with

Darcie Connors earlier this week. The clothes she was wearing, the look in her eyes when she walked into the room, even the small noises she made in the back of her throat when she was trying to build up the courage to ask me for help. But not just any help. A very unorthodox kind. Something she never dreamed in a million years she would ever willingly ask for.

"I've always trusted my husband," she had told me. "In the five years we've been married he never gave me any reason to doubt him." She sighed and rubbed her hands along the tops of her knees. "But then my sister told me what she saw at that party last week, after I had already gone home, and suddenly now it's all I can think about. The doubt has consumed me. I've wanted a baby for so long. And when we found out that I couldn't conceive naturally, I was crushed."

Tears began to well in her eyes, and I waited patiently for her to dab them away.

"But then, eventually the initial blow of it all subsided and we started talking about adoption. I was afraid he would be opposed to the idea. I know I was at first. It's just impossible to tell how you're going to feel about raising a baby that's not your own flesh and blood until it's the only option you have left. When Ben told me he would be just as happy adopting, a relief washed over me. I was ecstatic. I felt like I was finally going to get what I'd always wanted."

She had paused then and looked longingly out my office window, the moisture creeping back into her eyes. "But now, I don't know." She turned back to face me. "I can't bring a baby into a marriage that's not one hundred percent solid. I just can't do that."

I nodded, compassion and empathy rising inside of me. These were the kinds of assignments that made me feel good about what I did. Not that I wasn't happy to help everyone who came to me for answers. But it was assignments like this one that renewed my spirit, reminded me of my purpose, kept me fulfilled.

I could feel something cold and grimy under my fingers, and I realized that I was now gripping the bars of Shawna's jail cell. I quickly released them and wiped my palms on my sweatshirt.

"Ashlyn?" Shawna was standing in front of me now, her sparkly shadowed eyes watching me curiously. "Are you all right?"

I shook myself from the reverie of my flashback. "What? Yeah, I'm fine. What else did the file say about Benjamin Connors? About why he was here. In Vegas. What was he doing here?" The questions were flying out of my mouth, rushed and ineloquent. I already knew the answers, I just needed to hear some sort of confirmation. To assure me that my memories were trustworthy.

She squirmed in her uncomfortable costume and adjusted the seashells on her bikini top as she thought. "It just said that he likes to come to Vegas on his own to play blackjack. And that he knew he wouldn't be able to go as much after the baby arrived, so he was going to make the most of it."

Ding. Dong. Ding. Dong. Ding! Ding! Ding! Ding! Ding!

Suddenly the bells were back. And they were ringing louder than ever. In the back of my mind, I heard Darcie Connors's voice again. This time it came through with some kind of echo effect, almost ethereal: *I wouldn't be surprised if he stays up all night. Or at least until his money runs out.*

I pulled my cell phone out of my bag and checked the clock. It was two-thirty in the morning. If I was lucky, there was a chance it wasn't too late.

The scratchy sound of a loud, obnoxious throat clearing filled the hallway just then, and I glanced in the direction from which I'd come. The cheerful security guard was standing there with his arms crossed, indicating that my five minutes was up.

I turned my head hastily back to Shawna. "I have to go. But I promise I'll be back first thing in the morning." I glanced down at her outfit, then swiftly pulled my sweatshirt over my head and passed it through the bars to her. "In case you get cold tonight."

I turned toward the door, but her hand reached through the bars and touched my bare shoulder. "Wait!" she cried, her eyes still struggling to read my face for clues. "What are you going to do about Benjamin Connors?"

I paused for a moment as images of Jamie's face flashed before my eyes, but I did everything in my power to keep them at bay.

Sometimes in life you have to make exceptions. Sometimes you have to break the rules. Because not everything is clear-cut. Not everything happens the way you plan it. People are unpredictable. Things go awry. Messes are made.

And sometimes there's no one else to clean them up.

"I'm going to take care of it."

12

---

like riding a bike

The minute I stepped into the casino of the Palazzo Hotel, I was struck with an overwhelming sense of déjà vu.

It felt like decades since the last time I went undercover. Another lifetime.

Another *me*.

But nonetheless, there I was. Just like old times. Dressed in my sexy little dress and designer shoes and armed with nothing but a fake name and a hidden purpose.

My dress was slightly wrinkled from the plane ride, and my hair was far from perfect. I had found some mascara and lip gloss in my purse and was able to do a quick makeup touch-up in the cab on the way here, but I was still nowhere near the level of glamour that usually accompanied a night like this.

I attempted to smooth my hair as I approached the row of blackjack tables and discreetly surveyed the crowd.

It was surprisingly busy for three in the morning. Or maybe not so surprising given the nature of this town. Eight blackjack tables were currently in use, all of them full. The only time I had ever seen what Benjamin Connors looked like was when Darcie Connors first handed me his photograph and I placed it in the case file I assembled for Shawna. I knew that at this very moment, that file was sitting in a suite thirty-five floors above my head. The little cardboard key

that unlocked the door was being held captive with the rest of Shawna's personal effects at the Clark County Detention Center, and I
didn't have the time or the resources to figure out alternate ways to
gain access to her room.

I would have to rely on memory and instincts alone.

I circled the eight tables slowly, pretending to be engrossed in
each of the games as my eyes subtly scanned the faces of the players.
Not one of them looked even remotely familiar. I completed two
more laps around the cluster of tables before starting to resign myself
to the fact that Benjamin Connors might have run out of steam or
money or both and could have gone to sleep hours ago.

"Are these the only blackjack tables in the casino?" I asked one of
the pit bosses as I completed my third rotation.

He nodded, his jawline firm, as if smiling on the job were grounds
for termination. "But there are more in the Venetian."

My eyebrows rose. What if he had gotten bored with the tables
here and moved to a different casino? But if that was the case, he could
be anywhere by now. The Strip was huge, and it would take me six
hours to search every casino. Not only did I not have the energy, I
didn't have the time. It was coming on 3:15 in the morning already. I
had to bail Shawna out of jail in five and a half hours.

A sentence I never thought I'd ever hear myself say.

"Is the Venetian close by?" I asked.

He nodded again and pointed toward a large interior courtyard in
the distance. "It's connected to the Palazzo."

I thanked the man and started in the direction his finger had
pointed. Darcie Connors was fairly certain her husband preferred the
Palazzo, but then again, she was also fairly certain he would never
cheat on her, and look how that ended. I figured the possibility that
Benjamin Connors had decided to try his luck next door at the ad-
joining Venetian was high enough to warrant a thorough investigation of their blackjack tables as well. If I couldn't find him in half an
hour, then I supposed I would have to admit defeat.

I was almost to the clearing that led into the courtyard and could
see the signs above my head leading the way to the Palazzo's sister
hotel when a roar of loud cheering ripped through the space around

me. I turned my head to see where it had originated, and my eyes landed on a craps table at the end of the row. In all the times I had been to Vegas in my career, I had never fully understood that game. It always seemed to elicit the most enthusiastic responses of any table in the house. Every time I passed by a lively craps game, I felt as if I were stepping into the final fifteen seconds of overtime in a tied Super Bowl game.

The entire table was up in arms, high-fiving one another and making childish whooping sounds. I stopped walking for a moment, watching the group of people as they all held their breath and someone standing near the far end blew on a pair of dice and tossed them across the table.

Another eruption of cheers ricocheted off the walls, and I almost laughed at the spectacle of it all. That is, until my eyes landed on the man in the blue polo shirt and khaki pants standing three spaces from the center of the table. And all traces of amusement were wiped clean off my face.

I thought that it might be difficult to recognize him. I thought the fading photograph in my mind might leave me with doubt. But every bone in my body was telling me that this was Benjamin Connors.

Apparently, I was right: He *did* get bored with the blackjack tables here. But instead of changing casinos, he simply changed games.

My body stiffened as I watched him, unseen, from a few feet away. He was far too absorbed in what was going on at the table to notice me standing there.

As soon as I laid eyes on him, I could feel all my old instincts start to kick into gear again. My internal men-reading device seemed to know exactly what was happening and switched into active mode.

Darcie Connors had told me that Benjamin had just turned thirty in July and that they had been married for five years. She had told me about their struggle to conceive a child and their decision to adopt. She had even told me that they were once college sweethearts.

But these were just facts, numbers and dates and events. There were still so many other things that she didn't tell me. Not because she didn't want to, but because she *couldn't*. Because she didn't even know them herself.

I, however, was able to spot them instantly. Almost like magic.

Benjamin Connors once lived a picture-perfect dream life. It was effortlessly sold to him without the slightest forecast of buyer's remorse at the age of twenty-four. His marriage came a year after that, along with a monthly house payment, a barbecue in the backyard, and the promise of children someday.

This was what life was about. And he was fine with that. After all, if it had been good enough for his two brothers who settled down before him, it was good enough for him.

Then he turned thirty.

And something changed. At first, he didn't even know what it was. A feeling. A constant buzzing in the background that was tolerable but not silenceable. Over the next few weeks, the buzzing got gradually louder, eventually making it hard to concentrate at work, while watching TV, even during sex. And the talk of babies and adoption and picking out a crib for the nursery only made it worse.

He found himself often waking in the middle of the night in a panic, beads of sweat appearing across his forehead, breathing shallowly. He couldn't understand what was happening to him. He considered seeing a doctor. Or maybe a shrink.

Until one night he woke in his usual anxiousness, gasping for breath, and he looked over at the woman sleeping next to him, the only woman he'd ever loved. And that's when he realized what the buzzing sound was. It was a question. And it demanded to be answered:

Is this really what I want out of life?

He assumed the feeling would eventually pass. He wrote it off as being some strange rite of passage that comes to all men who enter their third decade of life.

And he was right.

He certainly wasn't the only man to turn thirty and feel the sudden urge to take inventory of his life. There were many men in the world like Benjamin Connors, who had, at one point or another, wondered what else is out there.

Some of these men resolved to find it. Others just continued to wonder.

And now it was up to me to determine which category Benjamin Connors fit into.

I peered into my purse and checked my financial situation. I had approximately three hundred dollars in cash left over from the ATM withdrawal I'd made before we left for Cabo. I hoped it would be sufficient to keep me in the game long enough to make that determination.

I took a deep breath and one step forward. Then another deep breath and another step. Until I found myself standing directly behind Benjamin Connors at the craps table.

It's just one time, I told myself repeatedly. *Just this once.*

This was it. One year of retirement, and I was back. Unofficially, of course. And only out of necessity. I tried desperately to remember what I was supposed to do. The way I was supposed to act. Deep down, there was a small fear that after being out of commission for nearly a year, I would be rusty and out of practice. And an even bigger fear that it would show and blow my cover.

But I swallowed down both of them and squeezed my way up to the table, claiming the space directly to the right of my first subject in over a year.

The minute his eyes acknowledged my presence, it all came rushing back to me. The flirtation tactics, the charm, knowing how much of my hand to show and how much to save for later. Almost as though I had never left.

It was just like riding a bike. And I immediately realized that mine was a skill that was not so easily forgotten. I guess there's just something about being an undercover fidelity inspector that stays with you. That never leaves.

And honestly, I couldn't figure out if that was a good thing or not.

I glanced casually in his direction, meeting his eye and flashing him a shy smile.

"Welcome to the table," he said, giving me a quick yet not-so-subtle once-over.

"It sounds like a lucky one," I remarked, keeping my voice light and playful.

The only direction I had given Shawna for this assignment was to sit next to him at the blackjack table and act as though she'd never played before. Clearly the game itself had changed, but I figured the approach was still valid. Plus, I had no idea how to play craps, so it wouldn't take much pretending on my part.

Benjamin Connors nodded. "Yeah, it's been pretty hot for the last ten minutes. You chose wisely."

I giggled in response, tucking a strand of hair behind my ear. As I clicked my tongue against the roof of my mouth, I leaned over the edge of the table, taking in the length of the playing field. It was covered in hundreds of various-shaped boxes and rectangles, all labeled with some type of cryptic, craps player secret language. My eyes skimmed over words like "Pass," "Field," and "Hard Way." And I couldn't help but marvel at how this long, complicated stretch of green felt seemed to be narrating my life. There I was, at nearly four in the morning, fresh out of retirement and back in the "field," trying to determine whether this man would "pass" or fail my reluctant inspection. It was pretty safe to say I had taken "hard way."

"And it looks like you came right on time," Benjamin commented, and motioned toward the table in front of me. I looked down to see six red dice staring back at me. The uniformed casino employee standing across the way had pushed them toward me with a long, hook-ended stick.

And suddenly all eyes at the table were on me. I felt a knot form in my stomach. Apparently, playing the role of the naïve and inexperienced craps player was already off to a believable start.

I looked to my neighbor for help. He chuckled at the bewildered look on my face. "You have to select two of the six. It's your roll."

"Oh no," I replied, snapping my body upright and holding out my hands in surrender. "I don't know how to play. I was just going to watch for a little while and see if I could learn."

"No way," he replied, motioning to the dice. "You can't learn craps by watching. You can only learn by doing. And don't worry, I'll help you."

I bit my bottom lip as I pulled my wad of cash out of my bag and placed it in front of me. Within seconds, my money had magically transformed into three equally sized stacks of red Palazzo-monogrammed chips.

Benjamin leaned in close to me—close enough that I could smell what was left of the cologne he had applied earlier in the evening—and told me to place four chips on the pass line. I immediately obliged. Then he instructed me to pick up the dice and throw them toward the other end of the table. I did as I was told, watching the swirls of white spots on red plastic as the dice floated gracefully in the air.

"Winner eleven," the man with the long stick called out as soon as they had settled on the far side of the green playing field. Everyone at the table broke out in another round of cheers and applause.

I didn't have to fake the confusion on my face as I asked what had just happened.

He laughed. "You won! We all won!"

I beamed. "You mean, I won for everyone?"

"Yeah, pretty much. Seven or eleven on the first roll wins all around."

I nodded, taking it all in. "Well, that sounds easy enough."

I proceeded to roll four more elevens in a row. The crowd gathered around the table was going crazy, and I was starting to understand what all the fuss was about in this game.

But the only reaction I was really interested in was that of Benjamin Connors. Because as much fun as it was to watch my stack of five-dollar chips grow exponentially before my eyes, I was here with a purpose. And I was determined to stick to it.

My next roll was a nine. Benjamin clasped his hands together and rubbed them fiercely. "That's all right, baby. Nine is good. Nine is easy."

"What happens now?" I asked, staring at the numerous piles of chips that were being placed around the table. "I didn't roll an eleven."

"Now," Benjamin explained, clearly enjoying his role as the craps master, "you have to roll another nine *without* rolling a seven. Think you can handle that?"

I smiled deviously. "No problem."

"That's my girl!" Benjamin shouted, and pointed at me. "Right here, my Lady Luck. She's gonna make me a rich man tonight."

I smiled and pretended to blush under the attention. Then with a quick shake of my hand, I tossed the dice in the air. One landed on four and the other on five.

"Winner nine!" the stickman announced.

And with this, Benjamin actually picked me up off the ground and twirled me around in his arms. "What did I tell you?" he cried to no one in particular. "Lady Luck, right here!"

I giggled girlishly. My face was so close to his that I could smell the alcohol on his breath. And when he put me down, I could feel his fingertips pressed softly into my side as his hands lingered momentarily around my waist. My stomach flipped.

I was really doing this. This was really happening. Benjamin Connors's hands were really touching my body. And I was letting them. Because that's what I was here to do. To let them.

After a twenty-minute-long winning streak and several more fairly intimate moments celebrating my luck with the dice, Benjamin invited me to step away from the craps table and grab a drink. "You just won me five thousand dollars. I think it's time to quit while I'm still ahead."

The moment my butt hit the wooden bar stool, I could feel the fatigue setting in. I managed a subtle glance at my watch. It was close to five. I had been awake for nearly twenty-four hours and been running off pure adrenaline for the last seven. I worried that a drink might do me in. But alcohol has always been a part of this job. If they drink, you drink, too. If they have another round, *you* have another round. If alcohol impairs their judgment, you kiss back.

"So does Lady Luck have a name?" Benjamin asked after we had gotten situated with two martinis.

I pulled the olive out of my glass and placed it in my mouth, rolling it around on top of my tongue. "Yes," I replied with a teasing smile.

"And what would that be?"

I chewed my olive and washed it down with a sip of my martini.

"Ashlyn," I replied coyly. The nostalgia of that name on my lips was staggering. She was back in full force, resurrected in all her glory. And the minute I felt her presence, it was almost as if she had never left in the first place.

As much as the Jennifer side of me wanted to fight her return, knowing how much trouble she had caused me in the past. I could feel my body slowly surrendering to her power. She had always found a way to simply take over, jump in the driver's seat, and seize control of the situation. *This,* after all, had always been *her* domain.

"Ashlyn," he repeated, sending chills of apprehension up my spine. "Pretty."

I shrugged, as if I had heard it a million times.

"And what brings you to Vegas?"

This was the part that I didn't have prepared. I would have to make up something. Or rather, *Ashlyn* would have to do what she did best . . . wing it. I decided the more generic the better. "Just here with friends," I replied nonchalantly.

He took a sip of his drink. "And where are these friends?"

"Ugh . . ." I sighed. "Totally passed out at like three. It was completely lame. I wasn't tired and I've always wanted to play craps, so I thought I'd come down here and learn."

"Well, you're a natural."

I smiled and took another swig of alcohol. "I had a good teacher."

It didn't take long for Benjamin's hand to wind up on my leg. He placed it there as casually as if he were simply placing an empty glass on a cocktail napkin. And the strangest part was, it didn't feel strange to me. As sinful and wrong as I knew it *should* have felt, there was an overwhelming sense of familiarity about the whole thing. The numbness in my entire body was back. The same numbness that had comforted me and carried me through a two-year career of letting men like Benjamin Connors touch me.

"What about you?" I asked, running my fingertip around the edge of my glass. "Why are *you* in Vegas?"

He shrugged, avoiding my eyes. "Just like to gamble." Then he nodded toward the glass in his hands. "And drink."

I laughed in agreement. "Vegas is always a good excuse to drink more than you should."

"It's a good excuse to do a *lot* of things you shouldn't." His eyes slowed down for a moment as they met mine with purpose and conviction. "Don't you think?"

I knew this was the turning point of the conversation. Every conversation of this nature has one. It's the moment when the night goes from innocent to something else. And it's a moment that every good fidelity inspector can spot like a black dot on a white page.

"I do," I whispered, knowing that the statement rang all too true . . . for both of us.

And then in one fluid motion, Benjamin Connors downed the remaining half of his martini, reached his hand around the back of my head, and pulled me toward him. As his lips met mine, I tried to fill my mind with nothingness. Empty space. It was my old tried-and-true trick for coping with the kissing part.

But as hard as I tried, the nothingness simply wouldn't come. Apparently, this was a skill that *had* managed to fade with time. Because all I could think about was Jamie. His face, his eyes, his hands. The fact that right now he was sleeping alone, in another country, with absolutely no idea that in one night, I had managed to revert to a person I had willingly abandoned long ago.

Or maybe I had never really abandoned her. Maybe she was just lying dormant inside of me. Waiting to be reawakened by the touch of a married stranger.

As Benjamin's tongue darted in and out of my mouth, I fought to block out the image of Jamie's face and replace it with the face of Darcie Connors, Benjamin's wife of five years. She was why I was here. I was doing this for her. She wanted answers to her questions, and I was going to give them to her. No matter what. That was the promise I had made when I opened the doors of the Hawthorne Agency. And that was the promise I made to every single woman and man who walked through them.

She had come to me asking for the truth. Asking if this was really the man she wanted to raise children with. And the next eight words that Benjamin spoke told me exactly what the answer would be.

"Would you like to come upstairs with me?"

I nodded. I knew I would never be able to get the "Yes" out of my mouth. It would be forever stuck there, trapped behind the emotional battle raging inside me.

But the nod was enough.

I followed him through the casino to the elevator banks. As we rode to the tenth floor, Benjamin's lips were on my neck and the sides of my face. Exactly where Jamie's had been less than seven hours ago when this runaway evening had begun.

I quickly pushed the thought from my mind and concentrated on pretending to enjoy *this* moment instead of being hung up in another. The last thing I needed tonight was for the subject to get suspicious. If he bailed out now, it would mean that everything up until this point had been for nothing.

And it couldn't be for nothing.

It had to be for something. For *everything*.

When we entered Benjamin's hotel suite, he didn't waste any time leading me straight to the bed. And believe it or not, I was grateful for his hastiness. Anything to make this night end faster.

We fell onto it, and I felt my mind start to leave my body as Benjamin's lips again met mine and his hands started to wander down the outside of my dress. His kiss was intense and tasting of vodka. It was a now-or-never kiss, the kind that married men use on women who are not their wives. If death row inmates were allowed a last kiss in place of a last meal, this is what that kiss would feel like.

I closed my eyes and reluctantly kissed back.

An intention to cheat. That's all I had to prove was there. That Benjamin Connors had every intention of having sex with someone other than his wife. And as soon as his hands started to slip under the hemline of my dress, I considered it confirmed.

I knew, professionally, I could have taken it further. The dress could have come off. That last PG-13 moment could have been reached. But I knew, emotionally, I would never make it that far. Not without vomiting, anyway.

I placed my hand on his chest and gently pushed him away. "I'll be right back," I said with a flirtatious wink. "I just have to use the restroom."

He smiled and rolled off me as I stood up and adjusted my dress. "It's by the front door."

"Perfect," I replied sweetly.

And it was.

I walked softly to the bathroom and flicked on the light, followed by the fan, then I peered back into the bedroom to see Benjamin unbuckling his belt and unzipping his pants. I closed the bathroom door from the outside and turned ninety degrees until I was face-to-face with my escape. My end to this seemingly never-ending night.

As quietly as possible, I turned the handle and pulled the front door open a crack. The Palazzo tower was a brand-new hotel on the Las Vegas Strip. It hadn't even survived a full tourist season yet. Which, fortunately for me, meant that the hinges on the door hadn't yet inherited the ability to alert tenants of a possible runaway. As I slid the door a quarter of the way open, it let out no squeaking complaints. I squeezed through the small space and ever so carefully shut it behind me, keeping the handle fully engaged until the last possible moment to avoid the *click* of the closing door.

Once outside, I took a deep breath and made my way to the elevator, relishing in the conclusiveness of my actions.

The front desk didn't seem at all fazed by my request for a room at five in the morning. In fact, their reaction made it seem rather commonplace. With my new key card in hand, I dragged myself back to the elevator and up to the seventeenth floor, where my room was waiting.

I had to be back at the jail in four hours, but I was still overjoyed to climb under the white cotton sheets of the king-size bed.

I could finally go to sleep. I could finally close my eyes. This night had *finally* come to an end.

But I knew, without a shadow of a doubt, that my mind would not rest.

13

guilt becomes her

"One starfish hairclip. One pearl necklace, blue. One seaweed boa, green."

I watched as the morning security guard removed from a plastic box all of Shawna's costume accessories that had been confiscated the night before and placed them on the counter in front of us.

"One seashell purse. Two coral earrings. And one cellular telephone." She pulled the last item from the box and placed it on the table next to the others.

Shawna, now dressed in my yellow sweatshirt with her glittering mermaid skirt underneath, scooped everything into her arms with a scowl and turned to me. "Please, let's get out of here."

I handed all the signed paperwork back to the bailiff and led Shawna through the front door and into a waiting cab.

We made a quick stop at the Palazzo so that she could pack up the rest of her stuff, and she was very grateful to be able to change out of her costume. I had picked up a pair of jeans and an overpriced T-shirt at the Palazzo shops earlier that morning.

As we made our way to the airport to catch an eleven o'clock flight back to L.A., I promised Shawna that I'd talk to some lawyers first thing in the morning to see about sorting out all the details of her arrest so she wouldn't have to come back for a court hearing. Then I told her to take the week off and get some rest, but she insisted that getting back to her usual routine as soon as possible would be the only way to keep her sane.

Jamie had called my cell phone around eight-thirty that morning to tell me that he was going standby on an earlier flight back to L.A. and that I should text him my flight information so he could pick me up at the airport when I arrived.

Once I got on the plane, I spent the first half of the flight home convincing myself that telling Jamie the truth about what happened the previous night (or, more accurately, earlier that morning) was the best course of action, and I spent the second half of the flight convincing myself that he would forgive me.

But the moment I saw his face as he stepped out of the car to greet me at the curb, every convincing word that I had spoken silently to myself at an altitude of thirty-five thousand feet instantly vanished into a black hole in the back of my mind.

His eyes were so trusting. His smile was so genuine. His face was so happy to see me. There was just no way that honesty was the best policy here.

It would only hurt him.

And that was something I could *not* convince myself to do.

Besides, there was no way I was ever going to do it again. So there was really no point in telling him about it. Exigent circumstances. That's all it was. I was dealing with a crisis. Extinguishing the flames of an unforeseen fire. I was doing what the president of any successful company would do. And the bigger deal I made about it, the bigger deal it would become.

So I lied.

"Everything okay now?" Jamie asked as he pulled me into a tight embrace.

I nodded into his warm chest. "Yes. Shawna's fine. A little shaken up, but she'll be okay."

He gave me a quick kiss and a squeeze and then opened the passenger-side door for me. I collapsed into the seat with a heavy sigh.

"So what happened after you got there?"

I shrugged, somehow feeling as though this casual gesture might possibly relieve some of the guilt. It didn't work.

"Not much," I replied. "I mean, I went to the jail, I was too late to bail her out, so I just talked to her for a while. When the guard kicked me out, I booked a room at the Palazzo and fell asleep." I nestled the back of my head against the soft leather of the passenger seat and closed my eyes. Although I admit, it was more out of not wanting to look Jamie in the eye than pure fatigue.

"And so what ended up happening with the second assignment?"

My eyes suddenly flew open and my pulse started to rise. He knew. He had to know. Why else would he ask that?

"What *second* assignment?" I asked warily, trying to gauge exactly how much he knew and what he was referring to. It's a common mistake when telling a lie—giving yourself away by assuming the other person actually knows more than he does. Amateurs end up falling for that trap all the time. Fortunately, I was no amateur when it came to creating complicated webs of deceit. Something I was not proud of. Especially not at this moment.

"You mentioned before you left that Shawna was double-booked last night. So I was just wondering what happened with the second one after she got arrested."

I was relieved to find absolutely no trace of blame or accusation in his voice. Jamie's response was casual and informally inquisitive. Clearly just the genuine reply of a loving, caring, *supportive* boyfriend—sorry, fiancé—who was trying to make conversation and fully understand the nuances of his girlfriend's horrible midnight rescue mission.

Which of course made me feel even more wretched than I already did.

"Um," I started, closing my eyes again. "That *was* the second assignment, actually."

We cruised to a red light and Jamie smiled tenderly at me, reaching out to touch the side of my face. "You look tired, baby."

Feeling his hand on my skin made me want to cry.

He didn't doubt my story for a second.

He didn't even blink.

He trusts me blindly.

The rock that seemed to be growing in the pit of my stomach

started to pulsate. I closed my eyes and willed it to stop. *It's not cheating if you didn't enjoy it,* I told myself, feeling rather resolved in my logic even if the pulsation refused to cease.

"I am," I finally said after a few moments of silence as Jamie continued to speed down Sepulveda Boulevard toward the freeway.

"Am what?"

I turned my head and looked out the window, watching the gray November sky follow us home. "Tired."

Jamie dropped me off at my place so that I could rest while he went home to unpack his bag, promising to come back later around dinnertime. Except I didn't rest. I didn't even try. I knew that it was a lost cause. As soon as I dumped my suitcase in the bedroom, I took a quick shower and changed into a fresh pair of jeans and a T-shirt that didn't have the Palazzo logo emblazoned on the front. Then I grabbed my keys and was back out the door in a matter of minutes.

I had to keep myself busy and my mind occupied. I feared idleness would be my worst enemy right now. So I drove around town, making up errands as I went. I definitely needed some more dental floss and toilet paper from the drugstore. And maybe an oversize bottle of Advil and some sunless tanning lotion. And oh, one of those master chopping mechanisms that I saw on TV. And I was sure I had at least *something* at the dry cleaner, even if the old Chinese man insisted that I'd picked everything up on Friday. I made him check again. Then I swung by Whole Foods and kind of just wandered the aisles for a good thirty minutes, picking up random items, examining the packaging thoroughly, and then throwing them into my basket regardless of whether or not I ever planned to consume them.

When I finally ran out of things to do around seven in the evening, I reluctantly headed back home, praying that something interesting would be on TV so that I could continue to distract myself from my thoughts until it was time to go to bed. At which point I had every intention of employing a prescription sleep aid.

I pulled my Lexus SUV into the garage and noticed that Jamie's Jaguar was already occupying the second parking spot. I fought hard to take a steady breath as I placed the car in park and killed the engine.

I didn't really want to face Jamie tonight. I wanted to be alone. But at the same time, I knew that not being around him would cause me pain. My mind felt as if it were being tugged in a hundred different directions.

But there was one thing I was sure of: I had to work past this. I had to learn how to swallow the guilt and keep it from regurgitating in my mouth in the form of a confession. Jamie was a big part of my life. The biggest. And he was going to be around. I couldn't *not* get over this.

After a cursory glance in my rearview mirror and a disturbing shudder at my tired reflection, I clasped my house keys and stepped out of the car, promising myself that this would get easier. Eventually time would do its job and I would forget.

And then things would slowly return to normal.

All I had to do until that day came was pretend everything still *was* normal. That nothing had changed. Because to Jamie, nothing *had* changed. I was still the same Jennifer Hunter he had fallen in love with and asked to marry.

So I would have to pretend to be her.

No matter what it took.

"Hey, where you been?" Jamie called from the kitchen, eyeing my armful of superfluous purchases.

I stumbled past the dining room and struggled to place everything on the counter. "Just running some errands for the week."

He reached into one of the shopping bags and pulled out a mysterious blue carton. "Hemp milk?" His face twisted in confusion. "What'd I miss?"

I shrugged, refusing to meet his questioning eyes. "Everyone says it's better than soy milk. And it supports the hemp farmers. It says so on the box."

"So," he said, placing his arms around my waist and pulling me close to him. "We have something to celebrate tonight."

"Hmm?" I mumbled, looking down at his shirt collar and fiddling with the edges. "What's that?"

He nodded toward the hallway that led into the bedroom. There were two suitcases and three small cardboard boxes sitting there. "Where'd those come from?"

He grinned. "I figured if I bring a few things over every day, I'll be fully moved in by the end of the week."

Oh, right, I thought. He's moving in. I wasn't sure how that could have slipped my mind. Actually, I could. But I was trying to forget about that.

"My Realtor thinks I can sell my place fully furnished, which means we won't have to figure out which furniture to keep."

I forced a smile. "That's great."

Jamie pulled me closer to him, and his arms tightened around me. Then his lips pressed hard against mine, and judging by the bulge quickly forming in the front of his pants, this wasn't going to be just a kiss. It suddenly hit me that *this* was how he was planning to "celebrate" the boxes and suitcases in the hallway.

I closed my eyes, trying to soak in even an ounce of his intensity. But unfortunately, my passion-o-meter seemed to be stuck at "cold fish."

Jamie, however, was oblivious to this fact. His hands were already digging into the sides of my waist, and before I knew it, my T-shirt was being whipped over my head and he was now kissing the tops of my breasts, moaning with a sound that resembled someone devouring an ice-cream sundae in the middle of a crash diet.

"We never got to finish what we started in Cabo," he cooed.

"Jamie," I protested, pushing gently at his shoulders. "I'm not sure if we should do this—"

"In here?" he interrupted. "You're right."

And suddenly, my feet were no longer on the floor. Jamie literally swept me off them and was now carrying me fireman style over his shoulder into the bedroom.

I yelped and clung desperately to his shirt. "Jamie! Oh my God! Put me down!"

And he did. Right smack in the middle of the bed. Then he was on top of me. And his hands were everywhere. Except I couldn't feel them. I mean, I could feel them on me. But they weren't Jamie's hands.

They were Benjamin Connors's.

And the lips that were sweeping along my stomach, making their way down to my top of my jeans, weren't Jamie's, either.

My breathing started to quicken. Jamie interpreted it as a sign of arousal and moaned into my abdomen.

But the only moaning sounds I could hear were the ones still stuck in my head from last night. The ones that I *thought* I had effectively extinguished with pointless errands and internal monologues. But there they were, louder than ever. And they seemed to be echoing from all corners of the room. Like Benjamin Connors in stereo.

I heard a voice whisper, "You are so sexy." But for the life of me, I couldn't figure out whose voice it was. Was it Jamie's? Was he the one saying that? Or was it part of my Saturday night flashback, presented in Dolby Digital Surround Sound?

"I can't believe how sexy you are."

Who the fuck is saying that?!

Apparently, what happens in Vegas doesn't really stay there.

Jamie was unbuttoning my jeans and kissing the skin just below my waist. Beads of sweat were appearing across my forehead, and the room was starting to spin. Slowly at first and then much faster. Like a merry-go-round gone postal.

Someone stop the spinning! I want to get off!

And then I looked down at the top of Jamie's head, trying to focus my attention on the man I loved. Trying to regain control over the situation. But my vision continued to blur, and the cloudiness in my head continued to hover. And then finally, he stopped and looked up at me. Except I could no longer see his face.

The only face that appeared in front of me belonged to Benjamin Connors.

"Stop!" I screamed. "Make it stop!"

Frantically, I pushed Jamie off me and bounded from the bed, nearly kicking him in the face in the process. I stood helplessly in the

middle of my bedroom in my bra and unbuttoned jeans, not knowing what to say or where to look. So I chose the floor.

I didn't know what I was doing. My body didn't feel like my own
anymore, and my mind seemed a million miles away. As if it had
completely abandoned me to fend for myself and I was failing miser-
ably.

When I found the courage to look up at Jamie, I caught sight of
his wide-eyed gaze and quickly looked away, feeling ashamed and
embarrassed.

Who was this person? Certainly not me.

For a moment, neither of us spoke. Jamie was too stunned to say
anything, and I was too freaked out. The merry-go-round in my
bedroom eventually started to slow down, and I felt my heart rate
return to normal.

"I'm sorry," I finally offered in a quiet, feeble voice.

Jamie wrinkled his forehead and ran his fingers through his hair.
"Um. What was that?" The tone in his voice was searching for
patience, but when it came up short, it seemed to settle for slightly
annoyed.

But I just stood there, my body shivering slightly, despite the fact
that I was far from cold. "I don't know."

Jamie fell onto his back and stared up at the ceiling. "You don't
know," he repeated numbly.

I shook my head and awkwardly ran the tip of my toe across the
hardwood floor. "I'm sorry. I guess I just freaked out a little."

"Apparently."

Once the shaking had subsided and the feeling returned to all of
my limbs and extremities, my mind was nagging me to find an excuse. To make something up. I couldn't just leave it at that. I had to
make it better. I had to fix it.

"I'm just stressed," I attempted, feeling less than confident about
my cover-up.

Jamie rolled onto his side and propped himself up on one elbow.
"Stressed?"

Clearly he wasn't confident about it, either.

But I couldn't back out now. I was committed to the lie. So

I nodded. "Yes. With work and Shawna's arrest and Katie out on that nanny assignment and Sophie's wedding in two weeks, and you know she's been calling me every fifteen minutes with drama and . . ." I let my voice fade away as I inhaled a deep breath.

Jamie studied my face, seemingly deciding whether or not he was going to believe me. I struggled to maintain eye contact with him. Any waver or shift would surely give me away.

"And that's it?" he asked, his voice full of doubt. "It's *just* stress? It has nothing to do with anything else? Like, say, my stuff in the hall-way?"

I swallowed hard and shook my head. "No, of course not. It's just stress. I promise."

Jamie considered this for a moment. And then finally he pulled himself off the bed and went over to me. Cautiously, he placed his hand on my waist and kissed me on the forehead, his lips lingering on my skin for a good five seconds. As if he were trying to suck the truth right out of my brain.

I closed my eyes and prayed for finality. That we would never again have to speak of this moment.

When I opened them again, Jamie was already in the kitchen making dinner.

14

sentencing

By the time I got to work on Monday morning, the dark circles under my eyes were starting to resemble ominous caverns. I'd barely slept at all last night . . . again. And the Ambien I had taken around two in the morning did little to remedy the situation. Apparently, it's only effective if your conscience is completely clear. Something that I firmly believe should be indicated on the label.

So it was safe to say I was in no frame of mind to deal with the appointment I had in fifteen minutes.

"Ashlyn?" Hadley's voice came through my intercom after a startling buzz. "Darcie Connors is here to see you."

Make that right *now*.

Damn it. She was early. Not that fifteen minutes would have made any sort of difference.

"Okay, send her in," I replied into the speaker. Then I stood up and pulled my suit jacket taut around my shoulders, as if this simple act might help pull the rest of me together as well.

With my eyes glued to the door and my fingers gripping the edge of my desk, I waited for the moment I had been dreading since I'd walked out of Benjamin Connors's hotel room less than thirty-six hours ago.

Breaking bad news to a client is never easy. In fact, it's always been one of the hardest parts of this job. But today it felt worse than

I'd ever remembered. I don't know if it was because of the guilt that I would forever associate with this assignment or because I knew that in just a few seconds, I would have to tell this woman that her dreams of having the child she's always wanted with the man she's always wanted to have it with were now officially shattered.

There was just no easy way to do that.

The door creaked open and Hadley announced my visitor. Then she stepped aside, allowing Darcie Connors to enter.

"Hello," I said, still maintaining a death grip on the edge of my desk. "Mrs. Connors," I sang. "Lovely to see you again." I could hear the obvious falseness in my words, and I quickly attempted to cover it up with an even falser smile.

After stabilizing myself on the desk, I slowly made my way to her and held out my hand, which I prayed wasn't as cold and clammy as it felt. She shook it.

"Would you like to sit down?" I gestured to the sofa.

Darcie Connors took a seat, staying perched on the very edge of the couch, almost as if she were afraid to get too comfortable. I didn't blame her. Clearly, I was now living proof that you should *never* get too comfortable. Because something is always waiting around the corner to turn your life upside down.

I struggled to keep my composure and appear relaxed. I'd broken a lot of bad news within the confines of this office, and today should have been no different. Just another choreographed routine of reassuring smiles, compassionate glances, and tender pats on the hand. That was what usually went down inside these four walls. At least five times a week.

But nothing about this moment felt routine.

The fact that I had personally been the one to prove the unfaithful tendencies of Benjamin Connors was irrelevant. It doesn't matter whose bare skin he touched, whose slightly glossed lips he kissed, whose short, provocative dress he tried to remove. What mattered was that he *did* all those things. With someone other than his wife.

This thought gave me a fleeting burst of strength, and I decided to seize the moment before it sizzled away and I was left once again with the total disaster that had stared back at me from the mirror this morning. I folded my hands in my lap and looked into the eyes of the woman sitting across from me, a serious yet empathetic expression etched into my face. "I'll be honest with you, Mrs. Connors, I don't like to draw out these meetings any longer than I have to."

For your sanity and *mine.*

"I know how difficult this is for you, so I'm just going to get right to it."

She nodded, her eyes wide with anticipation and fear. I could almost see the tears preparing for their call of duty. Lining up in the trenches of her eyelids like an army ready to go into battle, ready to deploy upon command.

"As we discussed, my *associate*"—I paused, shifting uneasily in my seat—"conducted a fidelity inspection on your husband, Benjamin Connors, on Saturday night at the Palazzo Hotel and Casino in Las Vegas."

Her lips were pressed hard together, soft pink pigment slowly giving way to a spreading sea of cold and lifeless white as she awaited my next words with eagerness.

"Your husband," I began slowly, "unfortunately did not pass the inspection."

Darcie drew in a sharp breath, held it for an unnaturally long time, and finally blew it out again. Even from across the coffee table, I could feel the soft gushes of warm air on my face.

"Oh God," she said, dropping her head in her hands. "Oh God."

That was all she managed to say before the sobs started.

Normally, I knew exactly how to respond in these situations. Normally, I'm a freaking database of supportive catchphrases and pep talks, complete with hand gestures, corresponding facial expressions, the works. But not now. Now I was just an empty mess. Nothing in my head was making sense. It was as if it were all written in a foreign language and I had lost my translation filter.

And for the life of me, I couldn't find a way to comfort Darcie Connors. All I could do was stare, dumbstruck, at her quivering body. After a few moments, my hands finally unfroze and my brain functioned long enough to grab the box of tissues from the table next to me and offer them to her.

Darcie lifted her head and plucked a tissue from the box. She blew her nose loudly and wiped under her eyes. "It's really happening, isn't it? My worst nightmare. It's happening."

I wasn't sure how to respond to this, either, so I just took a deep breath and reached out to touch her knee. She seemed to find comfort in the gesture, and strangely, so did I.

"I'm sorry I'm such a mess." She blew her nose again. "It's just that two weeks ago I had everything I ever wanted. A husband who loved me and the chance at a baby. I feel like I just lost my entire family in the course of five minutes." She let out a strange, nervous laugh. "It almost sounds funny when I say it aloud."

I nodded, feeling helpless. This had always been the dichotomy, trading the pain of the present moment for the hope of a happier future. But now I wasn't so sure. Was all this pain and agony really worth it? Not only hers, but my own as well?

"I'm just sorry it had to happen like this," I muttered, staring down at my hands.

And I was. I *was* sorry it happened like this. I'm sorry Ken Littrell's idiot best man felt the need to falsely accuse Shawna of prostitution. I'm sorry that I was able to charter a last-minute flight to Vegas. And I'm sorry that I was the one who had to feel Benjamin Connors's lips on mine.

Darcie's hands were clasped so tightly around the straps of her handbag, the pink pigment of her knuckles was starting to give way to that same pale white color that had recently overtaken her lips. "Yes, well, what's done is done. And once you know, you can't really go back, can you? As much as you might want to."

All I could do was nod my head again. I couldn't verbally express my agreement because it felt like I was betraying Jamie all over again.

Apparently my nod was good enough, because Darcie was quickly out of her seat, standing tall and rigid in front of me. "I'm sure you'll excuse me for not staying any longer," she choked out, surprisingly pleasant. "But I have to make a call to our adoption lawyer." She grabbed a few extra tissues from the box and then walked right out my office door.

My body slumped against the back of my chair, and my arms fell dangling over the sides. I felt as though a train had been coming straight at me for the past ten minutes and all I could do was stand in the middle of the track and welcome it with open arms.

Her words lingered in my mind like an annoying song that refuses to be forgotten.

. . . you can't really go back, can you? As much as you might want to.

But *did* I want to? And would I have done things differently if I *could*?

I immediately realized the futility in my own question—or more important, the futility in spending any time agonizing over the answer. Obviously it was outside of the realm of possibility. I couldn't turn back time. I couldn't repeat the events of Saturday night.

But for some reason, I *had* to answer the question. I had to know just how much I really *regretted* my decision. Because in my mind, it held the key to my self-inflicted sentence. The answer would determine just how deep the guilt went and how long I would have to punish myself for it.

As I sat there contemplating, I suddenly realized I was not alone in the room. Darcie Connors was back, standing precariously in the doorway, staring back at me with a pensive look on her face. Startled, I jumped up and struggled to straighten my body in the chair.

"I just want you to know," she began, seemingly failing to notice my dramatic shift in posture, "that I'm grateful for what you did."

I cocked my head to the side and stared at her intently. The doubt in my eyes was apparent. And although I never asked the question aloud, she confirmed it with a nod. "Yes. *Eternally* grateful."

There was a brief silence between us, and she glanced down at her feet, struggling with her next words. "I . . . um . . . there's something I didn't tell you when I first came in here last week."

I continued to stare at her, my mouth slightly agape as I studied her timid body language and uneasy stance.

She took a deep breath. "My parents got divorced when I was fifteen. My mom cheated on my dad. It completely destroyed him. It destroyed all of us. Our entire family fell apart. And I promised myself that I would never put my children through that."

She paused and pressed her lips together before continuing. "I had every intention of keeping that vow. But it wasn't until two weeks ago that I realized I was only half of the equation. I could be as faithful as a Buddhist monk until the day I died, but I couldn't control what my husband did or would possibly do. And that's when I decided to come to you. It was the only way I knew how to keep my promise to my future children. So thank you." And then after a deep breath, "You and your . . . associate."

I could feel the tears start to well in my eyes. Normally, I would fight them off at any cost. Never show emotion in front of the client. Never get personally involved. But her words hit too close to home. Her plight felt all too familiar.

Any words that I might have thought to say were immediately caught in my throat. But I didn't really mind. I knew that they wouldn't do my feelings justice anyway.

When she left the second time, I didn't collapse back into my chair as I had before. Instead I stood up and walked to the window. There was a distinct electricity surging through my body. It made me feel vibrant, alive. More alive than I'd felt in a long time, actually.

I thought back to my original question. The one that promised to condense all of my feelings, all of my emotions, all of my regrets, into a simple yes or no response.

If given a second chance, would I have done things differently?

And staring out at the ocean, replaying Darcie's final words of gratitude in my mind, I knew that I had my answer.

15

a nod to jane austen

By the time Friday arrived, I was physically and mentally exhausted.
I had spent the entire week trying to undo the damage caused by
Shawna's arrest. After a call to Gracie Katz, Ken Littrell's fiancée (or
now ex-fiancée), I was able to ascertain that Shawna's cover had, in
fact, been blown. Apparently, during her simultaneous bachelorette
party, Gracie got drunk and told all of her friends that she had hired
the agency to test Ken. Well, one of the bridesmaids, who also happened to be married to Ken Littrell's best man, got on the phone and
relayed the information to her husband, just in time for him to spot
Shawna dancing with the groom.

When I repeated all of this to a lawyer in the Las Vegas area, he
was pretty certain he'd be able to get the charges dropped. Especially
when, after some more digging around, he discovered that Ken
Littrell's best man is actually the son of a very prominent high roller
who frequents the MGM Grand, which was the only reason his "suggestion" that Shawna was soliciting sex was taken seriously.

The whole ordeal was an outrage and impossibly frustrating. But
by the end of the week, the situation was under control and settled.
The charges were dropped and Shawna's record was cleared.

When I got the news, I decided to duck out of the office early and
head home for some much needed R&R.

But just as I was pulling away from the valet station, my cell phone started ringing. I checked the caller ID and saw that the incoming call was from Willa Cruz, wedding planner extraordinaire. I had been screening her calls for three days now, and they were getting increasingly more frequent with each day that I didn't pick up. So I figured I should probably just answer and get it over with if I wanted any hope of a relaxing weekend.

I pressed the Bluetooth button on my steering wheel and spoke into the empty car. "Hello?"

"Jennifer!" Willa's voice came loudly and bubbly over the speakers, and I immediately jabbed at the volume button with my thumb.

"Yes, hi, Willa," was my slightly less enthusiastic reply.

"You know, I've been unable to get a hold of you for the last few days. Is something wrong with your phone, perhaps?"

I cringed. "Yes, perhaps."

"Well, the reason I've been so persistent . . ." Willa began.

I almost laughed at her choice of words. Two calls is persistent. Ten in three days is just plain harassment.

". . . is that I have located the most perfect of all perfect venues for your summer wedding."

I found it hard to believe that Willa Cruz would be able to pick out the most perfect of all perfect places for our wedding when the wedding questionnaire that I was supposed to fill out and fax back to her was still tucked away in one of my purses.

"You have?"

She sighed orgasmically. "So many brides have *killed* for this location, but it's always booked up years in advance. But I just got a call from someone I know on the *inside*." Her voice dropped to a conspiratorial whisper, as if this "insider" were in mortal danger for having made such a phone call. "Apparently, there was a cancellation. The groom ended up doing some *highly* inappropriate things on his last business trip, if you know what I mean."

Unfortunately, I knew *exactly* what she meant. "Yes, I think I get the picture."

"It was really quite scandalous," she continued in her hushed

tone, which in all honesty was starting to grate on my nerves. "It
turned out the bride actually hired some agency to test whether or
not he would be faithful to her. And he *failed*."

A lump formed in my throat as my grip on the steering wheel
tightened. "You don't say," I croaked.

Willa, who was clearly a big fan of wedding-related gossip, was
enjoying this immensely. "Yes. They sent some girl all the way to his
sales conference in Minneapolis. Can you believe that?"

I was hardly even listening to her because I was too busy yanking
my car off the road and rummaging through my briefcase until I
found what I was looking for: the case file Lauren Ireland had turned
in to me last week. I had brought it home this weekend in hopes of
getting some data entry done.

I flipped it open, and the lump in my throat immediately doubled
in size. I felt as though I might actually choke on my next attempted
breath.

There it was, right at the top of the client bio page. Eight rows
down from the top and clear as day.

BASIC INFORMATION
Case Number: 2371
Subject Name: Nathan Charles
Occupation: Software Developer
Client Name: Amanda Savant
Relationship to Subject: Fiancé
Associate Assigned to Case: Lauren Ireland
Inspection Location: Google Sales Conference in Minneapolis

I didn't have to ask what the groom's name was. There weren't
that many fidelity inspection agencies in town. I only knew of one,
and I had just left it. This was no coincidence.

I suddenly became aware of the fact that there was an expectant
silence in the car, and I assumed Willa was waiting for me to react to
whatever it was she had just told me. To be on the safe side, I went
with something generic. "That's crazy!"

"Isn't it?" she replied in awe. "Well, the bottom line is that the wedding is now off, and the most perfect of all perfect venues is now open for the date of August fourth! Their loss, *your* gain, right?"

"No," I replied quickly, without even thinking. The word just sort of flew out of my mouth. Because truthfully, it was the only word that made sense right now.

There was a stunned pause on the other end, and then she asked, "What do you mean, 'no'?"

"I mean, no, I don't want the venue. Or rather, *we* don't want the venue."

"But I haven't even told you what venue it is!" she exclaimed, the tone in her voice clearly indicating that she thought I was being unreasonable.

But I just wanted to get her off the phone. I didn't want to hear anything else about the most perfect of all perfect venues that was only available because of me. Or rather, because of my agency.

"Well, I don't want it. I think August fourth might be a bit too soon, anyway."

"But—"

"I'm actually really busy right now. Let's talk about this later."

"Okay, but I still haven't gotten your questionnaire yet—"

And then suddenly Willa's bubbly voice was cut off as I ended the call with the touch of a button, silencing her for good. Or at least for now.

I laid my head back against the headrest, trying to digest what had just happened. My wedding planner was trying to pitch me a venue that had just been abandoned by a couple that *my* agency broke up.

Honestly, what were the odds of that even happening?

Maybe it was a sign. Of what, though? That we shouldn't get married on August 4 in whatever perfect location Willa called to tell me about? Or that we shouldn't get married at all? Well, that was just ridiculous. Clearly it was the former.

There was really nothing more to read into it.

I refused to get married in a venue cursed by a failed fidelity in-

spection performed by my very own employee, and that was that.
The whole thing was just twisted and wrong.

Not to mention incredibly bad karma.

Jamie arrived "home" (I still hadn't gotten used to him calling it
that) around eight and brought with him my favorite vegetarian lettuce wraps and hot-and-sour soup from P. F. Chang's and a six-pack
of Tsingtao beer. We spread out our take-out feast across the coffee
table and ate dinner in front of the TV.

It was exactly what I needed.

A reminder of *why* I had given up the tumultuous, drama-laden
life of a fidelity inspector in the first place. For the quiet and comfort
of Chinese take-out with the man I loved.

We ate in silence, watching an episode of *Deal or No Deal* while
we crunched on lettuce wraps and slurped on soup. Then, once we
had finished, we pushed our plates to the end of the coffee table and
leaned back on the couch, covering ourselves with the crocheted
afghan that I keep in a basket under the end table. We tangled up in
each other's arms like interlocking puzzle pieces, fitting together
perfectly, as if his body were specifically made to intertwine with
mine.

It wasn't difficult to picture the rest of my life like this. And I
didn't feel as if I were forfeiting anything if this was what the rest of
my life would look like. I felt safe with Jamie. Protected.

And although he hadn't yet unpacked all the boxes that had accumulated in my hallway over the past five days, I was still happy
that they were there.

Jamie seemed to sense my contentment, because he squeezed his
arms tighter around me as if to say, "Me too." Then he grabbed my
hand and brought it to his lips to kiss. He likes doing that, kissing
my hand. The way they do in period pieces where the women wear
long, flowing gowns and tight tendrils frame their faces and the men
are dressed in tailcoats and sweep into respectful bows whenever
they enter the room. It started out as a joke. Ever since we rented

Pride and Prejudice on DVD, he would say things like "But of course, my lady" in a really pathetic British accent and then bow and kiss my hand. But then it later became more than a joke. It became kind of like our thing.

I suppose the gesture was pretty archaic and probably sexist. Yet somehow when Jamie kissed my hand, it always managed to make me feel beautiful . . . and loved.

Like some kind of unspoken magic between us.

I waited for the familiar touch of his lips on my skin. But a few moments passed and there was nothing. And when I looked up at him, I realized that Jamie was no longer preparing to kiss my hand, he was just kind of holding it awkwardly in front of his face, as if he were checking my skin for suspicious aging spots.

"What's the matter?" I asked, tossing him a strange look while discreetly trying to pull my hand away.

But Jamie maintained his grip and continued to stare questioningly at my fingers. "Where's your engagement ring?" he finally said.

I didn't have to look into a mirror to know that my face had turned a ghostly shade of white. The force I had been using to try to pull my hand away from his tightly clenched fingers was instantly sucked out of me, and my entire arm fell limply against his leg.

My mind started racing back through the steps of my day.

I had taken it off before I pulled up to the valet station at work and placed it in the same inside pocket of my bag. My eyes darted toward the dining room and landed on my Louis Vuitton briefcase, which had been tossed onto one of the chairs during my exhausted return home earlier that evening.

Shit, shit, shit!

That phone call with Willa Cruz on the way home had completely thrown me off. I always put my ring back on after I parked in the garage. But I guess in the distress and horror that followed our conversation about the venue, I had simply forgotten.

"Um," I began shakily, pointing toward the next room. "It's in my briefcase." Then I pulled myself onto my knees and prepared to stand. "I'll get it!"

But Jamie's hand landed firmly on my upper arm, and I got the feeling that I was supposed to stay put. "Why is it in your briefcase and not on your finger?"

I scrambled to find the right way to say what I was about to say. But there really wasn't a right way to say it. "Because I took it off . . . at work."

A hush fell over the room. The only sound was Howie Mandel asking some overweight contestant if he wanted to make a deal or not. But after a round of applause and screaming from the studio audience, Jamie eventually picked up the remote and muted the TV.

Now the room was completely silent. Unnervingly so. And I was pretty sure I preferred Howie.

After a long pause, Jamie asked, "And why did you take it off at work?"

I swallowed hard, feeling my heart start to beat hard and heavy. I knew I had to come clean about the ring. I couldn't lie to him. Not again.

"Well," I began carefully, "I didn't think it would be appropriate to wear at work because of what I do. You know, with the fidelity inspections and everything. So I've been taking the ring off when I get to work and then putting it back on as soon as I get home."

"Obviously not as *soon* as you get home," he added somewhat coldly as he nodded toward my empty left hand.

"Yes," I admitted willingly. "Today I seem to have forgotten, but that's only because I had such a hellish day. I was working really hard to get the charges against Shawna dropped, and then I got this totally unnerving phone call on my way home about—"

"Yeah, Willa Cruz told me that you hung up on her."

What? I could feel the disgust spreading across my face.

Willa Cruz told him that I hung up on her? Did she report back to him at the end of every day or something?

It took me a minute to gather my thoughts before I replied, "First of all, I didn't hang up on her, I just told her I didn't want the venue she had suggested, and then I told her I had to go. And second of all, why is she calling you after she talks to me, like you're my boss or something?"

Jamie shrugged but continued to face forward, his rigid body language clearly affirming his discontent. "She was just confused as to why on earth you would turn down such a *perfect* venue without even hearing what it was first."

There was that word again. *Perfect*. The perfect venue. The perfect wedding. She even had Jamie saying it now. There was *nothing* perfect about a venue that became available because of a fidelity inspection performed by *my* agency. And even though I couldn't very well explain this to Willa, I was just about to enlighten Jamie to the fact when he said, "She also told me you haven't faxed in your wedding questionnaire yet."

"It's ten pages long!" I shot back with frustration. "I have a business to run that's currently minus one full-time employee and another I've been trying to keep out of jail, so I don't exactly have the time to write a ten-page description of my ideal wedding."

"You barely even filled out one question in her office," he pointed out rudely. "I saw your clipboard."

I felt trapped and helpless, and that usually puts me on the defense. Today was apparently going to be no exception. "I'm sorry if I haven't been planning my perfect wedding since I was twelve years old. I'm sorry I don't automatically just *know* without a shadow of a doubt that I want a freaking vegetable garden for my theme! I don't know about these things. I wasn't born *knowing* what kind of cake I want. And I've been trying to find a free minute to sit down and give it some honest thought, but I've been totally swamped this week!"

"This week or every week?"

I turned and looked at him. "What do you mean by *that*?"

Jamie shrugged again. But this one was jam-packed with passive-aggressiveness. "I just mean that I'm not sure you want to plan a wedding . . . at all."

His comment stung—and not to mention rendered me speechless. I didn't know how to respond to that. Or even if I was supposed to dignify it with a response. "That . . . what . . . you're . . . that's crazy!" I finally spat out. "I don't fill out a questionnaire for *one* week and suddenly I don't want to get married?"

Jamie sighed audibly and finally turned to face me. But his eyes didn't reveal the same compassionate, understanding patience they usually did. Right now they just looked tired and frustrated. "It's not just the questionnaire, Jen."

"Then what else is it?" I asked, unable to imagine what on earth could have prompted this line of attack.

He shook his head slowly. "It's everything. It's the wedding planner. It's the ring . . ." He nodded toward my empty left hand, and I quickly tried to hide my bare finger between my legs. "And more importantly," he continued gravely, "it's . . . *you*."

"Me?" I shot back. "What about me?"

Jamie looked at me as if I were crazy. As if he couldn't believe I didn't know exactly what he was referring to. "Your little . . . meltdown the other night when we were about to have sex."

I lowered my head. "Oh, that."

"Yes, that," he replied indignantly. "Something changed in you when you went to Vegas. I don't know what it is. But you've been different since the day you got back."

I closed my eyes. Who was I to think I could fool him? Who was I to think I could pull this off? Hide the truth from the only man I've ever loved. That's crazy. And absolutely ridiculous.

But as much as I ached to tell him what really happened that night in Vegas, my mouth remained clamped shut.

So Jamie kept talking. But this time, his voice was significantly softer and gentler. "Look, my Realtor told me that an offer on my loft came through today. But before I accept it and go into escrow, I need to make sure that this is what you really want. And honestly, I'm a little worried. I think you may have some commitment issues."

And now my once clamped mouth was hanging wide open. "What?" I finally gasped, feeling this intolerable desire to defend myself. "I do *not* have commitment issues! Trust me, I *had* commitment issues. I know what it feels like. If I still had commitment issues, believe me, you wouldn't even be here."

And suddenly, Jamie's gentle demeanor was back. The patience on his face seemed to indicate that he actually felt sorry for me right now. He reached and took both of my hands in his. "It's okay, Jen," he said gently. "You've been through a lot. I don't expect you to be perfect. With your parents and your father and—"

"Why are you bringing up my father?" I snapped. "How did he suddenly find his way into this conversation?"

But Jamie just tilted his head and studied my face, clearly not believing me for a second. "So then, you've called him and told him about the engagement? And you've asked for the two of us to meet him and his new wife like we talked about?"

And just like that, he had trapped me. Like a small, helpless, ensnared rabbit, I was stuck.

But fortunately, I knew exactly what it was going to take to get out of it. Because his words were more than just a form of entrapment; they were an irrefutable challenge. He was daring me to pick up the phone and prove him wrong. And if that was what it was going to take to make Jamie believe me, then I was willing to accept that challenge.

"Is that what this is about?" I asked, scrambling to my feet. "Calling my dad? Fine, I'll call him right now. I'll invite him and his *third* wife to dinner. The four of us will go. It'll be a double date."

I stomped my way into the kitchen and grabbed the cordless phone from its charger. Then I marched back into the living room and stood before Jamie, phone in hand, my eyes glaring at him as if we were about to participate in some kind of telephonic face-off.

Jamie hoisted himself over the arm of the couch and looked up at me but said nothing. He simply continued to study me with curiosity. The way a scientist might study a bubbling beaker, trying to determine whether or not the liquid inside would eventually explode.

"Right," I said, clearing my throat. "So here I go." I pressed the "Talk" button and checked for a dial tone, half hoping that maybe the phone line would be dead. Because I forgot to pay the latest bill or because there was a sudden outage in the area.

"There's a dial tone," I announced to Jamie, as if I were required to give him step-by-step directions of how to use a phone. He continued to watch me, but I couldn't tell if his expression was one of disbelief or just plain old-fashioned concern. The kind of look you offer a recovering alcoholic who just walked into a cocktail party to discover they've run out of soda water.

I started punching in the numbers. I was aware that I was moving at a snail's pace, but I played it off, pretending to rack my brain for the right digits.

With my finger positioned on the final key, I looked down at Jamie again. His eyes bored into me, and I could feel my fingertips get sweaty. *Just press the freaking number,* I instructed myself. *Just press it!*

I flashed Jamie a weak smile. "I think it's 2127. But it *could* be 2128. For some reason my mind is blanking."

I'm not sure why I said that. I knew the last number was a 7. After all, I had gone through a similar difficulty-of-dialing routine just last week when I tried to call my dad the first time. But I guess I kind of hoped that during my prolonged hesitation, Jamie would suddenly shrug and say, "No biggie, you can just call him tomorrow," and then unmute the TV and go on with our night as though nothing had happened.

But he didn't. He just kept staring at me.

"Definitely a seven," I said with a nervous giggle as I pressed the key and listened to the corresponding tone that went with it.

I slowly brought the phone to my ear and waited. "It's ringing," I announced after a few moments.

Then I heard my dad's voice on the line. "Hello?"

"Hi, Dad," I said brightly. "It's Jen."

"Jenny! How are you?"

I glanced over at Jamie. "I'm fine. Just fine. Everything's good. I was just calling to see if you and . . . and . . ."

Oh God. Suddenly I was completely blanking on the *third* wife's name. It was something with an *S*. Suzanne? Susan? Summer? It wasn't as though I used the name on a regular basis. I generally tried to avoid her name altogether, substituting the generic title of "the new wife."

"Simone?" my dad offered.

Simone! Yes! At least I was right about the *S* part. That had to have awarded me some points on whatever rating system was used to judge this kind of thing. "Yes, Simone," I repeated indignantly, as if I really didn't need to be reminded of her name and was actually offended that my dad would just *assume* I had forgotten it. "I was thinking that maybe you, me, Jamie, and *Simone* could all go out for dinner sometime soon. You know, whenever you're free, no hurry or anything. Next month would probably work for . . ."

I looked down to see Jamie's face start to break into a frown. "I mean, next *week*," I clarified quickly. "Can you two have dinner next week?"

"Really?" my dad asked with genuine surprise. "You want the *four* of us to have dinner?"

"Yes!" I replied with forced enthusiasm. "Of course! I mean, I've never met her and you've never met Jamie. So I think it's about time the four of us all got together. Don't you?"

"Yes, I know, but . . ." my dad started to say. But whatever protest he was about to make was decidedly dropped, and he finished quickly with, "No, you're right. We *should* get together. Let me just ask her. She's the keeper of the schedule." He threw in a laugh for good measure, and I tried to reciprocate, but it came out sounding completely fake and remarkably like a dying chicken.

There was silence on the phone, and I translated the latest to Jamie. "He's asking the new wife . . . I mean, Simone."

Jamie simply nodded in response.

My dad got back on the phone. "She says Tuesday night would work."

"Great!" I exclaimed. "Tuesday it is, then."

My mind was already calculating how many days of agonizing I would have to endure before then. Four, if you didn't count today. But who was I kidding? It's not like I would be able to hang up and not think about this until tomorrow.

I didn't bother checking with Jamie about the date. I just wanted to get off the phone. If he was going to be so insistent that we all get together, he would have to rearrange his schedule accordingly.

As soon as I hung up, I felt a huge knot already starting to form in my stomach. *What on earth did I just agree to?* Was I crazy? Had I lost my mind? My dad and my fiancé in the same room, for the first time ever. And if that wasn't terrifying enough, he was bringing his new wife! I couldn't even bear to hear my dad *talk* about her over a plate of fried calamari, what made me think I could actually meet her in person?

"There you go," I said triumphantly as I plopped back down on the couch next to Jamie and placed the phone on the coffee table. "Who's got issues now?"

But Jamie didn't really respond to that. He just sort of laughed weakly, shook his head, and unmuted the TV.

As the voice of Howie Mandel flooded back into the living room, filling the awkward silence between us, Jamie reached down and grabbed my left hand again and brought it to his lips.

This time he did kiss it. But the magic was gone.

16

brand-new body style

I've often heard that women tend to be attracted to men who remind them of their fathers. It's inherent in our biological makeup or something. Sigmund Freud even went so far as to give it a complex. The female gender equivalent of an Oedipus complex, or as Carl Jung later termed it, an "Electra complex," after the Greek myth of Electra, who killed her mother to avenge the death of her father. That all seems really messed up and complicated to me, but one thing I do know is that Freud wouldn't find one ounce of Electra in any bone of my body. I'm definitely one of the few women who can say with certainty that when I meet a man who reminds me of my father, I run the other way.

Actually, that's not entirely true. Most of the men I've met who have reminded me of my father were ones I encountered on one of my fidelity inspections. So I had to stay put because I was being paid to.

But I think it's safe to say that what I fell in love with about Jamie was the fact that he was *nothing* like my father.

My relationship with my dad is a complicated one. He cheated on my mother for as long as I can remember, and I'd only just made amends with it and learned to forgive him about a year ago. That's not to say that we're now magically superclose and share our innermost thoughts and feelings. We don't. We don't really share much of anything. We have dinner, make polite conversation, hug, and say good-bye. And that's it. But that's more than we did two years ago. It's a relationship in progress, to say the least.

But now that my father was about to meet Jamie for the first time, and I was about to meet my new stepmother for the first time *and* break the news that I was getting married, it was confirmed: This "relationship in progress" was about to be put on permanent fast-forward.

The restaurant where we had arranged to meet was called Wilshire, after the street on which it was located. I found the title incredibly unoriginal, but I hardly had any energy left to dwell on it because I was too busy dwelling on the forthcoming dinner that I had so foolishly agreed to participate in.

I arrived at the restaurant ten minutes early. The entire drive there, I had been listening to a meditation CD I had bought at one of those overpriced bohemian-chic stores on Montana Avenue earlier that afternoon, hoping that the soft, soothing sounds of reeds and ocean waves would rub off on me and help me get through this night in one piece. I usually prefer not to leave restaurants in a stretcher.

"Hunter, party of four?" the hostess confirmed after I gave her my name.

I nodded politely, even though my mind was still trying to digest the implication of her statement. Party of *four*. Not two . . . but *four*. Tonight it would not be just me and my father. Tonight there would be four of us. Because Jamie was coming and she was coming. The *third* wife. The one who had replaced my mother three and a half years after their divorce. Although I'd be willing to bet money that given my father's established reputation with respect to relationships, this woman had replaced my mother a long time before that.

The hostess showed me to our table, and I ordered a glass of Chardonnay and attempted to browse the menu. Although I was far too nervous to absorb any of the entrées I was reading about.

My mother had been my dad's second wife. And he had cheated on the one before her, too. Apparently, my father had a hard time with commitment. No, actually, that's not true. He committed just fine.

After all, he'd managed to walk down the aisle *three* different times. It's honoring that commitment that seemed to be the problem.

What I couldn't understand, though, is why any woman would *want* to marry someone like that. She has to know. How could she not know? Jane Seymour, the third wife of Henry VIII, knew *exactly* what had happened to the two before that. The first one was divorced and left to rot in solitude until she died, and the other was beheaded. Yet she was still more than happy to become the next Mrs. Henry VIII. And look what happened to her. She died of something called puerperal fever a year later. Clearly, she was cursed to begin with.

So I wasn't sure what this woman could have been thinking. Did she honestly believe she was different? Special? That she possessed some kind of bewitching power that would keep my dad's attention for longer than a few minutes? I love my dad. I really do. It's taken me a long time to be able to say that, but it's true. However, that doesn't change the fact that my dad is who he is. I've learned to accept him despite his apparent flaws. I just wasn't sure I was ready to accept his new wife despite hers.

Jamie called to tell me he was running about fifteen minutes late, and I was somewhat relieved. The thought of meeting this woman under the watchful, analyzing eye of my fiancé/shrink made me even more nervous. Especially after everything that had been going on between us. All I needed was for Jamie to find another reason to question my ability to commit to him.

Neither of us had actually mentioned the argument we'd had on Friday night, but we did both agree that we should postpone our next appointment with Willa Cruz until I had a chance at least to complete the wedding questionnaire.

There was a large part of me that didn't want to deal directly with whatever was going on between us. Eventually, I knew it would all work itself out. I just needed enough time to prove to Jamie that I was completely devoted to him, that I *didn't*, as he so wrongfully speculated, have commitment issues, and that I *did* want to marry him.

I was hoping that if I could just get through tonight's dinner without suffering some type of mental breakdown (at least not an outward one), I might be one tiny step closer to proving my case to Jamie.

But the longer I sat waiting for my dad and *third* wife to appear, the more unrealistic that goal seemed to be.

Then at five minutes past seven, after I had thoroughly *not* read the entire menu at least four times, I saw them.

My dad was following the hostess through the restaurant, and I could just make out brief flashes of black fabric behind him.

When he reached the table, a woman in a tight-fitting dress stepped into view, and I laid eyes on my new stepmother for the first time.

The first thing that popped into my mind was *blond*. The second thing that popped into my mind was *young*. Two things that my mother was not. Blond and young. The only thing she was missing to make the cliché complete was a set of $10,000 double-D's. I never thought I'd be so happy to see a woman's modest B-cup-size chest in all of my life.

"Hi, Jenny," my dad said, leaning down and kissing me on the cheek. "This is Simone."

I struggled to make eye contact as I stood up and politely extended my hand, but apparently, she wasn't having any of the polite pleasantries. Instead, she pulled me into a tight and slightly awkward embrace. Although I must admit, it was only awkward because I couldn't find it in myself to return the gesture. So instead my arms hung stunned and lifeless at my sides while her tiny, Pilates-enhanced limbs wrapped tightly around my body.

"It's just so nice to finally meet you," she cooed earnestly into my ear. Her voice was soft and breathy. Not *exactly* like a phone sex operator, but not exactly like a non–phone sex operator, either.

When she finally pulled away, I was able to speak. "Lovely to meet you, too," I offered with an attempt at sincerity. "My dad has told me so much about you."

A complete and utter lie. But she didn't have to know that.

I sat back down in my seat and watched her float gracefully into hers. As I did so, I tried desperately to discern her age. I searched for a wrinkle, a crow's-foot, anything that would put her in at least the

35–44 age box, but there was absolutely no evidence of that. She was clearly a proud member of my 25–34 box.

"Well," she began breathlessly, as if this whole meeting exchange were the equivalent of running a 10K marathon, "your dad just can't stop talking about you, either. He's extremely proud." She reached out and rested her hand on my father's leg. Not in the safe, appropriate, knee portion of his leg. That I could have handled. I'm talking mere inches from his crotch.

Why couldn't she have started with an arm or a shoulder? Something PG to ease me into the evening? Did she have to go straight for the groin? Actually, I was surprised she didn't just bypass her own chair altogether and climb onto his lap.

Calming sounds. Ocean waves crashing. The music of Mother Nature.

I took a deep breath and forced out a grin. "That's sweet."

"So where's this studly boyfriend of yours?" she asked, glancing eagerly around the restaurant.

I fought a cringe. "Oh, he's just running a little late. He'll be here any minute."

My engagement ring was still stuffed in the inside pocket of my purse from when I'd come into the office that morning. I had planned to wait until Jamie arrived so that we could announce the news together, and then I would put on the ring and let Si-*moan* fawn over it for an hour.

"So your dad tells me you run an agency that finds nannies?" Simone said, resting her elbow on the table and her chin in her palm.

I nodded, glancing past her toward the front door. "Yes. That's right. And housekeepers and tutors, too."

"That sounds fascinating," she replied, her eyes wide. For a minute, I thought they might pop out of her head, so I was careful to make good eye contact. I really didn't want to miss that.

"Tell me more about that."

I pulled a piece of bread from the basket and began smearing butter on it. I thought about Katie at the Stanton residence with those obnoxious twin boys, just biding her time until Mr. Stanton officially made a move on her.

"Nothing to tell, really," I said with a modest shrug. "I interview the families and try to match them with the right nannies." And then for an extra ounce of credibility, I threw in, "I just placed one of my girls with a very nice family in Beverly Hills that has nine-year-old twin boys. It's a fun age."

"I had a nanny once," she replied, looking dazedly off to the side. "She was really nice. I think she was from Sweden. Or maybe it was Norway. You know, one of those countries. She was always dating like seven different guys at once. One of *those* types, you know?"

"Mm-hmm," I replied, taking an oversize bite of bread.

Definitely not a day older than thirty-two.

"So, how did you go from investment banking to finding nannies? That seems like a pretty big change."

I immediately launched into the spiel I had created specifically for my parents when I decided to form the Hawthorne Agency. Investment banking was getting to be too stressful, this job allows me to keep more regular hours, I feel like I'm helping people, blah, blah, blah.

She nodded understandingly. "Definitely. I mean, everyone needs to find good help, right?"

My dad smiled lovingly at her and leaned over to kiss her bare shoulder. "That's right, baby."

I felt nausea creep up in my stomach, and I forced it down with another bite of bread, despite the fact that I hadn't yet completely chewed and swallowed my previous bite.

Who was this woman? Where on earth did my dad find her? He was fifty-nine. And she was barely in her thirties. Did it not bother him that she was practically my age? And did it not bother *her* that when she's forty-five, he'll be collecting Social Security?

The only logical explanation was money. And my dad did have plenty of it. He may not have been Donald Trump, but he could certainly afford to buy her plenty of Botox. But I just couldn't understand how my dad was capable of marrying such a cliché. A blond, thirty-something named Simone with a 900-number voice? Did he not realize how ridiculous he looked flaunting her all over town?

Although I had to admit: To other fifty-something men out there, he probably looked like fucking James Bond.

"So how is everything?" my dad asked, reaching out and gently tapping the table in front of me. Clearly he could tell that my attention was elsewhere.

"Oh," I said, refocusing. "Fine. Just fine. You know, same old, same old." I thought about the ring hiding in my purse. The quicker I got it out, slipped it on my finger, and let everyone gush about it, the quicker I could get out of here. But I knew I couldn't tell them until Jamie was here.

"Work is good?" my dad prompted.

I smiled sweetly. "Oh, it's great. Never been better." I took a long swig of wine. "And how about you . . . um . . . *two*? How is everything going?"

My dad shrugged and started to reply, "Oh, just—"

But he was quickly interrupted with another of Simone's verbal orgasms. "Oh," she gasped, "absolutely amazing. Things have been great. Jack just took me on this gorgeous Alaskan cruise, and of course, I thought, you know *cruise*, time to show off my new favorite bikini! So there I was in like *Nova Scotia*, with a suitcase full of nothing but sarongs and minishorts, and oh my God, was I freezing! But thankfully we had time to do some shopping in Vancouver, and I bought some really nice sweaters. But the glaciers up there? Oh my God . . ."

I was trying really hard to be objective about this whole thing. So what if the girl didn't know that Nova Scotia wasn't anywhere near Alaska? Maybe she was just nervous. As I listened to her rattle on, I tried to put myself in her shoes. She was meeting *me* for the first time, too, and she probably felt a lot more pressure to impress me than I felt to impress her. Maybe she wasn't really like this. Maybe once you got to know her, she was actually very likable and calm. Some people, like me, get quiet and reserved when they're nervous. Maybe she just gets really . . . annoying.

I braved another glance at her hand in my dad's lap. It was actually moving farther *up* his leg. I didn't think that was possible. And with every sentence she spoke, she somehow felt the need to accentuate them with a squeeze of his upper thigh.

Let's face it, I was sitting across from every twenty-nine-year-old girl's worst nightmare. A new stepmom I could handle, but this was too much. I saw enough of it at work. I didn't need it at my so-called family dinners as well.

It's unbelievable. The older a man gets, the younger the woman he needs to make himself feel validated. Just look at Todd Langley. In his late forties and just couldn't wait to get twenty-five-year-old Keira Summers into his hotel room.

And then, as I half listened to Simone jabber on about the glaciers in Alaska and how global warming really is such a pity, a disturbing thought struck me. Jamie was eight years older than me. And he had been married once before . . . to someone his own age. And when he met me, he was technically still married.

Suddenly the room got very cold. I pulled my cardigan sweater tighter around my body.

My thoughts were stabbing at my brain like tiny icicles floating around in my head. Was it possible that Jamie had fallen for me for the same reason that my father had fallen for Simone?

For the past year, I had been so convinced that Jamie was nothing like my father. But what if the exact opposite was true? What if Jamie was actually *just* like my father? *And* even Todd Langley, for that matter?

Then what did that make me? His *Simone*?

I barely had time to entertain the disturbing notion when I saw Jamie hurrying across the restaurant toward our table. "Hey! I'm so sorry I'm late! Traffic from Century City was brutal. They closed two lanes on Santa Monica."

Jamie gave me a quick kiss on the cheek, and I introduced him to my dad's cliché. (Although I was careful to use her real name.)

As I watched him, too, get mauled into one of her apparently trademarked bear hugs, I studied his face for any sign of surprise or disapproval. Surely this situation had to bother him. *Surely* he could spot the colossal age gap between the two of them, and something to that effect would register on his face.

But I saw nothing. His smile was as genuine as I'd ever seen it. And his handshake as he met my father was as respectful as if he had been greeting a foreign ambassador.

Simone and everything she represented did not appear to concern Jamie in the slightest.

"So did you tell them?" he said, taking his seat and looking excitedly from me to my dad.

I smiled back and shook my head. "Not yet."

Simone gasped dramatically. "What? Tell us what?"

Jamie's grin beamed off his face as he grabbed my hand and squeezed it. "I think you should do the honors, Jen."

I could feel the words in my mouth, but I just couldn't force them out. What if Jamie *was* like my father? What if I was just the younger, newer, hotter model that replaced his ex-wife? Just as Simone had been the new model that replaced my mom. And if that was the case, how long would *I* get to park in the garage before he traded me in as well?

Jamie laughed at my silence and patted my hand. "Jen's still a bit overwhelmed by it all."

I looked into the anxiously awaiting eyes of my dad and his *third* wife, and I dug deep down inside of me and finally found the strength to say, "We're engaged."

In my mind, the sentence had ended with an exclamation point. But when I heard myself speak it aloud, somehow a simple period found its way to the end instead. At a moment like this, I wanted so desperately to be one of those exclamation-point girls. You know, the ones who throw them into practically every sentence because everything in life is just that exciting. "Here's that file you asked for!" or "Maybe we can carpool!" and, of course, "We're engaged!!!!"

But apparently, right now, just getting the words out was difficult enough. Conjuring up exclamatory punctuation was a near impossible task.

The screams came. Well, really it was just one. And it was coming from the brand-new BMW 7 Series sitting across from me.

My dad's reaction was a little more subdued. Still, I had never seen him look happier. He stood up and came around to my side of the table and kissed me on the top of the head. "Oh, Jenny. I am so happy for you."

"Where's the ring? Where's the ring?" Simone chorused.

"Oh, right," I said, still somewhat dazed as I reached into my bag and pulled out the diamond.

Simone frowned. "Why was it in your purse?"

And as I snuck a sideways glance at Jamie, I couldn't help but notice the dissatisfaction on his face as well. I opened my mouth to plead my case, but my dad beat me to the punch. "Because she wanted to surprise us," he explained.

"Exactly," I confirmed, stealing another glance in Jamie's direction to see if that heartbreakingly judgmental look had vanished from his face. But as far as I could tell, it was still there. Maybe it was just me. I had seemed to be viewing the world through judgment-colored glasses recently.

"If I showed up at the table wearing it, you would notice it right away." I was looking at Simone when I said it, but the statement was directed entirely at Jamie.

I slid the ring onto my finger and held out my hand for my dad and Simone to see. She grasped it and practically pulled me across the table in an effort to get a better look.

My dad then stepped over to Jamie and opened his arms to him. "Welcome to the family," he said in a deep, mobster voice.

Jamie laughed and stood up to hug him. "Thanks, Jack."

My dad patted him firmly on the back in that classic "man hug." "I guess you're one of us now."

I laughed politely along with everyone else at the table and then drew in a long, deep gulp of my wine, praying that my dad was anything but right.

After dinner I drove home in a haze.

I didn't know if I was being paranoid or incredibly perceptive. My dad was clearly stuck in some kind of pattern. He married his first wife when he was only twenty, then left her at age thirty to marry my mother, who was only twenty-one. And the moment she, too, began to feel less than novel, he started cheating on her with my twenty-year-old babysitter. And now, at age fifty-nine, three and a half years after my mom finally divorced him, he was married to a woman who could easily have been one of my classmates.

It was as if my dad suffered from some kind of relationship ADD. Never being able to stay satisfied with one woman for more than a few years.

I thought back to pictures I'd seen of my mother when she and my dad first got married. She was so beautiful and radiant and . . . young. I guess my mom might now be a used 1978 Toyota Corolla, but at one point, *she* was the shiny new model.

She was the cliché.

So what did that make me?

I turned up the volume on my meditation CD and tried to calm myself with the enchanting melody. But for some reason, now it was feeling more haunting than anything else.

I couldn't help but think that maybe the Electra complex was inevitable. That we really had no control over who we fell in love with. And that somehow, despite my years of bitterness and resentment toward my father, I had still managed to fall in love with a carbon copy of him. Without even realizing that I was doing it.

I was planning to broach the subject with Jamie when I got home, but the minute I walked in the door and saw him sitting on the couch in his Adidas track pants and white undershirt, I was struck with an overwhelming sense of foolishness. Clearly I was just being paranoid. This was *Jamie,* for God's sake. Not some random guy I had just met in a bar. He was the sweetest, kindest, most genuine man I had ever known. He didn't suffer from relationship ADD. And I felt stupid for allowing my unfounded anxieties to convince me otherwise. Especially when he hadn't done anything to give me reason to doubt him. And weren't actions supposed to speak louder than paranoid thoughts?

All of this *third* wife stuff had taken my mind for a delusional joyride. It had awoken suspicions inside of me that I never knew existed.

So what if Simone was a brand-new BMW 7 Series that my father would probably trade in for a newer model in a few years? In Jamie's eyes, I was a classic. One of those 1955 Chevys you see at old car conventions that everyone stands around and gawks at, praising the owner for keeping it up so well. Those cars never get traded in for newer models because they just keep getting more valuable with time.

Yes, that would be me. No matter how old I got, Jamie would never dare get rid of me.

By the time we got into bed that night, I had convinced myself that all I really needed was a good night's sleep to clear my head. Things always looked different in the morning. New, more grounded perspectives always seemed to magically materialize somewhere in the middle of the REM cycle.

And I was confident that when I woke up the next day, all of my senseless fears would be gone. And Jamie would go back to being the man I had agreed to marry. Someone who was *nothing* like my father.

17

maid of questionable honor

But it didn't exactly happen that way.

I woke up in the middle of the night in a full-on panic attack. My chest and the back of my neck were damp with sweat. My lungs felt as if they were banging violently against my ribs with each breath, fighting to break free from the cell that had kept them prisoner since birth.

I looked over at Jamie. He was sleeping soundly, his own torso rising and falling in smooth, even pulsations. Almost as if they were mocking me.

I winced against the pain and brought my hand to my chest. Jamie stirred next to me, and I quickly decided to move into the living room. The last thing I wanted to do was wake him up and explain why I felt as if my lungs were trying to escape from my body. Especially when I couldn't explain it to myself.

I gently pushed the covers off me and stood up. The bamboo-wood floors creaked under my feet, and I cursed the day I'd decided that wooden floors were more elegant and sophisticated than carpet. Elegant, maybe. Functional when trying to sneak out of a room without waking a sleeping fiancé? Not so much.

Jamie stirred again, and I decided to make a run for it.

I dashed out of the bedroom, closing the door softly behind me, and then scampered down the hallway—weaving my way in and out of the growing pile of boxes of Jamie's stuff—until I was in the safe confines of my kitchen. I dumped some tap water into a mug and popped it in the microwave.

I tossed a chamomile teabag into the mug, walked into the living room, and collapsed onto the couch. As I held the hot tea close to me and felt the steam rise up and warm my face, I prayed that the heat and condensation would seep into my skin and calm my pounding heart.

But it didn't seem to be working. My breathing was still shallow and quick, and my neck still felt clammy with cold sweat.

What the hell is the matter with me?

But I couldn't answer that question. Or maybe I just didn't want to answer it. Life was so much easier when you didn't answer questions like that. When you just ignored them and pretended they didn't even exist—phantom words swirling around in your head that just *happened* to come together to form a complete sentence.

I sipped my tea and closed my eyes, trying to take deep breaths.

Eventually, I turned on the TV. Some unfamiliar TV movie was playing, and I muted the volume.

As I continued to stare at the silent images dancing around my screen, my breathing slowly began to steady itself. I set my mug on the coffee table and closed my eyes. Feeling the stability of my breath finally start to overcome me.

The next thing I knew, Jamie was shaking me awake.

I opened my eyes to a bright, sun-filled living room. "What time is it?" I asked, blinking against the light coming in from the windows.

"Quarter after eight."

I pushed myself up and heard my neck crack. "Oh."

Jamie eyed the horizontal body–shaped indent on the couch. "What happened?"

I yawned and stretched my arms. "I couldn't sleep, so I made myself some tea and decided to watch TV. I guess I fell asleep."

He nodded, appearing to believe that was the whole story. I really didn't see any point in telling him about the whole exploding chest sensation. I was just grateful that at least now my lungs seemed to be perfectly content with staying inside my chest.

"Is everything okay?" Jamie asked.

I pulled myself off the couch and headed down the hallway to the bedroom. "Oh, yeah," I said, hoping it sounded convincing. "I think I just need to take a long, hot shower."

"Well, then I should probably say good-bye now. I might not be here when you get out. I have an early client meeting."

I spun on the balls of my feet and returned to the living room. "Okay, then," I said, kissing Jamie on the lips. "Bye."

We didn't see each other much for the next few days. Being at Sophie's beck and call kept me out of the house for most of the week. And I never thought I'd be so grateful to be Sophie's maid-of-honor gofer. Because honestly, I needed some time away from Jamie and that whole mess I had created to clear my head and try to think rationally. Things had been weird between us, to say the least, and my mind had become such a kaleidoscope of perspectives lately, I didn't know which one to focus on.

But Sophie's last-minute wedding details kept my thoughts otherwise occupied.

Thankfully, the groom's sister had come to her senses and dyed her hair back to its original mousy brown color (or a shade Sophie deemed to be "close enough"), and the caterer, despite his persistent threats, was still on the job, but Sophie had managed to come up with a whole bunch of new pressing issues for us to deal with during those last few days leading up to Saturday.

But by the time Friday night arrived and the rehearsal dinner had come to a close, everything seemed to slow down, and for the first time in my life, I saw Sophie relax. Zoë, John, and I were all bunked up in her bridal suite for a little slumber party to celebrate her last night of singlehood.

"She looks calm," I remarked about my friend as if she weren't sitting right next to me on the king-size bed. Her back was leaned up against the headboard, her knees tucked up under her chin. "Too calm."

John nodded from a nearby armchair. "Yeah, what did you slip her? Valium? Zoloft? Got any more?"

Sophie rolled her eyes and laughed at us. "No one slipped me anything. I just feel calm." She shrugged and hugged her knees tighter to her chest. "I am capable of being calm, you know?"

"Since when?" John mocked.

Sophie pulled a spare pillow off the bed and smacked him with it.

Zoë let out a strange gurgling sound just then, and I turned toward the couch she was sitting on and noticed a cell phone tucked between her hands. She was staring at the screen with a smitten look on her face.

"Zoë?" I said accusingly. "What are you doing?"

Her head popped up, and she looked at the three of us with a guilty expression. "Nothing," she said, trying discreetly to slide the phone to the side and push it between the couch cushions.

But I wasn't fooled. I recognized the symptoms right away. "Are you flirt-texting someone?" I asked playfully.

Zoë glared at me with irritation. "No," she growled. "I was just checking an e-mail. From work."

"You were not!" Sophie screeched, joining the game. "You're so right, Jen. Look at her face. She was totally flirt-texting."

"I don't even know what that is."

Sophie and I exchanged a look of mutual skepticism, and after a subtle, knowing nod, we sprang into action. Sophie leaped toward the couch and landed directly on Zoë's lap, her body sprawled out horizontally across the couch to hold Zoë's arms down while I went for the phone buried between the couch cushions. Zoë fought against Sophie's stronghold, and John quickly joined forces to keep our prisoner contained. She struggled fruitlessly against both of them. "Stop! What the fuck are you doing?" Then she saw me with the phone. "Jen! Don't. Please. Give it back."

Maybe it was the three bottles of champagne we drank, or maybe it was my unyielding desire to be a part of someone else's drama for a change, but I was a girl on a mission. And I was deaf to Zoë's protests as I scrolled through her list of recent text messages. Fifteen in total in the last hour. All from the same number.

"Ooh," I said dramatically. "Someone has been busy." I opened up a random text in the middle of the list and read it aloud to the group. "Can't wait to slip you out of that pouffy pink bridesmaid's dress."

John and I simultaneously let out a whooping sound while Sophie expressed her offense. "My dresses are *not* pink! And they're not pouffy! I made a specific effort to pick out *non*pouffy dresses."

Zoë finally broke free and snatched the phone away from me. "Give that to me!"

"Who was that from?" John demanded.

She tried to play the whole thing off with one of her aggravated eye rolls. "No one."

"Is this the same no one who was too good to come to my wedding?" Sophie asked.

"He couldn't come. He had a business trip."

"Yeah, right," she argued, clearly still upset about the dress comment. "That is such a lie. You never even asked him."

I plopped down on the bed and propped myself up on my elbows. "What's the big deal, anyway, Zo? Why won't you at least talk about him?"

Zoë let her long blond hair down from its claw clip and shook out the kinks. "I'm just not ready to talk about him yet," she replied matter-of-factly.

Sophie pulled her legs up onto the sofa and curled up next to John. "At least tell us his name."

But Zoë shook her head adamantly. "Not a chance."

Sophie turned to me. "What was the name on the text message?"

I stifled a laugh as I looked over at Zoë, who shot me the most menacing "Don't you dare" look I've ever seen. I promptly ignored it. "It didn't have a name. It just said 'Footlong.'"

John and Sophie both burst into laughter. *"What?"* John screeched. "Are you joking?"

I shook my head. "Nope. That's what it said."

"I can't believe you, Jen!" Zoë cried scornfully. "Is nothing sacred to you?"

I couldn't help but laugh. "No, Zoë, I'm sorry, I don't find the sacredness in 'Footlong.'"

"Now, is that nickname in reference to the kind of sandwiches he orders at Subway," John asked, feigning innocence, "or the size of his . . . package?"

"Maybe he's just a big fan of fruit by the foot," I suggested helpfully.

John nodded, humoring me. "Yes, Jen. I think you're right. Although if that is the case, then I believe the more appropriate nickname for him would be Dick by the Foot."

And we all broke out into another fit of giggles. Well, all of us except Zoë, who had fallen onto her back and pulled the pillow over her head. "There!" came her muffled voice. "You have your stupid details. His penis is really huge." She pulled the pillow off her face and glared at me. "Now drop it."

And we did . . . after another two hours of footlong jokes, of course.

The ceremony was to be held in an old Catholic church in Redondo Beach. Neither Eric nor Sophie was particularly religious, but according to Eric's devout Catholic mother, getting married in a church, by a priest, was the only thing that was nonnegotiable.

Zoë and John left early for the ceremony so that they could stop at a drugstore and pick up some emergency hairspray to keep on hand for the reception. So it was just Sophie and me in the limousine during the quick ten-minute drive to the church. Her unusual calmness from the night before seemed to have vanished sometime in the middle of the night, because now she was having a hard time sitting still, despite the comfortable, plush leather seats in the back of the stretch Lincoln.

"Relax," I told her patiently as I rested my hand on her knee. "Everything's going to be perfect."

She struggled to take a deep breath and stared out the window as we drove. It was at that moment that I first really noticed her. I mean, yes, I saw her in the hotel room when she was getting her hair and makeup done and when she slipped into her dress and I buttoned it up for her and as we were walking through the hotel lobby and everyone stared. But I don't think I really *saw* her until now.

Her brown hair was swept back dramatically into a complicated twist that was fastened with a diamond-studded clip at the top. Her makeup was subtle yet feminine, with pale pink eye shadows that brightened her eyes and matching pink lip gloss. Her strapless corset-style dress fell in layers around her small frame and flowed luxuriously along the floor of the limo like a foaming sea of white, flooding the inside of the car.

She looked more beautiful than I had ever seen her.

Yet while I was looking at her, there was a sudden pang inside my chest. Something was wrong. Really wrong. I mentally scrolled through my maid of honor checklist and was successfully able to tick off every item.

So what was it, then? Why was my heart beating so fast? And why could I not escape this sense of utter dread that was pulsing through my veins?

"What's wrong?" Sophie asked, noticing the uneasy expression on my face.

I shook myself from my trance and forced a smile. "Nothing! Nothing at all. I just can't believe you're actually getting married!"

She smiled and exhaled dramatically, placing her hand on her stomach, which I'm sure was doing multiple flips. "I know. It's crazy. But you know what's even crazier?"

I smiled back at her endearingly. "That you didn't give yourself a stroke?"

She nodded and let out a small laugh. "Well, that, too. But even more so . . ." She paused and looked me up and down, almost as if she were seeing me for the first time, too. "You're next."

The old stone church was beautifully decorated with lilacs and calla lilies, tied up in long white satin sashes. As I made my way down the aisle, I noticed Jamie right away. He was beaming from the aisle of the third row, snapping pictures of me like a crazed member of the paparazzi. I flashed him a hasty smile and then turned my head toward the front of the church and clung tight to the elbow of Eric's younger brother. I tried to focus all my attention on walking straight and not tripping on my gown. The last thing I needed right now was to end up on YouTube under the title "Bridesmaid Disaster." Sophie would never forgive me if I face planted in the middle of the aisle.

Eric's brother escorted me to the right of the altar and then took his place on the left. The organ began playing the "Wedding March," and everyone rose. I watched as Sophie made her way toward me, looking radiant and glowing. I had honestly never seen her look happier. And that was exactly how it should be. Your wedding day *should* be the happiest day of your life.

I suppose all that stress of finding the right location, selecting the right linens, choosing the right wedding dress, and picking out the right theme is eventually worth it. So maybe I needed to stop putting it off and just do it. Just call Willa Cruz and set a date. Pick up a pen and fill out that damn questionnaire. What the hell was I waiting for?

The priest breezed through the introduction and a few prayers and then said, "Eric and Sophie have decided to write their own vows to each other. Sophie, will you please recite your vows to Eric."

I stood up straighter and paid attention. Sophie had been stressing about writing these vows for the past month. And although I'd heard them at least fifty times and probably could have recited them myself, I knew I didn't want to miss this part. This is the part of weddings that you remember. The most important part. The rings, the kiss, the unity candle, they're all just formalities. They happen at every wedding. But vows are unique. They come from the heart.

"Eric," Sophie began, "when I met you, I was always wandering. Most of the time, I didn't know what direction I was going, but I always knew that I was headed somewhere. Toward something. Now I know that that *somewhere* was you. You are the night-light that leads me through the dark. And you are the water and sunshine that make me grow."

I stole a glance toward the pews and caught sight of Jamie in the third row. I could have sworn I saw mist in his eyes. Was he *crying*? But it wasn't even *our* wedding. Those weren't even *my* vows. Then I looked behind him: A row of faces I had never seen before. And another behind that. And another behind that.

Who *were* all these people? Where did they come from? How had I managed to know Sophie nearly my *entire* life and never met even half of these people? Were they long-lost relatives? Friends of the family? Wedding crashers?

I turned my attention back to the bride.

"I want nothing more than to spend my life with you. I want nothing more than to wake up to you every day and go to sleep with you every night. I love you more than you'll ever know because I love you more than I'll ever be able to tell you with words."

I glanced toward the pews again, and suddenly the gravity of her statement hit me. She wasn't saying these words just to Eric. She was saying them to *every single person* in this room. She was pledging herself to him in front of everyone she knew, and probably a few she didn't.

I could barely tell my dad and his *third* wife that I was engaged. How was I ever going to announce to a room full of half strangers that Jamie was the night-light that led me through the dark?

The priest was speaking now. "Sophie, please repeat after me. I, Sophie, take you, Eric, to be my husband . . ."

She did.

". . . to share this world with you through sickness and health . . ."

I could feel small beads of sweat forming on my forehead.

Is it hot in here? I wondered. *Or is it just me?*

I subtly glanced at Sophie's mother in the front row. She was covered in a wool pashmina that was held tight around her body.

Okay, it must be just me. It must be all these lights. It's like being onstage up here.

But when I looked above me, there were no lights. Just the sunlight peering in through the windows of the old stone church.

So where the hell was all this heat coming from?

"I promise to cherish you and devote myself to you fully," Sophie repeated. It sounded like it was coming from light-years away, from another dimension, even.

I turned my attention back to the altar. This was the most important day of my best friend's life, and I was busy obsessing about the lack of spotlights in the church. I was the worst maid of honor ever.

"I promise to never lie to you and always be faithful to you," she repeated diligently.

To never lie to you and always be faithful to you.

I wondered just how strict that "never" and "always" really were. Obviously there were extenuating circumstances. Because no one can *never* or *always* do anything. But I supposed that if the priest had asked Sophie to "almost never lie" to Eric, it wouldn't be quite as effective, would it?

But it's a known fact that some things are out of your control. And some things sound a hundred times worse aloud than they really are, so clearly *those* things should stay in your head.

Right?

Suddenly my vision seemed to be blurring. And the more I tried to concentrate on the back of Sophie's beautiful beaded white dress, the more fuzzy everything became. I blinked frantically, assuming it was just the sweat from my forehead dripping into my eyes. But I couldn't quite shake it.

Sophie's words were echoing over and over in my head.

You're next. You're next. You're next.

I don't think she meant for them to sound so ominous. In fact, when they left her mouth, I'm almost positive they were blanketed with love and adoration. But by the time they reached my ears and managed to bypass my skewed mental filter, they sounded like a death sentence a doctor might announce to a terminally ill cancer patient.

You're next.

Next to wear the white dress. Next to ride in a limo from the hotel to the ceremony. Next to wonder if the tilapia is fresh or frozen.

Me!

But was I really ready to be next? Was I even *next* material?

"Sophie, do you promise today before God in heaven to love Eric . . ."

Oh, good. We're already on to the question-and-answer portion of the ceremony.

Soon it would be over, and I could run to the bathroom and splash some much needed cold water on my face.

". . . to comfort him and keep him, to honor him and care for him . . ."

Why was the priest still talking? How long were these vows? Why can't someone just say, "Yes, I promise everything that's written in that little leather-bound book of yours, now let's eat cake?"

I caught sight of Zoë standing next to me. She had the oddest look on her face. Her eyebrows were all furrowed and she was staring at me as if I were a crazy person on the street who had just woken up from a booze-inspired nap. But maybe that was just the way it appeared through my blurred vision. She was probably just smiling.

When I finally managed to make eye contact with her, she mouthed, "Are you okay?"

But I couldn't really respond. My heart felt as if it were suddenly pumping out large, heavy rocks instead of blood. The room was spinning now, and a strange buzzing sound filled my ears. It seemed to get louder with each passing second.

". . . and do you promise to stay true to him for as long as you both shall live?"

By the time Sophie pronounced that fateful two-word answer, I could no longer hear her. Because blackness had started to creep into the sides of my vision, and the buzzing was now deafening. To the point where I could hear nothing else. And before I could even start to comprehend what was happening to me, the room suddenly went dark and I hit the floor.

I can only assume that her answer was, "I do."

18

human lie detector

If you thought tripping down the aisle was the worst thing a maid of honor could do at her best friend's wedding, you thought wrong. It turns out fainting at the altar is about a hundred times worse.

When I came to, the entire church had been cleared out except for a few people. Someone had managed to move my unconscious body to a nearby pew, and I awoke to the feeling of cold, hard wood against my back. The first things I saw when I opened my eyes were the rafters on the ceiling. They confused me at first, because I completely forgot where I was and why I was there. There was a mysterious throbbing feeling on my left temple, as though someone had taken a sledgehammer to it.

The second thing I saw was the unfamiliar face of an attractive, dark-skinned man hovering over me. He was looking down at me with intensity in his eyes. "Jennifer? . . . Jennifer, can you hear me?"

Oh shit, I thought. Do I have amnesia? Is this my boyfriend and I can't remember his name or face? Am I going to have to learn how to walk and write and read all over again? I really don't have time for that.

But then a face that I actually did recognize popped into view, and I immediately felt a wave of relief wash over me. It was Jamie.

And I knew for sure that *he* was my boyfriend. So then who was this other guy?

"Babe, are you okay?" Jamie asked.

I tried to nod. "Where am I? What happened?"

"You fainted at my wedding!" I could hear Sophie's voice come from somewhere behind me.

"Shhh," a voice urged her. "Don't upset her right now, honey."

Suddenly it all came rushing back.

The wedding. The ceremony. The buzzing sound.

I had passed out right in the middle of Sophie's wedding.

She's going to kill *me.*

The man with the dark hair reappeared and shone a flashlight into my eyes. "Who are you?" I asked, blinking against the light.

"My name is Gary. I'm an EMT."

"You called an ambulance?" I cried as I struggled to sit up, but the throbbing in my left temple intensified immediately, knocking me back down with a wince of pain.

"Whoa, whoa," Gary said, placing a gentle hand on my shoulder. "Don't try to get up. There's a chance you could have a concussion. You hit your head pretty hard when you fell."

"On what?" I asked dazedly.

"On the steps of my altar!" I heard Sophie's voice shout again, and once again someone quieted her.

"What?" I heard her mumble in defense. "Clearly she's fine. She's awake and talking. And there are a hundred and fifty people outside wondering what the hell is going on in here."

"Soph," I tried, "I'm so sorry. I don't know what happened to me. Suddenly everything just faded to black."

"It's okay," Jamie reassured me, grabbing my hand and squeezing it. "No one's mad at you."

The EMT now had his hand on my wrist and was checking my pulse. "Do you have any idea why you might have fainted?"

"Maybe she's pregnant!" I heard a voice scream from somewhere at the other end of the room. It was definitely Zoë.

I looked up to see Jamie's eyes narrow with concern. "I'm not pregnant," I assured him.

At least I didn't think I was. Although I guess that would have explained a lot.

"Maybe she's anorexic," came another distant conjecture. This time it was John.

I sighed in frustration. "I'm not anorexic, either. I don't know what happened. The last thing I remember was Sophie saying her vows and then the room started to spin and the next thing I knew I was lying here on this bench."

I might have been paranoid, or maybe the smack to my head had altered my judgment, but at that very moment, I could have sworn I felt Jamie's grip on my hand loosen. And when I turned my head to meet his eyes, he was no longer looking at me.

"Okay," began EMT Gary. "We're going to take you over to the hospital and have a doctor take a look at you, make sure you don't have a concussion."

"But what about the reception!" I heard Sophie whine.

But before I could respond with another dazed apology, I was being lifted onto a stretcher and wheeled right down the aisle from which I'd come.

The doctors quickly determined that I did not, in fact, have a concussion but were also just as quick to lecture me about the dangers of skipping meals and fasting in order to lose weight.

To be fair, they didn't just *assume* that I was a crash dieter who had inevitably crashed. I sort of told them that I had been trying to lose weight for the wedding so that I could fit into my bridesmaid's dress. I figured it was a believable excuse. Women are prone to doing crazy things like that when there's a fitted dress in the equation. So when they grilled me in the hospital room about why I just happened to faint when there was clearly nothing physically wrong with me, I had no choice but to lie. Particularly because Jamie happened to be sitting right there next to me the entire time. I couldn't very well admit that the real reason I passed out in the middle of my best friend's wedding vows was that the very thought of saying my own wedding vows literally made me lose consciousness.

The doctors discharged me on Sunday afternoon, and by the time I arrived home I had at least two dozen voice mails from Sophie from the night before. She had called every fifteen minutes to give me updates on the wedding reception, which I found incredibly endearing. In each message she was slightly more intoxicated, until the very last one, which, according to the voice mail lady, was recorded at 2:45 A.M. In this message, she was obviously completely wasted and bawling hysterically into the phone about how sorry she was for yelling at me for fainting.

The sound of her tears suddenly made me want to cry as well. I had missed my best friend's wedding. The whole thing. And that was something I would never be able to undo. Sophie would only get married once in her life (if she was lucky), and I hadn't even been there. I didn't get to see her cut the cake or share her first dance with Eric or drink too much champagne and make a complete fool of herself on the dance floor (although that was something she did often enough, so I probably didn't miss much there).

After I listened to the very last message from her and hung up the phone, I made a mental note to figure out some way to make it up to her when she got back from her honeymoon. I wasn't sure if there was anything on earth that could possibly make up for missing a wedding, but I would have to at least try.

My head ached for a few days after the incident, and I had a pretty big bump above my left ear where my skull made contact with the stone steps of the church, but for the most part, I felt fine. The doctors sent me home with a prescription for some kind of painkiller—basically just a stronger version of aspirin—and I was instructed to get plenty of rest for at least two days. So I called Hadley and told her to cancel my Monday and Tuesday appointments and postpone the weekly staff meeting until Wednesday.

But by Tuesday afternoon, I had come down with a severe case of cabin fever. I had watched every single show on my TiVo . . . twice and half of my DVD collection. I had devoured every gossip magazine that Jamie could find at the supermarket and a few back issues of *Fortune* that I had found in one of the boxes that were still sitting in the hallway. Needless to say, I was going out of my mind.

So when Jamie came into the living room that night, all decked out in a spiffy navy suit topped off with the designer cuff links I had bought him for Christmas last year, my hopes of an escape from my condo prison instantly rose.

"Where are you going looking so hot?" I asked after giving a low whistle. I figured flattery was the best chance I had of getting off this sofa.

Jamie stood in front of the mirror by the front door and straightened his tie. "I have a dinner meeting with a potential new client. The CEO of Chandler Cosmetics."

I crinkled my brow. "Never heard of them."

"That's exactly why they're thinking of hiring us. They want to re-brand their entire line and skew it younger. You're essentially the target demographic."

I pursed my lips thoughtfully. This was my chance. "Well, then you should definitely let me come."

"I don't think so," he said, coming over to the couch and kissing me on the top of the head. "You need your rest."

"No, I don't. I'm plenty rested." I pushed the afghan off my legs and sprang from the couch. It was probably a bit too fast, because I immediately felt the wooziness settle in on the perimeter of my vision, but I fought hard to conceal it. Fainting a second time would do little to help my chances of getting out of this house tonight.

Jamie shot me a skeptical look. "I don't know. The doctors said—"

"I feel great," I insisted, attempting to steer him away from any argument beginning with "The doctors said." Those are always impossibly difficult to refute. "I need to get out of this house. I can be your arm candy. Beautiful women are a highly effective form of negotiation, you know?"

Concern flashed over his face. "Are you sure you're feeling up to it? It might be a pretty long dinner and—"

"I'll be fine. Just give me ten minutes to throw something on."

And before he had a chance to argue, I was already halfway down the hallway, mentally rifling through my closet for the perfect outfit for my parole.

Jamie and I didn't talk much on the drive to Beverly Hills. There was a definite uneasiness between us. I could feel it in the air and in the perfunctory small talk that we exchanged. I don't think Jamie ever really bought the crash-dieting excuse that I gave the doctors, and I saw the way he looked at me when they announced that all my test results were negative and that I didn't in fact have a brain tumor or any other medical explanation for my collapse.

It was almost as if he *wanted* there to be something wrong with me. So that he wouldn't have to face the growing suspicion that everything that had happened recently was somehow connected. And truth be told, I almost wanted there to be something medically wrong with me, too. How much easier would that have been?

Once we got to the restaurant, everything just sort of magically returned to normal. Jamie was sweet and affectionate and adoring. We played the role of the blushing bride-to-be and doting fiancé flawlessly. And frankly, it was nice to live in a state of ignorant bliss for a few hours.

The business talk was incredibly boring. Although I had to admit, it was better than the alternative: lying lifelessly on the couch for the third night in a row.

"Well," Jamie was saying after setting down his knife and fork, "I really do think that the package we presented to you contains everything that your company will need to get your new product line off the ground. With the brand awareness campaign we're suggesting, you really can't do any better."

Hank, who had been introduced to me as the CEO of Chandler Cosmetics, tapped his pinky finger thoughtfully against the linen tablecloth. I couldn't help but notice it was adorned with an oversize gold ring. "I agree, your proposal is definitely appealing," he replied. "But I must tell you, one of the other firms we've been talking to is offering a very strong package as well. At a price that's significantly less."

I was mesmerized by the tapping of his finger. *What respectable businessman wears a gold ring on his pinky? No wonder his brand doesn't appeal to young people.*

Upon closer inspection, I noticed that it was actually a class ring, and I struggled to make out what school and year were written in the blue text. Not that it mattered. But it was the only thing keeping me entertained.

"And so you can see why it's very hard for me to sign with you guys when I have such a tempting other offer on the table," Hank continued.

I tilted my head to the side to get a better angle on the ring. *It looks like it says Class of Seventy-something. Seventy-five, perhaps? Is that a 5 or a 6? If only he would stop tapping his finger against the table so rapidly. I might be able to read it.*

"I see," Jamie replied thoughtfully. "Well, if you tell me exactly what the counteroffer was, I might be able to beat it or at least match it."

Hank's Class of Seventy-something ring was just a gold-and-blue blur now as his pinky finger drummed briskly against the table. I eventually gave up trying to read the stupid thing, as it was obviously a lost cause. But just as I was attempting to come up with my next creative two-minute distraction, I heard him say, "Well, the other firm we're considering is willing to offer us the same services, the same design consultation, and the same marketing platform for three hundred and seventy-five thousand dollars. And that's with consulting fees included."

Jamie inhaled a sharp breath. Clearly, this number was not going to help improve his night.

But I suddenly wasn't all that interested in Jamie's reaction. I was far too preoccupied with the reaction of the man sitting across from me. I looked up from his rapid pinky movement and studied his face. I must have been staring a bit too intensely, because when Hank glanced over at me, he squirmed a little in his seat. But I didn't care.

Something was happening.

A warning light was suddenly flashing inside my head, accompanied by an obnoxiously loud honking sound. Like one of those red alerts you see in movies right before the entire secret subterranean military base goes on full lockdown.

The feeling was nothing new to me. I had felt it many times over the past three years. But most of the time it was back when I used to come face-to-face with cheating husbands. The unmistakable warning sound that accompanied my ability to read men.

And right now that underutilized superpower was telling me only one thing.

Hank Chandler was lying.

I continued to scrutinize him as he droned on and on about how hard it is to sign with a company whose price is not competitive with the industry. Then I glanced over at Jamie to see if he, too, had caught on to what was happening. But he was just nodding, his lips pressed tightly together, clearly oblivious to the fact that Hank was playing him.

I eyed Jamie's BlackBerry sitting on the table and excused myself to use the restroom. As soon as I got to the bathroom hallway, I ducked around the corner and dug my cell phone out of my bag. I dialed Jamie's phone number and pressed the phone to my ear, leaning my head around the corner to peek back at the table. Jamie's BlackBerry vibrated against the tablecloth, illuminating the screen. I watched as he tilted it toward him to get a view of his incoming call. After a befuddled look, he held up one finger to Hank and answered the call.

"Is everything okay?" he spoke into the phone.

"Yes, just listen," I said urgently. "I'll explain everything later, but for now, you need to just play along. Tell Hank that it's your senior partner calling to check in on the negotiations."

There was a wary pause, and for a minute I feared that he might not go along with my plan. That he might just assume that my knock to the head had left some kind of permanent damage. But then finally I saw Jamie pull the phone away from his ear and cover the receiver. "It's my partner," his muffled voice came through the line. "He's just checking in on our progress."

Jamie removed his hand and spoke directly to me. "Everything's fine, Carl. Thanks for checking in. Hank and I are just going through the deal terms now."

"Good, that's good," I encouraged him softly, feeling like an undercover spy trying to save my partner from being made by a pack of Russian terrorists. "Okay, now whatever you do, don't lower the bid. He's bluffing."

"What do you mean?"

"I mean he's lying. There is no lower bid. And I'd be willing to bet that there probably is no other company, either."

"Uh-huh," he said into the phone, accompanied by a thoughtful head bob. "Yes, I see. Well, that's definitely an interesting conclusion. I would love to hear your reasoning behind that."

I cupped my hand over my mouth and spoke in a low voice. "I can't explain that right now, I just *know*, okay? You have to trust me. Now, tell me that Hank is talking to another firm and then ask me if there's any wiggle room in the price of our bid."

As I glanced at the table from my hiding place in the hallway, I could see Jamie nervously massaging the back of his neck with his free hand. Then he cleared his throat and reluctantly obliged. "Well, it's a good thing that you called because Mr. Chandler and I were just discussing some of the options in our proposal, and I was wondering if there's any chance we can negotiate a better price for him. He seems to have gotten a lower offer from one of our competitors."

I watched Hank's reaction to this. He looked mighty pleased with himself. Satisfied that he seemed to have successfully dodged a bullet.

"Good," I said to Jamie. "Now, I know you're not much of an actor, but do your best. I want you to look disappointed in what I'm saying right now."

I watched Jamie's face as the emotion registered.

"Nod understandingly," I commanded him.

He complied. "Yes, I understand."

"Then in a few seconds, I want you to say, 'Thank you, I'll convey your thoughts to Hank,' and then hang up the phone and tell him that unfortunately the current bid is the most competitive one your firm can offer."

Jamie paused, looking uncertainly down at the table. I could sense his hesitation from halfway across the restaurant. "*Please* just trust me," I assured him again.

"Well," I finally heard him say, "I hope you're right about that."

"I am right."

He nodded again and finally said, "Yes, well, thank you, Carl. I'll convey your thoughts to Hank."

Then the line went dead. I watched from the hallway as Jamie relayed my message. I couldn't hear the conversation, but I could definitely make out the drastic change in Hank's expression. It was as if someone had just told him that his $40 million lotto ticket was a fake.

There was a quiet yet intense exchange between them as I assumed Jamie was once again trying to assure Hank that their final price was well worth every penny and that they really were the best company for the job.

I danced impatiently in the hallway for a few minutes before returning to the table and sliding back into my chair. "What'd I miss?"

Jamie turned to me with an incredulous look on his face. "Quite a bit, actually. Mr. Chandler has just agreed to accept our offer."

"That's great!" I said, taking a sip of my water. "Congratulations to both of you."

Jamie was trying hard to hide his strange combination of elation and mystification, while Hank was trying to hide his embarrassment at being called on his bluff.

I, on the other hand, was simply basking in my victory.

"Okay, how did you do that?" Jamie asked the moment I sat in the car and shut the door.

"Easy," I replied, toying with him. "I simply pulled on the door and it shut. Would you like me to do it again in slow motion?"

"Ha-ha," he indulged me. "Now, tell me how you did that?"

I shrugged. "It was fairly obvious he was lying."

"Not to me!" he cried. "I was about to offer him a fifty-thousand-dollar reduction in our fees!"

I leaned back in my seat, enjoying Jamie's awestruck attention. "Well, that would have sucked, now, wouldn't it?"

He sighed loudly and slouched his shoulders, looking dejected.

I finally gave in. "Fine, I don't know how I knew, I just knew. It just came to me. He was talking about that other offer and every bone in my body was telling me he was lying."

"Really?" Jamie was clearly unconvinced.

I nodded. "Yeah. Really."

"It was just a hunch?"

"No," I replied with determination. "It wasn't a hunch. I *knew* he was bluffing."

"So it's real, then? This men-reading superpower of yours."

I shrugged again. "I guess. It's the same way I know the subject of a fidelity inspection is a cheater."

Jamie was silent for a moment. "You mean it's the same way you *used* to know the subject is a cheater," he clarified with a blank look on his face.

I suddenly felt the temperature in the car drop ten degrees, and I attempted to rub the chill from my gooseflesh-covered arms. "Right," I said, smiling weakly. "*Used* to know. That's what I meant."

Jamie studied me for a moment. His voice said nothing, but his eyes were far less discreet.

Eventually, he turned away and started the car, then pulled away from the curb and maneuvered through the streets of Beverly Hills toward home.

I faced out the window and stayed quiet. But I could feel Jamie's eyes on me as we drove, glancing periodically in my direction like a police officer staking out a suspected felon. Certain that any minute now I might do something worthy of an arrest.

And if I did, he would be ready and waiting to bring me in for questioning.

19

byte-size emotions

Having been on official bed rest for three days, I was anxious to get back to work on Wednesday morning. I looked at it as my return to normalcy. My chance to start fresh and erase everything that had happened in the past few weeks. I found comfort and relief in the habitual task of listening to my associates deliver their verdicts in the morning staff meeting and handing out their new assignments for the week.

There were only five of us in the conference room, as opposed to our usual six, because Katie was still shacked up at the Stanton residence, and according to her biweekly e-mail updates, there had yet to be any developments to conclusively determine the status of Dean Stanton's fidelity. And after two and a half weeks, I was starting to think that it might be time to pull the plug. I hated to keep Melissa Stanton's invoice accumulating if her husband wasn't showing any signs of disloyalty. I had offered her a discounted rate from our normal fees, given the unusual circumstances, but the final bill still wasn't going to be cheap by any stretch of the imagination.

So after the meeting was adjourned and before my first appointment showed up, I decided to call Katie for an update.

"Are you able to talk?" I asked as soon as she answered her cell phone.

She sounded surprised to hear from me. Probably because we had agreed to communicate solely by e-mail in order to protect her cover. But if I was going to make the right decision about this case, I needed to hear the details straight from her.

"Hi, yeah, I can talk. Mr. Stanton is on a business trip, and Mrs. Stanton is out planning some charity event fund-raiser."

"Well, where are the kids?" I asked, concerned.

She groaned. "Killing each other in the backyard. But don't worry about them. They don't listen to anything I say anyway."

I laughed. "I was actually referring to the fact that you were alone with them. Mrs. Stanton assured me that you wouldn't be doing any actual supervising. Has she not been keeping her word on that?"

"Technically she has," Katie replied bitterly. "The housekeeper, Juanita, is usually here, too, but she doesn't speak a word of English and the boys know that and walk all over her. Besides, she's always busy with laundry and cleaning and stuff, so I'm usually the one watching the little bastards."

I wasn't entirely pleased to hear that, but I let it pass. I wasn't sure how long I'd have with her on the phone, and I wanted to get to the point. "Well, I was calling because I want to talk to you about the case. Have there been any further developments since you last e-mailed me?"

"I'm afraid not," she said hurriedly, and then I heard a muffled sound as her hand covered the receiver. "Cooper! Henry!" she screamed. "Don't touch that! You'll burn your freaking fingers off!"

She returned to the line. "Sorry about that. Anyway, no, there haven't been any developments. But he's been gone on a business trip for the last few days. So it's hard to tell."

I took a deep breath. "Well, I've been thinking—"

But Katie interrupted me with a frustrated sigh and a mumbled curse word. "Ashlyn, I'm sorry. Hold on a sec."

I heard the phone clank against something, and then in the distance Katie's voice bellowed, "Henry! Do not point that thing at your brother! Put down the gun. Right now! Do you want to sit in the naughty chair?"

She was breathless and irritated when she came back on the phone. "Sorry again. They like to play with water guns even though

Mrs. Stanton doesn't approve. She says she doesn't condone violence in the house. Apparently *outside* the house is fair game, though."

I stifled a laugh, finding it incredibly ironic that the girl who could outsmart, outwit, and outmaneuver any man in the world had suddenly met her match in twin nine-year-old boys.

"So what were you saying?" Katie asked, catching her breath.

"I was just going to say that you've been there for nearly three weeks and he still hasn't shown any clear signs of unfaithful tendencies. I think it might be time to declare it a 'pass' and pull you out of there. I know we could use your help back at the agency, and I'm sure Melissa Stanton doesn't want to be paying for—"

"No!" Katie objected, sounding rather frantic. For a minute, I thought she was addressing the children again. But she quickly composed herself and said, "I mean, I don't think I should leave yet."

My face clouded over with confusion. "But I thought you said there have been no developments."

She stammered slightly. "Well, no . . . I mean, yes . . . sort of."

"Sort of," I repeated, skeptical.

She sighed, and it sounded like she was losing her patience. "Well, he's flirty . . . you know, when his wife's not around, which leads me to think that given enough time, he might take it further. So I'm . . . uh, hesitant to pull out now." And then she added hurriedly, "At least not until he gets back from his business trip."

I jotted down a few notes on my legal pad and then tapped the pen thoughtfully against the paper. "So you're saying that if he *has* been doing inappropriate things with his former nannies, then he took his time doing it."

"Um . . . yeah." Katie's voice was distant, her mind clearly elsewhere. Most likely on the two rowdy children shooting each other with water guns in the backyard.

"Well, how have you been responding to his flirtations?"

There was a pause on the other end of the phone, and then Katie replied in a rushed tone, "Um, good. I mean, flirty back, you know. Following his lead just like always."

"Okay, then," I concluded, setting my pen down. "I guess we'll give it another week or so and see if anything changes."

"Great," Katie breathed. "Look, I gotta go. I'll send another up-date soon." And then she hung up.

Julie Bleeker was a young woman, mid- to late twenties, with sandy, highlighted blond hair that was cut in a stylish bob. She struck me as the kind of girl you would imagine to have been captain of the cheerleading team in high school. Cute, bubbly, with a million-dollar smile that came easy to her. Much easier than frowning.

Well, on any other day, at least.

Hadley led her into my office, and she quickly took a seat on the couch and tucked her hands under her legs, as if trying to keep them warm.

"Would you like something to drink?" I asked, eyeing her hands. "Maybe a coffee or hot tea?"

But she shook her head. "No, thank you, I'm fine."

I pulled my legal pad off my desk and settled into my seat. "So," I began in my usual compassionate tone. "What brings you into our agency today?"

She took a deep breath. "Someone referred me. An old friend."

I nodded and smiled. "And may I ask her name?"

The woman hesitated, shifting uneasily in her seat. I was used to new clients being less than forthcoming about their personal life. So I spared her the agony and moved on. "That's all right. It doesn't matter. Let's just talk about why *you're* here."

She appeared grateful for the change in direction. "Well, it's my husband," she began to explain. "Ryan."

"Mm-hmm," I murmured as I began to take notes. "And how long have you been married?"

"Three years."

I wrote this down. "And what is your primary concern about Ryan?"

She tucked a strand of hair behind her ear and then quickly pulled it back into place. "He just doesn't seem to be as 'into' the relation-ship as he used to be. He's been distant. Not returning phone calls. He says he's just really swamped at work."

I nodded as I scribbled. "Okay. Well, in my experience I've found that women's intuition is one of the strongest forces on the planet, and you're wise to listen to it and find out for sure."

I continued to ask Julie my usual repertoire of questions about her relationship, her husband's likes, dislikes, hobbies, and any upcoming special events that would make for a good location for the assignment.

"Well," she began, rubbing the palms of her hands on her skirt, "he's supposed to be at the W Hotel in Westwood next Wednesday. One of his friends is staying there from out of town, and he's going to meet him for a drink."

I frowned at the mention of the date as I reached behind me and pulled my iPhone off my desk and navigated to the calendar. "Oh, I'm sorry," I replied. "But I'm afraid next Wednesday isn't going to work. I've been short one associate for the past few weeks, and the rest of my staff is booked up until the following week. But if your husband is local, I'm sure we can find another suitable location to conduct the assignment—"

Julie raised her hand timidly in the air, bringing my sentence to a premature halt. "Actually, um, I was hoping that *you* could do the test."

My eyes widened in surprise. "Me?"

"Yes. My friend told me I should ask for you. That you performed her inspection and . . ."

I let out a nervous chuckle. "Yes, well, I'm sorry, but I haven't taken on any assignments myself in over a year. But I can assure you, Mrs. Bleeker, that all of my associates are very capable."

But Julie was persistent. She shook her head. "I really wouldn't feel comfortable with anyone else. This is not the kind of thing I would normally do. You have to understand that." Moisture was beginning to mist her eyes as she spoke. "And when my friend told me how you changed her life for the better, for the first time in a long time, I actually felt hopeful about something. I need you to do the same thing for me."

I didn't know what to say or how to respond, so for a good thirty seconds I didn't say anything at all. I just sat there, staring wide-eyed at the woman perched on the edge of my sofa, hope and desolation performing a spellbinding tango across the surface of her face.

After everything that had happened in the past few weeks, I knew I couldn't possibly say yes to her, but somehow I just couldn't bring myself to say no. I also knew that something about this woman and her ridiculous request was making me extremely uneasy, and I had to get her out of my office as swiftly as possible.

Because it *was* ridiculous. Absolutely, positively, beyond all doubt . . . insane.

"Well, I'm gonna have to give this some thought," I finally admitted, rising to my feet and practically shuffling Julie Bleeker out the door.

"Okay," she replied warily, standing just short of the hallway. "Just let me know as soon as you can, I guess."

"Yes, I'll call you," I assured her, placing my hand on her lower back and giving her body a gentle nudge.

She walked hesitantly out the door, and I closed it firmly behind her, not even bothering to point her in the direction of the lobby. She was a smart girl, she'd eventually find it herself.

I knew I had to do everything in my power to create a diversion. Distract myself until this unsettling feeling in the pit of my stomach passed. So I decided to tackle all the data entry work that had been piling up over the past few weeks.

After every assignment is complete, every case file is updated, and every associate report is written and turned in, I assume the unenviable task of entering all the details of each inspection into a secure, highly confidential database on our remote server. The official "Fidelity Files." Every piece of information about every client and every subject is entered manually and stored behind a login and password that only I know. It's a total bitch to maintain, but the information is far too sensitive and classified to trust anyone else to do it. So the job remains mine and mine alone.

Eager to do something other than replay Julie Bleeker's words in my mind over and over again, I hastily clicked the icon on my desktop that launched the database program. I entered my login information and selected the option to start a new record. Then I pulled

a stack of folders out of my briefcase and plopped them down on
the desk next to my computer. With a deep breath, I flipped open
the first folder and got to work filling in the empty fields on my
screen.

Case Number: 2378
Subject Name: Jarod Cunning
Occupation: Video Game Programmer
Location: Seattle, WA
Client Name: Lisa Bailey
Relationship to Subject: Girlfriend of 2 years
Primary Concern Warranting Inspection: According to client,
subject has unhealthy obsession with playing video games (Interga-
lactic Battle Quest is current favorite), and client worries that obses-
sion could translate to infidelity should subject be presented with
female player who shares similar passion.
Associate Assigned to Case: Lauren Ireland
Inspection Location(s): Online and Seattle
Result: Failed
Notes: Associate posed as local gamer and engaged in online play
with subject. Rapport with subject was built quickly using game's
instant-messaging feature and occasional e-mails. After one week of
interaction, subject requested face-to-face meeting at a local Internet
café, and associate flew to Seattle for the encounter. Subject invited
associate to his apartment and then initiated physical contact.

Enter. Done. Next folder. Create new record. I could feel the distraction working already. Numbing my mind, muting my thoughts.

Case Number: 2380
Subject Name: Jocelyn Sandover
Occupation: Housewife and Stay-at-Home Mother
Location: Santa Monica, CA
Client Name: Richard Sandover
Relationship to Subject: Husband of 9 years
Primary Concern Warranting Inspection: Client claims that

relationship with subject has been "rocky" for past few months, and they are currently seeing a professional therapist. Client, however, worries that subject will seek additional consolation from a member of the opposite sex.

Associate Assigned to Case: Cameron Kelly

Inspection Location(s): Rockwell Elementary School and subject's home

Result: Failed

Notes: Associate posed as fellow parent experiencing difficulties in his marriage and interacted with subject outside elementary school. Subject invited associate to coffee shop and subsequently her home, where she initiated physical contact.

Every time I tackled this aspect of my job, I marveled at how strange it was. The most intimate details of a person's life—the story of their relationship's demise—fitting neatly into eleven pre-set data fields.

To my keyboard, these were just names, cities, and empty words. A series of letters and spaces that had no meaning. But in reality, these were people's lives. Their broken hearts. Their dashed dreams of happily ever afters. And now they were being effortlessly translated into tiny, byte-size pieces of information to be stored on a giant, lifeless machine, in a cold, dimly lit server room somewhere in the middle of a town with a name not even worth remembering. And with just the tap of a mouse, these stories of betrayal and heartbreak were forever immortalized as nothing more than a string of 1's and 0's.

I admit, it wasn't the most uplifting experience in the world, but it had to be done. And I was grateful for the distraction.

Two hours and fifteen cheating spouses (and one faithful one) later, I had finally reached the last file in the stack. My legs were numb from sitting and my neck was sore from staring at the computer screen, but I pushed myself to keep going, stretching my head from side to side in an attempt to relieve some of the stiffness in my shoulders.

Just one more to go.

I took a deep breath, opened the final folder, and began typing.

Case Number: 2383
Subject Name: Benjamin Connors

My fingers slowed significantly and eventually came to a stop just after the "s" in his last name. I stared at the open folder in front of me. All the information that leapt off the page and into my tired, bloodshot eyeballs was more familiar than I ever would have imagined. Because for the first time in over a year, the record I was about to create and store away in the depths of cyberspace for all eternity was my own.

The notes were written from *my* point of view. The details were part of *my* memories. *My* past.

Benjamin Connors's path had irrevocably intersected with mine. And that one night, that one seemingly accidental meeting, had left a permanent mark on both our lives.

But for Benjamin Connors, the meaning of this file, this record of data, seemed conclusive. As with everyone else in the stack, it represented the end of his marriage. The loss of a wife and a child and a future he'd once envisioned for himself.

Whereas I, on the other hand, still hadn't figured out the significance of this file for me. For my envisioned future.

Because for the past two weeks, my mind had been clinging desperately to the memory of Darcie Connors standing in the doorway of this very room, expressing her undying gratitude to me. For what *I* did. What *I* was able to give her. That gratitude had invoked some kind of sensation in me that I hadn't been able to shake. A rare sense of fulfillment. As if someone had reawakened a side of me that I didn't even know was sleeping.

And it had been so long since I had experienced that feeling. Since I had *personally* been the one to expose a cheater.

As I stared at her name on the page in front of me, once again tasting that glorious flavor of purpose, I instantly understood that *this* is what I had been craving for the last year. This is what I had been trying so hard to replace. First in forming the agency and later in agreeing to be an expert witness. I needed to feel that I was actively making a difference in people's lives. That I was still using my superpower for good. But unfortunately, my paltry substitutes weren't enough. They didn't do the trick.

I felt like a recovering drug addict who had no idea what substance I was addicted to until someone accidentally injected it into my arm.

But now that I had identified what was missing in my life, I didn't know how I was going to be able to continue to resist it. Especially when I knew *exactly* how and where to get it.

Especially . . . when it had just left my office less than three hours ago.

"No!" I said aloud as I forced the thought from my mind and focused on finishing the task at hand. Data entry. Dull, stupid, tedious data.

I glanced again at the open folder on my desk. I had to think of it as just another file. Just another record. Nothing more.

And I knew that if I ever had the chance to put this whole thing behind me for good, it was now. Because once that data was entered, once that "Submit" button was clicked, I never had to see it again. The original file goes into the shredder and the original memory hopefully goes into some type of mental shredder as well.

With shaking hands, I carefully copied the text word for word from the file onto my screen. I didn't change one detail. Not one word, name, or even comma. Although the file clearly wasn't an accurate representation of what happened that night, it was the only representation that I wanted to be permanently stored.

Occupation: Advertising

Location: Sherman Oaks, CA

Client Name: Darcie Connors

Relationship to Subject: Wife

Primary Concern Warranting Inspection: Client fears unfaithful tendencies in subject after subject was witnessed acting inappropriately at neighborhood party. Client wants to confirm or deny suspicions before moving forward with present plans to adopt a baby.

Associate Assigned to Case: Shawna Miller

Inspection Location(s): Palazzo Hotel and Casino in Las Vegas, NV

Result: Failed

Notes: Associate met subject at a craps table in Palazzo Casino and allowed subject to supply instructions on proper play. Following the game, subject invited associate to have drinks and subsequently to join him in his hotel room. Once inside, subject proved intention to engage in sexual activities.

Enter. Close program. Done.

I stood by and watched ceremoniously as the electric shredder next to my desk hungrily ingested the file, the blades slicing its pages into minuscule, incomprehensible pieces that not even the most accomplished member of the CIA could possibly make sense of.

The shreds of paper floated gracefully into the clear plastic canister below, like white glitter coming to rest inside a snow globe.

There was something very conclusive about the whole process. Finite. And I prayed that I could now put the whole thing behind me. That somewhere in the midst of that shredded confusion lay all the ambiguous feelings I associated with the name Benjamin Connors.

But when I got back from lunch and sat behind my desk, determined to start preparing next week's assignments for my staff, my eyes were perpetually drawn to the little black shredder on the floor. And when I reluctantly glanced over at it, I noticed a sliver of white paper stuck to the inside of the clear plastic bin. I could just make out the letter "C," typed on the front. Whether it was a *C* from the name Connors or a *C* from some harmless word like "coffee" or "car" or "credit card," I couldn't be sure. But it didn't really matter. What mattered was that it was there.

With sudden frustration, I jumped to my feet and yanked out the plastic container from underneath the shredder. Then I stormed out of my office, down the hallway, and toward the double glass doors of the reception area.

Upon seeing me emerge, Hadley leapt to her feet. She eyed the bin in my hands. "I can empty that if you want!"

"It's okay," I huffed, trying not to let my unstable emotions taint my tone. "I needed something to do."

The elevator was crowded when I stepped inside, and I scurried to take my place near the back, cradling the container protectively in my arms. When we reached the ground floor, a few strange looks followed me out and I headed straight for the security guard's desk.

"Where's the Dumpster?" I asked the uniformed guard, who stood upon seeing me approach.

He reached for the bin. "I'll take care of it, ma'am," he offered with an amiable smile.

But I clenched it tighter against my chest. "That's okay. I need to do this."

He eyed me with apprehension, and I swear I saw him eye his security phone as well. But then he eventually pointed toward a door in the back of the lobby and said, "In the alley, behind the building."

I flashed him my most gracious smile. "Thanks."

Once I reached the big blue Dumpster outside, I wasted no time, emptying the contents of my bin, shaking and tapping the sides violently in an effort to make sure every single last fragment of a piece got exactly where it needed to go. And as I watched the million tiny specks of paper drift into the abyss, I prayed that this would be the end of it. That this would give me the strength to walk back into my office, pick up the phone, and tell Julie Bleeker, without a hint of doubt in my voice, that I could not under any circumstances be the one to take on her case.

But as I stood in the alley behind my building, holding the empty shredder bin in my hands, I could see her face in my head. I could hear her words pleading with me. The desolation in her voice was poking holes in my resolve so rapidly that I couldn't possibly patch them all up fast enough.

And I knew that eventually I had to accept the fact that maybe my resolve just wasn't all that solid to begin with.

20

---

my better half

This is not who you are anymore.

That was my first thought as I stepped hesitantly into the lobby of the W Hotel in Westwood on the following Wednesday night. Although it was less of a thought and more of a mental reproach from my hyperactive mind. It had been running on overdrive for the past week. I was actually surprised it hadn't exhausted itself and given up already.

You should just turn around and leave.

Another direct order promptly ignored. I was getting good at that. Ignoring my own authority.

Because I didn't turn around. I didn't leave. I just kept on walking, farther and farther into the hotel and the unprecedented night that lay ahead of me. Both seemed to have this kind of ominous glow around them, like something out of a bad horror film. And I felt as if someone should cue the fog machine.

It was that woman's voice that kept propelling me forward. It was replaying in the back of my mind like fuel being tossed repeatedly atop a dying fire. Every time my mind tried to impart one of its adamant injunctions—*get in your car, drive straight home, lock the door behind you*—the sound of her voice and the desperation that saturated it immediately drowned out any and all sense of reason.

It was an epic battle. Legendary. One that was fought by all people, in all countries, at any given hour of the day. Good vs. evil. The angel and the devil campaigning tirelessly from opposite shoulders.

It was the timeless fight between what I *wanted* to do and what I knew I *should* do. Or in this case, *shouldn't*.

I wanted to help her. The way I had helped so many women before her. I wanted to once again feel that fleeting sense of fulfillment that had washed over me when I revealed the truth to someone and knew without doubt that it would change that person's life for the better. Like a roller coaster, it was a rush beyond words and over too soon. I had been craving it every day. Yearning for it. And now it was waiting for me somewhere in this hotel. On a silver platter.

Then there was the *should*. The promises I had not only made, but vowed to keep. The person I had been struggling to become for the past year.

It was Ashlyn vs. Jennifer all over again. My past and my future coming to a head. Someone would have to win the battle. Someone would have to claim victory. And as I stepped farther into the lobby of the W Hotel and my eyes zeroed in on the entrance of the hotel bar only a few short paces in front of me, I had a feeling I knew where to place my bet.

Go home! my mind commanded. *This is all wrong!*

I pushed forward, trying to drown out my ever intrusive conscience. I thought about Julie Bleeker. Her sad, frightened eyes. Her trembling voice. Her fidgeting hands. She needed me right now. She needed me to be *here*.

I had called her back that same day. I should have known I couldn't fight this. I should have known that "yes" was the only answer I would ever be able to give her.

The picture of Ryan Bleeker she had given me was tucked away in a small compartment of my purse. I had removed it from the case file before I left as an insurance policy. In case I had trouble recognizing him and needed a last minute visual confirmation. Besides my impromptu assignment with Benjamin Connors a few weeks back, it had been a long time since I'd matched a real live face in a dimly lit hotel bar to a two-dimensional photograph.

At the thought of Benjamin Connors, my mind instantly seized the moment and attempted once again to talk some sense into me.

Yes, Benjamin Connors! Remember what happened after that? Remember what happened when you got home? And that wasn't even planned.

It was right. My mind, that is. Benjamin Connors *wasn't* planned. It was a last-minute, split-second decision. And this was entirely premeditated. The result of a torturous internal debate. One that was apparently still raging in my head.

But I had already made my decision. My mind just needed to shut up and go along with it. It had been defeated, and now it was time to surrender with dignity.

"Can I get you something to drink?"

I looked up to see the bartender smiling as he placed a cocktail napkin in front of me. I had made it all the way to the bar, an accomplishment in and of itself. Now came the waiting.

It's not too late, you know? You can still back out. You can still leave.

I nodded. "Yes, I'll have a Heineken," I told the bartender.

According to his wife, it was Ryan Bleeker's favorite beer. And ironically enough, it was Jamie's as well. But I purposefully avoided that reflection. It would be foolish to willingly hand ammunition to my enemy.

I slid onto an empty bar stool and twirled it around so that I was facing out into the room. Wednesday night at the W Hotel was a happening time. I knew the growing crowd would only make Ryan Bleeker more difficult to spot. I would just have to pay extra-close attention.

I opened my purse and peeked inside. Ryan Bleeker's smiling face was staring back at me. I studied his features, committing them to memory for the one hundredth time this week. Or maybe I was just checking to make sure it was still there. That this was still real.

Before closing my bag again, I stole a quick glance at my cell phone, giving it a swift tap with the tip of my index finger to light up the screen.

It was blank. No new messages. No new texts.

There was a part of me—the rational *should* part—that wanted

Jamie to call. As if hearing his voice would be like some kind of sign that I shouldn't go through with it.

Things had been so awkward between us during this past week. It was as if we were simply coexisting. Going through the motions. "How was your day?" "What do you want for dinner?" "Are you ready for bed?"

Empty questions with even emptier answers.

We hadn't had sex—or, rather, *started* to have sex—since that day I came back from Vegas. And neither of us had mentioned our lack of physical intimacy. In fact, neither of us had mentioned much of anything lately.

I was somewhat relieved when Jamie told me on Sunday night that he had to go to Phoenix for a few days for work. And when he left this morning, the apartment felt lighter somehow. As though a heavy, menacing cloud had drifted away and for a moment it finally felt safe to breathe.

To be honest, his absence only made it that much easier to come here tonight. Because I knew I wouldn't have to lie. . . .

You're still going to have to lie to him.

At least not to his face.

A group of guys walked into the bar, and I mentally scanned their faces for a match. I knew from my meeting with Julie Bleeker that Ryan was thirty-two years old, six feet tall, and about a hundred and eighty pounds. I also knew that the friend he was coming to visit was around the same age, same height, but slightly bulkier. The men who were now entering the room were far too young to fit either description.

I took another sip of my beer and stole another glance at the photograph hidden in my purse. And as I did, I let my finger *accidentally* drag along the screen of my phone once again. It activated obligingly. But there was still nothing for it to display.

Why do you keep checking your phone if you've already made up your mind?

It was a valid question. One I did not have a valid answer for. So I simply opted to let it hang.

Another group of people flooded through the entrance of the bar, but still no sign of Ryan Bleeker. I was starting to feel antsy. I couldn't sit still in my seat. I thought about getting up and walking a few laps around the hotel lobby or maybe even stepping out by the pool to get some fresh air. But I didn't want to miss him.

I had come this far. I wasn't going to let Julie Bleeker down because of a stupid oversight.

She had asked for *me*. She had asked for *my* help, not anyone else's. Why shouldn't I give that to her?

Just then, I felt my phone vibrate in my bag. As if it were directly answering the question I had just posed. My entire body jolted, and I nearly fell off the bar stool.

What if that was him? What if it was Jamie? What would I do then? Would I answer it and lie about where I was and what I was doing? Or would I simply let it ring and deal with it later?

Or will you leave because you know you shouldn't be here?

There it was again. The *should*. Following me every step of the way like a pestering time-share salesman. Why couldn't I just make a decision and stick with it? Why did I have to be haunted by some ghost of supposed morality?

Because you know deep down inside that you're making the wrong choice.

That last one stuck with me. So much so that I had to pause and think about it. I stared down at the beer in my hand and then up at the crowd in the bar. It had nearly doubled since I'd first arrived. Men were talking, women were laughing, music was playing. I knew how loud the noise in the room must have been, but I couldn't hear a thing.

Suddenly, my surroundings reminded me of an old silent movie. Mouths moving but nothing coming out.

Fine, I eventually yielded to my other half. *If that's Jamie calling, I'll walk out of here right now. I'll leave and never look back. But if it's not . . .*

I didn't finish the thought. I didn't have to. That rational, highly outspoken part of me got the point. And it quietly succumbed to the acceptable compromise.

The noise in the room came back with sudden force. My phone

had already stopped vibrating, and as I slid my bag over my shoulder, I could feel the subsequent single vibration alerting me to a new voice mail. I scooted off the bar stool and hurried back into the lobby. If it was Jamie, I wanted to be somewhere quiet enough to hear his message.

And you'll want to be closer to the exit.

The contrast of the crowded bar and the relatively calmer lobby was severe. And I welcomed its tranquillity. The hordes of people had started to make me feel claustrophobic.

I took a deep breath and slid my purse off my shoulder, feeling in its straps the weight of the bargain I had just made. If it was Jamie who had called, this night would be over before it even began. And I would have to tell Julie Bleeker that I wouldn't be able to help her after all.

But if it wasn't him, I would walk back into that bar and continue on with no regrets.

With an audible exhale, I unzipped the bag and pulled out the phone, knowing that whatever name was displayed on that list of missed calls would send my heart into palpitations.

I sucked in a breath and peered at the screen. Just as I expected, my heart started pounding.

But not because I had to leave . . . because I had to stay. And my mind could no longer put forth halfway convincing arguments to persuade me otherwise. It had lost the bet, and now all was deathly quiet.

The screen of my iPhone was small, but seeing my dad's name displayed on it made it feel bigger than the JumboTron at Dodger Stadium.

Fitting, really. That my dad would be the one to win this wager for me. I almost had to laugh.

Almost.

I knew exactly why he was calling. He wanted to have that obligatory postdinner conversation. The one where I'm forced to "review" his *third* wife as if she's the long-awaited follow-up novel from a best-selling author and I'm the infamously hard-to-please *New York Times* book critic.

But I couldn't deal with that now. I had a job to do. And now that the war in my head had been won, there was no more doubting. No more second-guessing. It was time to march back in there and do exactly what I had come here to do.

I slung my bag over my shoulder and turned back in the direction from which I'd come. Very soon, Ryan Bleeker would be walking into that bar, and I would be ready and waiting for him.

But before I could complete the rotation, my eye caught sight of someone entering through the front door of the lobby, walking straight toward me. I whipped my head back around in astonishment and stared at him, my eyes blinking rapidly to make sure my vision hadn't suddenly been impaired.

Air stopped flowing through my lungs. Blood stopped pumping through my veins. Every inch of me, inside and out, was frozen.

I didn't need to check the photograph in my bag again to verify. This was definitely *not* the person I had come to see.

It was the person I had left behind.

21

---

wide-open spaces

The world around me stopped cold. As if someone had pressed pause on the entire hotel lobby and Jamie and I were the only two things in it that were still moving. Except neither of us flinched. We just stood there staring at each other. My heavy breathing was the only sound for a thousand miles.

Our eyes were fiercely locked, like two contenders in an eighteenth-century duel. Each waiting for the other to make the first move, take the first step, draw the first weapon.

As much as I tried to derive meaning from his stare, his eyes were void. Like two empty portals—long, dark, expressive, and yet leading to nowhere.

I approached him carefully, now standing a mere arm's length away. And for the first time, I looked away, casting my eyes at a downward angle.

Jamie was the first to speak. "Looking for someone?"

And then it suddenly hit me. He doesn't know why I'm here. How could he possibly? I could easily come up with a believable explanation for being here. An associate was in trouble and I came to help. Zoë broke up with her mystery man and asked me to meet her here for drinks at the last minute. A long-lost friend was in town. There were a hundred innocent excuses to choose from. All I had to do was pick one and go with it. Ryan Bleeker was still nowhere to be found. I could just leave here and pretend none of it ever happened. Pretend I had never even agreed to come.

Of course, my seemingly brilliant plan had only one apparent flaw. It didn't account for the reason that *Jamie* was here.

And then suddenly every thought in my mind was turned upside down. He was supposed to be in Phoenix tonight. What on earth was he doing *here*?

My heart lurched inside my chest as I realized that I might not be the only one hiding something.

I swallowed hard and attempted to answer his question with a noncommittal shrug. "Just a friend," I stated, casually glancing around.

"Hmm," Jamie replied thoughtfully, sweeping his eyes across the hotel lobby. "Anyone I know?"

My mind was torn. I couldn't figure out what was more important right now, catching Jamie in his lie or covering the tracks of my own. It was a dangerous intersection.

I shook my head. "No, I don't think so. Just an old friend who's in town, called me up to see if I wanted to have a drink."

I was just about to turn the question back on him, ask him who *he* was looking for. What *he* was doing here. And more important, why he wasn't in fucking Phoenix, where he'd said he would be.

But I didn't even have the opportunity. Because the moment I was about to open my mouth, he said, "His name wouldn't happen to be Ryan Bleeker, would it?"

As hard as I struggled to keep the reaction from spreading across my face, to keep the shock from escaping my lips, it was no use. My mouth flew open, the horror in my eyes registered, and the gasp that left my mouth echoed across the lobby.

I was trapped. And it was in that moment I realized that my lie and his lie were one and the same. They were intricately interwoven.

"How do you know that name?" I whispered, the words barely managing to flee my rapidly closing throat.

"Well," Jamie began. His voice was calm. Too calm. Bordering on icy. "Ryan is my middle name, and Bleeker is my mom's maiden name."

I could feel the tears welling in my eyes. I managed to blink a few of them away. But the rest fell rebelliously down the sides of my face. My eyelids closed, but it did nothing to stop them. "You sent her. You sent Julie Bleeker to my office."

"Yes," he replied softly. "She's a receptionist at the office. An aspiring actress. I paid her."

The words came out of his mouth at a normal, conversational level, but as soon as they reached my ears and started echoing around in my head, they were positively deafening. An aspiring actress? A decoy? Well, she certainly wasn't aspiring anymore. She deserved an Oscar for those believable emotions.

Or maybe they were believable to me only because I wanted so badly to believe them.

A painful realization washed over me as I mentally replayed the scene in my office. The same one I had replayed at least a dozen times this week. But this time, I inserted a fake Julie Bleeker into the equation.

Someone referred me. An old friend.

That's what Julie Bleeker had said, but technically, they weren't *her* words. They were Jamie's. And I couldn't believe I hadn't seen it earlier. The night we got engaged, he had asked me point-blank, "But what if the client doesn't want one of your associates? What if the client wants *you*?"

Of course it was a setup. All the signs were right in front of my eyes. And yet, just like every subject I'd ever tested, I was far too blinded by what I *wanted* it to be, I couldn't see what it really was.

"You were testing me," I whispered.

"And you failed."

I shook my head, the grief penetrating every inch of my body. "You don't understand—"

"Oh, I understand just fine," Jamie interrupted in a tone that I had never heard before. It made me feel like a stranger. Someone he had just met on the street and decided rather quickly that he didn't care for at all. But then again, Jamie was always fairly nice to strangers, even ones he didn't care for. So that made me something else. Something worse.

"I understand that you sacrificed our relationship for *this*." He motioned to the general area around him, as if this one random hotel lobby represented everything that I gave up for him. Everything that I used to be. And everything that used to define me.

And I suppose, in a sad, pathetic way . . . it did.

"No," I begged him. "It wasn't like that."

"Why, Jen?" he insisted, his tone once again harsh and foreign. "Why would you do this? We had a deal. You made me a promise. No more assignments. No more cheating men. But clearly that was too hard for you to keep. *Clearly,* this lifestyle was too hard for you to give up."

The tears were falling even harder now. They had taken on a life of their own, and for the first time since I'd walked through those doors, I noticed that people had begun to stare. I placed my hand desperately on Jamie's arm and pulled gently. "Please, don't do this here. Let's go somewhere quiet and talk about this."

His arm flexed beneath my grasp, and his jaw tightened. "There's nothing to talk about, Jen. I now understand where your priorities are. I'm just glad I figured it out before we got married."

Without another word, he turned and walked out the front door. He didn't hesitate. He didn't glance behind him for one last, longing look at my tear-streaked face. He didn't even slow down. He just left.

And he didn't come back.

I stood in the middle of the lobby, feeling small and helpless. The grief slowly gave way to humiliation as I felt several pairs of eyes on me. Hotel clerks at the front desk, bellhops, customers. Tonight the lobby of this happening Westwood hotel was bustling, and I was the main attraction.

"Is everything okay, ma'am?"

A warm hand landed on my arm, and I whipped around to see a man in a dark suit standing next to me. His hotel name tag informed me that he was the night manager. I had little doubt that his inquiry after my well-being had less to do with actual, genuine concern and more to do with avoiding any kind of "incident" on his watch. But maybe that was just the kind of cynical mind frame I was in.

"Yes, I'm fine," I replied coldly as I wiped the tears away with the back of my hand. "I was just leaving."

I didn't drive straight home. After collecting my car from the valet, I circled the streets of Westwood aimlessly, my body shuddering in anguished sobs. I admit I wasn't in the best condition to drive, but I just kept going.

Two hours later, I found my way back home.

The front door opened willingly, welcoming me back with open arms. But I didn't feel I belonged there. Not now. Not at this moment. In fact, I wasn't sure if I belonged anywhere at this moment.

I stood in the foyer, staring out into my beautiful three-bedroom condo. The warm and spacious living room to my left, the chic and modern dining room to my right, the bright and open kitchen behind that. I had lived here for nearly three years, and for the first time since the day I moved in, it felt like a stranger's house.

And I felt like a stranger in it.

An intruder.

But I was not alone.

I heard noises coming from the bedroom, and then Jamie stepped out from the hallway into the light of the living room. We stared at each other blankly for a few seconds. When he finally spoke, his voice was calm and collected, although still absent its usual warmth. "Just tell me how long it's been going on. How many more have there been?"

I shook my head slowly. "Just one," I murmured. "I swear. It only happened once."

He bowed his head, and a cynical laugh escaped his lips. "Of course," he mumbled to himself, suddenly understanding everything. "Vegas."

I nodded but continued to stare at the ground.

"Shawna wasn't arrested during her *second* assignment, was she?"

When I didn't respond, Jamie kept talking. "Well, that explains a *lot*."

"But I didn't have a choice," I begged, feeling the urgency start to rise up once again in my chest. "The client was going to adopt a child the next week. She needed to know—"

"There's *always* a choice, Jen. In that situation it was her or me. And you chose her. And every day that you kept it a secret, you continued to choose your job over me. Don't you get it? You would rather expose someone else's unfaithfulness than stay faithful to me. Do you realize how messed up that is?"

The tears were suddenly falling again. I couldn't even feel them anymore. My eyes were numb from all the crying, and the skin on my cheeks had been rubbed raw from wiping them away. But I knew they were there.

"I swear that was the only one," I whimpered, clinging to this one argument as if it might actually save me. "The only time."

"Until tonight," he pointed out maliciously.

I was cornered. There was nothing more I could say. He had set a trap and I had walked right into it. There were no more excuses.

"You just can't resist it, can you?" His voice suddenly changed, only slightly louder than a whisper now. It almost sounded as though he felt sorry for me. "You can't resist being that person you used to be. The one who exposes the cheaters. And it's ironic, really. Because it's that very obsession that turned you into one."

With this, my torment instantly morphed into anger. And I violently wiped at my face. "I'm not a cheater! It's not the same thing!"

"It is *exactly* the same thing," he shot back, the drastic shift in emotion registering on his face. "You took off your ring, you kissed another man, and then you lied to me about it. Blatantly. To my face, as if it were nothing. As if deceit is just a part of your DNA. Something that comes naturally to you. And after everything that's happened with your father, that might not be too far from the truth. Don't you see, Jen? You're just as bad as the rest of them."

My whole body stiffened, my fists clenched at my sides. "That is not true," I asserted through gritted teeth. "And I can't believe that you would actually compare me to any of them. Yes, I lied to you. Yes, I broke our promise. And that's something I'll always have to live with. But at least I know that what I did was for a cause. That I was helping someone."

I could feel the rage burning inside me, except I wasn't sure if it was true rage or just a bad combination of guilt and helplessness that when mixed in the right proportions can lead to a false sense of wrath. But I didn't feel like waiting around to figure it out. So I stalked forward, brushing angrily past him, and started down the hallway to the bedroom, ready to slam the door behind me once I reached it.

But I never got that far. I stopped midway down the hall when I realized that something was missing. Something that I never thought I would actually *miss*.

Jamie's boxes were gone.

The ones that had seemed to take up permanent residence in this hallway for the past three weeks. They were nowhere to be seen. And the sinking feeling that was already occupying the majority of my chest immediately spread to my stomach, my thighs, my knees, even my toes. I stared at the empty wall space that lined the path to the bedroom. Funny how only yesterday those boxes had made the whole hallway feel so cluttered and claustrophobic, making the entire trip to the bedroom feel like some elaborate obstacle course. And now that they were gone, there was all too much space surrounding me. An unnecessary amount. Making me wonder why they even made hallways this wide when clearly you can get away with half the width.

It had taken him an entire week to move in all that stuff but apparently only a matter of hours to get rid of it. I didn't know how that was even possible. I guess it's just one of those strange breakup phenomena that the laws of physics can't really explain.

I turned back to Jamie, who hadn't moved an inch. "Where's your stuff?" I asked warily, praying that he would simply shrug and tell me that he finally got around to moving it all into the guest room.

He didn't reply. He just continued to stare straight ahead. But in that silence, I got all the answers I needed.

"You never sold the loft, did you?" I asked with sudden realization. "You never took that offer."

Jamie shook his head so subtly that to an unknowing bystander, it probably would have looked like an innocent twitch. But I could practically feel the gust of air that the motion of his head produced. And it nearly knocked me over.

Everything became very clear in that moment. Jamie had lost faith in me. Long before he'd ever decided to set me up. Long before he'd ever sent someone pretending to be Julie Bleeker into my office. In the back of his mind, something told him that I would let him down. And he had planned accordingly.

Knowing that the person you love has taken out an insurance policy on your relationship is like a sucker punch in the stomach. It happens just as fast, and it knocks the wind right out of you upon impact.

"Okay," I said quietly to the back of Jamie's head as he continued to face away from me. "If that's what you want."

And then I slowly turned back around and took broad, zigzagging paces toward my bedroom, making sure to cover every square inch of the wide-open, unrestricted hallway. Just to prove to myself that those boxes would not be missed. That I *did* need every speck of space the original floor plan had provided. Even though, deep down, I knew it was a lie.

I shut the bedroom door behind me and slid to the ground, hugging my knees to my chest and crying uncontrollably into the small crevice between my kneecaps.

When I finally peeled myself off the floor an hour later and reluctantly tiptoed down the dark, deserted path into the living room, Jamie was gone.

And as it had in the hallway, his absence left an empty space far too big for just one person to live in.

22

moldy expectations

When I didn't show up to work the next morning, my phone started ringing. But I didn't answer. Eventually, by nighttime I simply shut off the ringer. I knew I had a whole schedule full of people waiting to hear the fate of their relationships. But I didn't care. I found it hard to care about anything at this point. Especially when the fate of my own relationship was so dismally grim.

Plus, I really couldn't bring myself to get off the couch. I just lay there for three days straight, with my head on my pillow and my heart lying in a million shattered pieces on the floor. Sometimes I would watch TV, but most of the time I would just stare numbly at the wall or the ceiling.

Once again, I was alone.

Which ironically was exactly how I always imagined my life to be before I met him. Alone but never lonely. Single but never desperate. Unmarried but never unhappy.

But now I felt nothing but loneliness, desperation, and over-whelming unhappiness.

Which only made me convinced that I was better off not know-ing him at all. Better off just living my life the way I always thought I would live it.

By Sunday, I had reached an all-time low. Four days and no con-tact with the outside world. I had consumed just about everything in

my fridge. Or at least I had tried. Half-eaten evidence of my unsuc-
cessful attempts to nourish myself were lying scattered throughout
the room. I had no doubt that some of the more perishable items
were now growing layers of mold, but the thought of doing any actual cleaning made me want to lie down and take another nap.
Which was exactly what I did.

It was around seven on Sunday evening when a key turned in the
lock and the bolt on my front door twisted.

"Oh. Sweet. Lord," was John's appalled reaction to my current
living arrangements. Then he glanced behind him and announced,
"She's alive!"

I barely even turned my head as John, Zoë, and Sophie all filed
into my living room thanks to the use of Sophie's spare key.

Sophie was hardly through the front door before she was up in
arms. "So first you *faint* at my wedding, then you don't even call me to
welcome me back from my honeymoon, and *then* I call you for three
straight days and get nothing. I thought you were dead, Jen. Seriously.
I thought the bump on your head got infected and you died of pneu-
monia in your sleep."

I rolled my eyes and pressed the back of my head hard into the
pillow. "Go away," I muttered.

"What is the matter with you?" Sophie said, still exasperated as
she eyed my disheveled appearance.

John came and sat on the couch, instantly regretting his decision
to get that close to me. "Ugh, you stink!" he shouted, holding his
nose dramatically, as if he were driving past a manure farm.

Zoë glanced around the room, taking in the used Kleenex, dirty,
food-crusted plates, and overall disaster that had become my living
room. "And this place is disgusting. Did your maid quit on you or
something?"

I grabbed a throw pillow from the floor and smashed it into my
face. "No," I mumbled, my voice muffled. "Jamie did."

It took my friends a good ten seconds to fully understand what I
had just told them. I couldn't see their faces because my head was
still buried in the pillow, but I recognized Sophie's reaction first. It

was a strange combination of a gasp mixed with a strangled cry. *"What?"*

"What the fuck are you talking about?" That was Zoë.

John's reaction came last. "He *quit* on you?"

I removed the pillow and tossed it off to the side. "Yes, okay. He's gone. It's over. No more engagement. No more anything."

Sophie ran to me and cradled my head awkwardly in her arms. "Jen, oh my God. Tell me what happened."

I couldn't look any of them in the eye. But with Sophie sitting to my left, Zoë hovering over the couch to my right, and John planted firmly by my feet, there was really nowhere else to look but straight up in the air. Back at the ceiling. A familiar landscape for me these days.

"I broke my promise to him," I said vacantly. "I took on an assignment. Well, technically it was two, but the second one turned out to be a setup."

Sophie twisted her face in confusion. "What do you mean, a setup?"

"I mean, he suspected I would start taking on assignments again, and so he sent some woman into my office to request a fidelity inspection and for *me* to conduct it. I guess he always thought I wouldn't be able to resist the chance to get back into the game again. And apparently I couldn't, because I said yes and I went. And Jamie was there waiting for me."

"But that's entrapment!" Zoë protested.

I shrugged in response. There wasn't a day that went by that someone didn't accuse my agency of entrapment. And I denied it until I was blue in the face. Every single time. But the truth of the matter is, it doesn't really matter what it is or what you call it. I still failed. And now I had to live with the consequences. End of story.

"But why did you do it?" Sophie's voice was strangled. Troubled, even. I looked up at her and could see the struggle in her eyes. She wanted so badly to be on my side. To support me through my hardship, because as my best friend, that's what her job description required of her. But I could tell from the look on her face that it was no longer a simple task.

I launched into an explanation about Vegas and Shawna and the arrest and Benjamin Connors's inspection. I told them about Darcie Connors's visit to my office, the things she said to me, and how her gratitude had made me feel whole again. And right about then was when fake Julie Bleeker came to see me.

Then I fell silent. And I let the weight of my words sink in. Not only for them . . . but for me. Somehow, narrating it all in sequence like that made everything seem so transparent. As if I were somehow destined to be lying here on this couch with Jamie no longer in the picture and my friends doing their best to console me.

As if this whole chain of events had somehow been inevitable.

"I don't know," I whispered, answering some unspoken question in the room. "All I've ever wanted to do was help people. Offer them the truth. I guess I just wasn't capable of letting someone else do it for me. I guess that just wasn't enough for me."

I glanced up at Sophie, trying to gauge her reaction to all of this. But she wouldn't even look at me. My answer to her question hadn't facilitated her plight to comfort me.

I could feel the disappointment emanating off of her, and I knew that I had let her down. Because in her eyes, I had always been above this. My history and my past and everything that I'd seen in my life had put me on some type of moral pedestal. And now I had fallen off of it.

No. Worse. I had jumped.

I looked to John and Zoë, who thankfully appeared to still be on my team.

"Well, what did he say when you explained all that to him?" Zoë asked, perching herself atop the back of the couch and looking down at me.

I shook my head and closed my eyes against the pain of reliving that night. But in the blackness, the memories were only stronger and more vivid. Replaying against the backdrop of my eyelids, like a projector blasting the images onto a blank screen in a darkened room.

"He said I chose my job over him. That I would rather expose someone else's unfaithfulness than stay faithful to him."

As soon as the words left my mouth, I felt myself waiting for the refutation. For someone to tell me that was crazy, ludicrous, and totally untrue. Maybe not Sophie, but John or at the very least Zoë. Someone was going to defend me. Someone was going to take my side on this.

But none of them said anything. They all just kind of looked at one another, completely speechless. I suppose they didn't really have to say anything.

I used every ounce of what was left of my strength to push myself up and prop myself against the arm of the couch. "You think that, too, don't you?" I accused all of them, glaring from one person to the next. But they all avoided my eyes. "You think I sacrificed my relationship with Jamie for my job."

Zoë was the first to speak. And she was uncharacteristically gentle. "Well, you kind of did, Jen."

My eyes widened, and I immediately shot a look of disbelief at John and Sophie. They both nodded their confirmations.

"I mean," Sophie began, "you broke your promise to Jamie to help a client. Is there really any other way to categorize that?"

I immediately opened my mouth to protest, but nothing came out. So I quickly closed it again. As much as I might have wanted to fight the accusation to the death, I couldn't seem to find a valid argument to fight with.

Maybe Jamie and my friends were right. Maybe I *did* choose my agency over my relationship. After all, I had managed to convince myself that breaking my promise to Jamie was less important than keeping my promise to Darcie Connors. Or to the fictional Julie Bleeker, for that matter.

On that fateful night in Vegas, when the choice came down to giving Darcie Connors the answers she was looking for and keeping my word to Jamie, I chose Darcie. And although the guilt immediately overwhelmed me from the moment the decision was made, I soon realized what a gift I had been able to give her. And then I never looked back.

Worst of all, I was willing to do it all over again.

So what did that mean? And what kind of person did that make me?

Three years ago, I had made a vow to help people. And I had forsaken everything else to keep that vow. But then one day I decided I didn't want to live that life anymore. That I wanted to be Jennifer Hunter and nobody else. So I made another vow. This time, to someone else. Someone I loved. But when push came to shove, I had forsaken one vow for the other.

I was never meant to be a wife. Like the plates of half-eaten food scattered across my living room, that was a title I could never fully digest. My destiny had always been a fidelity inspector. And those two roles would never coexist.

I didn't need a law degree to recognize that all the evidence thus far had been leading to one conclusion. And it was a conclusion that I never wanted to face, but one that Jamie ultimately sensed regardless.

"I never wanted to get married." I said the words aloud. Not because I needed my friends to hear them, but because *I* needed to hear them. It was a truth that would never be fully accepted until it was freed from the deep, hidden corners of my subconscious.

John, Zoë, and Sophie exchanged worried glances. "You don't really mean that," Sophie asserted, grabbing my hand and giving it an anxious squeeze.

"I do." I turned my head and looked into her panicked eyes. "I was never like you, Sophie. My happily ever after never looked like yours. I was always content being alone. And I will be again someday. After I get through this, I'll be fine."

Sophie shook her head adamantly. "No," she insisted. "Where's the ring?"

I sighed. "It's still in the top drawer of my dresser from when I went on that last assignment. I spent more time hiding it than I did wearing it."

"You two will work this out. I know it. You'll apologize and he'll take you back and you'll be engaged again." Sophie's eyes were starting to brim with tears, and she stared at me with such intensity that I almost feared she might take longer to mourn this breakup than I would.

I cracked a gentle smile as I squeezed her hand back. "I don't think so, Soph."

"You're just saying that because you're upset!"

I slowly shook my head. "No, you guys were right. You were absolutely right. I did choose this job over Jamie. Because it's always been more than just a job. It's been my life's work. My quest. And clearly, it hasn't been fulfilled yet."

23

un-retired

These were the words that finally got me off the couch and back into the office on Monday morning. Not lagging, not disheartened, not even with puffy eyes and a red nose. No, when I strutted through the double glass doors of the agency that I *owned,* that I *founded,* that I poured my heart and soul into, I felt renewed and energized. I felt as though a weight had been lifted and a roadblock had been removed. After a year of detours and wrong-ways and trying to convince myself that the bumpiness in the road was normal, I had finally made it back to the path I was meant to walk on.

Hadley jumped to her feet the moment she saw me, shock and awe spray-painted across her face. "Ashlyn! You're here! Oh my God, are you all right? I didn't know where you were. I didn't know how to reach you. I don't have any number but your cell, and it was shut off. I was going to go to the police and fill out a missing persons report, but Lauren told me Ashlyn wasn't even your real name."

I shook my head. "It's not. And I'm sorry about that. I didn't mean to scare you. I had a little personal emergency that I had to deal with. I should have called. I apologize."

She continued to gape at me as if she didn't really believe it was actually me standing there, but maybe a femme bot dressed like me with a voice that sounded surprisingly human.

"So," I said, standing in front of her desk. "I'm assuming there were messages while I was out."

Hadley broke from her trance and sprang into action, gathering stacks of pink message slips from her desk and forming them into a neat pile. "After you didn't show up on Thursday, I was going to start canceling all your appointments because I didn't know when"—she gulped—"or *if* you were ever coming back. But Lauren kind of just took over while you were gone. She told me not to cancel anyone and that she would take your place and meet with the clients until you got back."

"Excellent," I said, feeling proud of my associate's initiative. It felt good to know that I had such loyal, trustworthy, responsible people working for me. That I could have a meltdown and the agency wouldn't fall apart. "Well, you can call her and let her know that I'm back."

Hadley glanced anxiously at me and then in the direction of my office. "Actually, she's in there now. You can tell her yourself." Then she jumped to add, "Or I could buzz her!"

I laughed at her ever endearing eagerness. "It's fine, Hadley. I'll go in and tell her myself. Thanks for these." I held up my stack of messages.

"You're welcome," she replied after a moment of stunned silence. She still couldn't quite believe I was there. And just before I left, she mumbled timidly, "Um, what *is* your real name, by the way?"

But I simply smiled in response and continued down the hallway.

Lauren seemed significantly less surprised to see me. When I walked in the room, she just flashed me this knowing smile, as if she knew it was only a matter of time before I took care of whatever mess was keeping me from the office.

"Welcome back," she said, rising from my chair and offering it to me.

"Thanks," I replied, taking a seat as Lauren pulled out her PDA and began catching me up on everything I had missed.

"A girl named Lexi Garrett keeps calling. Hadley says she wanted you to test her father, but you refused."

"Yes, she calls about once a week to see if I've changed my mind."

Lauren tapped on her screen with a stylus. "Katie called earlier this morning. She wrapped up everything at the Stantons' on Friday night."

"So I assume Dean Stanton finally failed his inspection?"

Lauren nodded. "It appears so, but Katie wasn't overly forthcoming on the phone. She assured me she'd give us all the 'juicy deets' at the staff meeting tomorrow."

I rolled my eyes. "After nearly a month, they better be juicy."

Lauren laughed, then continued with her debriefing. "These are the new client bios from the meetings I took last week." She placed her hand gingerly on a stack of crisp new crimson folders. "I was going to start formulating the assignment details for them this week, but I guess you can handle that now that you're back."

"Okay," I replied, visibly impressed by her diligence.

"And these," Lauren continued, indicating another neatly stacked pile of folders, "are the clients that have already been given the results of their assignments and are ready to be entered into the database."

"Great."

Lauren clapped her hands together definitively. "And I think that's it."

"Thanks," I replied, exhaling. "You did an excellent job keeping this place running. I really appreciate it."

"You're welcome."

I had pretty much prepared myself for an entire week of working frantically to get back on track, with many apologetic phone calls to clients and a mountain of unattended paperwork to sort through. It was a relief to come back to such organization.

It only made me that much more eager and excited about my decision to get back in the game and continue doing what I loved most. And now the agency had one more full-time associate to add to its repertoire.

After lunch, I finally got around to listening to all the messages that had accumulated on my cell phone during the four days that I had it shut off. There were seven from Sophie, ten from Hadley, three or four apiece from John and Zoë telling me to call Sophie so she would stop calling them asking if they'd heard from me, two from Willa Cruz, and one from my dad. It was the one he had left that night at the W Hotel. I had never gotten around to listening to it.

In the message, he asked me to call him back so that we could "chat." I didn't know what that meant, but I did know that I didn't feel like "chatting." Especially because at some point in the conversation, I would have to mention that Jamie was no longer in the picture, and then ten minutes later I would undoubtedly get a frantic phone call from my mother demanding to know if this was some kind of sick joke. And *that* was a conversation I wanted to have even less.

After work, I drove straight to Sophie's house. She had asked that I come over to look at honeymoon photos, and I had happily agreed. Not because I was looking forward to listening to Sophie's five-minute captions for each of her three thousand photos (ever since the invention of the digital camera and the two-gigabyte memory card, Sophie's photo presentations had become especially brutal), but because the thought of returning home to an empty house made my stomach cramp.

"Hey," Sophie greeted me warily as she swung the door open wide. "How are you feeling?"

I shrugged. "Better now that I'm back at work."

She seemed disappointed by this response. I'm pretty sure she was still hoping to find a basket case on the other side of her front door. "You know," she warned in her motherly tone, "you can't just distract yourself until the pain goes away. Sooner or later, you're going to have to deal with it."

I rolled my eyes and walked past her into the living room. "I *am* dealing with it."

She pouted behind me. "Not in a healthy way, though!"

I plopped down on the sofa and crossed my arms over my chest. "Can we just look at the pictures already?"

Sophie sat beside me and shot me a disapproving look. "Okay, but I also have some wedding proofs to show you. The sunset shots came out really good, and they might even change . . ." She stopped the sentence abruptly in its tracks. I got the feeling she hadn't meant to say that last part aloud.

"They might change my mind?" I ventured. Although it wasn't exactly a *wild* guess, as it didn't take much effort to get to the bottom of Sophie's schemes. I'm sure she had spent the entire day fantasizing about flaunting her beautiful wedding and honeymoon photos, and then I would magically leave here a different person. A changed person. The kind of person who wants nothing more than to be married and have a honeymoon of my own.

"Sophie, you know I would love to see the proofs from your wedding, but I'm not going to change what I want out of life just because of a bunch of sunset snapshots. So don't get your hopes up."

Sophie slouched in her seat. "Fine. But I know you'll come around eventually." She stood up and nodded toward the kitchen. "Wine?"

I nodded eagerly. "Yes, please." It was the most promising thing she'd said since I'd walked through the door.

Sophie disappeared into the kitchen to get the wine, and I glanced around the living room, taking in the new decorations and presumable wedding gifts that had materialized since the last time I was here. "Where's Eric?" I called out to her.

Sophie emerged carrying two glasses and a bottle of Merlot. "He's working the late shift at the hospital. He won't be home until after midnight." She motioned to the wine in her hands. "Red okay?"

I nodded. "Yeah, red's fine."

Sophie filled each glass to the top and handed one to me.

"Okay," she said, positioning herself on the floor and pressing a button on the digital camera that was rigged up to the TV. "You are going to *love* these pictures."

The screen immediately illuminated with a picture of Sophie and Eric standing in front of a gate at LAX with the word *Athens* displayed on the destination sign behind them. "John said he might stop by later, too," Sophie informed me. "But I didn't want to wait for him. So we can just do the whole slide show again when he gets here."

I took a much-needed swig of my wine and smiled. "What about Zoë? Is she coming?"

Sophie groaned and shook her head. "No, she's off with her mystery man again. Of course, she didn't tell me that. I just assumed as much when her excuse for not coming was, 'I'm going to the ballet.' Like Zoë would ever be caught dead going to the ballet. I swear, ever since she started dating that guy, she's gotten really weird."

"Yeah," I agreed. "But I'm sure she'll tell us about him in her own time."

Sophie shrugged. "I guess." And then she caught sight of a photograph on the screen, and her mind instantly switched gears. "So, anyway, this is us boarding the plane." Her avid enthusiasm, in contrast with her blatant disapproval of Zoë's recent behavior, was actually somewhat comical.

"The flight to Athens was superlong and boring," she continued animatedly. "Funny story, actually. So when we first got to the airport . . ."

Forty-five minutes later, we were just finishing up day two (of twelve) and I was already on my third glass of requisite wine. John had arrived shortly after me, and we were now both staring at a life-size photograph of a donkey's ass while listening to another winded narrative about their treacherous trek up to the top of some Greek mountain (evidently via donkey).

After about the tenth picture in a row of a house resembling a white sugar cube, John had had enough. "Okay, time for a break. Who needs more wine?"

He jumped off the couch and fetched another bottle from the kitchen. He popped the cork and diligently made his rounds to refill our glasses. I held mine up as he poured and attempted to make small talk. "So how was your first day back at work?"

I shrugged. "Pretty calm. I thought it was going to be hectic, but one of my associates did an awesome job of stepping in and taking over for me while I was gone."

"Uh-huh, uh-huh, that's nice. So what's the latest? Tell me all the juicy gossip."

My face was deadpan. "There is no juicy gossip."

But John wasn't having any of it. "There's *always* juicy gossip in your line of work."

I surrendered a sigh. "What do you want to know?"

John pondered my question gravely, as if his answer were going to decide the fate of a nation. "Hmm. Just tell me about the juiciest assignment you've seen lately. Besides the one where Jamie showed up."

"John," Sophie warned, tossing him a look. "Besides, I don't want to hear about cheating spouses. It's depressing."

I flashed her an empathetic look. "Tell me about it."

John stomped his foot like a petulant child. "Come on. You know I live vicariously through you!"

I leaned back against the couch and shook my head with a laugh. "Fine. Katie just got done posing as a nanny in someone's home because the client was certain that her husband had slept with all their former nannies. How's that for juicy?"

John arched one eyebrow and took a sip of his wine. "This is good. This is very good. Katie is the cute blond one, right?"

"Yes."

"Got it. Keep going," he urged.

But I shrugged. "There's really not much else to say."

He grunted, clearly irritated. "Details, Jen. Give me details! Did he fail?"

"Yes," I admitted reluctantly. "He did fail. But I won't know any more details until tomorrow."

"Ha!" John practically celebrated in his seat. "I knew it. They *always* fail."

"That's awful!" Sophie whined. "John, these are real people, not TV shows. His wife is devastated right now. Show some respect."

"What?" John replied defensively, feigning innocence. "It's not like I know her." Then his head jerked toward me. "Do I know her?"

I shrugged and sipped my wine. "Probably not. But you might know *him*. Apparently he's some kind of celebrity."

As soon as the words left my mouth, I regretted them. It was like slicing my finger open in front of a hungry shark. John was immediately thrown into a tizzy, jumping up on his knees and leaning toward me menacingly. "Oh my God, you *have* to tell me! I promise I won't tell. I swear to God, Krishna, Buddha, whoever!"

"No."

"Jenny!" he groveled shamelessly. *"Please!"*

"No."

Sophie giggled. "Okay, now I'm a little curious."

"See," John insisted, pointing at Sophie. "Even Prude Pants over here wants to know."

I set my wineglass on the table and crossed my arms over my chest. "If I tell you his name, John, you cannot tell *anyone*."

He drew an X over his heart. "Cross my heart and hope to die."

"Not your mother, not your shrink, not your gay lover of the week. *No one*."

He nodded. "I got it. Not a soul."

I sighed. "His name is Dean Stanton. He's the head of New Edge Cinema. And apparently, he sleeps with his nannies."

I half expected John to explode right out of his skin. But when I looked over at him, he was unusually quiet and pensive.

"What?" I teased. "Not the big celebrity you were hoping for? I'm sorry it wasn't Brad Pitt. Next time I'll try harder to impress you."

But he just shook his head absentmindedly and continued to stare off into space with a disturbing look on his face. "When did he fail the inspection?" he asked, his voice suddenly calm and serious.

"Friday," I replied, keeping a wary eye on him. "Why?"

But John just shrugged. "No reason."

"John," I stated in a warning tone, "what's the matter?"

He let out a little snort and looked at me as if I were going crazy. "Nothing."

"You're going to keep your word." It was more of a threat than a confirmation. "Because if this ends up in the tabloids next week, I *am* going to kill you, you know?"

He laughed at this. "I'm not going to tell anyone. Relax." And then before I could question him further, he turned to Sophie and said, "So are we going to finish this slide show or what?"

Sophie was more than willing to oblige and immediately launched into day three of Operation Honeymoon. But it was hard for me to concentrate on the photographs that filled the screen or the verbose stories that accompanied them. I kept stealing subtle glances in John's direction, trying to figure out what was going on in that scheming little brain of his. But I knew it was a pointless undertaking.

Eventually, I relinquished the battle and downed the rest of my wine, quick to pour myself another as Sophie reached day four. I swiftly finished that one off as well. And by the time the final Athens skyline flashed off the TV screen, I was completely inebriated and in no condition to drive.

John and Sophie helped me out of my business suit and into one of Sophie's T-shirts and a pair of ratty nineties-style sweatpants that she'd had since college. John headed home, muttering something about having work to do, and Sophie set me up with a pillow and blanket on the sofa. She kissed me tenderly on the forehead as if she were tucking in a child who'd played too hard on the playground that day and was now utterly exhausted and barely coherent.

Sleep came quickly for me that night, and I was relieved. Thankful that I no longer had the alcohol tolerance of a professional whiskey shooter. A year ago, that much wine never would have knocked me out like this. And I was grateful for small favors.

I knew there was no way I'd ever be able to admit to myself that I'd drunk too much on purpose. But I was happy nonetheless to be sleeping on someone else's couch for a change.

24

the blue pill

"Okay, first things first," I said, sliding into my chair at the head of the conference table the next morning. "I'd like to welcome back Katie from her extended tenure as the Stantons' live-in nanny."

Katie popped her strawberry bubble gum loudly. The smell of it wafting through the air was somewhat nostalgic. "Thanks, boss lady. It's good to be back. Did you miss me?"

I laughed politely. "Yes, you were definitely missed. Now why don't you tell us what happened at the Stantons'. I assume everything went smoothly since the last time we spoke."

"Yes," Katie replied confidently. "The nanny has officially left the building."

I smiled. "Good. What happened, exactly?"

Katie quickly launched into a long, dramatic telling of her nanny diaries and was careful not to leave out any excruciating detail about the "demon spawns" that she had to deal with on a daily basis and her expert opinion on how *not* to raise children.

"And so then Friday night," Katie was recounting, "Mrs. Stanton went to some charity fund-raiser event, and Dean claimed that he was feeling a little bit under the weather and opted to stay home. So after I had put the two monsters to bed, succumbed to all their demands for water, night-lights, action figures, and trips to the bathroom, I was just heading into my room when Dean asked if I wanted to watch a screening of a new film his company was releasing. Of course, I accepted his invitation and joined him on the couch, praying that he would finally make a move so that I wouldn't have to be there when the demon spawn woke up the next morning. And I guess my prayers were answered because about fifteen minutes into the movie—which was really bad, might I add. Just because you have access to a camcorder doesn't mean you should make movies." Katie paused a moment to grimace at the memory of her cinematic experience. "Anyway," she continued, giving her shoulder-length blond hair a toss, "about fifteen minutes in, I noticed he was starting to subtly inch his way closer to me. And I had to struggle not to laugh because it was seriously so eighth grade. Then he kind of just leaned in and kissed me, and not long after that, he was climbing on top of me."

I nodded patiently as she spoke, all the while taking detailed notes so that I could report the entire story back to Melissa Stanton when she undoubtedly paid me a visit this week. "Okay, so then how did you end it?"

Katie just shrugged. "I didn't have to, actually. She did."

I stopped writing and looked up at her. "What do you mean, 'she did'?"

"I mean, Mrs. Stanton came home and caught us in the act."

And immediately I stopped writing and put down my pen. Apparently, I wouldn't have to relay the details of the evening to her after all. She had already come face-to-face with the hard truth herself. "Really?"

Katie chomped ferociously on her gum and pulled her knees up onto the chair. "Yep. Personally, I don't think she even went to the charity thingy. I think she was just tired of paying to keep me around when I clearly knew nothing about child rearing and was giving her husband the opportunity to do what she already knew he would do. She was probably waiting outside the window the entire time. A little creepy, if you think about it, but hey, whatever the client wants, right?"

I glanced around the room. Everyone was fully engaged in Katie's story. Even Teresa had set down her latest issue of *Vogue* to listen in.

"So what happened after that?" Cameron asked, looking riveted.

I turned back to Katie. "I'm assuming you packed up and left at that point."

Katie smiled deviously. "Yes, and I wasn't the only one."

"She kicked him out?" Lauren joined in on what had now officially morphed into an interactive postassignment review.

Katie nodded, enjoying the attention. "Yep. He's staying at the Chateau Marmont as we speak." Then she looked at me and quickly added, "And the only reason I know this is because he whispered it to me as I was walking out the door, as if I might actually be interested in joining him there. I still don't think he knows it was a setup."

"Okay, then. I suppose that's that." I picked up a crimson folder from the stack in front of me and handed it to Katie. "Here's something new for you for this week."

"Let me guess," she conjectured sarcastically. "You've got me working at a doggie day care for the next six weeks."

I smiled. "Sorry to disappoint. It's just your run-of-the-mill happy hour this time. Adam Bennett likes to go out drinking with his male colleagues after work instead of coming home to his wife and kids. Meet him at their favorite bar tonight and find out what these so-called *work* functions consist of."

Katie breathed a sigh of relief. "Oh, thank God. Something normal for change."

I continued around the room for the next ten minutes, taking detailed notes on the outcomes of all the previous assignments and distributing folders with the details for the next ones.

For Shawna, I had scheduled the bachelor party of Graham Hawkins, a financial analyst from Arizona, who was getting married in two weeks and celebrating his last night as a single man with his closest friends in Hollywood this weekend. Lauren received an assignment in Toronto, Teresa was headed for the Hamptons, and Cameron was scheduled to start attending the same yoga class as Nick Warren's bored housewife.

By the time the meeting was over, I had successfully distributed all of the case files in front of me . . . with the exception of two.

These I had saved for myself.

After everyone had filed out the door and I was left alone in the empty conference room, I sat with the two glossy folders in front of me, fingering the tops of their smooth surfaces with my thumb.

"This is my choice," I said quietly to myself, picking up one of the folders and holding it between my fingers. "This is what I want to do. What I've always wanted to do."

I sat there for a few minutes, perfectly still, perfectly quiet, feeling the weight of my decision in my hand.

Then I got up, gathered my things, and headed out the door toward my office.

"Um, Ashlyn?" I heard Hadley's voice behind me, and I turned around to see her jogging to catch up with me. "There's actually someone here to see you."

"In my office?"

"No. In reception." She nudged her chin back in the direction of her desk. "She didn't have an appointment, so I told her she'd have to wait out here until you got out of your meeting."

I backtracked toward the reception area, genuinely intrigued. Mostly because when I'd passed by a second ago, I hadn't seen anyone out there except Hadley.

And I soon realized why.

The person who was waiting for me wasn't as tall as most of the visitors who entered this office. In fact, her head barely cleared the top of Hadley's desk. It was no wonder her four-foot-ten-inch frame had gone unnoticed when I'd stepped out of the conference room.

"Lexi Garrett . . ." I sighed as she stood up to greet me. "So nice to see you again." I made no attempt to inject my words with sincerity.

She shifted the weight of her backpack on her shoulders. "You're a bad liar, you know that?"

I nodded. "So I've been told. What are you doing here?"

She held up a tiny square piece of blue plastic, no bigger than a guitar pick. "I told you I'd be back when I had proof."

"A piece of plastic."

She rolled her eyes and let out an impatient sigh. "It's an SD card. I stole it from my dad's phone. Well, after I transferred his schedule for this weekend onto it." She looked mighty proud of herself as she described her Nancy Drew escapades. "I was trying to get to all of his scandalous midnight text messages, but apparently he's too smart to leave those on his phone. But he's going to Palm Springs with his friends this weekend for a 'golfing trip.'" She drenched these two words with so much skepticism, it almost sounded as though she doubted the authenticity of the words themselves. As if "golfing" and "trip" probably weren't even in an official English dictionary.

She slung her backpack off one shoulder, unzipped the top compartment, and pulled out a single piece of white paper, placing it atop the stack of items in my arm with a firm pat. "I printed out a copy for you. It's the perfect time and place for my dad's fidelity inspection."

Hadley was observing this exchange from behind her desk with great interest. When I glanced up at her, she quickly dropped her head and pretended to be absorbed in paperwork.

I reached out and placed a tender hand on Lexi's shoulder. "Honey, I'm not going to send someone to test your father. I'm sorry. If you're really that worried about your dad's behavior, you should talk to your mother."

"I'm not leaving here until you agree to take on my case," she grumbled as she planted herself back into one of the waiting-room chairs.

I raised my eyebrows. "And what happens when you don't come home for dinner, won't your mom get worried?"

Lexi grunted and crossed her arms over her chest, attempting to make some kind of statement. As though she were sitting in for gay rights or something.

I simply sighed and turned back in the direction of my office. If my fourteen-year-old niece, Hannah, had taught me anything about kids her age, it's that they thankfully have very short attention spans. And I fully expected her to be gone by lunchtime.

What I *wasn't* expecting, however—and what I never could have predicted in a million years, despite my knack for making predictions—was for my cell phone to ring at two-fifteen that afternoon and for Jamie's name to appear on the caller ID.

I held the phone in my hand and stared helplessly at the screen for a good five seconds, not knowing whether I was supposed to answer it or just let it go to voice mail.

I had already made the decision to move on. That was a done deal. But I was still desperate to know why he was calling. What if he wanted to apologize? What if he thought he had overreacted and wanted to work things out between us? How would I respond to that? Would I even *want* to work through it?

In the end, my curiosity got the better of me and I decided to answer the call. But by the time I came to grips with my decision, the phone had stopped ringing.

The voice mail chime dinged a few moments later, and I immediately jabbed my finger against the "Listen" button on the screen.

The voice mail lady announced the message with her usual introduction. Time, date, etc., and then Jamie's voice came on the line. The first thing I did was try to categorize his tone. "Hesitant" was the only word I could come up with that seemed to fit.

"Hey there, it's, um . . . me. Jamie. I just wanted to let you know that I was planning on stopping by your place later on today. Maybe around four."

My pulse quickened and my death grip around the phone tightened until I could swear my fingers were bleeding. I pressed it even closer to my ear as I drew in another breath.

Jamie's *hesitant* message continued. "I still have a few things there. Some clothes in the closet and, um, some stuff in the bathroom. I figured it would be easier if I picked them up while you were at work. Please let me know if this is a problem. Otherwise, I'll assume that it's fine. Oh, and I'll leave the key behind when I go. Okay, well . . . bye." There was an awkward pause, and then he added, "Take care," as if the "well . . . bye" wasn't painful enough. Then the line clicked.

Well, I guess that answered the question of whether or not he wanted to get back together.

After being in a relationship for more than a year, things belonging to the other person automatically start to accumulate around the house—most of the time without you even realizing it. A DVD on top of the television, a few books on the shelf, coffee mugs in the kitchen cabinet. These things don't necessarily stick out as foreign or out of place; they sort of just naturally assimilate into the environment, blending in effortlessly over time, until you forget whom they initially belonged to.

Which is why I couldn't even *picture* the stuff he was referring to. After the boxes disappeared from the hallway and his clothes disappeared from my closet, there was nothing left that particularly stood out in my mind as uniquely *his*. But I knew that the moment I walked through the front door later that night, the absence of those items would call out to me like a spotlight in a dark room, drawing my attention to the empty spaces that had once housed all evidence of my life as half of a couple. And those vociferous voids would insist on being acknowledged, forcing me to recognize the fact that no matter what I tried to fill those empty spaces with, it would never replace what had been there.

I listened to the voice mail lady ask me what I wanted to do with the message. Apparently, there were only two options, delete it or save it for later. When I didn't respond right away, she repeated the question. I knew that her voice hadn't changed—that it was just a computer program designed to sound like a human being—but the second time around, she sounded just the slightest bit more persistent.

And I suddenly felt as though it wasn't just the voice mail she was asking me to delete.

I was struck with an overwhelming influx of emotion that seemed to be oscillating between sadness and anger. And since the two felt so inherently different, I had trouble deciding which one to feel at any given second.

As more tears fell down my face, contrasted darkly by the fuming smoke I was sure was coming out of my ears, I searched for something to erase it all. Something that would dull both emotions. A magic pill that would swallow it all down to a place where I couldn't feel it anymore.

I glanced around my office and was immediately reminded of my purpose for being here. The very reason all of this marriage stuff wasn't meant for me. Because let's be honest here, you can't break up

relationships by day and try to keep one together by night. Somewhere along the line, you're going to run into . . . well, *this*.

Then my eyes fell upon something in the trash under my desk. It
was the printout Lexi Garrett had handed me earlier that morning.
The details of her dad's scheduled trip to Palm Springs. I had thrown
it out the moment I'd entered my office. And before my mind was
given the opportunity to start dissecting everything all over again, I
sprang into action. I pressed the number 7 on my cell phone and
listened as the voice mail lady confirmed my irrevocable decision:
"Message deleted."

Then I dropped the cell phone on my desk and buzzed Hadley
over the intercom. I didn't even bother with a greeting after she answered. I simply said, "Is Lexi Garrett still out there?"

Hadley sighed. "Yes. I've tried to talk some sense into her, but she
won't leave."

"That's okay," I replied hurriedly. "Would you please send her
in?"

There was a baffled silence on the other end, and then Hadley
confirmed, "Into your office?"

"Yes," I replied. "Tell her I've changed my mind."

She didn't respond right away, and I had a feeling she was taking
some time formulating a reply. Or maybe a round of questions to
verify my sanity. But I didn't want to take the chance that whatever
she came up with might cause me to second-guess my decision, so I
quickly added, "Tell her I'll take on her dad's assignment myself,"
and then shut off the intercom.

I grappled for a half-empty, week-old bottle of SmartWater that
was left on my desk and downed the last of it in one ferocious gulp.
Praying that the imaginary pill I had just swallowed was strong
enough to do what I needed it to do.

25

---

a twelve-year-old's intuition

I wasn't looking forward to testing Lexi Garrett's father. And I went back and forth several times on my decision to take on the case. But I finally convinced myself that there was no harm in finding out the truth about Dustin Garrett's intentions. If he passed the inspection, then there was nothing more to do. And then at least I could put this little girl's fears to rest by assuring her that her father is a devoted, caring, and loyal husband to her mother. Something I wish I could have been assured of at age twelve. Hell, at any age, really. On the other hand, if he failed the inspection, at least I could offer his wife some valuable information that she otherwise would never have known.

So after much deliberation and a short fifty-minute flight into the desert, I found myself standing in front of the bathroom mirror of my hotel room in the Hyatt Grand Champions Resort in Palm Springs. The same hotel where Dustin Garrett and his buddies were shacked up for an innocent weekend of golf, martinis, and cigars. Or so Dustin had told his wife and two children.

I suppose I would deliver the final verdict on the accurateness of the word *innocent*.

I finished applying a coat of jet black eyeliner around the inside of my lower lid and touched up my mascara. Tonight I was wearing a vapor gray strapless dress that fell to just above my knees and strappy black Manolos.

I adjusted the bobby pins that were holding my sophisticated updo in place, then took one final glance in the mirror before grabbing my hotel room key and my bag and heading out the door.

As I walked down the hallway toward the elevator, I felt confident and self-assured. My legs glided steadily underneath me as if they already knew exactly where to go, what to do, how to cross. Tonight marked my first official assignment as an unretired, unattached, full-time fidelity inspector. But the way my body moved and my head stayed clear and focused, it felt as though I had never left. I had spent almost a year sitting behind that desk, watching as my five trustworthy associates took on assignment after assignment, and I'd actually managed to convince myself that the life I had traded in was a good exchange. I'd *actually* thought that I was done with this lifestyle for good. But really, it was only a temporary vacation. A short hiatus. A brief diversion thrown at me for the sole purpose of being able to realize for myself who I really am. And finally come to terms with what I'm supposed to be doing.

As the elevator doors slid open and I stepped inside, I was overcome with a familiar sensation. As if I were stepping onto a stage, assuming the role that I had been hired to play. A role that had been designed specifically for Dustin Garrett.

Tonight I would no longer be Jennifer Hunter, I would be known only as Ashlyn, an overworked executive assistant, traveling with her boss on business and trying to get away for a few hours of relaxation and a strong martini.

Everything felt natural. Instinctive, almost. Not forced and artificial like so many of the emotions I had felt with Jamie in the last couple of months. I knew that I was made to do this. Made to walk into that hotel bar. Made to follow Dustin Garrett's lead until I had reached a solid conclusion about the man I was about to encounter.

When I exited the elevator and made my way into the lounge, I searched the room for a group of early-forty-something guys who looked as if they were enjoying a weekend retreat away from their everyday wives . . . I mean, *lives*. Lexi had e-mailed me a photograph of her father, but as for the rest of the men on this trip, I was completely in the dark.

When I didn't spot them right away, I decided to head for the bar and take a seat. It would be easier (and less suspicious-looking) if I continued to survey the room from there. Lexi had sworn she had overheard her father on the phone saying that they would be grabbing a drink at the hotel bar before their eight P.M. dinner reservation. I checked my watch: It was almost seven-thirty. But then again, all of my intelligence had come from a person whose generation considered Facebook their primary news source. I decided to give it until eight before I modified my strategy.

The bar was fairly crowded. After I had ordered my martini, I swiveled around in my chair so I could get a better view of the clientele. I took a sip of my drink, knowing full well that I would have to pace myself if I was ever going to get through a night of drinking with a bunch of middle-aged golf buddies. I supposed it was time to start building up my tolerance again.

As I sipped, I systematically scanned each of the tables in the room, numbering them in my head from left to right and making mental notes. It was the game I always used to play when waiting for a subject to show up.

Table 1: Middle-aged married couple. Probably celebrating a relationship milestone. Fifteen-year anniversary, maybe twenty.

Table 2: Two young men in their late twenties. One straight, one pretending to be straight. The man on the right has no idea that his friend is gay. Nor does he know that his friend will do just about anything to hook up with him.

Table 3: Girls' night out. Six total. Possibly a bachelorette party. But without the visual confirmation of a white veil or any other conventionally identifying bridal trademarks, it's difficult to be certain.

Table 4: Early-forty-something male with embarrassingly younger (looking) female. With her back facing me, exact age is only a guess at this point. But given her hairstyle (long and blond), dress choice (tight and pink), and body type (thin and shapely), my guess is mid- to late twenties.

Table 5: Mother and daughter bonding . . .

Wait a minute.

I suddenly stopped and jerked my head back a few inches to Table

4. As I glimpsed past the blonde in the tightly fitted pink dress and focused my attention on the man she was with, I narrowed in on his gray dress shirt, black slacks, and half-empty wineglass sitting in front of him. Why did he look so familiar? Did I know him from somewh—

Oh, God.

My eyes widened and my jaw almost dropped to the floor. I could only imagine how I must have looked to everyone else in the room, staring . . . no, *gawking* at a perfect stranger on the other side of the room.

But that was just the thing. He *wasn't* a perfect stranger. I knew exactly who he was. That was Dustin Garrett! I was certain of it. I hadn't recognized him when I first walked in because I'd assumed he'd be with a large group of middle-aged men with beer guts hanging over their khaki golf pants. But that wasn't the context of this situation at all, was it?

He was with a woman. And from the looks of it, a young one at that.

Okay, I told myself as I forced my mouth shut and struggled to appear normal again. *Maybe she's just a friend. Or a work colleague. Or a manager at the hotel, and they're discussing the unsatisfactory condition of his room and how she's going to make it up to him.*

Just because a man is sitting at a table across from a blond woman nearly fifteen years younger than him doesn't automatically mean he's—

And just then, Dustin leaned in and rested his hand on the girl's leg as he whispered something in her ear. She started giggling flirtatiously, tipping her head back and letting her long blond hair cascade down her back in soft layers. Then, as he pulled away, he allowed his lips to playfully drag against the side of her neck. She grabbed his face in her hands and pulled him in for a deep kiss. When they finally broke apart, she reached out and seductively wiped her lip gloss from his bottom lip.

Okay, well, that settles it.

There was no way Dustin Garrett was here with a bunch of amateur golf players. That was clearly a ruse to get out of the house. These two had come here together. And judging by the girl's sultry designer dress and the hint of lingerie straps underneath, she had packed for the occasion. This was not a random meeting in a bar. This girl hadn't beaten me to the punch by just a few minutes—she had beaten me to the punch by at least a few weeks. If not more.

I spun my chair around and faced the bar again, taking a long, much less inhibited swallow from my martini glass and grimacing as the chilled, bitter liquid oozed down my throat. So Lexi Garrett was right. In fact, she was more right than she even knew. She had a feeling something was off, something wasn't right, and she assumed that her dad was *capable* of cheating on her mom. As it turns out, he had already been doing it. And for God knows how long.

I marveled once again at the keen perception of that little girl. How could she have known that? How could she have seen something that her mom has been missing for quite some time? She was supposed to be focusing on clothes and gossip and shirtless boy bands. She was not supposed to be worrying about things like this. And she was certainly not supposed to know about them.

But now she would have to know. I would have to tell her. Because she was, after all, the client. And although I had refused to take her money, no matter how much she'd persisted, she had still come to me for an answer, and therefore I was obliged to give it to her.

I took another sip of my drink.

But what if she didn't have to know? I speculated suddenly.

What if I refused to tell her and instead insisted that I break the news directly to Mrs. Garrett? Clearly, that would be the responsible way to handle this. She may have had the awareness of a ninety-year-old soul, but there was no way Lexi Garrett could know about her father's affair before her mother did. Or worse yet, bear the burden of having to *tell* her mother what she knew. I knew from first-hand experience that this was definitely not an age-appropriate responsibility to bestow upon a child.

I had to admit, though. As confident as I felt walking into this bar tonight, I was extremely relieved that I wouldn't have to go through with the assignment myself. The intention to cheat had apparently been confirmed long before I was even brought into the picture.

I downed the last of my drink and set down a twenty-dollar bill for the bartender. At least now I could enjoy a nice, relaxing evening on my own. I would order room service, take a hot bath, curl up in one of those fluffy white robes they hang on the bathroom door, and spend the night watching pay-per-view movies. And right now, nothing sounded more appealing.

I spun around on the chair and adjusted my dress as I stood up. Dustin Garrett would never even know that I was here, yet my presence tonight would undoubtedly change his life forever.

As I passed by Dustin's table on my way back to the lobby, I took one final glance in his direction. He and his date were gathering their belongings and preparing to leave. I checked my watch: It was five to eight. They were probably heading off to that eight o'clock reservation that Lexi had overheard him talking about. If only she had paid a bit more attention, she might have caught on to the fact that the reservation was only for two.

As the blonde in the pink dress slowly stood up and turned to pull her cream-colored pashmina off the back of her chair, I finally managed to get a glimpse of her face. And it was at that exact moment that she happened to glance in my direction as well.

Our eyes met and both our bodies froze, her cream pashmina slipping from her grasp and floating gracefully to the ground.

I could feel my legs start to give out beneath me, and I reached out to grab on to the nearest thing I could find to steady myself. It turned out to be the shoulder of a man in a dark suit. He looked up at me with a quizzical expression, but I didn't remove my hand. I feared that if I did, I might fall over.

To anyone else in the bar, it might have looked as though we were bitter enemies. Timeless adversaries. Having once divided the country into two equal and separate sections with the distinct understanding that she would never infiltrate my territory and I would never infiltrate hers. And now one of us had had broken that code and was standing in enemy territory.

But that couldn't have been further from the truth.

Because the woman standing in front of me in the fitted pink satin dress, ready to be whisked away to a romantic dinner with the man I had been hired to test, was not my enemy. She was one of my best friends.

And she had clearly been keeping a very dark secret from me.

26

---

friends in low places

"Zoë?" I finally managed to get out after my eyelids stopped blinking rapidly in utter disbelief. But the question mark in my voice wasn't for the purpose of verifying that it was really her. I knew it was her. She was standing right in front of me. And despite the fact that she *never* wore pink, or owned a dress that even remotely resembled the one she was wearing now, I recognized her right away. The question was directed more at her reason for being here. In this bar. In this city. With *this* man.

My subject.

"Jen?" she asked immediately in return, with seemingly the same motivation behind her punctuation. "What are you doing here?"

But I lobbed the question right back at her. "No, what are *you* doing here?"

She glanced anxiously between me and Dustin, clearly wondering how much I could possibly know and how much she should divulge as a result. "I'm here with my, um . . ." she stammered slightly. "My boyfriend."

"The one you refused to tell us about?"

She shifted her weight uneasily. "Uh, yeah."

"And now I know why," I stated, my voice blatantly accusatory.

Zoë hesitated again, sneaking a wary glance at Dustin. "I'm not sure what you mean."

But I didn't feel like playing this bullshitting game. So I grabbed her by the elbow and steered her into a nearby corner. She looked apologetically back at Dustin and mouthed, "I'll be right back."

"I'm on an assignment," I hissed once we were out of earshot.

Zoë still insisted on playing coy and unassuming. "Really? Wow, what a coincidence."

But I simply rolled my eyes. "And *he* is the subject." I jabbed my finger back toward Dustin.

Shock spread across Zoë's face, and I realized that she hadn't understood just how much of a coincidence this was until right now. "Dustin?" she confirmed in disbelief.

"Yes!" I gasped.

Her skin suddenly turned a very pale shade of white, which happened to be the second uncharacteristic color I had seen on her tonight.

"Oh my God." Zoë's voice was quickly filling with panic. "Alice hired you? She sent you here?"

Now it was my turn to shift uneasily on my feet. "Well, not exactly."

"What do you mean, not exactly?"

"Actually," I began hesitantly, "Lexi hired me. She's the one who came to my office."

Zoë's eyebrows crumpled together. "Lexi, as in Dustin's *daughter*?"

I nodded. "She sensed something was going on with her dad, and I guess her friend overheard her mom talking about the agency, and so Lexi speculated that maybe her dad was a cheater."

"You took an assignment from a twelve-year-old girl?! Do you know no limits, Jen?"

I purposely ignored her jab. "Well, she was right," I pointed out, motioning toward the general vicinity of the bar.

"That's beside the point. I can't believe you would stoop that low as to take money from a child . . . for this!"

"First of all," I replied sternly, quickly losing my patience with Zoë's blatant subject avoidance, "I didn't take her money. I'm doing this pro bono. And second of all, more importantly, it doesn't matter *who* hired me. What matters is that she was right. Her father is a cheater."

Zoë placed her hands on her hips. "That's a really harsh word. With very negative connotations. I wouldn't go so far as to call him a 'cheater.'"

"Oh no?" I shot back. "What would you call him, then? He's married. With kids. And you're here canoodling with him in a hotel in Palm Springs, where he is *supposed* to be with a bunch of golf buddies. What part of that is *not* cheating, Zoë? What part of that doesn't make you the other woman? The *mistress.*"

Clearly she didn't like this word any better, because her eyes narrowed and I could almost see steam coming out of her nostrils. "Because it's different," she insisted. "He doesn't love his wife anymore. He loves me. And he's going to tell her about us."

I let out the most audible, irritated groan I could muster. "Oh, *please!* Do you realize how pitiful you sound right now? Do I even have to tell you that story is complete and utter bullshit? Because honestly, I thought you were smarter than that."

"I know how it sounds!" she snapped, immediately defensive. "But I believe him. I do. There's something really good between us. Something I've never felt before. I'm wearing pink, for Christ's sake! And I didn't tell you guys because—"

"Because you knew I'd flip out?" I interrupted, my voice getting louder. With a glance over Zoë's left shoulder, I could make out Dustin still standing by the doorway, looking incredibly awkward and nervous. There was no doubt he was starting to pick up bits and pieces of our increasingly heated conversation. "Honestly, Zoë, I can't believe that after everything I've been through in my life and *everything* I've seen in my career, you would actually date a married man. How could you do that to me?"

Zoë crossed her arms over her chest. "This isn't about *you,* Jen. This is about me. And it's my life and I'll date whomever I want. I promise I was going to tell you once he left his wife. Once we didn't have to sneak around anymore."

"Well, I think that day will be coming sooner than you think. Although my guess is she'll probably be the one doing the leaving."

Zoë's eyes widened. "You're going to tell Lexi about this!?"

I shook my head. "No. That's not exactly appropriate. But I *am* going to tell her mother."

Zoë's body language immediately transitioned from fury to pleading. "Jen, no, you can't do that!"

"Why not?" I asked coolly.

"Please don't. You'll ruin everything!"

I threw my hands in the air. "How will that ruin everything if he's already planning on telling her? I'm just going to make sure she gets the information from a trustworthy source."

"Because," Zoë cried, her eyes growing moist with desperation, "he has to do it at the right time. He has it all planned out."

I groaned again. "God, you sound like such a walking cliché, I can't even deal with it."

I started to turn toward the exit, but Zoë placed her hand on my arm. "You can't tell her. Please, I beg you."

But I brushed it away. "I have a duty to report my findings to my client, and if *this*"—I gave Zoë a disdainful once-over—"is what I found, then that's what she'll get."

And with that, Zoë immediately reverted to anger mode. "So you would betray our friendship? Just like that? With no regard for me or what I want or what I'm feeling? All because of some stupid client?"

I looked into her fuming eyes, my own pupils dilated with rage. But when I opened my mouth, my voice was as calm as a Buddhist monk's. "Yes."

"How dare you," she accused. "How dare you stand there and call *my* life a lie after the way you fucked yours up royally by . . . well, *lying!*"

I could feel the chills run up and down my spine as her comment touched a nerve, but I didn't respond. I just continued to glower at her.

Zoë snorted in disgust as she pushed me aside and stomped past me. "Fine!" she called back, drawing the attention of the entire bar—or the half that hadn't already started to eavesdrop on our argument. "Tell her. What the fuck do I care? I hope that makes you very happy. I hope you can sleep at night knowing that you sold out your best friend for a complete stranger!"

Then she grabbed a very nervous and inquisitive Dustin by the arm and literally dragged him out of the bar, thus ending the first fight Zoë and I had ever had in our ten years of uninterrupted friendship.

Needless to say, I didn't enjoy the relaxing evening I had originally planned for myself. Instead, I spent the rest of the night seething over what had just happened and replaying the argument over and over in my head, each time getting more enraged about the things she had said to me.

She *knew* what infidelity meant to me. She *knew* that my whole life had been built upon the crumbled and unsteady foundation that my father had left behind in the wake of his selfish affairs and half-hearted affections for my mother. Yet she'd stood there *defending* her decision to do the same thing to some other poor, defenseless little girl.

I had given up everything for this job—literally *everything*—to make sure that what happened to me didn't happen to other people. People like Lexi Garrett and her mother. People like Darcie Connors and her unadopted child. And Zoë knew that. She knew what I had sacrificed to make a difference in this world. And it was as if she didn't even care. She couldn't even be *bothered* to care. She was too selfish, too blinded by some bogus excuse for a relationship, to even see what she was doing.

It was as if she had taken an ice pick, stabbed it into my heart, and then just stepped over my lifeless, bleeding body with a shrug and a perfunctory, "Good luck with that, Jen," as she disappeared into the night to enjoy her eight P.M. dinner reservation with her married lover.

I attempted to distract myself with my planned pay-per-view movie and a room service cart full of fried food, but my appetite for both had vanished. And what finally calmed me down to the point where I wasn't literally pacing the hotel room, leaving zigzagging tracks across the carpet, was not a relaxing bubble bath or the hotel-supplied fluffy white robe, but the ultimate realization that this whole thing with Zoë was temporary.

There are two things that every woman knows about men (or at least should): (1) They don't change, and (2) they don't leave their wives. Obviously there are exceptions to every rule, but I happen to work in a job that pretty much proves that exceptions are meaningless in the grand scheme of things. Just as a statistician would study a set of data and systematically throw out the anomalies. Because they don't matter. What matters is what's in the middle. The majority. That section of the curve that 99.99 percent of all people fit into.

And you can't live your life hoping to land on the outskirts. Hoping to be that .01 percent exception.

Zoë would evidently have to learn this the hard way.

Tomorrow I would tell Lexi's mother the truth. And Zoë would be able to see firsthand what kind of man Dustin Garrett truly is. And when she did come around and realize the gravity in her mistake, I would be waiting with open arms to comfort her. Because she is my friend, and that's what friends do. They forgive each other's mistakes. Zoë could accuse me all day long of selling her out, betraying our friendship, whatever she wanted. But I knew the truth.

I was doing her a favor.

27

home turf

The next morning, I flew back to Los Angeles with resolve and determination. Zoë was living in a state of delusion. And chances are Mrs. Alice Garrett, Dustin's wife, was living in that same state. This was my opportunity to wake up two birds with one stone . . . so to speak.

So instead of driving straight home from the airport, I opened up Dustin Garrett's case file and inputted Lexi's home address into my car's navigation system.

I knew that trying to get to Dustin's wife through Lexi would have been too difficult. She would want to know the results herself first before she allowed me to speak to her mother, and I wasn't going to trust the delivery of this kind of information to a person who proudly describes herself as "almost thirteen." I also knew that getting Alice to come down to the office without telling her who I was or why I wanted to speak to her would be near impossible. So I decided that this, although highly unorthodox, would be the easiest, cleanest approach.

I used to do house calls all the time. When I was doing this job solo and didn't have an office to bring people to. I would visit the client's home once before the assignment and once after. But there was a reason I stopped entering people's homes. A very good reason. It was too much like entering their lives. After already having almost *slept* with someone's husband, the last thing you want to do is walk through their front door and see firsthand what you've just potentially destroyed.

However many times you remind yourself that what you did was for a just and worthy cause, these are still things that you don't need to see. And that's exactly why the clients come to me now.

Well, except for today. When the client happens to be twelve.

Twenty minutes later, I pulled up in front of a modest, one-story cottage-style home in Cheviot Hills. It was quaint and well kept. Nothing like the million-dollar mansions I used to visit back in the day.

The landscaping appeared to be a labor of love, with neatly sheared grass that reminded me of a marine's crew cut and a brick walkway lined with a rainbow of tulips.

My cell phone rang just as I was unfastening my seat belt and gathering my things. I checked the caller ID. It was John. He had been calling every twenty minutes since six A.M. this morning. And I had been ignoring his calls for just as long. I knew he had probably heard from Zoë either late last night or early this morning and was calling to get my side of the story. I groaned loudly and ignored the call once again. Then I shut off the cell phone and tossed it into my bag.

As I got out of the car and made my way toward the front door, I could feel my chest tighten and my breathing quicken. The nerves were settling in. Not because this was my first house call in over a year, but because, let's face it, this was no ordinary visit.

It was one thing to knock on the door of someone who's been expecting you. Who's been waiting impatiently for more than forty-eight hours to hear whatever news you've brought with you. It's quite another when the person on the other side of the door has no idea who you are. And the news I was bringing with me would definitely not be welcomed. In fact, I had to prepare myself for the fact that it might not even be *believed*.

I sucked in a deep breath and rang the doorbell.

Dogs barked in the background, and I heard a voice sternly telling them to shut up and sit. Not until the barking subsided and the

voice chorused in a round of "Good girls. Stay!" did the door finally
open.

Lexi Garrett's youthful face appeared on the other side of it.

I could tell that she was trying to place me. It wasn't that she
didn't recognize me. She did. She just didn't recognize me *here*. On
the front stoop of her parents' house, with her mother (hopefully)
just in the next room.

After a moment of stunned silence, she finally got out, "Ashlyn?
What are you doing here?"

And before I could even answer, her eyes opened wide as realization crossed her face. "Oh my God. He failed, didn't he? That's why
you're here. To tell me in person."

I smiled patiently and cocked my head to the side. "Is your
mother here?" I asked, purposely avoiding her question.

"I knew it!" was her only reply. "I just knew he would."

"Lexi," I warned softly, "that's not necessarily why I'm here. I
would like to speak to your mother. In private."

She tossed me a confused look. "I don't get it. Why can't you just
tell me if he . . ."

But her voice stopped suddenly, and I could see her body stiffen as
her hand clutched the doorknob.

"Lexi?" came a voice from behind her. A tender voice. A warm
voice.

An unassuming voice.

I felt my body tense up as well. For as long as I've been doing
this, for as long as I've been breaking bad news, you would think
that I would have seen it all. But this . . . this was new. This was
different. And this was making my heartbeat feel erratic in my
chest. As if it were beating for the very first time and still trying to
get the hang of it.

Then a face appeared. It was soft and feminine and framed with
shoulder-length waves of auburn hair. And its eyes were gentle and
innocent. The worst kind of eyes to see in this situation.

The moment I laid my eyes on Alice Garrett, I was overwhelmed
by the stark differences between her . . . and my best friend Zoë. I've
always said the grass is greener on the other side. Especially when it

comes to infidelity. And in this case, it couldn't have been more true.

Zoë was sarcastic and sassy and brooding and always enhanced by bold clothing choices and dramatic makeup. This woman was natural and minimal and exuding a soothing, uncorrupted energy. The kind of person who always assumes the best of everyone she meets, even after she's been scorned.

They were like night and day.

"Who is this?" Alice asked, looking adoringly at her daughter.

But for the first time since that child stepped into my office nearly six weeks ago, she was absolutely speechless. It appeared to surprise her mother as well, because a mellow laugh escaped her lips. The black, wet nose of a Labrador retriever pushed its way into the open doorway, followed shortly by another one belonging to a smaller terrier mix.

Mrs. Garrett nudged both of them aside with her leg and turned to me. "Can I help you?"

"Yes, hello," I said as politely as possible, feeling the nerves already starting to slip into my voice. "I'm a friend of Lexi's. Actually, she came to me asking for some help a few weeks back, and I'm hoping I might be able to speak to you about it."

Alice's eyebrows rose inquisitively, and she looked to her daughter for confirmation. Lexi's head dropped down to avoid eye contact and then eventually fell into a surrendering nod.

"Well, of course," Alice obliged, trying to hide the inevitable inquisitiveness in her voice. "Please come in."

"Thank you." I stepped warily across the threshold, bracing myself for all that was waiting for me on the other side.

Lexi followed quietly behind us into the living room and slinked into a seat on the far end of the couch.

"Lexi," I said kindly, "I think it's best if I talk to your mother alone."

She slumped in her seat and crossed her arms. "But—"

"Lex . . ." her mom began in a warning tone, but she didn't finish the sentence. Clearly the tone was enough, because Lexi reluctantly stood up and disappeared from the room. I had no doubt that she would stay close enough to eavesdrop, so I knew I had to speak softly.

I scooted in closer to Alice. "This is a little difficult for me," I admitted honestly as I clasped my hands in my lap. I couldn't help but marvel at how our roles were suddenly reversed. I was usually the calm one, the one in control, while the person sitting across from me, whether it be in my office or in her own home, was usually the restless one, unable to sit still. But I had to stay professional here. Regardless of how hard this was for me or the fact that it was *my* best friend who was with this woman's husband last night.

"I feel as though I'm in a bit of an awkward position here," I continued.

Alice cocked her head to the side and studied me. "You said Lexi came to you for help?"

I nodded. Yes, that was a good place to start. I would start there. "She did."

"What kind of help?"

I took a deep breath and started apprehensively, "You see, Mrs. Garrett, I run a very special kind of business. With very special kinds of clients, of which Lexi . . . is definitely not the norm."

God, I sound like a madam managing an upscale whorehouse.

Confusion flashed over her face. I definitely wasn't off to a very good start. I decided the best way to do this was to just blurt it out and answer questions later.

"I run a company that provides fidelity inspections for distrustful spouses. Kind of like a private investigation agency, but focusing solely on infidelity."

Alice nodded as if she understood, but the puzzled look on her face gave her away.

So I kept talking. "Lexi came into my office because she was concerned about her father—"

"Wait, Lexi went to a private investigator's office?"

I nodded with caution. "Yes, apparently she got the name of our agency from a friend who overheard her mother talking about it. At least that's the story she told me."

I could tell that Mrs. Garrett was starting to catch on. At least the anger lines that were appearing around her mouth and forehead were suggesting as much. "She came to you because she was worried that her father was cheating on me?"

I struggled with her summarization. "Technically, no. Lexi hired us—well, me, rather—to test whether or not her father, your husband, *would* cheat on you."

Now the words made sense. All too much sense, because Alice shot out of her seat and glared at me with a look so intense, I had no choice but to look away. "You took money from a twelve-year-old girl to do some kind of infidelity sting operation on *my* husband?!"

Okay, when she put it that way, it didn't sound all that kosher. But I immediately raised my hand to defend myself. "No, Mrs. Garrett, I did not take Lexi's money. I told her I would take on her case for free because she was concerned that—"

But she didn't let me finish. The disgust was spewing forth from her mouth like verbal vomit. "Who the hell do you think you are? Dragging a child into her parents' *private,* personal relationship matters, which are frankly much less *your* business than hers! What kind of a sick, fucking person even does that?"

The two dogs that had been lying disinterestedly at our feet suddenly caught wind of her excitement and raised their heads inquisitively.

I could tell this conversation was already getting out of hand. I hadn't even been able to tell her yet about Zoë (or rather, the nameless, unknown stranger I would refer to her as), and already she was dropping the F-bomb. And something told me this woman did not readily curse in everyday conversation. Even the dogs were becoming agitated. I had to wrangle this in if I was ever going to successfully divulge all the information I had come with.

"Mrs. Garrett," I pleaded, "please calm down so we can talk rationally about this. I didn't say I went through with it." Which was technically the truth, but at the same time a slight exaggeration of it.

But apparently my tactic was the right one, because she deliberated momentarily before sitting down and forcing out a jagged, "Sorry," through her clenched teeth.

"I understand that this is upsetting. I was upset myself to see her in my office. Obviously she's not one of my everyday clientele." I forced out a weak laugh in hopes of lightening the mood a bit. It didn't work. Alice continued to glare at me, her fists clenched at her sides.

I cleared my throat and continued, "The reason I wanted to speak to you in private is that you're right, this isn't any of Lexi's business. It's yours and yours alone. And that's why I'm here."

Alice eyed me with skepticism, her nostrils flaring as she inhaled heavy breaths. But she didn't speak. And I suppose I should have been grateful for that. I really wasn't looking forward to being called a "sick, fucking person" again.

"You see, when I flew to Palm Springs this weekend to conduct the assignment"—I paused, easing into the rest of the sentence—"I noticed that Mr. Garrett was not with the group of people that he was supposed to be with."

I waited for a reaction, but Alice's face was pure stone. She was beyond letting my words affect her at this point. At least not outwardly. But her eyes told a different story.

So I kept talking. "Lexi told me that he was supposed to be on a golf trip with some of his friends. But instead I found him with . . . a woman."

Alice continued to glare at me, rage simmering just below the surface. And I was more than confident that my next words would bring her to the boiling point. But they had to be said. Even if they were the last words I uttered in this room, they were the most important.

"It was very clear to me, when I saw them together, that Mr. Garrett was having an intimate *relationship* with this woman." I paused momentarily, searching her face for a sign that I should continue or just stop there. I received no confirmation either way. "I wanted to tell you this in person because I firmly believe in my heart that it's the right thing to do. That you deserve to know. That's why I started my agency in the first place, because I wanted to help people—"

And before I could finish the sentence, I felt the sting of Alice Garrett's right hand making contact with my cheek, and my head whipped around so fast from the impact, I nearly lost my balance.

My head went fuzzy, and I couldn't follow my stream of consciousness. Not that I had much of one at this moment. My hand rose instinctively to touch my throbbing face as I struggled to come to terms with what had just happened.

But I wasn't given much time.

"Get out." Her voice was unyielding and striving for impassiveness. But the slight waver in her tone suggested it was a losing battle.

I slowly lifted my head to look at her, my whiplashed neck screaming in protest. "Mrs. Garrett . . ." I started softly, still in shock.

"Get out of my house, *now!*"

One of the dogs let out a distinctive bark that seemed to perfectly echo Alice's calm yet alarming intensity.

It was definitely time to go. And my pulsing, red hot cheek couldn't have agreed more. I quickly rose and reached for my bag. "If that's what you want," I said obligingly.

"What I want?" she repeated, the revulsion dripping off her tongue, but her voice never rising past the level of a simple indoor conversation. The combination was staggeringly intimidating. "You think any of this is what I *want?*"

I put up both my hands, palms facing out, in what I prayed would come across as a peaceful gesture. "That's not what I meant. I'm sorry. I know that this is shocking news. . . ."

"No," she stated firmly, walking toward me menacingly. Her composure was slipping at an exponential rate. "What's shocking to *me* is that *you,* a complete stranger, think that it's *your* place to walk into my life, fuck everything up, and then act like you're doing me some kind of favor. *That's* what's shocking. I think you need to get off your high horse for one second and take a good long look at your life, because whatever *good* you think you're doing here is a delusion. One that you've obviously created for yourself to help you deal with your own fucked-up issues. You're not helping people. You're destroying them. You're meddling where you shouldn't be meddling. And all the while, you're trying to plug some kind of emotional leak that's so deeply rooted in yourself, you can't even remember where the hole was to begin with."

By now she had backed me all the way up to the front door. I could feel the cold, hard metal of the doorknob jab against my spine.

But that didn't stop her. She was still coming closer, the space between us shrinking with every ominous movement of her body. The fury in her eyes had completely transformed the innocent, unassuming person who had answered the door only a few minutes ago. She had become something else. A creature, almost. Talk about a wolf in sheep's clothing.

I could just see the headlines tomorrow morning: FIDELITY INSPECTOR HACKED TO BITS AND FED TO DOGS.

My hand made contact with the doorknob, and I twisted it hard. It opened and I pulled it toward me, closing the infinitesimally small gap between us even more. "I'm so sorry to bother you, Mrs. Garrett," I sputtered. "I'm just gonna . . . you know, go."

In the crowded space between her, me, and the doorway, I somehow managed to spin around and squeeze through the narrow opening that had appeared. The moment I was outside, I expected the door to hit my ass as it slammed behind me. But when I didn't hear anything, I snuck a quick glance over my shoulder as I hurried down the tulip-lined walkway.

Alice was just standing there, the door open wide behind her. Her eyes followed me all the way back to my car. For a minute, I feared that she might be memorizing my license plate, taking mental notes on the make and model of my car. And then as soon as I was gone, she'd call in a favor to one of her Mob connections. At this point, I wouldn't put anything past her.

I threw the car in gear and peeled out onto the street. I didn't need to steal a glance in my rearview mirror to know that she was still there, watching me like a mother bear who had just chased a predator from her den and was now making sure I didn't come back.

But she needn't have bothered. There was no way in hell I was ever going back there.

28

empti-mess

By the time I pulled into my garage later that night, my cheek was still throbbing. I had spent the rest of the day wandering around Brentwood with an ice-blended caramel macchiato pressed to the side of my face in an effort to alleviate some of the burning sensation.

But it really wasn't the impression Alice Garrett's hand had left on my skin that was bothering me. It was the impression her hurtful words had left on my mind:

. . . you're trying to plug some kind of emotional leak that's so deeply rooted in yourself, you can't even remember where the hole was to begin with.

And it's true—these were not words spoken by someone in a calm, rational frame of mind. These were words spoken by a spiteful woman who had just been given the shock of her life from a complete stranger . . . whom she had just slapped.

But like my bruised cheek, they stung nonetheless.

No . . . they burned. Burned deeper and more painful than any words had ever done before. And believe me, I've had *many* insults thrown my way in the past three years. It kind of comes with the territory. I've been glared at, splat at, bribed, attacked, and even condemned to hell on a few occasions. This is definitely not the kind of business to go into if you're a fan of flattery.

But this was different somehow. This was personal. This hit home.

Or at least the home I thought I had. But walking through my front door now that night had fallen and Alice's words were still haunting me, I wasn't even sure where my home was. Or who was supposed to live there.

When I looked at myself in the mirror nowadays, the reflection wasn't the same hopeful, determined person who had moved into this place three years ago. And it wasn't the same person who had fallen in love inside these very walls, despite her persistent efforts not to. It was someone else. Someone who had suddenly become lost along the very path she'd always thought would get her where she wanted to go.

And then there was him.

He was gone.

His stuff was gone.

Even his smell was gone. Despite the fact that I'd refused to call the maid service in almost two weeks in a desperate attempt to keep his memory there as long as I possibly could.

But it was fading fast.

I headed into my bedroom and creaked open the top dresser drawer. I pulled out the familiar blue velvet box and popped the lid. The diamond inside sparkled with the same unparalleled brilliance. It was amazing how it never dulled, even though the love behind it was gone.

As I carefully removed the ring from the box and slid it on my finger, I half expected the power and intensity of it to overtake me and knock me off my feet. But it was just a ring. Just a piece of jewelry. Constructed in a factory somewhere by an underpaid worker who knew nothing of my life.

Maybe a diamond was just a diamond. Maybe it didn't mean anything. How could it represent anything if it refused to stop sparkling? If its essence refused to dwindle away just as his had?

And the hole he had left behind—not only in my heart, but in my house—was still gaping. I was so foolish to think that I could ignore it. That I could *talk* myself out of feeling it just by insisting that I was better off without him.

Maybe Alice was right. Maybe I was just trying to plug some kind of emotional hole that was slowly draining me of life. How unsettling it was to think that a perfect stranger had been able to see through me with such clarity, while my own outlook was so terribly opaque.

The thought sent shivers through my body, and I returned to the living room and plopped down on the couch, reaching for the afghan under the end table. I wrapped it tightly around me, as if I were swaddling a newborn baby, and fell ungracefully onto my side, curling into a ball.

My house was a mess. Dirty laundry scattered throughout, coffee mugs and cereal bowls strewn about the coffee table, dust settling on the furniture. It was a scene that normally would have made me hyperventilate. But right now, I didn't mind the clutter. It seemed like an appropriate extension of the clutter in my mind.

I pulled my legs tighter against my chest and buried my face in the soft yarn of the blanket.

And that's where I found it.

The one place where Jamie's smell still lingered. Nearly two weeks and a thousand secret tears hadn't washed it away. Maybe yarn was more resilient like that. Maybe it clung to scents better than any material in the world.

I breathed in deeply, trying to use his scent to conjure up other memories in my head. Like his face, his hands, his hair, the way his arms felt when they wrapped around me.

There were no tears. It was almost as if this kind of sadness was beyond crying. Beyond all conventional reactions to pain.

There was just . . . emptiness.

I woke up the next morning with the worst hangover of my life. I hadn't drunk a drop of alcohol, but the emotional indulgences that I had partaken in had left me with a far worse headache and overwhelming sense of nausea.

I lifted my head just enough to peer at the clock on the cable box. It was nine in the morning. I hadn't moved for twelve hours straight.

I didn't want to go to work. For the first time in my life, I felt there was no point. If I was really just trying to "plug some hole" in my pitiful existence, then why ruin other people's lives in the process? The way I had apparently ruined Alice Garrett's. Because, let's face it, who was I really kidding here? I wasn't helping people. I wasn't "waking" them up from a bad dream. I was putting them in one.

Todd and Joy Langley would still be married if it weren't for me.

Darcie Connors would be holding a brand-new baby in her arms.

Alice Garrett would still be blissfully happy. Maybe she'd be blind to the truth, but she'd still be happy. And what's wrong with being happy?

I was happy once. And it was amazing. And now it's all fucked up. And that's what I did for all those people. I fucked up their happiness.

I had no desire to go into the office, but my sense of obligation finally pulled me off the couch. I had a ten A.M. meeting with a potential new client and another one later that afternoon. Both appointments felt like thorns in my side. Nails in my coffin. Whatever.

I could call them all off and hide out in this house for the rest of my life, or I could fulfill the commitments I'd already made.

I dragged myself down the hall, into my bedroom, and into a pair of sweatpants and a questionably clean T-shirt that I found crumpled on the floor of my closet. I didn't even bother showering or putting on any makeup. My usual motivation to look presentable and well put together was buried somewhere beneath the rubble of all my destructive thoughts.

I trudged through the front door of the agency dressed as though I were on my way home from a slumber party, with a cup of Starbucks coffee in one hand and my oversize sunglasses covering the ugly purple bruise that was starting to form around my left eye.

Hadley noticed my new "look" right away. She studied me curiously from the door as I mumbled some kind of greeting and then breezed right by her on my way to my office. I collapsed in my chair, spilling the coffee down the front of my T-shirt. I made a half-assed attempt to wipe away the stain and then simply shrugged and took a sip before resting my head against the back of the chair. I guess now there was no question whether or not the shirt was dirty.

It didn't take long for Hadley to appear in the doorway, a blatantly concerned expression plastered across her face. She approached my desk slowly, almost tiptoeing, as if she were afraid the slightest movement might startle me. She was completely silent. Not a word. And as she inched closer, I picked up my head and watched her, wondering what she might do. What do you even say to a sight like me?

Hadley studied me for a minute. I could feel her eyes on me. And I was already planning out in my head what I would say to her if she mentioned my current state . . . or ensemble. Nothing.

I simply wouldn't reply. It was none of her business, anyway.

But apparently she didn't need to ask. Something I probably should have expected by now. Because when she spoke, all she said was, "He'll be back."

I yanked my chair around to face her. So hard, in fact, that I almost spun in an entire circle. I had to catch myself on the edge of the desk and compensate back to center. I never told her that he had left. I never even told her that he *existed*. I hid it from everyone here. I never even—

"The ring." She nodded toward my left hand, seemingly reading my thoughts like some kind of freaky tarot card–wielding psychic. My eyes darted downward to the hand that was still gripping the edge of my desk. Yes, there it was. Jamie's diamond engagement ring. The one that refused to stop shining. The one that I had slid on my finger the night before and forgotten to take off.

The very one I had forgotten to put back *on* only a few short weeks ago.

"You never wore it before," she explained. "When you looked so happy."

A small laugh escaped my lips. Not because the situation was funny, but because it was so far from being funny that the only thing I could do was laugh. "Right," I said solemnly, understanding her logic perfectly. Even though to anyone else, it would have failed to make any sense at all.

"Maybe if you called him," Hadley suggested timidly.

"No," was my obstinate reply. "He doesn't want to be with me anymore."

Hadley cocked her head to the side in a silent question mark. I could tell she was considering a counterargument, and my eyes pleaded with her to just let it go.

She eventually conceded with a nod and turned back toward the door. "Your ten o'clock appointment should be here any minute," she reminded me, eyeing my outfit.

I swung my chair back to face the window again and nodded absently. "I know."

"Would you like me to postpone?"

"No."

Hadley pursed her lips thoughtfully for a moment and then shut the door behind her.

I pulled up my legs and hugged them to my chest. Then I sat, unmoving, in the silence of my office, watching the waves on the shore and the busy morning traffic of Ocean Avenue. From way up here, the world actually appeared to have some sort of order to it.

But I knew better.

Zoë was right. I *had* crossed the line. This time I had gone too far. I let a twelve-year-old child talk me into testing her father. All because I needed to prove to myself that I had made the right choice. That choosing my work over Jamie was the right thing to do.

God, could it really get any lower than that?

My thoughts were interrupted by the buzz of my intercom.

"Yeah," I replied, barely turning my head toward the speaker.

In a perplexed tone, Hadley said, "Um, the new associate is here to see you?"

I continued to stare out the window as I replied numbly, "What new associate?"

Then I heard something that sounded like a struggle and a familiar voice saying, "Just give me the phone," and then more clearly came, "It's John! I *have* to talk to you. It's very important."

There was another apparent struggle for the receiver, complete with grunts and hissing, and then Hadley was back. "Sorry about that. He says you hired him last week. Do you want me to send him in?"

My head collapsed back against my chair. "Fine. Whatever."

John trudged into my office a few seconds later, zeroed in on my location at the desk, and headed straight toward me with an intensely determined look on his face. "You," he stated ominously, wagging his finger in my direction. "You and I need to talk."

I didn't even turn around. "No, we don't."

"Why haven't you been answering your phone? Or returning your calls?"

Without moving my head, I glanced in the direction of my bag. I suddenly remembered shutting off my phone before entering Alice Garrett's house yesterday. "Oh yeah," I muttered dazedly. "I forgot to turn it back on."

John sighed dramatically. "Not cool. I've been trying to get a hold of you!"

When I didn't respond, he marched over to my chair and turned it around to face him. Then he leaned in close to me, and I could smell the McDonald's McGriddles on his breath. "I'm sorry about showing up here like this, but you left me no choice. *You* have a problem."

I closed my eyes. "I know."

He put his hands on my shoulders and shook them. "No, I mean a serious problem."

I pushed him away from me and stood up, stalking to the far end of the room. "John, I know," I growled. "I'm a terrible person. I never should have ratted out Zoë's boyfriend. I never should have cheated on Jamie. I never should have done anything. Okay? What do you want from me?"

He furrowed his eyebrows and shot me a confused look. "What are you talking about?"

I groaned. "What are *you* talking about?"

"I'm talking about your associate. The cute blond one."

I swung my head around and stared at him. "Katie?"

"Yes. Katie."

"What about Katie?"

John sighed and removed a manila folder from the green-and-black messenger bag that was strapped across his chest. He dropped the folder on my desk and opened it. From across the room, I could just barely make out what looked like a stack of eight-by-ten black-and-white photographs. The kind that private detectives take to prove that someone is in cahoots with the Mob. I squinted at the photos, trying to make out their contents.

"What are those?" I asked, completely exasperated and having no patience for John's games.

"They're pictures of Katie at the Chateau Marmont," he stated matter-of-factly.

I took a few steps closer. The photographs were almost in complete focus now. "Well, what is she doing in them?" I asked warily.

John watched my reaction carefully, almost as if he was expecting me to faint again and preparing himself to catch me. "She's walking out of Dean Stanton's hotel room."

29

traitor in our midst

I stood motionless for a full minute, my eyes trying to absorb everything that they were seeing while my brain tried desperately to compute it. Neither one seemed to be keeping up with the other. I stared down at the black-and-white photo that sat on top of the pile in front of me. I hadn't dared touch it.

No matter how many times I tried to come up with an alternative explanation for what was being represented, my mind kept coming back to the same conclusion. The only conclusion. That the woman in this photograph was Katie Morgan. My associate. And the man she was kissing outside of a hotel room door marked with the number 812 was Dean Stanton. I had recognized him not only from the picture in his case file, but from the pictures I had seen multiple times in *Variety* magazine as I was researching his case.

When my hand was finally able to move, I reached out and flipped over the photograph to reveal the one underneath. A similar shot, still black and white, still taken from somewhat of a distance using some type of zoom feature, but still the same two subjects: Katie and Dean outside room 812. This time they weren't kissing. Instead, he had his face buried in the side of her neck and she was laughing.

I squeezed my eyes shut and tried to think back to the details Katie had given me last week about the Stanton assignment. I could almost swear she'd said that Melissa Stanton caught them making out on the couch and then she packed up her things and left. Yes, that's definitely what she said. Although why did the Chateau Marmont sound so familiar? I opened my eyes and reached for the yellow legal pad on my desk, flipping back through a dozen pages until I landed on the right one. My eyes scanned the scribbles until I came face-to-face with the words *Chateau Marmont*. That's where Dean said he was staying after Melissa kicked him out. Katie had said something about how he'd whispered it into her ear as he was leaving, hoping she would stop by later, not knowing that this whole thing had been a setup.

Oh God.

I leafed through five more photographs. More of the same.

My head popped up. "John, where did you get these?"

"I took them," he said proudly. As if the artistic value of the photos were the primary concern here.

"When?"

He walked around the edge of my desk, tracing it with his fingertip as he walked and finally plopped down in my chair. "Yesterday morning."

"Yesterday morning?" I repeated, my voice strained.

"I *tried* to call you," John countered defensively. "But someone wasn't answering their phone."

My head was spinning. And now I felt as though I really *might* faint again. I fell into a guest chair behind me and gripped the armrests. "But how did you know . . . why were you even there?"

"Well," he began, leaning back in the chair and folding his hands over his stomach, "I was at the Chateau Marmont for a party two weeks ago—"

"Two weeks ago?" I interrupted. "You knew about this for that long and you didn't tell me?"

John sighed. "If you'll just let me finish, I can explain."

I slouched in my chair. "Fine. Go. Finish."

"So I was at the Chateau for a party with this smoking hot new guy that I met named Chad. I've been trying to hook up with him for the past *month,* but he keeps blabbing something about having a boyfriend in London or someplace like that. I mean, really, that's ten thousand miles away and I'm *here*. Hello?"

"John!" I screeched. "Get on with it."

"Right. So we were just leaving the party, which was in this amazing suite in the Chateau, and we passed by this couple that was walking to their room. A late-forty-something guy with silvery hair and a little blond girl." His head nodded toward the photos in front of me, and my stomach flipped.

John continued, "I remember thinking, Okay, total Hollywood stereotype. Older guy, younger girl, Chateau Marmont. Can we get any more cliché? But then after they had disappeared into a suite, room 812"—he nodded again toward the photographs—"Chad whispers to me, 'Do you know who that is?' and I don't, so I go, 'No,' and then he tells me it's Dean Stanton, the head of New Edge Cinema. And then of course I feel really dumb because I know I *should* know who that is, given that my boss has totally met with him on more than one occasion. But whatever, I was drunk and that's beside the point."

He stopped talking, and for a moment, it appeared as though he had concluded his story. I waved my hand. "And?"

John looked confused. "And what?"

"And that's it?" I cried, exasperated. "How did you get these fucking pictures?"

John's face suddenly lit up with recognition. "Oh, right. Sorry." Then he shot me a disapproving glance. "Testy, testy. So anyway, when I first saw the girl he was with, I thought she looked kinda familiar, but I couldn't really place her. And when Chad told me who *he* was, I just assumed she was some D-list actress I had seen on TV somewhere. But then that night at Sophie's when you told me that your associate Katie had tested Dean Stanton and I remembered those PI photos you showed me last year before you hired her . . . well, I realized why she looked so familiar."

"Then why didn't you say something?" I blurted out.

"Because I couldn't be sure. I mean, I was so wasted when I left that hotel. As was Chad. That guy we saw could have been anyone. I needed to make sure before I told you. So I decided to go back and stake it out. I went by the hotel every night after work, but I didn't see anything for an entire week. Room 812 was dead silent, and I thought maybe he had already checked out. But then finally, on Saturday around midnight, I saw Dean and Katie in the lobby. I couldn't get a clear shot of them without being noticed, so I came back early in the morning and staked out the hallway until she finally came out around seven and I got these shots."

"Did they see you take them?"

John shook his head, again, extremely proud of himself. "Nope. I'm just stealthy like that." He got up from his chair, walked around the desk, and thumbed through his handiwork. "I thought the black and white was a nice touch, don't you? Very early forties detective movie."

There was a tightness in my chest, and suddenly I felt as though I couldn't catch my breath. John noticed and immediately came over and put his arm around my shoulders. "Jen, breathe. Take a deep breath."

"What does this mean?" I cried, feeling defeated, betrayed, saddened, and infuriated all at once.

John cracked a smile. "What do you mean, what does it mean? It means she broke the cardinal rule. She slept with him."

I ran my fingers through my dirty, tangled hair. "I know *that*, but it just doesn't make sense. When she told me what happened at the staff meeting, she said she made out with Dean on the couch and then his wife walked in and kicked him out and he went to the hotel. Why would she just *go* with him? Just like that? No one's that good a kisser!"

"Easy." John shrugged. "That wasn't the first time they'd kissed."

My eyes widened, and a strangled gasp escaped my lips. I hadn't even thought of that option. "What?"

John shook his head and laughed at me. "You know, Jen, for someone who makes a living off of other people's relationships, you certainly aren't very good at figuring them out."

My thoughts were a blur. Details from the past few weeks were whizzing through my head as I tried desperately to sort them all out and rearrange them into a conclusion that didn't make me want to throw up right there in my trash can.

"You're saying she was having a *relationship* with Dean Stanton?"

"Um, yeah," John stated, as if it were obvious. And maybe it should have been. Maybe if I hadn't been so preoccupied with my own personal dramas, I would have actually noticed the clues. Because there had to be clues, right?

Suddenly my mind flashed back to that conversation I'd had with Katie nearly three weeks into her assignment. When I told her I wanted to pull her out of there and mark the whole thing down as a pass. She was so quick to dissuade me. Too quick, actually. She'd insisted that she needed more time.

Was it possible that she was *sleeping* with him that whole time? And that's why she didn't want to leave? Because she was actually *enjoying* herself? And all that time, Melissa Stanton was *paying* for her to be there?

Oh God, the nausea was here. I couldn't hold it back any longer. I leaned forward, grabbed the trash can from under my desk, and vomited into it.

John instinctively took a few steps back from me and turned his head, either to give me privacy or to avoid puking right alongside me.

The intercom on my desk buzzed just then, startling both of us. "Ashlyn?" Hadley's voice came through. "Your ten o'clock is here."

Horrified, I looked at the phone on my desk. There was no way I could meet a client now, looking like this. Then I turned to John. He seemed to understand and spoke into the speaker. "Uh . . . Jen's not feeling very well. I think you should probably reschedule it."

"Okay," Hadley replied, sounding wary of his response. After all, to her, John was just some strange guy who had barged in unannounced, claiming to be a new employee, and was now answering my intercom for me. "Should I reschedule all of her appointments today?"

John looked to me, and I nodded. He relayed the message to Hadley and then clicked off the phone.

I fell back into my seat and closed my eyes. This was all starting to feel like a bad dream. Everything was wrong. Every decision I had ever made in my entire life was *wrong*.

I had given up so much for this job. This agency. This life. And it had betrayed me. My own employee had deceived me. And if Katie was capable of that kind of betrayal, who's to say the others weren't, too? Who's to say they weren't already betraying me?

With Jamie, I'd had something real. Something wonderful. And I'd traded it all in for this. A corrupted world full of dishonesty, lies, and most of all . . . infidelity. When you boil it down—strip off the layers and fancy titles and designer clothing—that's all this job was. A business of cheaters. Nothing more.

And I had lost the only thing that could have saved me from it. The only person who had ever represented everything that this world was not.

And now it was too late.

universe idol

"It's *not* too late," Sophie insisted from behind her iced vanilla soy latte.

After I had entered a comatose state in my office where I pretty much mumbled incoherently for ten minutes while staring into space, John had to practically carry me from the building. Not knowing what to do, he'd plopped me down in the front seat of his car and driven me to the Starbucks near Sophie's work, where the three of us now sat.

Although my location had changed, my current state hadn't improved much. The incoherent mumbling had stopped, but I was still just staring into space like a psych-ward patient who had been injected with too many brain-numbing drugs.

"Drink your tea," John instructed me.

I looked down at the cup of hot liquid sitting on the table in front of me, but I didn't touch it. I just fidgeted with the string on the end of the teabag. John looked anxiously to Sophie. "She's been like that for almost an hour now."

"Well, I don't blame her after what you did to her. Why are you always the one to bring her the bad news?" Sophie reached out and poked him in the ribs with her index finger.

"Ow!" he yelped, rubbing his side. "What are you talking about?"

Sophie nudged her head subtly toward me. "The Web site," she whispered. "Remember? You're the one who told her about that stupid Web site with her picture on it last year. That nearly ruined her. And now this!"

"I don't know," John shot back defensively. "I'm just observant, that's all. Are you saying I *shouldn't* have told her that her own associate was lying to her?"

"Will you guys stop talking about me like I'm not even here?" I grumbled.

Sophie put on a cheerful face and smiled brightly at me. "You know," she began, quickly changing the subject, "you can still try to get him back. It's amazing how far a simple 'I'm sorry, I was wrong, please forgive me' can go."

"It's too late," I repeated again, my voice empty and lifeless. I'm pretty sure this was the statement I had been babbling over and over again while John was dragging me from my office.

Sophie reached out and rubbed my arm. "You don't know that. What if Jamie is sitting alone at home right now, just *praying* that the phone will ring and it'll be you calling to apologize?"

"He's at work," I stated matter-of-factly.

Sophie rolled her eyes. "Or at work! Whatever."

I attempted to shake my head, but the movement was so slight, I doubt the meaning of the gesture came across. So I verbalized it with a blank, "No."

Sophie frowned. "You have to at least *try*! You have nothing more to lose. You've already lost everything!"

John shot her a look. "Sophie!"

"Sorry," she mumbled as she lowered her head to take a sip from her straw. "But she has."

I looked at her incredulously. "I'm not going to call him."

She considered my statement for a second and then responded, "No, you're right. That wouldn't be appropriate. It has to be a drop-by."

I sighed. "A what?"

"You have to drop by his house," John translated. "Calling would be a complete cop-out. If you're going to beg for him back, it has to be in person."

For the next fifteen minutes, John and Sophie proceeded to plot out a full-fledged strategy for getting Jamie back, complete with scripts and multiple scenario variations depending on Jamie's reactions to each of the statements they had planned out for me to say. It was starting to sound like they were writing one of those *Choose Your Own Adventure* books. I suppose it failed to dawn on them that I hadn't agreed to any of this. Either that, or they didn't really care whether I agreed to it or not.

"So there you go," Sophie said, turning the cocktail napkin she had been scribbling on so that I could read it. "Your guide to reconciliation."

But I didn't even bother to look. "No," I said again.

Sophie banged her fist on the table. "Come on, Jen. What else are you going to do? Sit around your house and mope until you're eighty?"

I feigned consideration. "Yep. Pretty much."

She groaned. "No, you're not. We're going to fix this. We are going to get him back."

"We?" I asked with skepticism.

She nodded resolutely. "Yep. I'm going with you. We'll stake out his place in Century City and wait for him to come home from work."

"Uh-huh," I indulged her sarcastically. "And then are you going to come inside with me and chaperone?"

"No," she replied, frustrated by my antics. "I'm going to wait in the car."

"Well," I said flippantly, nodding to her ink-covered napkin, "since you seem to already have the conversation all figured out, maybe *you* should just go up there and *I'll* wait in the car. Or better yet, why don't I just stay home and you can go all by yourself. Then you can text me and tell me how it went!"

Sophie exhaled a defeated sigh. "We just want you to be happy, Jen."

I looked to John, and he nodded his agreement. Then my face

softened. "I know you guys do. And I love you for that. But I'm not going to Jamie's house. End of story.

Although apparently it *wasn't* the end of the story, because six hours later I found myself sitting in the passenger seat of Sophie's car, staring at the front of Jamie's building. I'm not sure how she was even able to talk me into this in the first place, but sometime between Starbucks and now, I caved. It probably had a lot to do with a full day of listening to Sophie's incessant whining and pleading and listing her million and a half reasons why she was right and I was crazy. I swear the girl should work for the government. I bet she could crack suspected terrorists in under ten minutes with that nagging voice of hers.

The "plan" was to wait for Jamie's car to turn the corner and pull into the underground garage before using the key that I had yet to return to him to get through the street-level entrance. Then I would take the stairs to the second floor and wait in the stairwell for him to get off the elevator and enter his loft. Then I would knock on his front door.

I glanced at the clock on the dashboard. It was already almost eight. "What if he's working late?" I asked Sophie.

She shrugged. "I have nowhere to be. Do you?"

I shifted in my seat. My butt was starting to fall asleep. "Well, what if he's on a business trip? We could be here for several days."

"He's not," Sophie stated confidently.

"How do you know?" I countered.

She pointed through the front windshield at the second floor of the building. "That's his loft, right there."

I leaned forward to look up. "Yeah, so?"

She pointed again. "His bathroom light is on. People don't accidentally leave lights on when they know they're going away for several days."

I turned and stared at her. "Do you do this often?"

She simply shrugged. "Let's just say it's not my first stakeout."

I had to crack a smile at this. My first one all day. "Why does that not surprise me?"

A silence fell between us, and Sophie turned on the radio. She flipped through a dozen or so stations on her satellite radio until she found one called Sirius XM Chill. The station stayed true to its titular promise as a soothing female voice filled the air, backed by a sultry African-inspired drumbeat. I felt my body start to relax.

I leaned back against the headrest and took in a heavy breath. "You haven't said anything about Zoë," I pointed out.

Sophie was quiet for a moment, seemingly contemplative before she said, "I know. I figured we'd deal with one thing at a time."

I nodded my understanding. "Yeah."

"Plus, friendships are more resilient than romantic relationships. I know that you and Zoë will work things out on your own. But *this*—" She motioned to the car and our immediate surroundings. "This you need help with."

I had to laugh. It was a weak laugh, but it felt good nonetheless. "You're probably right about that."

"But if you want to know what I think . . ." Her voice trailed off. It wasn't a question, but she was still waiting for my permission to continue.

"I do," I confirmed.

"I think you're both wrong."

"So she told you?"

Sophie nodded. "She called yesterday. Obviously I don't condone her sleeping with a married man. But I also don't condone you taking on the assignment or telling his wife. It's one thing if someone comes to you asking for that information, it's quite another for you to deliver it unsolicited."

"I know," I agreed softly. "I learned that the hard way."

Sophie looked at me, surprised by my concurrence. "Are you going to tell Zoë that?"

"Eventually. Like you said, one thing at a time. Besides, I don't think she'd even answer the phone right now. I figured I'd give her some time to cool down. We didn't exactly part ways amicably."

Sophie laughed. "Well, we could always do another stakeout at her place after this one."

I flashed a faint smile. "Maybe."

We spent the next hour and a half talking and listening to the radio. Sophie told me more stories about her honeymoon in Greece and recounted details from the wedding that I'd missed because I was stuck with my head in an MRI machine. I could tell she was trying to distract me from the fact that it was almost eleven at night and Jamie still hadn't shown. It was only partially working.

Finally, at 11:25, I saw the familiar headlights of Jamie's Jaguar turn the corner and his car pull into the garage. My pulse instantly quickened.

Sophie reached out and clasped her hand around my wrist. "This is it," she said, excitement building in her voice.

I wasn't sure I could go through with this. I had agreed to come on the stakeout, but I hadn't necessarily agreed to go upstairs. What if he said no? What if he slammed the door in my face?

Then I thought of the alternative: driving home now, after we'd been sitting here for nearly four hours, without even trying. And I figured getting rejected at Jamie's door was far less lame.

"Okay," Sophie commanded as the garage door started to close, "it's showtime."

I took a deep breath and placed my hand on the doorknob. My throat was suddenly feeling scratchy and tight, and I wondered if I would even be able to get any words out if I did manage to get out of this car and follow the plan.

"Do you want the script?" Sophie asked, holding out the crumpled cocktail napkin.

I rolled my eyes. "I don't think so."

I stepped out of the car and closed the door behind me. With unsteady feet and uneven breath, I walked the few paces to the front door of the building. I removed the key from my pocket and placed it gingerly in the lock. For a moment, I hoped the door wouldn't open. That maybe for some reason the HOA had changed the locks. But the key turned smoothly, and I pressed forward.

I turned back to Sophie, and she gave me an enthusiastic thumbs-up through the front windshield. I waved back awkwardly before walking into the building and heading toward the stairwell. Jamie's unit was only three floors up from the garage, but he almost always took the elevator. Usually because he was carrying his heavy laptop bag with him, or a suitcase from his latest business trip, or, until recently, a bag full of stuff from an extended stay at my place.

I climbed the two flights to the second floor and waited in the stairwell, peering through the small window in the door for Jamie to pass by. My heartbeat was racing now, pumping out blood faster than my veins could keep up.

And that's when the panic started to set in.

What on earth was I doing here? Did I actually think this was going to work? That a simple apology was going to change things? But when I thought about the small, infinitesimal chance that Jamie might actually take me back, that he might actually forgive me, somehow it all seemed worth the risk.

I heard a faint ding indicating the elevator's arrival, and my breath caught in my chest. I had a feeling I wouldn't be able to take a real breath until all of this was over. And depending on the outcome, I knew there was a chance I might never feel the satisfaction of a true deep breath again.

The footsteps were audible now—coming from the direction of the elevator—and then I heard Jamie's voice. I figured he was probably on his phone, talking into his Bluetooth earpiece as he always does. I used to make fun of him. Because often when he was in need of a haircut, his thick, wavy brown hair would cover the earpiece completely and he looked as if he were talking to himself. Like a crazy person on Hollywood Boulevard.

The thought brought a nostalgic smile to my face. As did the sound of his voice.

God, I really did miss him.

As the footsteps and voice got closer, I could start to make out what he was saying. He was telling one of his really bad jokes. I remember he'd told it to me on one of our first dates. And then I had to listen to him repeat it over and over again at parties and group dinners and work functions for the past year. And every time, I had to pretend as if I hadn't heard it before.

But somehow now it was funny again. And I found myself laughing quietly to myself as he got to the punch line, remembering the way his face always looked when he delivered that last line. His eye-brows raised, his lips curled into an expectant smile. It was beyond adorable.

And then suddenly I realized that I wasn't the only one laughing. My body froze as I pressed my ear to the door. So hard that I thought I might push it open. But then I heard it again.

A second voice. A second set of footsteps. A second person.

And it was distinctly female.

I pulled my ear away from the door and smashed my face against the glass window. And that's when I saw them.

Both of them. Jamie and a woman. I couldn't see her face, because by the time I pulled my ear away from the door, they had already passed by the stairwell and were on their way to Jamie's front door. But I could see her hair, and I could see the back of her dress. Both nauseatingly sexy.

I pressed my face harder against the glass as I strained to follow them with my eyes. But unfortunately, Jamie's unit was on the same wall as this door, limiting my field of vision. The last thing I was able to see was Jamie's hand as it touched the small of her back and led her inside.

The world around me was suddenly in black and white. There was no more color. I blinked rapidly, but it didn't help. I felt like I was stuck in one of those PI–style photographs that John had deliv-ered to my office earlier today.

Oh, God, had that really been *today*? Had all of this happened to me in one fucking day? The universe couldn't possibly hate me *that* much. Or maybe it could. Maybe this was all a game. And I was just an unfortunate contestant on some type of cosmic reality show. Like those people who audition for *American Idol* and honestly think they can sing. Meanwhile, everyone at home is laughing their asses off. Maybe God was laughing *His* ass off at me right now. Sitting on His couch with all His heavenly buddies, drinking beer and ridiculing the fact that I *think* I can survive in this world, when clearly I don't have a clue.

I could barely feel my feet as I stumbled back down the stairs and outside to Sophie's car.

"So? What happened?" she asked anxiously before my whole body was even in the front seat.

"Just drive," I replied numbly as I leaned back against the headrest and closed my eyes.

But the engine didn't start. The car didn't move. Sophie just sat there, staring at the side of my face. "Jen," she commanded sternly, "tell me what happened. What did he say?"

"You were wrong," I said, feeling the moisture start to sting the backs of my eyelids. "It really is too late."

31

the last person on earth

Sophie tried her best to console me on the way home. She even offered to let me sleep on her couch again so I wouldn't have to be alone. But it was no use. I was inconsolable.

"At least let me come in and stay the night here," she said as she pulled up to the curb in front of my building.

I shook my head. "I'll be fine, Sophie. I just want to be alone."

But that was a lie. I didn't want to be alone. I couldn't even fathom the thought of it. Which is why I didn't actually go home. After Sophie dropped me off, I slipped down the stairwell into the garage and headed straight for my car. As soon as I was out onto the street, I pulled my cell phone out of my bag and navigated to the address book.

I didn't have the heart to tell Sophie the truth. That it wasn't about wanting to be alone. It was about not wanting to be with *her*. It wasn't personal. There was only one person I could talk to about this. And it was the last person in the world I ever thought I would call in a time of crisis, let alone a *relationship* crisis.

"Hello?" the male voice answered after two rings.

"Dad?" My voice was weak, frail, probably not like he had ever heard it.

Alarm immediately registered in his tone. "Jenny? What's wrong? What's the matter? Is it your mother?"

I held the phone tightly against my ear. "No," I assured him. "Mom is fine. But I need to talk. Can you meet me?"

There was silence on the other end of the phone. No doubt a stunned one. When was the last time his daughter ever called him up at eleven-thirty at night to "talk"? Or better yet, when was the *first* time?

"Of course," he finally responded. "I'll meet you in the lobby of the Huntley Hotel."

"Okay," I replied, flipping my car into a U-turn to compensate for the new direction. "I can be there in seven minutes."

I drove in silence. No radio. No cell phone conversation. Nothing. The streets were dead. And the stillness of the deserted night seemed to add an extra level of eeriness to the unusual quiet in my car. As if the world around me were taking pause, stopping to acknowledge the sheer rarity of such an occasion.

Jennifer Hunter, driving through the night to speak to her previously estranged father about her broken heart.

Definitely something you don't see every day.

But the truth is, he knew a thing or two about betraying loved ones, messing up relationships, regrets. He was really the only person who made sense right now.

What did Sophie or Zoë or even John know about stuff like that? They didn't. So they couldn't help. Because they couldn't even begin to understand what I was feeling right now.

My problems were officially out of their league.

I cruised through every stoplight, passing only a handful of moving cars along the way, until I finally turned right onto Second Avenue and pulled into the valet station of the Huntley Hotel.

It had always been one of my favorite hotels in Santa Monica. Set back two blocks from the ocean, it was sort of a hidden gem. While most L.A. visitors opted for the beachfront properties like the Loews or Shutters or Casa del Mar, the Huntley's lack of beach-going tourists made it feel slightly more upscale. More exclusive.

I handed my keys to the valet attendant and headed inside the pristine, modern lobby. My eyes swiveled, searching for a familiar face. I spotted my dad reclining awkwardly on a striped leather chair that looked like a hollowed-out mushroom cap.

He struggled to push himself to a standing position and walked over to me.

As we came face-to-face, I could tell that he wasn't sure how to greet me. This was a very unorthodox event in the history of our relationship, and proper protocol had yet to be established. But I didn't hesitate. I fell into him and buried my head against his chest. My dad responded immediately by wrapping his arms around my body and squeezing tightly.

As much as I thought it would feel uncomfortable, foreign even, it was the exact opposite. I felt right at home. As though I had been waiting seventeen years to do exactly this. And the strange part was, I always assumed a moment like this would come after some kind of unexpected reconciliation between us. Where he apologized for everything that he'd ever done to our family and swore on his life that he had changed and become a better person.

But now that the moment was here, I realized that it wasn't *him* who had changed. It was me. All this time, I had worried that Jamie might be just another version of my father. But in actuality, I was the one who had lied. I was the one who had broken my promise.

I was the replica.

And that's how I knew that my father was the only person in this city who wouldn't judge me right now.

The tears started to fall and soak into my dad's unadorned gray T-shirt. He bent and gently kissed the top of my head. "Shhh," he cooed. "It's okay. Let's go sit down and talk."

He led the way through the lobby to an empty lounge. The bartender was just finishing his nightly cash-out procedure, and upon seeing us, he sighed and his shoulders slouched.

My dad waved away his concern. "We're just going to sit. We're not going to order anything."

We found an empty banquette in the back, and I plopped down onto it while my dad fetched a stack of cocktail napkins from the bar. He handed me one, and I wiped the skin under my eyes. "Thanks," I said, sniffing.

He waited for me to speak, keeping his eyes glued to my face. Almost as if he were afraid to blink in fear that he might miss something.

"It's Jamie," I finally managed.

My dad let out a small laugh. "I figured as much." Then his eyes softened. "Did he cheat on you?"

I kept my head down as I shook it. I couldn't bring myself to look into his eyes. "I cheated on him," I whispered.

My dad sucked in a sharp breath, and I finally lifted my head and looked at him. I could see the struggle on his face. This was a blow that he wasn't quite expecting. Although I was never able to read my father the way I was able to read other men, tonight it wasn't hard. He was blaming himself.

But I knew that my actions were my own, and I hadn't come here to pass the blame.

"Dad," I urged softly, placing a hand on his shoulder, "this has nothing to do with you."

He smiled at my attempt, but I could tell he didn't believe me. And for a moment, as I stared into his eyes, I swore I saw tears forming. But he blinked them away before I could be sure.

"Do you want to tell me about it?" he finally said.

I nodded. I did want to tell him. I wanted to tell him everything. But I wasn't sure how much he would want to hear. How much he was ready to hear.

"All of it?" I asked softly, my voice breaking.

"Yes," he confirmed, sounding confident. "All of it."

So I took a deep breath and started from the very beginning. From the moment I first walked in on him cheating on my mother. The moment I've always felt defined me and every choice I've made since. I had never told anyone about that night. Not my mom, not my friends, not even Jamie. And certainly not my father.

I watched his reaction carefully as I spoke; his face was emotionless, but his eyes gave him away. They showed remorse. And although it wasn't my motivation for telling him, it still felt good to have him acknowledge it.

But I didn't stop there. When I reached the part about becoming a fidelity inspector, his face finally registered. He didn't say anything, but I knew right away that he understood. And that he didn't blame me for doing what I did. For becoming what I had become. In fact, a small piece of him blamed himself.

I kept going. Talking until I reached the bitter end. Until I arrived right here, right now, at this very moment. As the words poured out of me, the relief came with it. Never had I told this story from start to finish. It had always been bits and pieces here and there, doled out on a need-to-know basis, depending on who was listening and what role they played in my life.

But sitting in that darkened, empty lounge, telling my dad everything, I knew it was exactly what I needed.

When at last I stopped, I took a deep breath and waited for him to speak. I didn't know what he would say—in fact, I hadn't a clue—but for the first time in my life, I wasn't scared. I wasn't cringing in anticipation of his reaction, the way I had when I first told Jamie what I did for a living or when I first told my friends. I was afraid of the way they would look at me. Afraid of being forever changed in their eyes.

But not now. Not here. Not with him.

I felt safe.

Wordlessly, my dad pulled me into his arms and held me. I snuggled into his chest and allowed myself to feel vulnerable. Wide open.

He began to sway gently back and forth, as if he were rocking a newborn baby. And the comparison wasn't too far off. Everything felt new right now.

We stayed like that for longer than I can remember. For a moment, I might even have fallen asleep. Right now there was such a hazy, blurred line between sleep and awake, they almost seemed to be one and the same.

When I started to come back to awareness and take note of my surroundings, I opened my eyes and caught sight of the deserted bar. The empty bar stools, the bottles of wine that lined the shelf, the cash register. And that's when our current location first struck me as somewhat odd. Why had my father agreed to meet me *here*? Was he afraid of waking Simone? But this hotel was at least eight miles from his house in Malibu. I had been so distracted by my grief when I called, I didn't even stop to think about where he had suggested we meet. It was only a seven-minute drive from my house in Brentwood, but he had been waiting for me when I got there. Had he already been here?

Oh, God, I thought with sudden panic. Was he here with another woman? Was he having an affair here?

The realization made me feel sick to my stomach. And I felt my old instincts start to kick in once again.

Don't ask if you don't want to know. Avoid the subject. Avoid. Avoid. Avoid.

But those days were over now. I had just spilled my entire life story to the one person who, up until a year ago, didn't know anything about my life at all. I think it was safe to say that we were well past avoidance.

I lifted my head and looked up at him. "Dad, why were you at the Huntley?" I asked point-blank.

My dad bowed his head in shame, and I felt the queasiness start to overtake me. I was right. He *was* here with another woman! And God knows what I had interrupted when I called.

I fought to keep my eyes glued to his face. To not look away. Because that's what my gut was telling me to do. What I had always done.

"Simone and I are over," he admitted softly. "She kicked me out last week. I've been trying to call you to let you know, but you haven't been answering your phone lately." He stopped long enough to give a quick nod toward the tears on my face. "Clearly, you've had a lot on your plate."

I felt some relief. Immediately followed by guilt. "So you're not here with another woman?"

He let out a sarcastic laugh. "No. I'm here alone." Then, after a beat, he added, "Although, since we're being honest, I should probably tell you that Simone kicked me out because I cheated on her."

I nodded, finally understanding. I'm just not sure why it took me this long to accept it. My dad was never going to be the sitcom father

I used to watch on TV. He was never going to be the home at six, flowers on special occasions, faithful, loving husband I always wanted him to be.

But you only get one father. And he was mine.

And I wasn't really one to throw stones. Especially when the glass house I had inhabited for so long was now lying in shattered pieces at my feet.

"So what happens now?" I asked, wiping under my nose with a crinkled cocktail napkin. "Does she get the house?"

He nodded. "Yeah, it was the least I could do. She was so crushed. And honestly, Jenny, I was, too. I really thought this time was going to be different. I loved her differently. It just felt right. But I guess it was me who wasn't different."

"It's okay, Dad," I said, reaching out and patting his shoulder. After all the consolation he had given me in the past hour, the least I could do was return the favor. "Don't be so hard on yourself."

He chuckled at that. "Right."

"You just need to stop getting married. Or you'll never find a permanent place to live."

He smiled at my attempt to lighten the conversation. But it was fleeting. His face suddenly turned serious again. "Actually, that's something else I needed to talk to you about."

His tone sent a shiver through my body. Although I couldn't imagine how he could drop anything worse in my lap than "I cheated on my *third* wife and she kicked me out."

But apparently, I was wrong.

"I'm moving to Paris."

"What?" I choked out, feeling the room start to spin. Just when I thought I had finally gotten that spinning problem under control. "You're doing what?"

"My firm wants me to head up their new offices out there. I just found out last month. I wasn't going to take it. Simone wanted to stay here. Apparently, she's been thinking of starting an acting career, I don't know. But after what happened between us, I figured, why not? Fresh start. New country. And besides, infidelity is practically expected over there. So I suppose I'll fit right in."

A small laugh escaped my lips, but my head was reeling. He couldn't leave. He couldn't go to Paris. Not after everything we'd just gone through in the past . . . well, ninety minutes! We had finally made some kind of breakthrough. We had finally reached the point where I thought we could have a *real* relationship. Not the fake, artificial, don't-talk-about-anything-personal kind that we'd been having for the past year. And now he was going to leave?

"I know it's bad timing," he said, responding to my stunned silence. "But I think it's for the best. I just need a change of scenery. You understand that, right?"

I nodded. I did understand. More than he knew. If anyone needed a change of scenery, it was me. If anyone needed a fresh start in a new country, it was me.

"I really want for you to come visit, though," he was saying. "As often as you want."

But I was hardly listening. I was too busy trying to contemplate the words that were bubbling up inside me, ready to pop out of my mouth without regret, without consequence, and most of all without looking back.

But there was really nothing to think about. Contemplation is only necessary when you're faced with multiple options. A crossroads of numerous possible paths. For me, there was only one.

"I'm coming with you."

32

false friends

The only person I contacted before I left was Lauren Ireland. And the only reason I called her was to tell her that I was closing the doors of the Hawthorne Agency and could she please relay the news to everyone else. She begged me to reconsider, but I was resolved in my decision. I no longer wanted anything to do with that world. It had chewed me up and spat me out and made it very clear that I wasn't welcome. So I was leaving.

When I refused to change my mind, Lauren suggested that perhaps she could take over the agency instead. I agreed without reservation and told her I'd have my lawyers transfer everything to her name. I warned her about the situation with Katie and Dean Stanton, and she took the news in stride. For some reason, it didn't seem to bother her as much as it had bothered me, and she calmly stated that she would take care of it.

Who knows, maybe she would be better suited for this business than I was. Maybe it would treat her better than it treated me. If she could cope with the pressure and the drama and the way it all messed with your head, then maybe she'd have a shot at surviving it. Or maybe she wouldn't. Either way, it wasn't my problem anymore. And that was more liberating than anything I had ever experienced.

Everything happened very fast after my late night soul-baring session with my dad. He was leaving in less than a week, and I was determined to leave with him. It didn't make sense for me to stay around any longer than I had to. The agency was gone. Jamie was gone. There was nothing left for me in Los Angeles.

I emptied my savings account into traveler's checks and paid some guy on Craigslist fifty bucks to unlock my iPhone so that I could use it abroad. I didn't pack much, just a few essentials and some of my favorite clothes. In staying true to my vow for a fresh start, I wanted everything in my life to be new, even my clothes. So much of my wardrobe and material possessions were tied to my old life. And I figured it would have been counterproductive to drag the past with me five thousand miles across the Atlantic Ocean.

Besides transferring ownership of the agency, there wasn't much left for me to do. And by Thursday morning, I was gone.

I didn't tell anyone I was leaving because I knew it would have made it harder. It would have led me to doubt my decision. And I didn't want to doubt it. I just wanted to go and not look back. I just wanted to do the first unpredictable, spontaneous thing I'd ever done in my life. And I didn't want anyone talking me out of it.

Because God knows they all would have tried. My mom, my niece, Hannah, Sophie, John, maybe even Zoë if she decided to pick up the phone and talk to me. They all would have told me I was being rash and overreactive and that I should allow myself some time to stop and think things through before I moved to any foreign countries. But I had been thinking things through my entire life. For once, I just wanted to do something and not think about it. For once, I wanted to let my emotions guide me instead of my head.

And if I called them from Paris, then it would be too late to convince me to stay.

From the moment we landed at Charles de Gaulle Airport, I felt an overwhelming mix of sadness and relief. Paris had always been my favorite city in the world, and I immediately found comfort in its sights and sounds and smells. It was *nothing* like Los Angeles. The culture, the language, the landscape. But I figured the more foreign the better.

I quickly fell into a new routine. After my dad left for work in the mornings, I would get dressed and stroll down to the café on the corner to enjoy a *thé au lait* (tea with milk) and a brioche while making small talk with Pierre, the friendly French waiter who worked the morning shift. Then I would turn on my iPod and just walk. I never planned where I would go. I never once looked at a map. I'd just start walking until I didn't want to walk anymore. And then I'd find my way back home using the Eiffel Tower as my guide.

Sometimes I would be gone for ten minutes, sometimes a few hours. It's amazing how Paris can kind of suck you in like that. Where you feel as if you could stay forever and be perfectly happy. I don't know any other city in the world like that. And the more I walked, the more I started to believe that I could one day be happy again. I guess that's why they call it a "magical" city.

The first few weeks flew by rather quickly. My dad and I went to dinner together almost every night and spent the weekends visiting nearby sites like Versailles, Mont-Saint-Michel, and the dark, musty champagne caves of Reims, where the world's finest bottles of champagne are born. We would talk about everything from religion to politics to culture and even relationships. There were no more taboos. No more minefield topics to step around. It was real and raw and authentic. The kind of father/daughter relationship I used to see in other people's lives but never dreamed I'd ever experience in my own.

The city seemed to welcome me with open arms. As if I were a lost, wounded soldier returning from war and Paris was the kind, gentle-hearted countryside woman who took me in, gave me shelter and food, and helped me heal. And it wasn't long before memories of Ashlyn, the agency, and everything that happened there faded into the background noise of people, traffic, and French sirens.

But the problem wasn't forgetting about work. Those memories left quietly and without a fight. The problem was Jamie. He was everywhere. In the drive from the airport to the city, in the beautiful stone monuments that I passed on my morning walks, sitting next to me in the café at breakfast. The memory of the trip we had taken here together only a year ago was still fresh in my mind, as if it had happened just yesterday. And seeing those same places that we had visited—standing in front of them, walking *through* them—only made it worse. And as much progress as I was making getting past everything else, the wounds that Jamie had left behind seemed to reopen every day, with every step. As if someone were constantly tearing out the stitches that had promised to hold me together. And every night I would find myself bleeding again.

Sophie and I e-mailed often, despite the fact that she vowed never to forgive me for skipping the country without telling anyone. In every e-mail, she asked me how long I was going to stay, and I repeatedly answered the same thing: "I don't know. As long as it takes, I guess."

Most of John's correspondence was laden with long-winded accounts of the local L.A. gossip. The biggest news, of course, was the story of Dean Stanton, the powerful head of New Edge Cinema, who had recently separated from his wife, was now dating one of his former nannies, and was rumored to have cast her in his studio's next film. I assumed this meant that Katie would no longer need her job at the Hawthorne Agency after all. Not when she had someone like Dean Stanton on hand to help launch that acting career she'd always wanted.

I sent numerous e-mails to Zoë over the first few weeks, most of them saturated with apologies and lengthy soul-searching paragraphs describing everything that I'd come to realize since we'd last spoken (or, more accurately, *screamed*), but I hadn't received a single reply. I wanted to believe that her e-mail simply wasn't working or that she had changed addresses and forgotten to tell me, but I had entered a new phase of honesty in my life. Refusing to lie to anyone . . . most of all myself. So eventually I had to admit that Zoë's e-mail was working fine. She just wasn't responding.

The only person I didn't attempt to contact was Jamie. And the memory of the last time I saw him—walking into his loft with another woman—continued to haunt me. But the fact that he had yet to reach out to me only confirmed my belief that he had moved on. And now it was time for me to do the same.

Sometimes during my walks, I would sit on a bench in a park or a garden somewhere in the city and just watch people as they passed.

Paris is the most wonderful city in the world for people watching because everyone is out on the street. Everyone's reaction to life is out in the open. From the moment I got here, I noticed that my ability to read people's minds had severely diminished. Maybe it was the foreign language or the unfamiliar culture, or maybe my burning desire to let go of all my attachments to the past had forced me to block it out, but the minds of the French men passing by me were unusually quiet. At first it terrified me. I had never heard such silence. But after a while, I came to appreciate the stillness and the mystery of strangers. It made people watching that much more fun. A challenge. For once I wasn't inundated with other people's problems. Other people's stories. And I hoped it meant I could concentrate on unraveling my own. Because God knows I hadn't done a very good job of it thus far.

When my Parisian sojourn reached its one-month mark, I decided that I needed to find something to do with my time. I had been wandering around the city for three weeks straight, and I was starting to crave some kind of direction. Although my dad had been paying the rent on the apartment here, I was still paying my mortgage back in L.A., and without a steady income I knew my resources would eventually run dry.

When I told Pierre, the waiter at my regular morning café, that I was looking for a way to make money, he told me that the weeknight bartender had just quit and the owner had been looking to replace him.

His suggestion intrigued me. Not only for monetary purposes, but for the experience of it all. My French was improving every day, and this would undoubtedly help. Plus, I liked that it was different. I liked that it was something that six months ago I never would have dreamed I'd be doing.

So the next morning, I took Pierre up on his offer and met with Carlos, the Spanish owner of Café Bosquet, and ten minutes later the job was mine. I didn't have a work visa, but Carlos seemed more than happy to pay me under the table in cash, and I was just happy to have a place to belong again.

I started working five nights a week. I would come in at six in the evening and leave a little after midnight. The café was never too busy, a dinner crowd that shuffled in around eight and fizzled out before ten and a few late night customers after that. It was a relatively quiet restaurant, in a relatively quiet section of town tucked away between the Eiffel Tower and l'École militaire (the Military School) in the seventh arrondissement. The neighborhood, or *quartier,* as the French call it, had a reputation of housing many French politicians and foreign ambassadors, earning it the nickname "the Washington, D.C., of Paris."

From day one, Pierre helped me learn the ropes. He introduced me to the staff, taught me how to use the impossibly confusing cappuccino machine that I swear you need a Ph.D. to operate, and corrected my floundering French when I made comical grammar mistakes. *Faux amis,* he called them. False friends. English words that you'd think would translate directly into French because they're so similar but in fact have completely different meanings. Like *préservatif,* which actually translates into "condom" and not the stuff the American vineyards put in red wine to help lengthen the shelf life. A mistake I made only once.

The job at Café Bosquet wasn't anything glamorous or important, but I found contentment in its simplicity. There was a beginning, a middle, and an end to every task that I undertook. I poured a drink, someone drank it, I cleaned the glass, and I placed it back on the rack for the next customer. When the icebox was empty, I went to the back to refill it. Small, uncomplicated cycles. No broken hearts, no crying, no betrayals. The most disappointing part of my night was when someone forgot to leave a tip. But even then Pierre explained that most French people don't tip.

I enjoyed the people aspect of the bartender life as well. Conversing with someone new every night. It was actually a much bigger part of the job than pouring drinks. And without fail, the conversations always found their way to the subject of relationships. Nearly every customer who made conversation with me would eventually talk about love. What's wrong with it, why they can't find it, why they can't manage to stay in it.

Maybe it was just me. Maybe lonely hearts sensed something in my past—an understanding of human nature—and were inevitably drawn to it.

Pierre and I would talk a lot, too. He normally worked the breakfast shift, but he would come by the café for a drink almost every night after the dinner rush and sit at the bar and chat with me until it was time to go home.

I quickly got used to his company. I considered him my first real friend in Paris. He was sweet and funny and easy to talk to. Plus his hilarious French antics and unusual sense of humor made me laugh. I've always loved how jokes vary from country to country. What's funny in French may not be as funny in English. Something about that unique French charm just gets lost in the translation.

It eventually got to the point where I would look forward to Pierre's visits. Especially on slower nights when there was nothing to do but stare out into the gradually emptying café and watch people clear out and return home to their lives.

One Monday night in early January was shaping up to be like that. It was just after nine-thirty, and the only people in the café were two businessmen—one French, one American—at the far end of the bar. They were speaking in English, which made it easier to catch bits and pieces of their conversation as I went about my side work behind the bar. Shining glasses, scrubbing down the cappuccino machine, and wiping down the leather-bound menus.

From the chunks of dialogue I was able to passively pick up every time I came by to check their drink levels, it was evident these two men were in the middle of an important business deal. And not a very interesting one at that.

I checked my watch and glanced toward the door. Pierre usually made an appearance between nine-thirty and ten, and I was anxious for him to show up and keep me company on such a dull night.

I studied the two businessmen out of the corner of my eye. The Frenchman was dressed in a light gray suit, a coral pink shirt, and a powder blue tie. It had taken me a while to get used to the French's colorful fashion sense. Especially when it came to the businessmen.

When I first arrived in Paris, I'd actually found it quite comical. They looked more like they were going to the circus than the office. But Pierre had explained to me that the French just liked and appreciated color. And that to a French person, the traditional American corporate attire looked drab and dreary. As if they were going to a funeral every day of their life.

And now I had to admit, when I glanced over at the American at the bar, dressed in his smart black suit, crisp white button-up, and conservative navy striped tie, he looked so . . . stiff. And boring.

The American swigged down the last of his wine, and I sidled over with the bottle. "Another glass?"

He nodded gratefully, and I poured.

"Well, I'm positive my client won't agree to those terms," the Frenchman was saying in impressively solid English. "He's not going to spend a half a million euros on tenant improvements for a five-year lease. It's just not worth it. He has no guarantees that you will renew the lease in five years or that your company will even make it here for that long."

"We'll make it," the American assured him, sounding cocky and confident as only a slick American businessman can. "Projections for the European market are extremely strong."

I finished pouring and indicatively held up the bottle to the second man. He nodded and pointed toward his glass. I began refilling it.

"But this is your first venture outside the United States," the Frenchman replied. "And projections are just that: projections. They are not guarantees. Now if you agreed to sign a ten-year lease, then I'd have something to go back with."

The American man shook his head, keeping his composure despite his evident aversion to this suggestion. "Look, we both know this space has been vacant for more than eighteen months. I'm sure your client hasn't enjoyed covering the mortgage out of his own pocket. He needs cash flow. And we can help. But if he doesn't agree to the terms, we'll have no choice but to set up the European headquarters in Brussels."

I stifled a groan as I listened to the conversation.

What a bunch of bullshit, I thought. Brussels? Yeah, right. It was so obvious that this man was absolutely *desperate* to set up his company's new offices in Paris.

"The Belgian landlord has already agreed to the five-year lease term *and* the five hundred k in improvements. All we have to do is sign the paperwork," the American was now saying.

I fought back a laugh. Another load of crap.

The wineglass in front of me was nearly full, but I just kept on pouring. I was hardly paying attention to what I was doing because I was too distracted waiting for the Frenchman to call the American's obvious bluff.

But he didn't. His expression remained grim and defeated, and he sighed in frustration, clearly not catching on to this blatant lie at all.

Then I heard a gasp, and I looked down to see a sea of red wine flooding the top of the bar and spilling over the edge. I jumped in surprise and pulled up the bottle. The two businessmen had leapt up from their seats to avoid a Cabernet shower.

"Oh God!" I exclaimed as I mopped up the mess. "I'm so sorry about that. I just totally blanked out."

"It's fine," they both assured me with smiles, although the Frenchman's was slightly less genuine. No doubt his head was still stuck on the ultimatum he had just received.

The American excused himself to use the restroom and try to reduce some of the stain's damage, and I continued to wipe up the spill and apologize profusely.

"*Je suis si desolée,*" I transitioned into French.

"*Pas de problème,*" the Frenchman repeated, wiping his pants with a spare napkin I had tossed to him. "The deal was going sour anyway. It was perfect timing, in fact."

I studied him intently, taking note of the disappointment on his face. Did he really not know the man was lying? Was it really not obvious?

My mind flashed back to the dinner meeting I had attended with Jamie. I thought Hank Chandler's bluff about having an offer from another company was the most transparent thing in the world, but Jamie didn't have a clue.

Ever since I had arrived in Paris, I had found it difficult to read

French men. But that man in the bathroom was American. And I had been able to read his true intentions as clear as day. Was it really just a question of language? Did the secret behind my special men-reading superpower all come down to nationality?

"You know," I began cautiously, eyeing the restroom for the American's return, "he doesn't have the option to go to Brussels."

He looked up at me with curious eyes. "What are you talking about?"

I continued wiping the bar with slow, purposeful strokes. "I overheard what he said. About putting the European headquarters in Brussels." I shook my head. "It's a lie. He has to put it in Paris."

The man continued to study me with apprehension. "How do you know that?"

I shrugged. "I don't know. I just do. To me, the lie is as obvious as that wine stain on your shirt."

He glanced down at the front of his soiled pink shirt, wiping it haphazardly with his napkin. He was far less concerned about the stain than he was about the questionable information I was imparting to him.

"And I'm sorry about both," I offered quietly. "The stain *and* the lie."

Another stunned silence. He wasn't sure what to make of this new development. Or if he should even believe it. "So what are you suggesting I do?"

I tossed the now-red rag into a bucket of soapy water by my feet. "Don't give in to his demands. He'll rent the space regardless."

The American returned from the bathroom just then and tossed a fifty-euro bill down on the bar. "Let's get out of here," he said. "I've got an early call tomorrow morning with the New York office."

The Frenchman nodded absently and followed his drinking buddy out the door. He took one last inquiring glance in my direction, and I smiled back, happy to have offered some advice that didn't have to do with someone's love life. Whether he took it or not.

Pierre showed up a few minutes later and ordered his usual Kronenbourg beer. Like every night, tonight he stayed with me until it was time to close up. It was all part of our usual routine. I sometimes wondered why he never seemed to have anything else to do than come down here five nights a week and drink beer at the bar. But I always assumed it was because he enjoyed my company as much as I enjoyed his. He would always tell me funny stories and jokes while I cleaned up the bar and counted out my cash register. And then after Carlos locked the door behind us, he would usually offer to walk me back to my apartment, which I would always insist was unnecessary since I lived only a block away. Then we would part ways with a double-cheek kiss. Very French.

Yes, he was attractive, and I definitely noticed how the American female tourists and even the French local women looked at him when they came into the café. But I never saw him as anything more than that: a double-cheek kiss.

And he seemed perfectly fine with our casual, platonic relationship. Never crossing the line, never implying or hinting that we could be anything more than just friends.

Which is probably why I didn't see it coming when he asked me out.

Although in retrospect I probably *should* have. You would think that someone who had flirted with men for a living would have been able to pick up on something like that. But whatever the reason, I was caught completely off guard.

Carlos had just locked the door behind us and I was still buttoning up my coat when Pierre said, *"Tu veux dîner avec moi demain soir?"*

I stopped midbutton, and my hands fell lifelessly to my sides. My head slowly tilted toward him as I struggled to keep the look of panic from registering on my face.

I knew what the sentence *translated* to: "Do you want to have dinner with me tomorrow night?" *Dîner* is one of those classic French verbs that you learn early on because it's easy to remember and its conjugation is regular.

But I couldn't be sure what kind of "dining" he was referring to. Because obviously it was one thing to grab a ham-and-cheese sandwich from one of those carts on the sidewalk, but it was quite another to sit down to a candlelit meal at some romantic French bistro. Plus, he was so casual about the whole thing. Just slipping the question into the conversation as if it were nothing. What if *dîner* was just another of those "false friends" that I kept learning about? And in this context it actually meant "to visit an educational museum in a very platonic, nonsexual way"?

Pierre laughed at my stunned silence, and it was then that I realized my mouth was hanging open. "Can I take that as a yes?" he asked hopefully.

I quickly shut my gaping jaw. "Um," I stuttered, trying to find the right words. They didn't really teach you how to let someone down easy in high school French class. "I . . . I don't think so," was my eloquent reply.

"Pourquoi pas?" he immediately asked, his face dripping with evident disappointment. French men certainly didn't have any problems showing their emotions. An admirable quality. Just not for me. Not now.

I knew that after I said no, things probably wouldn't be the same between us. That's how it always is when someone reveals secret feelings that turn out to be unrequited. And the thought of losing Pierre as a friend saddened and frustrated me at the same time. Because knowing that all his helpfulness and affections and funny jokes had probably been just one big ruse to take things to the next level suddenly made me feel somewhat betrayed. As though *he* had been the *faux ami*.

I continued buttoning up my jacket, this time with considerably more fervor than when I had first started. "Because I just don't think it would be a good idea."

Pierre looked at me with a slightly confused expression. "Do you have a boyfriend?"

I yanked my gloves out of my pocket and slid them over my hands. "No."

"But you used to," he speculated observantly. Then, upon seeing my silent reaction, he added, "Very recently."

Emotionally transparent *and* astute. What a combo.

"Yes," I replied curtly, wrapping my scarf tightly around my neck as if I were preparing for a mile-long trek across town, not the fifty paces it took to get to my dad's apartment from here. "I used to, but not anymore."

He cocked his head to the side and studied my distressed expression. "That's why you're here, isn't it? In Paris."

I stared down at the ground, kicking my left toe against the sidewalk. "I'm here for a lot of reasons."

Pierre sensed my uneasiness and placed his hand gently on my shoulder. "I can help you forget him. French men are good at that sort of thing."

I chuckled politely. But it wasn't because what he said had been funny. It was because the very same thought had crossed my mind the minute he asked me to dinner. I knew that Pierre was the kind of man who *would* make me forget about Jamie. Or at least distract me long enough for the pain to dull. And believe me, it was tempting. As tempting as a lifeboat in a tumultuous sea.

I hesitated, fingering the frayed ends of my cashmere scarf. "I'm sorry, Pierre," I replied as graciously as possible. "I just don't think I can."

I expected his shoulders to slouch, his head to drop, and his hands to shove into his pockets in bitter defeat. But instead he just flashed me this coy little smile, as if he knew something I didn't, and leaned forward to kiss me on both cheeks.

"You'll change your mind," he assured me. The way he said it wasn't in any way foreboding or threatening. In fact, it was actually somewhat endearing. He was so confident of himself, as though he had been given a rare glimpse into the future. I had to laugh.

He grinned back at me. *"Oui?"* he presumed, misreading my amusement.

I laughed again. *"Peut-être,"* I finally admitted with a shy smile.

And it was true. Maybe I would change my mind. Maybe someday I would wake up in the morning and the first thought that popped into my head wouldn't be about Jamie. And maybe one night I would fall asleep to the fantasy of someone else's arms wrapped around me. But I knew I couldn't depend on anyone else to save me. I had to get there myself. In my own time. With my own lifeboat.

33

. . . a window opens

When I got home from the bar that night, my dad informed me that someone named Zoë had called for me on the landline while I was gone.

My immediate response was disbelief. Zoë hadn't returned any of my calls or answered any of my e-mails since I got here more than a month ago. "Are you sure it wasn't Sophie?" I verified, standing in the middle of the living room with skeptical eyes.

My dad pursed his lips. "Pretty sure she said Zoë." He nodded toward a piece of paper on the kitchen counter. "I took a message and told her you'd call her back when you got home."

I felt nerves boiling up in my stomach. I checked my watch. "What time is it there?"

My dad glanced at the clock on the stereo. "A little after three in the afternoon."

"Thanks!" I said as I grabbed the landline phone from the cradle and skidded down the hallway toward my room, dialing Zoë's number as I went.

The line rang twice before she picked up. "Hi," she said in a low voice without any formalities.

"Hi," I returned in an equal tone, even though my heartbeat was racing. "I'm glad you called. I've been wanting to talk to you for so long and—"

"I know," she interrupted, clearly not wanting me to keep going. "I need to tell you something, and I need you not to speak until I'm done."

There was a certain firmness to her voice that caught me off guard. It didn't sound like Zoë. She was too calm, too reserved, and I had a feeling I was in for a harangue. But I also had no doubt that I deserved it. And if listening patiently while she got a month's worth of frustration off her chest was what it was going to take to get my friend back, I was more than happy to do so.

"Okay," I obliged softly.

Zoë took a deep breath that I could hear from across the entire Atlantic Ocean. "Dustin and I broke up," she stated. I imagined this was the part where I was supposed to stay quiet. So I did.

"After you told his wife," she continued, the emotional struggle apparent in her voice, "things were pretty good for a while. We didn't have to sneak around anymore, and I felt like I finally had the relationship that he'd been promising me since we started dating.

"But then Alice filed for divorce. And he panicked and tried to leave me. He mumbled something about losing his kids and his house and the only family he'd ever known. I tried to remind him of his promise to me, that he was already planning to leave her. And he *did* promise me that. And I really think that he meant it . . . at the time. . . ." Her voice trailed off for a moment, as if she were trying to muster the strength to continue. "But as soon as the reality of it all set in, as soon as it was *her* who was doing the leaving, then suddenly it wasn't so appealing anymore."

She exhaled loudly and painfully. "Apparently, Alice told him that she'd take him back if he left me and started seeing a shrink. And that was that. I was dumped. Like a hooker he had picked up on Hollywood Boulevard. I was no longer useful."

There was a time not too long ago when I'd willed this day to come. When I'd fantasized about how good I would feel when it did. Satisfied, triumphant, pleased with myself. But I felt none of that now. My heart did not rejoice. It only broke for her.

"Oh, Zoë," I cried, wishing I could reach through the phone and comfort her. "I'm so sorry. I can't belie— Oh wait, can I talk now?"

She laughed weakly. "Yes. Go ahead."

"I can't believe he would do that to you," I continued.

"Yes, you can," she stated matter-of-factly. "It's exactly what you said would happen."

I bowed my head in shame. "I'm so sorry about what I said and what I did. I shouldn't have sold you out like that. I should have supported you. The way you always supported me, through all my horrible, not to mention *unethical,* mistakes."

"I know," Zoë stopped me before the apologies started flooding out with no foreseeable end. "I got your e-mails."

I could hear the faint smile on her lips, and I smiled back. "Right."

"But you were right," she pointed out. "About all of it. And if you hadn't told her, I would still be with him. And this horrible breakup would have been prolonged even longer. Possibly years. And I can't even imagine how much that would have hurt."

Even though Zoë was letting me off the hook, I couldn't seem to do the same for myself. I still felt the need to earn her forgiveness. "I still should have chosen you," I whispered.

"Yes," she agreed. "And I should have told you about him from the beginning. I was afraid of what you might say. Because I knew I would have to deny it, and yet deep down, I also knew that you would be right."

"Trust me when I say that this brings me no joy."

She laughed. "I trust you." Then after a brief pause, "Now, can we forget this sappy bullshit and start talking about real stuff?"

I laid my head down on the pillow and smiled into the phone as I began to fill her in on everything that had happened to me in the past month.

Zoë was back.

When I arrived at Café Bosquet the next night for my shift, Carlos informed me that someone was waiting for me at the bar.

A knowing smirk stretched across my lips as I tied my apron around my waist and crossed the restaurant. I had been feeling anxious about seeing Pierre all day, wondering how he would react to our conversation last night. Wondering if he would even continue to come in and see me.

But when I reached the bar, I saw that it wasn't, in fact, Pierre who had been waiting for me, but a man I didn't recognize.

"*Bonsoir,*" he said politely, rising from his bar stool.

"*Bonsoir,*" I replied warily, trying to figure out who he was and why had supposedly told the owner that he was here to see me.

"I don't know if you remember me," he transitioned smoothly into perfect English with just the trace of an accent. "I was in here last night with an American man. We were discussing his company's plans to open a European headquarters in Paris—"

"Of course!" I interrupted, recognition instantly flashing across my face. "The guy with the *big* opportunity in Brussels." There was clear mocking in my tone as I remembered the bogus ultimatum the American had given him. Well, at least it had been bogus to *me*. If I remembered correctly, this guy didn't doubt its authenticity for a second.

The man in front of me smiled. "Yes. That one. I wanted to talk to you about it."

I made my way to the side of the bar and ducked under the lift-up countertop. "Sure. Would you like something to drink?"

He nodded gratefully. "Yes. A glass of Bordeaux would be great."

I smiled and turned to grab a glass from the rack.

The man reclaimed his seat as he watched me pour the drink. "If I may, I'd like to ask how you knew he was lying. About being able to set up the deal in Brussels."

I slid the wineglass across the bar to him. "I'm just perceptive, I guess . . . about men."

"Yes, very," he agreed, sipping his wine.

I chuckled and leaned back against the counter behind me. "It seems to work better on Americans than anyone else, I've recently discovered."

He leaned forward, intrigued. "So you just have this sense when men are lying?"

I shrugged. "Yeah, I guess you could put it that way." I didn't feel like telling a perfect stranger that it was a bit more than just a sense. That I actually had the ability to read men's minds.

Unfortunately, my answer didn't seem to satisfy him. "But how did you know that the French distributor would only work with him if he was located in Paris?"

I scrunched up my mouth in confusion. That part I certainly didn't remember. "I didn't. I don't know even know what you're talking about."

Frustration flashed briefly over his face. "But when he was in the bathroom, you told me that he had to put the headquarters in Paris. I remember."

"Oh, right," I replied, suddenly recollecting that part of the conversation. "Well I didn't know exactly what all the details were, but I could just *sense*"—I chose his word—"that he had to put the offices here."

The man gazed at me, awestruck. "But how?" he insisted.

I shrugged again, starting to feel uncomfortable under all this scrutiny. "I don't know," I said. "I just did. I could hear it in his voice and see it on his face."

"Well, how is it that you were able to see and hear those things and I wasn't?" The man's frustration was back. Clearly I had him doubting his keen negotiation skills.

"Maybe because I'm a woman," I stated simply.

He found humor in this and laughed. "You're probably right." He took a long gulp of his wine, not bothering to swish it around in his mouth to absorb the flavor. "Well, I just wanted to come by and tell you that you were spot-on. He *was* lying. And when I told him this morning that my client wasn't going to accept his terms and that he should probably just take the deal in Brussels, he caved."

Unable to hide my contentment, I felt a sly, satisfactory smirk stretch across my lips. Not that I needed him to come here to tell me that I was right. My instincts were rarely ever wrong.

"Then I found out the French distributor that he had agreed to partner with wasn't going to work with him unless he was located in Paris."

"Well, there you go," I said, crossing my arms over my chest. "Congrats on winning the deal."

He shook his head, his expression troubled. "But that's just the thing. I wouldn't have won if it weren't for you. My client probably would have been the one to give in."

I smiled, thinking about how I had saved Jamie's firm $50,000 in pretty much the same way. But then the thought of Jamie started to make my stomach wrench, so I struggled to push it from my mind.

The man finished off his wine and I offered to pour him another, but he declined politely. "I have to get home for dinner. My wife's cooking." He stood up and removed a ten-euro bill from his wallet and a cream-colored business card from his pocket, then placed them both on top of the bar. "But I wanted to leave you my card."

I took a step forward and slid the card over to me. "Alain Dumont," I read the name on the front.

He grinned. *"Enchanté."*

"A corporate real estate broker?"

"Yes. My firm does a lot of work with American corporations coming to Europe."

Jean-Luc, one of the café waiters on duty tonight, approached the bar just then and ordered two drinks for one of his tables. "A vodka soda and a Heineken, *s'il te plaît.*"

I smiled graciously and placed the man's business card in my pocket before turning to prepare the drinks. "Well, I'll be sure to pass along your name to any American business owners who come into the bar."

He seemed to find amusement in that. "No," he replied, shaking his head. "Actually, I was hoping I could hire you."

I nearly dropped the bottle of vodka I was pouring from. *"Hire* me? To do what?"

He looked at me as if the answer were obvious. "To help me negotiate. To use that sixth sense of yours or whatever it is."

Jean-Luc glanced uneasily between the two of us, knowing that he had missed some important piece of this conversation. I hastily finished off his drink order and splashed them down onto his tray. He hoisted it up and disappeared around the corner.

I turned back to the man now identified as Alain Dumont. He was staring at me expectantly. "Well?"

I threw up my hands. "Well what?"

"I have another deal with an American company coming up in a few days, and I could really use your help. I'll pay you well. A percentage of my fee." He glanced around the bar. "I assure you it'll be more than you're making here."

I slinked back against the counter, disbelief on my face. "You really want to *pay* me just to tell you if a man is lying?"

Now it was his turn to shrug. "Pretty much."

I nodded slowly, taking it all in.

He picked up on my hesitation. "Look, you have my card. Take your time. Think it over and get back to me."

And with the flash of a smile, he was out the door, leaving me wondering what the hell had just happened.

I continued to lean against the back of the bar, staring out into space and trying to process the conversation that had passed between us. A stranger had just offered me a job. Just like that. And I had to admit, it was a highly intriguing offer. A chance to use my men-reading superpower *without* ending up in a hotel room at the end of the night? I didn't even know a job like that existed.

But then again, I didn't know that fidelity inspectors existed until I actually became one.

So I suppose it was fitting.

And although the magnitude of what would eventually transpire from Alain Dumont's offer would not become completely apparent until much later on, I had a feeling something was about to change.

Looking back, though, I suppose it was fairly obvious.

I had found my next calling.

Or rather, it had found me.

Epilogue

---

new beginnings

Three Months Later . . .

I step out onto the balcony of my new two-bedroom apartment in the Latin Quarter of Paris. The morning March sky is gray and somewhat gloomy, but by now I've come to appreciate the characteristic weather of Paris. It wouldn't be the same city without the rainy mornings and dreary afternoons. And I've been told the months of May and June make the long-drawn-out winter worth every drop.

I pour myself a cup of tea in the kitchen and sip it slowly as I sit down in front of my laptop and begin scrolling through my morning e-mails. Five total. Three personal and two business related.

More requests for my services, no doubt.

Ever since I started working for Alain Dumont three months ago, my new career has taken off at a steady pace. At first I simply sat in on the meetings and quietly informed him when the other party was not being entirely truthful. But then eventually I started to get the hang of the negotiation process and was able to run a few meetings on my own.

When it became pretty obvious to Alain that my "sixth sense" (as he liked to call it) about lying men was not just a fluke, he started recommending my services to his friends. Not only other real estate brokers, but sales reps, ad men, consultants, small corporations, basically anyone who did business with Americans and were looking for the competitive edge that I was apparently able to provide.

Who knew freelance negotiators who could read American men were in such high demand in Europe? Almost as much as fidelity inspectors in the States.

Within two months, my income was enough to support me full-time, and I quit my job at the bar and signed a lease on my own apartment in the fourth arrondissement. Not that I didn't enjoy living with my dad, but it was nice to have a place of my own again. And with my condo in Brentwood currently being rented to a lovely young newlywed couple expecting their first child, there was something to be said about the feeling of permanence that came when I signed the lease on my new Parisian home.

I read and respond to the personal e-mails in my in-box first, because they're more important. I've learned a thing or two about priorities over the past few months. Friends and family come first. Everything else can wait.

The first e-mail is from Sophie. I tap on it and skim the text, although I already know exactly what the e-mail is pertaining to. For the past few months, she's been planning a trip with Zoë and John to visit me in Paris, and with the departure date rapidly approaching in less than two weeks, my in-box has been flooded with questions about what to pack, where to exchange money, and what my thoughts are on the latest Paris-related articles in *Condé Nast Traveler*. The usual international travel provisions. But of course, with Sophie in the equation, it's always a much more urgent affair.

Today her e-mail is contesting the appalling weakness of the American dollar against the euro. As if I am personally responsible for setting the exchange rates on the international currency market and she is lodging a formal complaint.

I shake my head with amusement and quickly tap out a reply before continuing to the next message. This one is from Zoë, a much more concise e-mail (albeit half of the text consisting of profanities) updating me on the new hot guy she met at the gym, who, she was happy to report, has never been married and has not fathered any children . . . that she knows of.

I tap out an enthusiastic reply and keep going.

The last e-mail is from John. And the subject line reads, "HAVE

YOU SEEN THIS???" in all capital letters with about twenty question marks following it. He appears to have maxed out the number
of allowable characters in the subject line field. As I scroll down further into the message, I have a feeling I know exactly what all of this
exaggerated punctuation is referring to.

And when I see a blue link leading to an online article from the
L.A. Times, I realize that I was correct in my assumptions.

I don't need to click on the link to know what is written on the
other end of it. I came across the article myself just a few days ago,
and although the shock of its contents has still not worn off completely, I have spent the past forty-eight hours making peace with it.

It's a story in the *L.A. Times* about an unknown little company
called the Hawthorne Agency, which specializes in exposing infidelity. And apparently, it's taken the nation by storm.

I remember the way I felt the morning I first laid eyes on the full-
size color photograph on my screen. It was a picture of none other
than Lauren Ireland (whom the article refers to as "Bella Grace"),
and the caption read, "President Bella Grace, who inherited the
agency from an anonymous previous owner, calls her business the
next frontier in private investigations."

Apparently, as I was attempting to piece my life back together,
Lauren—or rather *Bella*—was working hard to build public awareness around the agency I left behind. And this article is the direct
result of those efforts.

My eyes skimmed wildly over the text as I caught sight of key
phrases like "intention to cheat test," "fidelity inspector," and "hopes
to open offices in New York and Chicago later this year." And the
most shocking part of all: a Web site, www.thehawthorneagency.
com.

I sigh as I type out a response to John, explaining that yes, I've
seen it and I'm fine.

Which is true. Of course, it was disconcerting at first. All that
time and energy I spent trying to keep the agency a secret. Clearly,
it was necessary only to protect my own identity. Because Lauren
quickly made a decision to put it all right out there in the open, and
what do you know? It worked.

Just goes to show she was a better woman for the job after all.

I skim through the rest of my e-mails and then wander into my bedroom to shower and dress for my appointment this afternoon with a new client.

Although I suppose it's hard to describe him as "new" when I've known him my entire life. But to be perfectly honest, I never really *got* to know him until recently.

My dad called me a few days ago and asked if I would come in and help him with a last-minute negotiation he had just set up. Apparently, an American man he had once done business with was looking to renew their partnership.

I am scheduled to arrive at his offices in the *La Defense* district of Paris in two hours, which leaves me just enough time to drop by my favorite café and enjoy a brioche and a quick chat with my favorite French waiter.

Pierre and I continue to hang out occasionally, although obviously not as often as we used to since I no longer work at the bar. And once I began booking early client meetings, my leisurely mornings of brioche and long conversation were limited to once or twice a week.

He continues to ask me out on a regular basis, and I continue to say no. Yet his confidence never falters, and I'm repeatedly impressed with his unyielding persistence. Every time I turn him down, he simply vows that one day I will change my mind. But after four months of living in Paris without a single date, I am still pretty sure that I want to be on my own for a while.

I finish dressing, drying my hair, and applying my makeup, then slip out the front doors of my seven-story classic Haussmannian-style building, with my briefcase in hand. I hop in a cab and direct him to Café Bosquet near the École militaire, and he steps on the gas.

After a quick breakfast of my usual *thé au lait* and brioche and a few delightful jokes from Pierre, I get into another cab and settle in for the drive to the outskirts of the city, where the metropolitan business district of Paris is located.

As I slide into a seat at the conference table, my dad says to me, "I'll probably just stick around for the introduction and then slip out and let you handle the negotiations. I think it'll go much smoother if I'm not around to interfere."

I pull my legal pad out of my briefcase and set it in front of me. "No problem. That's fine. I've done plenty of these things on my own," I reassure him as we wait for the other party to arrive.

My dad leans back in his chair, looking extremely at ease. "Sounds good."

"So tell me what the story is with this guy again?"

He folds his hands in his lap and explains, "We formed an LLP about a year ago, but things got complicated and he said I wasn't keeping up my end of the deal. The partnership eventually dissolved a couple months back."

"So why are we here, then?"

My dad shrugs. "He called me a few days ago and said he wants to try to reconcile. You know, set up a new agreement."

I jot down a few notes on my legal pad. "And you're cool with this?"

He nods. "Yeah. I've always thought it would be a good partnership. I'm just glad he finally came around and realized it, too."

My dad seems to find amusement in his last statement, and a knowing smile creeps its way across his lips.

I shoot him a strange look. "What?"

But he simply shakes his head and continues to smirk. "Nothing."

I roll my eyes. "Whatever, Dad."

He laughs at this. "Is that part of your sophisticated negotiation vocabulary?"

But I just smile in return. "Yeah, I suppose it is."

A few moments later, the door opens and my dad's assistant enters. She speaks in a rich French accent, the elongated syllables rolling off her tongue like an enchanting melody. "Mr. Ree-shar has arrived. He is in the restrooms."

"*Merci,* Yvette," my dad responds with a courteous smile.

I lean closer to him. "What's this guy's name? Ree-shar?"

He laughs. "No, that's just the French pronunciation. Yvette sometimes has a hard time with the American names."

I nod understandingly. "So how *do* you pronounce his name?"

"It's Richards in English."

I scowl and lean back in my seat. "Ugh. That's Jamie's last name."

Another knowing smile stretches across my dad's face. "It is, isn't it? I forgot that. Common name, I guess."

"Yeah," I mumble as I drop my head down and start doodling on my notepad.

But when I look up again and study my dad closer, for some reason he doesn't seem like himself. He seems . . . I don't know . . . smug or something. I am just about to comment on the fact when the door squeaks open once again and into the room walks Mr. Ree-shar himself.

Except it isn't just any other person with that name.

As common as it might be, the man who enters that conference room is the only Richards *I* have ever known.

And his first name is Jamie.

I sit paralyzed in my chair, a stunned expression plastered on my face.

I'm dreaming. I have to be dreaming.

There's no other explanation for this. Jamie only appears in my dreams. In my late-night fantasies as I'm lying in bed trying to find something to sleep to. He doesn't appear in my real life.

Our eyes meet, and I wait for a similar (if slightly less frantic) expression to register on his face. But it never does. He simply flashes me a polite, professional smile and then turns his attention to my dad.

As if he doesn't even recognize me.

As if he's seeing me for the first time.

Does he have amnesia? I wonder. Has he been in a terrible accident and lost all of his memories? That would certainly explain the absence of a phone call or e-mail in the past four months.

My dad leaps into action, rising and offering his hand for Jamie to shake. "Hi, Jamie. Good to see you again."

"Good to see you, too, Jack."

Then my dad turns to me. "This is my associate, Jennifer Hunter. She's here to assist with the negotiations."

I stare blankly up at my dad. *What on earth is he doing?* Does he have amnesia, too? This is Jamie standing here. *Jamie!* The man I lived with. The man I once agreed to marry. Has it been so long since the two of them met that he can't even put two and two together?

"Pleased to meet you, Ms. Hunter." Jamie extends his hand to me, his face once again void of any recognition.

But I don't shake it. I just sit there gawking at it. As if it's a foreign object I've never seen before. But in actuality, it's a hand I once knew very well. A hand that once caressed me, held me, comforted me.

My dad nudges me with his elbow, and I blink rapidly to wake myself from my trance. With cautious, unsteady fingers, I reach out and shake the hand that is extended toward me, feeling a million tiny tingles shoot up my arm.

Jamie sits down, tugging at the lapels of his jacket. "So," he begins, his voice all business, "shall we get started?"

But my dad doesn't return to his seat. He simply looks down at me and says, "I think you can take it from here, Jen. I have a lot of work to finish up, so I'll leave it to you." He gives me a reassuring pat on the back.

Jamie flashes a tight-lipped smile. "Good to see you again, Jack."

My dad points a finger at him. "You, too, Jamie."

My head bobs frantically between the two of them, trying to figure out what the hell is going on in here and why I don't seem to be in on it.

"Are you kidding?" I finally sputter out, speaking (or more like *spitting*) for the first time since my amnesiac ex-fiancé entered the room.

But my dad just looks at me as if he has no idea what I could possibly be referring to. "Is something the matter? If you have any questions, I'll be right down the hall."

I look back at Jamie, and he offers me an innocent little shrug.

Okay, maybe it's just me. Maybe *I* am the delusional one with the mental malfunctions. Maybe the man sitting across from me is just another stranger I've never met and I'm sitting here imagining the entire thing. I mean, it certainly wouldn't be the first time I pictured Jamie walking back into my life with no warning. But during most of those fantasies, I don't sit there with my mouth hanging open like an idiot. I jump into his arms and make out with him passionately.

But this feels so much more real than any of the others.

"Um, nothing," I mumble, staring down at the table. "I'm fine."

My dad smiles. "Good." He motions toward a phone in the middle of the table. "Just call if you need me." And then he steps out the door, leaving me alone with the one man I never thought I'd ever see again. Especially not in a scenario where he doesn't even seem to recognize me.

"Okay, then," Jamie begins, his voice once again completely professional and detached. "I think we should start by discussing the dissolution of the previous agreement so that we can identify the key problem areas and work to resolve them in the new one."

I nod my head timidly but make no sound. Well, except for the small gurgle that comes from the back of my throat. But that's completely involuntary.

Is he seriously going through with this? Obviously this is some kind of joke. A gag. A prank.

But if it is, Jamie clearly isn't in on it, because he proceeds to remove a thick and rather daunting-looking document from his briefcase and plops it onto the table with a loud thud. Then he flips calmly to a flagged page about twenty sheets in and starts reading. "In section two C of our previous business agreement, it was stated that 'in creating this partnership and in the general spirit of all partnerships of this nature, both parties explicitly agree that every effort will be made to keep the other party fully abreast of any and all developments that hold relevance to the partnership.'" His voice is unnervingly impassive, like a robot's.

He stops reading and looks directly at me, his eyes penetrating mine with a steely expression. "It is my understanding that you—as a representative of your client—were in direct violation of this section."

I can barely understand anything he is saying. *What partnership? What agreement?* My dad told me that we were meeting with some guy he tried to form an LLP with last year and the partnership eventually fell through. But when did my dad go into business with

Jamie? And why did no one tell me about this? Did they do it behind my back?

When I don't respond, Jamie interprets my silence as permission
to continue. "Moving on to section four F." Mechanically, he flips
to another flagged page and continues reading in that same cold,
aloof tone: "In this section, it was explicitly stated that you were to
abandon your previous business practices once the partnership was
formed, as they were in direct conflict with the goals and objectives
set forth by our agreement." He takes a breath and looks at me again.
"It is my understanding that you were in direct violation of this section as well."

Wait a minute. My mind is suddenly flooding. *Abandon your previous
business practices?* Why would my dad sign an agreement that required
him to quit his job? He loves his job. He would never agree to that.

Something is not right here. Something is not adding up.

"Do you agree that you failed to abandon your conflicting business practices in accordance with this agreement?"

"What?" I blubber, feeling frustrated to be so out of the loop.
"No. I don't agree. I mean, I don't know what you're talking about.
Jamie, what is going on here?"

He looks back at me questioningly, his eyebrows raised in innocent speculation. "So are you contesting this section as a valid reason
for the dissolution?"

But I ignore his annoying business jargon and just ask him point-
blank, "Did you go into business with my dad and not tell me? Was
it while we were dating?"

But he remains silent, refusing to say a word. And this infuriates
me even more. "I want to know what is happening here. And don't
pretend you don't know."

Jamie's voice is patient but still detached. "I thought we all understood our purpose for today's meeting was to renegotiate a new and
improved partnership."

My eyes narrow and I stare at him intently, trying to extract just
one ounce of sense from his words. My superpower was always use-
less on Jamie. But you would think that after all the time that has

passed, after everything I've been through to get to this point in my life, I would be able to read just one smidgen of a thought in his brain. Except I draw nothing but a blank.

And just as I'm about to rise up and storm out of this office in vehement protest, I catch the smallest twinkle in his eye and the faintest smirk on his lips.

And then suddenly his words repeat in my mind and everything starts to fall into place. *Abandon your previous business practices. Direct conflict with the goals and objectives set forth by our agreement. New and improved partnership.*

The agreement he's referring to isn't between him and my father. It's between him and me.

Jamie is here to *negotiate* me back.

"Isn't that why we're here?" Jamie asks, forcing me back into the conversation.

I sit up a bit straighter, feeling a burst of electricity run through my body. My head is spinning and my heart is pounding in my chest, but I manage to match his professional tone and businesslike manner when I say, "Yes. That is why we're here. Please continue."

He nods appreciatively. "Thank you. So do you or do you not contest the violation of these agreements and accept responsibility for the resulting dissolution of the partnership?"

There is no way I could ever contest it. Or ever *would*. It's a responsibility I have been accepting fully for the past four months of my life. The responsibility that won't let me sleep at night. Won't let me walk the streets of Paris without seeing Jamie's face everywhere I go. *I* am the one who broke my promise. *I* am the one who hurt him. And now is my chance to tell him. And apologize.

I nod firmly. "I do take full responsibility for the dissolution of our previous partnership. And I am remorseful for the violations of our agreement and my blatant errors in judgment. But I am eager to renegotiate a new contract and prove my ability to maintain a successful partnership."

Jamie nods back. "Although it should also be noted that my party accepts partial responsibility for the dissolution as well. We acknowledge that the use of certain testing methods to analyze the durability of said agreement was dishonorable and in bad form. We also acknowledge that alternative methods utilizing communication between the two parties should have been employed instead."

I fight back a smile. "I acknowledge your acknowledgment."

"Good," Jamie states. "Then let's talk about the reconciliation."

My face is tight and rigid, matching Jamie's body language meticulously. But inside, I'm screaming. My pulse is racing at max speed. My stomach is churning.

"I think the key to the new partnership is to create an agreement that is fully amenable to both parties. And which both parties are comfortable upholding."

"I couldn't agree more."

"Very well, then," he continues in all seriousness. "I've given the reconciliation much thought. And I've come to the conclusion that the fundamental problem with the previous partnership all comes down to a question of language."

"Language?" I confirm curiously.

"Yes. It appears that your previous business practices did not lend themselves well to the establishment of a permanent, *traditional* form of agreement. And it was essentially the definition of the partnership that was ultimately problematic."

"I see," I reply, nodding pensively. "So what exactly are you offering as a proposed solution?"

Another deadpan smile. "I'm glad you asked." He reaches into his briefcase and removes a single sheet of white paper and places it face-down on the table in front of him. "I've created a proposal for a new and highly *untraditional* form of agreement that I hope you'll find suitable to your specific needs."

Slowly, he slides the paper across to me. "As you can see, it's significantly shorter than the previous one."

I stare down at the white page in front of me, feeling my throat go dry and my nerves go haywire.

"Go ahead," Jamie encourages me. "Take a look."

With shaking hands and uneven breath, I slowly flip the paper right side up and glance down at it. The page is completely blank except for one line in the middle, carefully typed in a basic Arial twelve-point font.

Will you not marry me?

And with that, I simply can't hold myself together any longer. My composure cracks and laughter escapes my lips. Glorious, liberating, joyful laughter.

"Do you not find the proposal amenable?" Jamie replies, his face still blank as a whitewashed stone.

I shake my head. "No, I do. It's . . . perfect." My voice breaks and the tears come. "I love you," I whisper.

At last, Jamie's professional, emotionless façade comes crashing down. And in its place is the warm, gentle smile that I thought I'd never see again. Except in my memories.

"I love you, too."

We rise from our seats at exactly the same moment and walk the length of the conference table until we meet in the middle. Our fingers touch first, then our palms, and then our lips. It's the kiss I've been dreaming about for four empty months.

He pulls me close to him, and I collapse against his chest, feeling the familiar sound of his heartbeat. It's pounding almost as fast and as furiously as mine.

The unforgettable warmth of his skin thaws me instantly. Paris has been so cold without it.

"How did you know I was here?" I ask into the fabric of his suit jacket. "How did you find me?"

He leans forward and kisses the top of my head. His lips feel heavy and purposeful. "I saw the article in the *L.A. Times*. About the agency." Then he places his hands on my shoulders and pulls me away so that he can look directly into my eyes. "I couldn't believe that you had given it up. I never thought you'd be capable of walking away from that life. I always thought it had to come first for you. That it would always be your priority. That's why I left. When I read that you were no longer running the agency, I went to your place to find you. But a strange pregnant woman answered the door. She said you had moved to Paris.

I called your mom to confirm, and she told me what you had been doing here. The negotiator thing. And then she told me you had come here with your dad. Another shocking discovery. I could hardly believe it. It was like you had turned into a whole different person."

I laugh. He is absolutely right. I *have* turned into a different person. And definitely a better one. "When you left, everything changed," I say softly, feeling more tears well up. "Nothing made sense anymore. And it didn't take long for me to realize that choosing my past over my future with you was the wrong choice."

Jamie wraps his arms back around me and squeezes me tightly. I bury my face under his chin and we stay like that for a long time, locked in each other's arms in the middle of the drab and dreary corporate conference room. I breathe in the sweet scent of him. It fills me with so much joy because I thought I had lost it forever.

My mind flashes back across the last twenty minutes. The charade that Jamie set up to be here. Calling my father, flying halfway across the world. Just to ask for me back. I know it's something I'll always remember.

"I think I underestimated your acting skills," I say playfully, giving his chest a poke.

He chuckles. "I can pull out a noteworthy performance when it really matters." He exhales a heavy sigh. "I'm really proud of you, Jen. For who you've let yourself become."

I blush. Jamie has always had a way of making me do that. "I haven't *become* anyone else," I reply softly. "I'm just Jennifer."

"That's the only person I ever wanted you to be."

My eyes close as I try desperately to freeze-frame this moment in my mind so that I will be able to look back on it forever.

When they open again, I gaze out the window of my dad's office and can just make out the recognizable buildings of Paris in the distance. The cold, gray skies of March do nothing to cloud my mood.

"So this new 'partnership,' as you call it," I say, leaning back slightly and looking up at him. "Where is it supposed to take place? My life and work is in Paris now, and you still live in L.A."

But Jamie simply shrugs, as if this one tiny detail has never been an obstacle in his plan. "I think that part's negotiable."

acknowledgments

Well, well . . . here we are. Book two. I can hardly believe it. I never thought I would actually get to this point. There were many times while writing this book that I felt like a cyclist trying to complete the Tour de France . . . on a tricycle. Fortunately, I had a very fantastic support team, as evidenced by the next few pages.

Michael and Laura Brody, thank you once again for your constant (if not sometimes delusional) belief in me and my ability to actually make a living as a crazy person (aka "writer"). Charlie, thank you for keeping me (relatively) sane and making me laugh. You're the only person I know who has the ability to make bookends funny. To Terra, thanks once again for your fashion expertise.

I owe a tremendous amount of gratitude to my fabulous agent, Elizabeth Fisher, for your enthusiasm, sympathetic ear, and undying support. Thanks also to Monika Verma, Miek Coccia, Sasha Raskin, and everyone at Levine Greenberg for all your hard work on my books.

Thank you to my two amazing editors, Jennifer Weis and Hilary Teeman, for believing in Jennifer/Ashlyn enough to let her live on in a second book! And mucho thanks to all the fine people at St. Martin's for everything you do: Anne Marie Tallberg, Nadea Mina, Joseph Goldschein, Matthew Shear, Anne Bensson, Kerry Nordling, Jeanette Levy, Brittney Kleinfelter, Ellis Trevor, Christina Harcar,

326   acknowledgments

and everyone else who has worked on my books whom I've not yet
had the privilege of meeting.

I also really want to thank all the foreign publishers who have put
my work on bookshelves around the world and the incredible people
I've had the honor to work with, including but certainly not limited
to: Gillian Green, Hannah Robinson, Katie Johnson, Alex Young,
Louise McKee, Liz Marvin, Edward Griffiths, Sarah Bennie, and
Caroline Craig at Ebury Press in the UK; Deborah Drubah, Estelle
Revelant, Nicolas Watrin, Nicolas Cauchy, Mathilde Deprez, Cé-
line Gonzalez, Jean-Claude Dubost, and Francois Laurent at Fleuve
Noir in France *(Je ne me souviens jamais mon voyage incroyable à Paris!)*;
Anne Tente and Ursula C. Sturm at Heyne in Germany; Tsiu-lun Liu
at OctA in Taiwan; and everyone at Ast in Russia and Metafora in the
Czech Republic.

A huge shout goes out to Marina Grasic, Christina Hodson, Elyse
Lawson, Dominie Mahl, and everyone at Curious Pictures. Thank
you for believing in this concept and taking it above and beyond the
pages of a book. And thanks to Margery Walshaw for bringing me
to them!

To my wonderful and savvy entertainment lawyer, Mark Stankev-
ich. Just the fact that I'm thanking my lawyer means that he's obviously not your typical lawyer (I know, a low-ball, cheap shot at
lawyers, but I simply couldn't resist).

There are so many other people to thank as well that I simply cannot leave out: Jessen Gregory, for making sure my references to divorce law sounded at least *somewhat* plausible. Noémie Demol, for
making sure I didn't completely embarrass myself in front of the
French press. Alyson Noël, for doing equal parts to inspire me with
your success and help me procrastinate with your hilarious e-mails. I
guess it all evens out in the end. Ella Gaumer, my first (and most devoted) fan and my good-news magnet. You'll always have a spot under my umbrella.

Once again, everyone who helped with the book trailer, I am
incredibly indebted to you. Deprise Brescia, and Holly Karrol
Clark, you continue to sparkle and shine as Ashlyn. Carla Holden,
your beautiful voice, music, and lyrics took this book's trailer to

new heights! Jerry Brunskill, there would be no trailer without you. And I mean that quite literally.

I also want to thank everyone at Yahoo's *Primetime in No Time*—Corey Moss, Frank Nicotero, Jason Fitzpatrick, Michael Bachmann, Kyle Moss, and Nick Paschal—for putting up with my wordiness and allowing me to be just one of the guys (even if I'm *still* never invited to poker).

And last but never least, thanks to all the readers out there who took time out of their busy and important lives to read *The Fidelity Files* and now *Love Under Cover.* Your e-mails and Facebook messages are the reasons I keep writing. My only quest in life is to entertain you. I hope that I've succeeded.

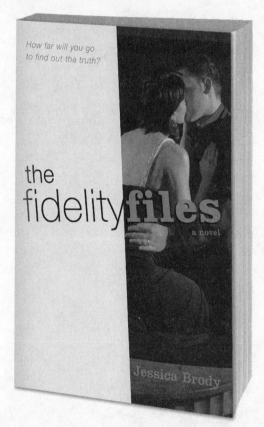